Disclaimer

www.vainqueurthedrag(

© 2019 Maxime Julien Durand / Void Herald

Table of Content

1: Vainqueur the Dragon

Vainqueur the Dragon, great calamity of his age, stirred as he awakened from his sleep.

This sixty-foot long beast of legends, with scales more radiant than molten rubies and great jet black wings, yawned as he stretched his body, pushing away some of the gold and jewels of his hard-won hoard. *How good,* he thought, his golden eyes opening and acclimating to the darkness of his cave, to rest on the wages of victory after a feast. He could spend another half a century here if he didn't feel the urge to eat some cattle this morning.

Vainqueur slowly stretched his mighty neck until his crown of horns scraped against the stone ceiling. He surveyed his cave deep within the southern mountains of Albain, marveling at the beauty of his shining conquests. A bed of rubies, diamonds and gold coins, looted from beastkins, mermaids, the retinue of an elven princess, and the corpses of armored manlings foolish enough to challenge him. A good hoard, but a small one; one he promised himself to double in size before going back to hibernation.

Maybe he should raid the dwarves next? He had heard they collected enough gems to fill underground vaults.

And here, on his left, one of his trusty, dutiful goblin minions cleaned up a silver rapier, one of the finest items of his treasures. It was a tall goblin, with smooth skin, a dirtied hood and a terrified expression as Vainqueur watched him...

Wait.

That was no goblin, but a human. A *manling.*

Vainqueur suddenly blinked in realization, and so did the manling who just realized he had woken up a dragon.

"A thief!" Moved to action by a flash of fury, Vainqueur roared and attempted to crush the manling with his upper arm, the terrified rogue jumping with the rapier to the side before he could make a dash to the exit. Vainqueur kept attempting to stomp the manling like a fruit, but the cloaked one had good reflexes.

No matter, the cave was too small, and the exit on the other side. The dragon quickly cornered the robber, trapping him between a wall and himself. The manling held the rapier as a desperate weapon, but only the threat of melting his treasure prevented Vainqueur from burning that treacherous animal to cinders.

Vainqueur quickly scanned his hoard with a glance, sighing in relief upon finding no missing piece. He had caught the thief right in the act.

"I swear it," Vainqueur cursed in dragonian. "You take a quick nap for fifty years—*fifty years*—and everyone forgets the food chain."

Even setting up his lair in the tallest mountain known to western dragonkind hadn't discouraged thieves.

And where were these damn goblins he had allowed to live in exchange for keeping watch? Did they run? Or did the thief kill them? Why was it so hard to find good help nowadays?

No matter. He would eat this fool and then raid the nearby villages for cattle; that would teach the manlings not to bother him again. "My sweet food," he told the thief in the manling's tongue, "What is your name?"

The manling's hideously small eyes bulged beneath the hood. "You can speak?"

"Yes, yes, sometimes I talk to my breakfast." Or to maidens he abducted back in his younger years. "Answer me manling, before I lose patience."

"I, uh..." The human trembled at Vainqueur's amazing majesty. "Victor, sir..."

"Vainqueur Knightsbane, First of his Name, Great Calamity of this Age and King of the Albain Mountains. But you may call me Your Majesty."

"Your majesty—"

"With a capital M," Vainqueur corrected his insolent food. "I can tell the difference."

"Your Majesty, I swear this is a mistake!"

"I do not think so, manling. Now, tell me, because I truly want to know. What made you think trying to steal from *me* was *ever* a good idea?"

The manling narrowed his eyes in recognition of his stupidity. Vainqueur knew little of manlings, but this one sounded young, barely an adult. "I swear," he said. "I didn't know this mountain was yours. Someone hired me to recover that rapier, and that was all! It was thought lost, not yours."

"Liar!" Vainqueur roared, his voice causing the ceiling to tremble, "You must have fought past an army of goblins to get there!"

"There… there's been no goblin activity in the mountains for decades, Your Majesty. They fled Barsino's great march through the Albain mountains twenty years ago."

What? Vainqueur hummed deeply, trying to smell goblin stench. His sharp senses didn't pick any, not even the faintest hint. The manling was right, no goblin had guarded his lair for ten years at least.

"Those moronic cowards, fleeing the very second I take a nap?" Vainqueur cursed in dragonian, the manling unable to understand the brilliant elder tongue. The dragon deigned to return to the creature's primitive language. "Do you have minions, manling Victor?"

"Minions?" Understanding the dragon would let him live so long as he answered, manling Victor answered. "I had a party once, but it didn't work out. Like I was the only professional with ambition beyond petty theft."

"Finding good help is hard everywhere," Vainqueur ranted to his audience. "I advise you never to hire goblins, even if you will not live long enough to. I will spare you this mistake."

"Wait, wait!" The manling panicked. "They will send someone else, even if you kill me! No one knows Your Majesty lives in these mountains!"

"They will, once I burn the countryside to cinders," Vainqueur replied, although the manling indeed piqued his curiosity. "But I am curious, who sent you? I will eat them after you."

"I don't know! It was an anonymous request in the guildhall of a town nearby," manling Victor said, "The reward was one thousand gold coins."

"A nice sum for such a dirty deed," Vainqueur condemned him, vowing to search for these coins once he had tracked down the mastermind as payback.

"Yes, but I mostly took it for the challenge," the manling admitted. "I thought I would gain a few levels out of it. Maybe even a special Perk from the climbing."

"Levels?" What was that, some kind of cattle food? That interested Vainqueur. "What is that?"

"You, you don't..." The manling shut his mouth. "How to explain... levels are powers you gain in a class, like Knight or Wizard or Outlaw, and which grant you extra power called Perks. You gain levels through work, experience, or killing stuff. I thought I would gain at least one or two."

What rubbish was that? "You cannot even begin to *fathom* the number of thieves I slew, manling Victor, and I never received any of these, 'levels'."

"Maybe you just didn't know," the manling pleaded for his miserable life.

That was stupid. Class? Like what, a thief? He was a great red dragon, the king of the mountains, the apex of creation! Surely the mighty dragonkind would have unlocked such a power long ago if it existed!

Congratulations!

What? Vainqueur thought, as words appeared right before his eyes.

*Through your sheer ego and noble dragon bloodline, you gained a level in the [**Noble**] class!*

+30 HP, +10SP, +1 STR, +1 AGI, +1 CHA, +1 LCK!

*You gained the [**Old Money**] class perk!*

What was this witchery? Math magic? The sight puzzled Vainqueur. "Old Money?" he said out loud, much to manling Victor's confusion.

*[**Old Money**]: double the chances of monsters dropping treasure after death.*

Ah. Nice. "Manling Victor," the dragon asked his food. "Do you self-identify as a monster?"

"Of course not!" the manling replied, and it didn't sound like a bluff, "Monsters are goblins or trolls or... or..."

"Or dragons?" Vainqueur finished the sentence, amused. Well, if that 'perk' worked on that damn, arrogant frost dragon Icefang in the northern lands, he might just triple the size of his hoard. The dragon narrowed his head until it was within an inch of the thief, who tried to present a strong face. "Take off your hood and cloak, manling, slowly. Look at me in the eye."

The manling did so, revealing his face. As Vainqueur had guessed, this was a young adult manling, with disgusting short black hair instead of mighty horns; how could these animals live with them Vainqueur would never understand. Still, the dragon liked the fear and the hint of low cunning in these small, amber eyes. The would-be thief also carried two metal toothpicks around his belt, not worth adding to his hoard.

That manling was no goblin, but it would make a nice substitute. "Manling Victor."

"Yes, Your Majesty?"

"Put the rapier back where you found it. You will lead me straight to this 'Guildhall' so I may see this request for myself. Since I am short on goblins right now, you will be my new minion until you pay back your life debt to me."

The manling couldn't believe the great honor bestowed upon him and thought himself undeserving of it. "I am wholly unsuited for this role, Your Majesty."

"I am a dragon," Vainqueur reminded the manling of this timeless wisdom. "You are now my minion."

The manling said nothing for a short while, before gracefully accepting his new role, "It is a great honor, Your Majesty."

"Very good. There is a great reward in doing as I wish. Namely, living. Any other dragon would have eaten you for your sinful crime and would never have taken a manling in their service, but I am forgiving and merciful."

"This is very generous of you, Your Majesty."

"I know, manling. Now, tell me more about these Perks..."

2: V&V

Victor had no idea what he had gotten himself into.

For the first time in his life, he flew outside the confines of a plane. Namely, the dragon carried him in palm—because his back was too good for Victor—as he flew north of the mountain, towards the Valbin village where he took that damn request. Victor hated the experience; not only did he take the icy wind head on in the face, the dragon held him tight and could crush him any moment.

Victor had had terrible luck streak lately, and no amount of Luck stat increase changed it. Dying on Earth to end up in this fantasy world, falling in with brigands to make ends' meets, narrowingly avoiding death half a dozen times, and then getting caught by a giant dragon on his very first adventurer quest.

This world sucked!

"Your Majesty!" Victor shouted, as the duo left the snowy mountain to the grasslands, the sight of the village coming to life under the morning sun. "I should go alone! The guard will sound the alarm at your coming!"

The dragon would have none of it. "Minion, a king sometimes must show his face to his subjects, so they may remember who rules them. Also, I do not trust you yet not to have lied to me, especially about this 'class system'."

In hindsight, Victor wondered if informing a giant red dragon about it had been his brightest idea.

How could he have known? Every civilized person on this goddamn planet knew about it! They even had Class Scholars!

As expected, as they reached the village's wooden ramparts, Victor heard the song of bells, the city watch sounding the alarm upon seeing the dragon. Not that it would help. Victor had heard a single dragon could devastate a country single-handedly, and Vainqueur seemed huge even by reptilian standards.

A few archers and wizards on the ground launched arrows and lightning bolts at the legendary beast; they bounced off Vainqueur's scales, who hadn't even noticed. "Minion, where is this guildhall?" the dragon demanded, as he circled the village, the inhabitants closing their windows at the sight of his dreaded shadow.

"The stone building with the bells, between the bell tower and the marketplace, Your Majesty."

Finding his target, the dragon landed on his last two legs in the middle of the marketplace, the flapping of his wings and his sheer mass blowing away most stands. Panic set among humans, beastkin, and elf merchants, as they hurriedly fled screaming, most of them not even grabbing their wares with them.

Vainqueur briefly glanced at the animal-like beastkins with what looked like hunger in his eyes, before focusing on the guildhall and its human-sized, closed doors. Without a care in the world, the dragon headbutted the entrance, smashing down the walls and most of the ceiling, so he could move inside.

Victor found himself in front of two dozen adventurers armed to the teeth, forming a wall between the dragon and Charlene, the pretty, plump receptionist Victor had hoped to take out on a date after his first quest. The mission board which caused this whole fiasco stood behind her back, Victor immediately noticing that damn request among them.

A powerfully built spearman led the adventurers, swinging his spear like a show-off. "My fellows!" he shouted, his white teeth shining as he flashed a smile, "Are you afraid of a flying lizard? Well, I am not! I am not afraid of an oversized drake, and I will prove it this second!"

That asshole braggart, Alain... Victor couldn't stand him, but that smug bastard was the highest level adventurer in town at twenty-five. He had killed a lot of drakes, even a giant. Maybe he had a shot at killing the dragon.

With a mighty roar, Alain charged with his spear, his sheer moxie inspiring the rest of the adventurers to follow suit.

With a gaze full of condescension, Vainqueur lazily moved his free hand in front of the incoming spearman, and flicked his fingers.

Alain went flying and crashed against a stone wall with a loud, morbidly amusing sound. He turned into a puddle of blood, brains and bones on impact, like a squashed mosquito.

... they were all doomed.

The adventurers immediately screamed as one. They dropped their weapons and fled by crashing through the windows and the staff backdoor, much to Vainqueur's smug amusement. Only poor Charlene stood behind her desk, too shocked to move, her poor colleagues probably hiding beneath it.

Finally, the dragon released Victor, letting him walk again. "Minion Victor, do the thing," the dragon ordered, Charlene briefly blinking at hearing him speak in common.

The poor rogue briefly glanced at the broken windows, realized they were too far off to escape, and cleared his throat. "Charlene," the terrified receptionist's eyes moved from the dragon to him, "I present you King Vainqueur the First of his Name, my new boss. Long may he live."

Her eyes widened in stark, raving terror. "Vainqueur? Vainqueur *Knightsbane*?! The Red Terror of Midgard?!" She clenched her fists in a mix of horror and fury, while Vainqueur looked proud that people remembered him. "You brought an ancient red dragon to our village! Are you insane?!"

"Yes, yes, of course I had a choice in the matter," Victor deadpanned, pointing at the giant behemoth right behind him.

"Minion Victor, who is this female manling and why do we need her?"

"She's the chief of staff and receptionist of this guildhall, Your Majesty," Victor explained, making discreet signs to Charlene to play along. "Charlene, please tell the giant angry dragon what you do."

The woman glanced up at the dragon, then wisely decided to play along. She dusted her robes, then adopted the same professional look she used with every would be adventurer, albeit while still noticeably trembling in fear. "I manage the paperwork and requests on behalf of the Gardemagne Adventurer Guild. I receive requests from clients and distribute them, and the rewards to adventurers and mercenaries willing to take them on."

"Minion Victor, ask manling Charlene to find and read the request that led you to my domain out loud."

Of course, the dragon couldn't read the language, even if he could speak it. Even Victor had taken a few months of intense study to learn it. "Your Majesty does not talk to other humans?" Victor asked the giant beast, curious.

"No, talking to animals is what a minion is for," Vainqueur replied. "Minion Victor, ask manling Charlene to read your request out loud."

"Charlene, would you kindly..." The secretary had already grabbed one of the paper sheet on the board behind her, clearly in no hurry to test the dragon's patience.

The woman cleared her throat. "Louise, Marquise de Carabas, offers a generous one thousand gold pieces reward for the return of her family's prized Silver Rapier, last reported in the hands of goblins in the Albain mountains. There is a drawing of the sword with it."

Since most goblins had fled the mountains years ago, Victor thought it would be easy money. That, and bringing the rapier back would give him the opportunity to scout the Carabas estate in case something caught his fancy.

Pity the locals had forgotten to mention the dragon's presence.

"It appears you spoke the truth, minion Victor. You shall be spared. You too, manling Charlene, if you tell where I may visit this Marquise and eat her cattle."

"Charlene, where is—"

"I heard," the angry receptionist cut him off. "Victor, give me your map."

The rogue hurriedly grabbed the old sheet of paper he kept around his belt, Charlene taking it from his hands, grabbing a feather pen, and marking a spot in the south-east of the Gardemagne countryside.

Vainqueur squinted, as he observed the board where Charlene took Louise de Carabas' request. "Minion, explain to me how it works."

"People, mostly nobles, merchants, or groups of peasants, send requests to the adventurer guild alongside promised rewards," Victor explained, "With the end of the Century War two years ago, many of them involve dealing with roving monsters or brigands."

"There were many lucrative requests and bounties to take Your Majesty down, decades ago," Charlene said. "Until you were declared dead."

"Oh? And all this time I thought your kind had a collective deathwish. Like sending your sick and your wounded to die honorably at my—" Vainqueur suddenly stopped mid sentence, as the words hit him. "Declared dead?"

Charlene winced as the dragon glared at her. "A-a group of Barinian adventurers brought back a red dragon skull twenty years ago after Barsino's march through the mountains, declaring it belonged to Vainqueur... and since no red dragon showed up for years afterward..."

"This, this is an indignity!" The news had infuriated the beast almost as much as Victor's attempted robbery, smoke steaming from his nostrils. "Minion, order manling Charlene to inform your primitive, credulous species that I, Vainqueur Knightsbane, am not dead!"

"I am sure the news will travel fast after Your Majesty's mighty show of force," Victor deadpanned, the dragon thankfully too incensed to notice the sarcasm.

"They better do!" Vainqueur calmed himself, his eyes fixed on the board. "What kind of requests does this manling get?"

"Charlene, can you read a few quests for His Majesty's benefit?"

A bit more confident due to being in her element, Charlene grabbed a paper sheet and read it out loud. "A clan of trolls calling themselves the Branded Barks has sacked the lands of the Count of Provencal and currently hide in the Woods of Gevaudan, east of his domain. The Count offers a great reward for the extermination of this vermin."

"You get 'experience' and 'levels' for this deed?" Vainqueur asked, before clarifying his true intention. "*I* could get levels?"

"You know about levels?" Charlene blinked, without waiting for Victor's 'animal translation.'

"His Majesty Vainqueur apparently leveled up in the Noble class," Victor told her. Fitting for a large parasite living off the gold he 'taxed' from people weaker than him.

"A dragon can level up in a class?" Whatever colors left on Charlene's face suddenly drained, as she realized the implications. "Oh, by the twelve gods, dragons can get class levels."

"Yes, my minion recently informed me of the existence of this class system." If glares could kill, Charlene would have murdered Victor twice over. "How much do you manlings get paid for this request?"

"Six thousand gold coins."

"Six thousand gold coins, to eat trolls?"

"This is considered a difficult quest, Your Majesty," Victor said. These were war trolls, brought by Prydain during the great war, crafty and strong.

"Trolls? You are afraid of *trolls*?" The dragon's bellowing hiss of a laugh made the walls tremble. "You manlings are so weak!"

"Yes, Your Majesty," Victor deadpanned, angered by his patronizing. "Maybe you should consider a career as an adventurer and show us the ropes? I'm sure you would do great."

He said this as a joke, but much to his horror, the dragon seemed to consider his words seriously. "Six thousand coins for a feast of trolls..." he mumbled. "Is this the most well-paid request available?"

"No, Your Majesty," Victor replied. "I think it was the kraken hunting bounty, right?"

Charlene nodded abruptly. "Killing the Kraken of Massaline is worth the equivalent of sixty-four thousand gold coins in emeralds."

The fires of greed lit up in the dragon's eyes. "Sixty-four thousand? That is almost as much as my entire—" He stopped himself, probably realizing that he had already said too much.

As much as my entire hoard, Victor guessed. Perhaps more. The rogue estimated quite a few of the items the dragon had collected had lost their luster over time.

Victor could almost see the gears turning in the dragon's head, and the exact train of thought his mind followed. And it terrified him.

Oh no. Oh please no.

"Minion Victor, I intended to burn this village to the ground for you manlings' crimes against my royal person," Vainqueur declared. "But I suddenly realize my usual method of building my hoard may be slightly outdated. All of this wealth sleeping without a good dragon to claim them is a sin, and if this Old Money perk does not lie..."

Oh by the gods, please no...

"I, Vainqueur the Dragon, will gladly answer requests and solve your inferior species' problems for your coins!"

Charlene, too, wondered if the dragon was serious. When it became that yes, he was, she didn't know what to do. "Your Majesty, Vainqueur, I am not sure a dragon can become an adventurer."

"Of course, I am overqualified," Vainqueur declared proudly.

"Your Majesty, this is not—"

"I am a dragon. I am, now, an adventurer. And you are starting to sound like food. Minion, is manling Charlene food?"

"Charlene, are you dragon food?"

Charlene, understanding the implied threat, searched under the desk for a huge pile of paperwork, putting it on the desk. "I will register you two as a new adventurer company. We will need both your signatures, and the paperwork done."

Vainqueur glanced at the pile of paper, then at Victor, who saw what came next coming from a mile away. "Minion Victor."

"Yes, Your Majesty?"

"I officially promote you to my minion chief of staff and living signature. You shall be responsible for managing this 'paperwork' thing on my behalf. This is a great and important responsibility, but you will do fine."

Victor guessed he wouldn't be paid for it, but wisely kept that for himself.

*Congratulations! By becoming the chief enforcer of a mighty dragon, you gained a level in the [**Monster Squire**] Class!*

Victor blinked at the notification. Monster Squire? He had never heard of that class.

+30 HP, +10 SP, +1 STR, +1 VIT, +1 SKI, +1 AGI, +1 INT, +1 CHA, +1 LCK!

*You gained the [**Monster Kin**] Class Perk!*

*[**Monster Kin**: you can now talk to and understand any monster, and gain a +20 charisma bonus when interacting with them!]*

Wow, he never received such a massive stat boost before. That Class must have had incredible growth potential.

Victor glanced at the name Charlene registered the adventurer company as, and froze.

V&V?

"Is this a prank?" he asked out loud.

Charlene glared at him, then at the dragon, then at the destroyed ceiling, then back at him.

Okay, maybe he deserved it. He supposed that also meant she wouldn't go out for a drink with him. Bugger.

"What is it, minion Victor?"

"Nothing, Your Majesty," Victor sighed as he completed and signed the documents on both his and the dragon's behalf, "Nothing."

"I would wish for you to go to hell, Victor," the receptionist said. "But I think you're already there."

3: First Quest

They gave him a lead plate tag with his name on it. *Him.* Like he was some *mammal.*

"This is degrading!" Vainqueur complained to his loyal lackey Victor, as they flew above the farmlands of Carabas. The news had put him in a foul mood. "Lead? *Lead!*"

"Every adventurer starts with a lead plate," Victor explained, the wind in his face causing his lips to move in ways Vainqueur found distracting. "That's the ranks. Lead, copper, iron, bronze, silver, gold, and starmetal. I'm a lead adventurer too, Your Majesty."

"But you are a *manling*!" Also, why the adventurer guild put that greenish unshiny starmetal higher than brilliant gold, Vainqueur would never understand. "I am a *dragon.* Can you manlings fly? Can you breath fire that melts stone? Can you live forever? No, so why is that not enough for gold?"

"You are a unique case, Your Majesty," minion Victor tried to assuage his wounded pride. "Forgive my poor species, who does not know how to deal with you."

"Just this once!" Vainqueur said, flying over a vast forest, smelling the presence of trolls, slimes, and other beasts below. Birds and harpies flew away in fear at his arrival. "Are these the troll woods?"

"Yes, Your Majesty. Trolls usually live in caves, if we look for one—"

"Minion, I will not sully my peerless scales with some troll's dung. I am a dragon, remember?" Vainqueur took a long, deep breath, and then dived towards the woods. The forge in his stomach lit up, the infernal power within turning the air into flames.

The great calamity unleashed his mighty dragonfire upon the forest, a torrent of bright, nearly white flames incinerating trees, animals, everything; Vainqueur flew in a straight line around the forest, intending to make a full ring of fire and trap the trolls – and whatever creatures unlucky enough to live with them – within.

Victor screamed in surprise, held close to Vainqueur's own maw. "Your Majesty, what are you doing?!"

"Fulfilling your kind's request," Vainqueur replied, after taking back some breathe and preparing for a second round. Thanks to the wind, the inferno spread through the forest far north, turning trees to candles and grass to embers.

Vainqueur dove again through a cloud of smoke, much to his minion's terror, smelling trolls below. A bunch of these savage, green-skinned giants attempted to flee the coming flames, only for the dragon to bombard them, spitting his fire in the shape of fireballs instead of a continuous stream. The projectiles exploded on contact with the ground, vaporizing the beasts, blasting the dirt and forming craters.

*Congratulations! You gained a level in [**Noble**]!*

+30 HP, +1 INT, +1 LCK!

Vainqueur awaited the declaration of a new Perk, but nothing came up. Maybe he hadn't burned the place enough. The forest bordered several hills forming a natural frontier, and so Vainqueur bombarded this area too, intent on devastating the entire forest instead of just the troll's lair.

After a few minutes of firebombing the land, Vainqueur finished remaking the Woods of Gevaudan into a nice, smoking hellscape. "There, troll problem solved!" Vainqueur said, happy with himself. "All we need is to claim the reward now!"

"Your Majesty, can I..." Victor pleaded, the ash-filled wind making him scoff, "Your Majesty, flight is terrible when you hold me in your palm. Especially when you breathe dragonfire down my neck."

"This must be your lack of scales," Vainqueur said. "I empathize with your situation, I truly do, but what can I do about this birth defect?"

"Can I... can I... can I ride on your back instead?"

Vainqueur looked down on his insolent lackey. "Minion, what kind of ungrateful demand is that? Have I not given you an honest occupation? When I found you this morning you were but a mere thief, purposeless, adrift. Now you are chief of staff. *My* chief of staff. Do not demand too much."

Victor sighed at his master's scolding. "I guess at least I got a level out of this."

"You did?" Was that not payment enough?

"Yeah, I got a level in Monster Squire when you made me your 'chief of staff,' and now I got another. I didn't even know this class existed."

"What is a squire? A manling term?"

"It's, uh, the apprentice of a knight or a noble. They help them get ready for battle, do menial chores for their boss, learn the tricks of the trade..."

"Ah, yes. A minion."

"Yes, it pays just as much."

Of course, the manlings would copy this honorable dragon institution. They learned from the best. "I did not get a perk this time, which I find confounding."

"It's only one per two levels, Your Majesty."

"Who decides that?"

"The gods, I think. Or maybe the Fomors."

"These good for nothing upstarts? They always claim they made the world when *everyone* knows dragons did it first. Tell me where I can find and reprimand them."

Victor gave him a strange, incredulous look. "Reprimand the... I don't know Your Majesty, I'm not a religious guy. Maybe we could ask a bishop."

"We will after you climb down and recover what is mine."

"After I *what*?"

"According to this Old Money Perk , the trolls below should drop treasures when they die. You do not expect me to get down and sully myself with ashes?"

Victor glanced down at the fiery crater below them, then back at his master. "Your Majesty, I am not immune to fire."

Not immune to—ah yes, he had forgotten. By the elder wyrm, how could the manlings avoid extinction so far? "We will delay my gratification after the fires die down," Vainqueur said. "After we obtain restitution for your previous employer's crime."

"Sure, sure, if we could just land somewhere safe so I could look at the map..."

No wonder that Marquise lowered herself to hire thieves. Vainqueur too would be bitter at living in a palace with only one tower.

And one on such a small hill at that. The female manling must seethe in jealousy upon seeing Vainqueur's own lair, made of the world's tallest mountains. That castle had little stone walls, overseeing villages from above its mound, and manned with manlings equipped with bows and arrows. They had fired a few of these toothpicks as Vainqueur and his minion landed on their front door, with the dragon retaliating by tossing a few of the primates on the ground with his tail. After they stopped,

Vainqueur had patiently waited for them to bring their master for a civilized chat.

The castle overflowed with the smell of cats and felines, including lions, tigers, and even a sphinx, according to Vainqueur's nose. A flag representing a cat with boots stood at the summit of the tower, much to the dragon's amusement.

Maybe they had good knights? It had been a while since Vainqueur hadn't lived up to his name.

"I have been wondering, minion, what does Marquise mean in your language?"

The minion finished stretching his legs, happy to be back on his feet. "That means she's a noble lady. Don't ask me where she ranks in the kingdom's hierarchy, I just know she's above the count that put the request for the trolls."

A noble lady? Vainqueur's head perked up, his Princess Sense stirring. "Is she a princess?"

"A princess? I don't think so, no. Why?"

Disappointing. "Old habits."

The manling's tiny eyes blinked. "Does Your Majesty kidnap princesses?"

"Sometimes, mostly elves," Vainqueur said, fondly remembering that particular hunting season he snatched the only elven princess of the current generation before his rivals. He had bragged to his fellow dragons for centuries afterward. "This is a very popular sport among dragonkind, since the black dragon Grandrake ransomed the manling Princess Genevieve a thousand years ago. Maybe I will take you minion on a hunting season someday."

"Do you..." His minion hesitated, as if afraid of the answer, "Do you eat them?"

"Of course not, do you take me for a savage? I release them back in the wild when I get bored of their whining." Or when he ran out of the food he had stored to keep them alive.

As if hearing their conversation, a chubby, two-legged cat the size of a manling joined the soldiers on the walls, wearing emerald and gold jewelry that Vainqueur immediately thought would look great atop his hoard; so would her golden fur. Two pretty manling maidens attended the cat, looking fearfully at Vainqueur.

Apparently, the owner wasn't a manling, but a catkin. "What business have you here, threatening my castle, dragon tamer?" the cat, Marquise Louise, asked the minion.

Vainqueur couldn't help but laugh. Humans, taming dragons? "I think you got our relationship backward!" Victor shouted back with modesty.

"*I* tamed *him*," Vainqueur made a face. Even if that talking cat was probably the Marquise, she didn't smell like a princess. She didn't even smell like a virgin! Not worth adding to his hoard. Still, since she was noble blood, Vainqueur deigned answer directly. "I am Vainqueur Knightsbane, King of the Albain Mountains, great calamity of this age! You sent ruffians after my silver rapier treasure, interrupting my long nap. I thereby demand half your cattle as restitution for the trouble caused, alongside the one thousand gold coins you offered for my possession."

"Half the cattle in my marquisate?" the catkin asked with her shrill, insolent voice. "This is preposterous!"

"I had to fly two hours to get here," Vainqueur emphasized his pain, "Two. *Hours*. I burned pounds of fat and smelled the dung of your peasants coming to this place."

"Also, Your Majesty burned the local woods coming here!" minion Victor shouted to the Marquise. "On request of the Count of Provencal!"

"Who owes me six thousand golden coins for this service!" Vainqueur pointed at the lead tag around his neck with his claw. "See this tag? I am an adventurer! The greatest your puny race has ever known!"

"Certainly, Your Majesty," Victor said. "Certainly."

The marquise let out a hiss as she squinted at the lead tag, then turned to whisper at one of her manling knights. "Bring me Count Gilbert for an explanation," Vainqueur heard her say thanks to his good ears, before she turned to the dragon. "If I give you what you want, you will leave my lands at once?"

"That depends, do you have more quests for me?" Vainqueur asked, eager for more gold.

"No, no, we do not," the marquise declared with haste.

"Also, if you have a Bishop on hands, Your Majesty has theological questions!" Victor added. "Important questions!"

"Good thinking, minion," Vainqueur said.

"Our chaplain is away on a diplomatic mission." The marquise then turned to whisper to the same knight as before. "Tell our cooks to prepare a feast for King Vainqueur. The 'troublesome guest' kind, with the special ingredient."

"I will tell the cooks to put the maximum dose," the knight added.

"We will provide you with a feast, and the reward for your noble deed!" the marquise told Vainqueur. "I hope you shall forgive us for our lack of courtesy!"

"Only if your cattle is good!" Vainqueur replied.

"You will find it most exquisite," the catkin noble replied with a strange tone, before leaving with her knight.

"She's..." Victor struggled to find his words. "Damn, she's a catkin. And here I thought she would be hot."

"Not as hot as me," Vainqueur rolled his eyes at his chief of staff's naivety. "You are too easily impressed, minion. My breath burns brighter than the sun. You have seen it. Of course, she would be lukewarm in comparison."

"Yeah, at least most of the staff is human. I wonder if one of the ladies-in-waiting is single."

"Of course they are not 'single', your noblewomen are rare in the wild, but not as much as princesses." Clearly, Vainqueur would have to finish the poor minion's education.

As the sun began to set, armorless manlings came out of the castle, bringing Vainqueur fat, cooked sheep, pigs, and cows on carriages. A fat, obese manling wearing brighter, cleaner clothes than the servants led the way, carrying purses and sweating. "Minion, is that manling part of the feast?" Vainqueur asked Victor.

"I'm not sure, Your Majesty…"

"No, no," the fat man sweated. "I am Gilbert, Count of Provencal."

"Ah, the one who issued the troll request?" Vainqueur's head perked up. The purses must contain his rewards.

"Yes, yes, I was petitioning the marquise for help getting rid of them before Your… Your Majesty solved the problem." The count gulped as he looked at the smoke rising on the horizon. "You were very zealous…"

"I am taking my duty as an adventurer seriously," Vainqueur agreed, swallowing a cow whole and spitting out some meat that got stuck between his sharp fangs. "You can eat the leftovers, minion. Let it never be said that Vainqueur starves his staff."

The minion glanced at the feast, then at the count, noticing sweat over his forehead. "No, no, I cannot share Your Majesty's meal," Victor replied. "It's all yours."

Such a dutiful manling. Why did Vainqueur ever bother with goblins? "You have come to deliver my reward?"

"Alongside the marquise's gift of apology," the sweating manling said. "She said this was my duty as her vassal."

"Indeed, what a good minion you are," Vainqueur said, feasting on sheep covered with a strange sauce. "Minion Victor, count the coins. And do not dare steal them!"

"Oh, very far from my mind, Your Majesty," Victor replied, taking the purses and doing as asked.

Congratulations!

*By stomaching the poison in the food like a champ, you gained the [**Lesser Poison Immunity**] Perk!*

"Poison? What was this? Manling seasoning?" The count smiled, although it strangely did not reach his ears, and sweated so much Vainqueur wondered if he would die of it on the spot. Was he ill?

"Yes, Your Majesty," minion Victor said. "It's a very bitter spice for special occasions."

"I did not feel the taste, bring more of it!" Vainqueur complained, the count hurriedly running to the castle and attend to his needs.

Maybe he would get a stronger Perk at the end of the feast?

4: Chief of Staff

When the marquise had invited Victor to a private breakfast in her apartments, Victor had expected everything *but* an actual breakfast. Maybe a poisoned meal, or being made into the breakfast, or maybe fed to a lion. Not an actual, pleasant breakfast with the lady of the house and the Count of Provencal.

Of course, she had four knights ready to chop his head off at any moment, alongside a few catkin butlers, but he was thankful for the meal all the same. It had been a while since he last ate beef and cooked vegetables with a fork.

Thankfully, he didn't taste any poison in the meal. He guessed yesterday's fiasco taught them a lesson.

"This is humiliating," the marquise said, lounging in a mink chair while petting a winged lion in one hand and sipping a glass of wine with the other. Victor guessed she had taken more than a few drinks. "A red dragon empties our pantry and then decides to take a nap at my front door. Why did the gods send this calamity? Is he still there?"

"Yes, my lady," an armored knight in full plate armor replied, glancing through the window. "He is resting on his back, with a hand on his belly. The poison should have killed him thrice over by now."

"Why did you have so much poison on hand in the first place?" Victor asked, too curious for his own good.

"Intense war politics," the marquise replied without giving more of an explanation, shifting uncomfortably in her chair. "I cannot take this anymore! Someone groom me!"

One of the catkin attendants, a thin, frail, humanoid cat wearing butler clothes, groomed the back of the marquise's ears with a paw, soothing her. "Victor, is it?" she asked him suddenly. "What is your level?"

"I'm level seven, madam." Five levels in Outlaw, two in Monster Squire.

"A level seven taming a dragon?" She sneered at him with resentment. "I do not believe you."

"Do I look like a dragon tamer to you?" Victor replied with a sneer of his own.

"He listens to you," the Count of Provencal said, having removed his sweat with a now wet handkerchief. "You saved my life."

"Listens is a bit exaggerated. That creature is a goddamn wrecking ball, all I can do is try to steer him in one direction and hope he doesn't burn too many houses."

"We could mount a surprise attack while he sleeps," a guard proposed.

"Yeah right, try to kill the invincible dragon who ignores arrows and thinks your best poison is pepper. Maybe you will give him a better perk this time." As he drew glares from the nobles and their guards, Victor cursed his tongue. When he had noticed Vainqueur didn't understand sarcasm, the adventurer could no longer help himself. It helped relieve the stress of dealing with the wyrm.

"Use another tone with your better, ruffian!" one of the guards spoke up, barely restraining himself from hitting him in the face with his iron gauntlet. His mistress interrupted him with a mere gaze.

"Where do you come from?" the marquise asked Victor. "Your accent is not Gardemagnian. It sounds vaguely Prydanian."

Her tone told Victor this wasn't a good thing to flaunt. The Fomors of Prydain had shed much blood in their attempted conquest of Gardemagne, and their Wild Hunt still attacked ships approaching their island. "I come from America," Vic admitted, before adding, "Earth."

"A Claimed," the marquise nodded. "Show me."

Victor pulled back the sleeve on his left arm, revealing a crimson, shining tattoo representing a twenty-faced dice. "The mark of Dice," the Marquise recognized. "I should have known only a chosen of the luck god could befriend a dragon."

Some luck. This world *sucked*. It was full of brigands, man-eating monsters, *dragons*, oh, and stuck in the Middle Ages! He hadn't been able to take a hot bath for months! All because he saved some girl he had a crush on from getting mugged, only to be stabbed and left to bleed in an alley. And if *death* hadn't hurt enough, getting forced to join a band of outlaws to survive right afterward had been just as harrowing.

But he understood where that comment came from. People from Earth reincarnating in Outremonde after being branded by the local gods were a known occurrence, and most sported unique perks allowing them to make a life for themselves. The phenomenon even caused the rise of a new religion, the Esoteric Order of the New World.

But Victor didn't care about becoming a hero or a local curiosity. He just wanted to survive, get laid, and return home.

Also, *befriend*? Victor would have run away if he could. Unfortunately, the dragon would probably track him down in no time, that beast had keen senses. "Look, lady, I'll try to lure him off your lands, but I don't promise anything. Just don't try to steal his stuff again, okay?"

"My lady, why did you ask for this rapier in the first place?" the Count of Provencal asked.

"This is a family heirloom," the marquise replied. "My ancestor, according to legends, befriended a manling adventurer and tricked a King of Gardemagne into giving the boy his daughter's hand. As a reward, the manling gave my ancestor his prized rapier and the marquisate of Carabas. Catkins ruled Carabas ever since."

Ah, that explained all the felines running around.

"Looters stole that rapier from my great grandfather's corpse during the Century War, but I had no idea it ended in the claws of a red dragon," the marquise said, a maid refilling her glass. "I did not know one befouled the country, let alone Vainqueur Knightsbane."

"He's got a reputation?" Victor asked, eager to know more about the wyrm.

"He was the bane of Midgard for centuries, before vanishing fifty years ago," the Count of Provencal said. "Legends say he fought a Wild Hunt party single-handedly and traded blows with a level sixty-seven elf knight."

From what Victor had heard, only the now legendary Shining Knight approached that level. Which meant the dragon might as well be invincible. "Yeah, and now he has taken two levels in Noble."

The marquise and the count exchanged worried glances. After all, like most aristocrats, they probably had levels in that class too. "A red dragon should not have access to a Rogue Class," the marquise stated. "How did this happen?"

Victor wisely decided not to mention his own responsibility. "No idea. He was already like that when I found him. Now he's set on becoming an adventurer because it pays well, and it's *easy* for him. Look at the forest."

"The monsters of Gevaudan plagued the regions for ages, especially with the chaos of the Century War," one of the knights said. "To destroy the entire area in minutes..."

Louise de Carabas nodded. "While the loss of my pantry is devastating, the economic gains do outweigh it. We might as well make use of the dragon's current fancy. If he wants to be an adventurer, we could send him on a fool's errand."

"My lady, you cannot be serious!" the count protested. "A dragon adventurer? What else, a troll prince?"

"The creature is toying with us," a guard agreed, clenching his fists. "How long until its natural instincts reassert themselves?"

"We could offer him a doomed request, like attacking the Fomors of Prydain or the demon lord Brandon Maure," the marquise ignored her advisers, her butlers moving to groom her back. "Either he will succeed and do the world a favor, or fail and get killed."

"Er, the lizard won't move unless there's a significant reward," Victor said, although the idea had merits. If the dragon was willing to fight other monsters for a price, then maybe he could steer him towards a better purpose. "You better be ready to deliver if he succeeds."

The marquise frowned, probably lacking the funds to assuage Vainqueur. "No matter," the marquise said. "My court's Wizard sent messages to His Majesty King Charles Gardemagne and the Shining Knight, who will dispatch their best warriors after him. After the news spread, this dragon's days are numbered. "

Victor doubted they would amount to much. Vainqueur's family name was *Knightsbane* after all.

But what should he do? Lure Vainqueur to his death, hoping an adventurer would get lucky? His gut told him it wouldn't work. No, Victor was stuck with the dragon for now, and from what he had seen he would better work with or around him than *against*.

The adventurer decided the best option was to make use of the dragon's fancy, as the marquise suggested. Even with the war's end, the kingdom of Gardemagne remained plagued by troublemakers, who killed people right now, instead of retreating to an island far away like the Fomors.

He might also make a nice profit out of this mess. He had gotten two levels in less than one day, after struggling for months to level up in his Outlaw class. Being around a dragon killing strong opponents he himself couldn't take on helped him level up faster. If he reached a high enough level while guiding and studying the dragon up close, maybe Victor could escape his grasp one day.

"Are there any troublemakers that need death by dragonfire?" Victor asked, drawing gazes at him, "This is a gamble, but if I aim him at dangerous enemies, maybe one will get lucky and kill him."

That greedy Vainqueur would never let him keep anything shiny, but if he managed to grab a noble title or magical items while at it...

"The main threats to Gardemagne's peace are the Scorchers, roving bandits and mercenary bands ravaging the countryside since the end of the Century War," the Count said. "Bands led by the kind of Ogron the Ogre, Gustave La Muraille, and François Vilmain are causing trouble in the south-west. Duchess Aelinor issued bounties on their heads."

"They are no match for a dragon, Gilbert," the marquise said. "Even Ogron is only level thirty-five or so, and while the duchess put a bounty on the Scorchers' leaders, they are low. Will they motivate a dragon?"

"Do you have the bounties on hands?" Victor guessed he would just guide Vainqueur towards that kraken. Considering the reward, he would have no trouble convincing the dragon. But it wouldn't hurt to take a look at the other options.

"Minion?" Victor winced, as Vainqueur's voice made the walls tremble. "Minion?! MINION!"

Vic sighed. Duty called. "Do you happen to have a large bag?" he asked the nobles. "And maybe a potion of fire resistance?"

"Have you not asked enough already?!" a knight lambasted him, the winged lion growling at his outburst.

"Otherwise, I tell him you have a hidden pantry under your tower," Victor replied, annoyed. "Your choice."

The marquise waved a hand in annoyance. "Fetch him what he wants, so long as they leave."

Victor figured babysitting a dragon had its perks.

5: Human-Sized Loot

"That feast was great," Vainqueur told Victor, as his faithful minion returned from the ash-filled ruins of the Woods of Gevaudan, having covered his mouth with a scarf and carrying a full bag on his back. Vainqueur could already hear the sound of his new treasures falling on his hoard. "We should come back one day."

The dragon wondered how that noble catkin would have tasted if roasted. Beastkins had varied tastes, and that one would have been fat enough to satisfy Vainqueur's ravenous appetite.

Yesterday's feast, and the ash-filled atmosphere of the burned woods, made Vainqueur hungry for a special barbecue. It had been a long time since he had eaten anything more varied than cattle or bland, unfulfilling knightly manlings.

What else could he eat? Elves were vegan food. They tasted like the grass they liked so much and made him sick. Dwarves were nice, fat and thick, but Vainqueur always got drunk after eating more than three. Goblins were little more than snacks.

Dragons then? Come to think of it, Vainqueur had never eaten other dragons. Vainqueur wondered how he himself would taste, with that sweet manling sauce and spices.

...

No, that would be cannibalism. Vainqueur wasn't a savage.

"We, Your Majesty?" the minion asked his master.

"Minion, you are my official guide," Vainqueur gave his chief of staff a new promotion. He had more than deserved it, and due to his current minion shortage, the dragon had many offices to distribute. "You take care of the trip, I take care of the food. Now, what have you found?"

"Quite a lot, actually. That [Old Money] perk is goddamn useful. No wonder nobles live the high life." The minion opened the bag, presenting Vainqueur's new treasures to the dragon, jeweled rings, necklaces, sounding horns, trinkets and other shiny stuff. "A [Ring of Fire Resistance], a [Horn of Wyvern Calling], a [Gold Statue of Mithras], a [Firebomb Necklace], a pair of |Solar Bracers] and a lot of gold pieces I haven't counted, probably twenty thousand or so."

Vainqueur marveled at the new additions to his hoard, especially the three foot tall gold statue of some manling king and the golden bracers. At this rate, he would double the size of his hoard within the week.

Since nothing should have resisted his flames, Vainqueur figured the Perk must have materialized these treasures after the incineration. The more he learned about this class system, the more it fascinated him. "You sound like an expert retriever, minion," Vainqueur said, noticing his chief of staff had identified each item by name, "I did not know this."

"That's thanks to my [Eye for Treasure]," Victor replied. "It's a Class Perk that allows me to identify magical items and their value."

"What about this [Lesser Poison Resistance] perk I received yesterday? You said I could only get one every two levels."

"Yes, for class perks. There are two categories of perks, class perks and personal perks. The first are obtained by leveling up, the others by fitting specific criteria, like eating too much poison. I heard it's very rare to get it this way."

"Who else but a dragon to unlock it?" Vainqueur declared proudly. He was just getting started. "Put the treasures with the rest of my earnings. We return to my hoard to add them to it, and then we go..." The dragon left the sentence hanging.

"Hunt the kraken of Messaline, Your Majesty?" Manling Victor suggested.

"Hunt the sixty thousand coins squid, my thought exactly, minion." Just the thought of eating that kraken and getting paid for it made him salivate. Maybe the creature would drop a greater treasure Vainqueur hadn't collected yet, like a throne or a crown.

Being an adventurer was awesome! Why didn't more dragons tried it?

"About that, Your Majesty," Victor cleared his throat, coughing due to the ashes, "I only survived the trip thanks to a potion of fire resistance the marquise gave me. What use to you have of that ring or the bracers?"

"They are shiny, and they will look good in my hoard."

"I'm just saying, I would perform my duties better with good equipment, Your Majesty. Especially if you have me search for items in ash-covered ruins every week. At worse, you could recover your *shiny* treasures from my corpse if I die in the line of duty."

"What equipment?" The demand confused Vainqueur more than anything. "You will not look better with bracers or a ring. All manlings look the same."

"Thank you for the kind remark, Your Majesty."

"You are welcome, minion."

"Anyway, the ring will make me resistant to fire, the horn can help me summon a wyvern in a pinch, and the bracers increase my strength under the sun. Only the necklace is more trouble than it is worth, and unless either of us worship the god Mithras, the statuette has no effect besides looking good."

Vainqueur gave his lackey a confused look. "You can get stronger by wearing bracers?"

Victor's face morphed into a strange expression, as if he had said something stupid. Vainqueur pushed further as he connected the dots. "Minion, are you telling me that you also became resistant to fire by drinking a potion?"

The minion shifted uncomfortably, as if he had something to hide. "Yes, Your Majesty, I did. For a time."

So all along, the foolish manlings trying to kill him didn't wear items to look less unremarkable? They could get more powers from magical items?

"Marvelous!" Not that Vainqueur would ever need a potion to survive a trip among flames, but the idea of his hoard making him more powerful appealed to him. Vainqueur already imagined himself with a golden crown making his breath even hotter. "And the bracers give strength? I will try them at once!"

"They're human-sized so they won't fit," the minion pointed out the obvious.

"Oh?" Vainqueur checked, and realized that yes, all of his new treasures were indeed manling-sized. He did not hide his disappointment, nor the anger boiling within him. "Why does my Perk brought me human-sized treasure? This is sabotage! A malfunction!"

"Maybe it was never meant to work with dragons, Your Majesty."

"Exactly, a malfunction." Who created these crappy, manling-centered Perks? He would have a word with the designers.

Unable to wear the items himself, Vainqueur considered manling Victor's offer. The minion was as weak as the rest of his kind - he couldn't even survive *fire* - but he had been an exemplary, reliable servant so far. Vainqueur decided he wanted to keep him around safe and healthy, at least until he could rebuild his minion stable.

"Fine, minion, I agree to loan you items you can wear. No need to thank me, my generosity knows no bounds." Of course, Vainqueur expected his lackey to thank him anyway, and looked at him expectantly.

"Thank you, Your Majesty," Victor replied, bowing so deeply Vainqueur wondered if his hair would touch the ashes.

"That [Eye for Treasure] Perk, how can I get it?" Vainqueur asked, curious and eager to marvel at his own treasures. "Does it come from your Monster Squire class?"

"No, that's from my first class, Outl—" Victor stopped himself, as Vainqueur squinted at him.

"You can be two classes at once?" Vainqueur caught on, suddenly very interested. "How many?"

The minion lowered his head in embarrassment, scratching the back of his head. "As many as you can achieve. The level cap is one hundred in total though. Afterward you become a god and ascend to heaven. I don't think anyone alive today reached level eighty, though."

Only because no dragon ever tried. "Then I, Vainqueur, will reach level one hundred!" the dragon boasted with enthusiasm, dreaming about the loot so many Perks could provide him, "And you, minion, will reach ninety-nine!"

"That's the spirit, Your Majesty."

Vainqueur let the minion read maps and papers, thinking about the minion taught him. If he could get stronger wearing enchanted items, the dragon wondered how he would look in an armor of gold. It would be like carrying his hoard all the time. A new world full of wonderful possibilities had opened itself to the dragon.

"Your Majesty?" the minion asked, after reading the papers, "On a second thought, I think the kraken can wait."

"What could possibly delay me doubling my hoar-" Vainqueur stopped himself mid-sentence, unwilling to reveal his hoard's size. The fact it seemed quite small when compared to what adventurers earned already shamed him, although he would never admit it openly. "Explain."

"According to the request, the kraken disrupts a sea trade route to the southern merchant empire of Barin, since its den is located on the way. Merchants want it gone to improve trade, hence the big reward, but if left undisturbed, the kraken doesn't disturb anyone. The Scorchers... not so much."

"Scorchers?" Vainqueur had never heard of them. "Are they a kind of knights?"

"Yes and no. They're former soldiers and mercenaries turned highwaymen when the war's end left them jobless. I have the bounty posters of three of their leaders, and they're an endless litany of murders, abductions, arsons, property damage, slaughters, and other war crimes perpetrated on the helpless peasantry."

A bunch of glorified thieves then. Vainqueur would have smote them on principle, but he never did anything for free. Not anymore. "I am listening."

"Gustave La Muraille," Minion Victor read the wanted poster of a knight with a black, horned helmet, "Twenty levels in Knight, four levels in Heavy Knight, three levels in Turncoat, total level twenty-seven. A human deserter from the Gardemagnian army leading a warband of twenty soldiers; wanted for the sack of the Poustagniac village and the massacre of its eighty-seven inhabitants. Duchess Aelinor of Euskal offers five thousand gold coins for his head. And that's the *nicest* of the three. Ogron the Ogre has a triple-digit body count, and François Vilmain is a corrupt priest who reinvented himself as a demon summoner."

While the manling's concern for his puny kind was almost touching, Vainqueur only cared about one thing, "How much?"

"Ten thousands for Ogron, since he's the toughest, and five thousand for Vilmain. Twenty thousand all together, officially."

"Minion, twenty thrice makes sixty," Vainqueur brushed him off, before catching on, "What do you mean by, *officially*?"

The minion smiled at him, as if sharing a secret. "They are enemies of the great and beautiful Duchess Aelinor, who will be very grateful if we get rid of them. I'm sure she will give you a much greater reward under the table."

"Why under a table? Is it a magic ritual?"

"Ah, no, it's uh, a metaphor, Your Majesty. Meaning that she will offer us a much greater reward that is not mentioned in the bounty."

"If she is willing to offer more, why didn't she put it in the request?" Vainqueur found the hole in the minion's logic. The dragon had the distinct feeling the minion was trying to sucker him into fighting these bandits, but on the other hand, Vainqueur still had much to learn.

"Because of royal taxes," Victor replied hastily. "The king takes a tenth of rewards offered through the Adventurer Guild, and that doesn't include the guild's own five percent fee."

Vainqueur almost choked. "A tenth?! That is theft! No wonder you turned outlaw, your puny race is led by a robber!"

"Indeed, Your Majesty," Manling Victor said. "Hence why I think she will probably offer the real reward outside the official channels, so it does not get taxed. Avoiding taxes is an ancient, respected human tradition... and Your Majesty is a dragon. I am sure she will enjoy rewarding you the same way the Marquise did."

"A noble endeavor," Vainqueur commented, before wondering about how this duchess looked like. "Aelinor, is she a princess?"

The minion shrugged his shoulders. "I dunno. Maybe."

The prospect of adding a princess to his hoard delighted the dragon almost as much as the promise of easy money. "Minion, we will hunt your thieving kind at once."

6: Food Chain

"Are we there yet?" Vainqueur asked for the hundredth time, as they flew over yet another stinking human village.

"Nope, sorry," manling Victor replied, his eyes set on the map he struggled to keep pace with the wind. "Ogron was last seen near Haudemer, and this is Pointin."

"How do you know?" Vainqueur lambasted his minion guide. They had flown all the way across the land, almost reaching the western sea; yet missed the target. "All of your dirty villages look the same!"

"Oh, Your Majesty, I believe the next one will be the right one."

"And how so?"

"Because of the fires, Your Majesty."

Indeed, a column of fire rose from the west, on the coast. Vainqueur squinted, noticing a small city under assault by a large group of manlings.

Vainqueur approached the city and circled it from above to take a good view of it and the nearby beaches. It was larger than the villages they had visited, with stone houses and a wooden extension leading into the sea itself; a port welcomed a dozen floating buildings the manlings called ships. Quite a few of the inhabitants hastily tried to board them.

A large group of manlings, around eighty, attacked the city from the north, axemen slaughtering people like pigs while bowmen set the roofs of nearby buildings on fire. Dozens of corpses littered the stony ground, while defenders used carts as improved barricades to slow down the invaders' progress.

A monstrous, fifteen-foot tall cyclops led the manling attackers, swinging a large two-handed axe which cut soldiers in half with each blow. Arrows and spears bounced off his thick green skin, as he tossed carts away with every step.

Incensed at them not stopping to marvel at his arrival, Vainqueur let out a mighty roar from above, and it did the trick. Everyone looked up at him, freezing at his crimson majesty, their faces draining of colors.

"A dragon!" one of the defenders shouted on the ground. "Ogron has a dragon!"

"Ogron? Aha, finally!" Vainqueur chuckled. "Minion, on whom do I land?"

"The attackers, Your Majesty."

Vainqueur descended in the streets below, the manlings fleeing at his sight; but not fast enough. His landing blew away nearby houses and crushed half a dozen latecomers.

Only the cyclops hadn't run, glaring at his men with its single eye. "Cowards! Dragons aren't scary!" he shouted at them.

"Of course not, they are amazing," Vainqueur replied, releasing his minion on the ground. The defenders cowered behind the barricades, unsure how to take this turn of events. "Which of you is Ogron the Ogre?"

The cyclops struck the ground with his axe, pulverizing stones and making the street tremble. "I am!"

Vainqueur looked at the cyclops, then burst out laughing, the one-eyed meat responding with a glare. "No seriously, which of you is Ogron?"

"Your Majesty, this is Ogron," the minion said.

"Minion, this is a cyclops, not an ogre. Ogres have two eyes."

"Yeah, I know, but that's Ogron the Ogre anyway. I've seen his poster."

"You goddamn righ'," the one-eyed ogre said with rising frustration. "Ain't no other Ogron! I traveled to this country to figh' and make war for Gardemagne! I bled dry, and instead of gold, the king gave me a dirt poor farm! Ogron ain't no farmer, he is a warrior! Ogron will not stop until—"

Vainqueur zoned out at that point, too confused by the eye paradox. All he could notice were isolated blabbering, "Ogron, Ogron, Ogron, pirate! Blah blah, flee the country! Ogrongron, knights!"

"—and that is why Ogron will sail these boats!"

"Minion, if he is a cyclops and not an ogre, why is he called Ogron the Ogre?" Vainqueur ignored the one-eyed ogre. "It doesn't make sense!"

"Ogron is called Ogron the ogre because..." the cyclops said with a low growl, swinging his axe with impatience and showing his bloodied teeth. "Ogron eats people."

"You too?" Vainqueur looked at the cyclops with a new, fresh gaze. He was just fat enough around the angles, with plenty of meat...

The cyclops let out a roar, raising his axe to swing it at Vainqueur. "You die—"

Chomp!

Vainqueur took a bit out of the giant's upper torso, swallowing a third of the corpse in one go. He sprayed blood all over his mouth, too ravenous to care. Everyone looked at Vainqueur as he digested the cyclops' eye and head, the manlings having all turned pale for some reason.

"Minhion, shyclopsh tashte like shalty pihg!" Vainqueur chewed on the giant's flesh, finding the taste too sweet to stop with one bite. "Sho good! I wansh more!"

"What about some human bandit snack to go with the taste?" Manling Victor suggested, pointing a finger at the cyclops' pale followers.

They looked a bit too sick now, but Vainqueur approached his muzzle to smell them closer; at least one of the archers had soiled himself, so the dragon made a face. The bandits panicked at his approach, running away from him screaming.

Vainqueur wondered if he should pursue them, then decided he would rather eat the rest of the cyclops than run. He absentmindedly grabbed a large chunk of a house's stone wall, and tossed it at the fleeing manlings, crushing many of them like insects. The others sped up even faster after that, and Vainqueur returned to his meal.

He ate the rest of the one-eyed ogre with two more bites and let out a belch.

*You gained a level in [**Noble**]!*

+1 STR, +1 VIT, +1 CHA, +1 LCK!

*You earned the Class Perk: [**Snobbery**]!*

*[**Snobbery**]: your attacks inflict five percent more damage on non-noble targets, and you receive five percent less damage from non-noble assaillants.*

"Minion, I leveled up!"

"Sweet, how many stat points did you win?"

"Four, minion," Vainqueur replied proudly, before realizing he had no idea what that meant. "Minion, where do stat points go?"

"You can check your class and stats by saying 'Menu' out loud."

"Really?"

"Your Majesty didn't notice?"

...

"Of course I noticed," Vainqueur spared the minion's feelings. "I *always* noticed. I was just testing your knowledge. And you have passed."

"Truly an honor," the minion replied with gratitude.

"Menu!" Vainqueur said, the word making hungrier than the ogre. A series of words appeared out of nowhere in front of him.

Vainqueur Knightsbane

Level: 3 (Noble 3)

Type: Dragon

Party: V&V

Health Points	5,315
Special Points	1,290
Strength	95
Vitality	88
Skill	11
Agility	39
Intelligence	9
Charisma	71
Luck	39

Personal Perks	Class Perks
Dragonfire Breath	Old Money
Fire Immunity	Snobbery
Red Dragon Lifeforce	
Dragon Arrogance	
Dragonscale	
Super Senses	
Virgin Princess Radar	
Lesser Poison Resistance	

V&V? Double Vainqueur!

A heavy silence had fallen on the area, and Vainqueur realized the manlings defenders looked at him with open eyes.

"Minion, the ambiance feels too heavy," the dragon said. "Sing my praise to cheer it up."

Manling Victor immediately raised a fist. "Vainqueur, best dragon!" He turned to the silent manlings behind the barricades, raising his other hand to encourage them, "Vainqueur, best dragon!"

"Vainqueur, best dragon!" a urine-smelling man said. Eventually, the other manlings joined in.

"Vainqueur, best dragon!" "Vainqueur, best dragon!" "Vainqueur, best dragon!"

Much better. "Thank you, thank you, I deserved it," Vainqueur said, licking the blood on his lips. "I, Vainqueur, am an adventurer coming to rescue you! See the plate? See the lead plate? Now bring me your cattle!"

They fed him only a cow and two pigs, which disappointed Vainqueur slightly, but he was too full from the cyclops to complain.

Vainqueur had made his nest on the beach next to the city, resting on the warm sand as he digested his meal. Even if he had saved the city, he noticed quite a few ships leaving it regardless, fleeing as far away from him as possible. The dragon ignored them and toyed with this 'menu' power.

"Menu," he said, the words appearing, before saying it again. "Menu." The words disappeared. He did again, finding the process strangely addictive.

After five minutes of playing, Vainqueur noticed the minion returning with two other manlings, one female—not a princess—and the other male. The former was an adult with large mammaries, long blonde hair and that strange clothing the manlings called a dress; the other was an old, frail male with a grey beard and a hat, but otherwise perfectly plain.

Vainqueur still had trouble telling one monkey from another. They all looked the same at first glance.

"Your Majesty," minion Victor said. "This is the mayor of Haudemer, and its innkeeper, Miss Lynette, and the village's Class Scholar, Henry Bright. I briefed them on your career choice."

"Your Majesty Vainqueur, on behalf of Haudemer," the female manling said, bowing deeply, "As thanks for saving the city, allow me to grant you the city's highest honors, the keys to—"

"Where is my money?" Vainqueur cut her off.

"Already covered, Your Majesty," Victor replied, while the female remained speechless from the blunt rebuke. "The local guildhall reported your deed to the Duchess, who will send men at arms to deliver the reward soon."

The mayor coughed. "Please allow me to offer you free lodging at my inn for a week, free of charge. It would be a pleasure to have you around."

"Is there a lava bath?" Vainqueur asked.

"A lava..." the female frowned. "No, Your Majesty, no, we do not have a lava bath."

No lava bath as a basic accommodation? They truly were backward peasants. "I will sleep on your hot sand, but my minion probably does not have my quality standards."

The female made a strange face, while the minion concurred, "Certainly not, Your Majesty. I will be sure to enjoy a good, warm bed."

Vainqueur brushed the matter off, focusing on that Class Scholar, who began to speak up. "Great Vainqueur, your friend Victor told me your majesty needed advice on the class system—"

"Majesty, with a capital M," Vainqueur corrected him. "Also, what is a friend? Some kind of minion?"

Henry blinked. "How can you... does Your Majesty have the [Super Senses] perk?"

Vainqueur checked his menu, noticing it among his 'personal perks.' "Ah, yes, I do. How do you know?"

"It's a Perk common among highly perceptive species, such as beastkins."

"Henry is our city's class expert, advising us on how to develop our career, stats, and perks," Lynette told the dragon. "Although I didn't know a dragon could get one."

"Me neither!" Henry exclaimed, "This a new discovery! I couldn't wait to discuss with Your Majesty about it!"

"Me too," Vainqueur nodded. "Now, what is this system exactly?"

"It's a powerful supernatural system unlocked by the god Dice during his first rolling spree, back when it was still a sentient dice artifact," Henry explained, already losing Vainqueur's attention. "Classes represent powerful roles, which grant us immense powers when we tap into them."

"Are you sure dragons did not create it?" Vainqueur pointed the obvious hole in his logic.

"Your Majesty, historical research show the class system appeared with Dice, who is the very first recorded instance of an intelligent being gaining a level in a class. Even if Dice never claimed to have created it, evidence shows that it activated it first."

"So you have no proof dragons did not create the system first," Vainqueur replied.

"Er, yes, maybe, but this would go against every research we ever did, all species combined."

"So this is a dragon-created system to grow stronger and richer, I get it," Vainqueur said, minion Victor putting his hand on his face for some reason. "Now, manling Henry, I want to get more levels in Noble."

"Are you sure?" the manling sounded confused, "The noble class is a hit or miss, with either situational ones like [Aristoradar], which help sense true or false nobles, or strong ones, such as [Stipend], which grants money every month."

"Free money?" Vainqueur's head perked up, the sudden gesture startling the manling trio, "When?!"

"Noble level nine!" the scholar cowered.

"And then? I gain diamonds at eleven? Tell me!"

"None of the other perks of the noble class increase money gains," Henry continued, trembling under the dragon's gaze, before adding hurriedly. "But there are very good perks, like [Privilege], which allows you to ignore one attack a day."

"Why would I need it? I already ignore your attacks all the time!"

"That is true indeed," the minion said.

"What else can make me *richer*?"

"Merchant," Victor said with a laugh. "Or Banker."

"But merchant is a minion's work!" Vainqueur protested.

"Crafter classes tend to get better material rewards, compared to other classes," Henry said. "But maybe it would be better if I started from the beginning, please?"

Vainqueur sighed, already bored by the professorial tone. "Go on..."

"Classes are divided into five categories. Fighters, the best at direct combat and warfare; Spellcasters, who gain strong magical abilities; Rogues, who focus on tricks and social perks; Crafters, who create items or empower existing effects; and the rare Monster classes, which are only available through deals with monsters. If Your Majesty wants to get richer, Crafter classes like Alchemist or Merchant would indeed work better."

"A dragon does not hold a shop," Vainqueur replied proudly. "What else? How many classes can I get?"

"As many as possible, although one cannot get farther than level 100 in total, everything combined. When a person reaches level 100, they level up into the God class, becoming true deities, but no longer able to grow further. Also, the higher your total level, the harder it is to gain new levels, even if a class's entry conditions are low. You will need ever greater challenges to reach a new level. I see with my Class Screen perk that you have three levels in Noble, so you could probably level quickly to level nine with a good training regiment."

"The Scorchers are pressured by knights of the Shining Crusade, adventurers out for their bounty, and men of the King," Lynette said. "Ogron's band attacked us to board ships to escape the country, and Haudemer is less defended than other ports. Which means they may return."

"Good, free experience," Vainqueur replied. "That way I won't have to burn fat to chase them."

"Oh, by the way, I gained a level in Monster Squire when King Vainqueur made me his chief of staff," Victor butted in the conversation. "Ever heard of it? It might come in handy."

"Monster Squire?" Henry frowned. "No, I never heard of this class. What kind of perks does it have?"

"Monster Kin, which makes me buddy-buddy with monsters."

"This may be a monster class," Henry said. "Monster classes are classes which are usually only available through deals with intelligent monsters or fiends. Somehow, your promotion fulfilled the class' entry condition. Amazing."

"Yes, yes, all my minions bask in my brilliance," Vainqueur said, impatient. "Now, what class can make me rich in a good, dragon way?"

Henry frowned, thinking. "Gamblers have good, balanced stat growth for an unpromoted class," he finally said. "C in Health Points, C in Special Points, D in strength, D in vitality, A in skill, C in agility, A in intelligence, B in charisma, and, the best for last, S in luck. A jack of all trades with a strong focus on luck, and several useful perks to farm gold."

"What is this gibberish?" Vainqueur started having a headache. "Unpromoted?"

"Every time Your Majesty gains a level in a class, your stats have a chance to increase according to that class' stat growth," the manling continued. "D is a one in four chance, C one in two, B three in four, and with A, you always win a point. S means you always get two points instead of one, and E means you never gain anything. Promoted classes are classes only available if you reach sufficient level in another class, so Gamblers open the path to—"

Boring! "Minion Victor, you are now my official class manager," Vainqueur said when he couldn't take it anymore, "This is a very important job, the most important you will ever receive. You deal with this."

"Me?" manling Victor frowned. "Didn't you want to learn everything about the system yourself, Your Majesty?"

"I, as a dragon, have too much on my hands to learn every single detail... that is why we dragons have minion laborers do it."

Lynette and Henry exchanged glances, with Vainqueur tiring of their presence. "Leave," he said, resting in the sand. "Minion, stay a bit longer."

The two monkeys left hurriedly, leaving the dragon alone with his favorite audience. "Merchant," Vainqueur complained. "I am not paid enough for this, minion."

"What? But it went so well!" the minion tried to cheer him up, "Free lodging, Your Majesty! I even got an anonymous letter from an admirer! With so many single maids in town, maybe I have a shot."

The manling sighed at Vainqueur's puzzled look. "A shot at getting laid, Your Majesty."

"Getting laid?" After some deep thinking, Vainqueur guessed the meaning. "Ah, ah, you want to *breed*! To put your eggs in a female manling!"

The minion said nothing, then gave him a strange, empty stare. "You had to say it like this," he complained. "Your Majesty's phrasing ruined it for me."

"No, no, minion, the problem lays elsewhere," Vainqueur corrected him, "You will never succeed unless you take a bath."

"A bath, Your Majesty?"

"Minion, I wanted to spare your feelings before your fellow monkeys, but you stink like beetle dung! You will never breed with that smell!" Manling Victor lowered his head in shame, his master deciding to cheer him up. "Minion, I swear to you as your master, I will do everything in my power to ensure you breed and perpetuate your species."

The minion's head sprung up so fast, Vainqueur thought he would snap his neck. "Wait, what, really?"

"Of course I will! That way I can renew my stock of minions within the year." The minion didn't get it, so Vainqueur detailed his logic. "If you breed well and your females lay their eggs before winter, then I should have a new tribe of minions available by next summer. No more goblins, all manlings. I will even let you use my cave for a nest if you need it."

"We humans don't grow as fast as—Wait, goblins lay eggs?"

"All the time," Vainqueur nodded. "Manling, I, Vainqueur, order you to take a full bath, for your own good. These peasants have no lava bath, but there's the sea right next to us."

"I will settle on a hot bath at the inn, Your Majesty."

"Then go breed, and sin no more!"

7: Gather the Minions

Victor let out a moan of pleasure, as he sank in the warm, hot bath. So good!

Lynette's inn was a top-notch establishment, a stone mansion renovated into a resort for adventurers and merchants; he had his own room with a king-sized bed and full access to a private bath in the back.

Victor had left his clothes and weapons nearby, just in case. He had had a nasty experience with a naked ambush in the past, and it didn't hurt to be paranoid.

Victor glanced at the copper plate around his neck. Following Ogron's 'last meal,' the adventurer guild had upgraded him and Vainqueur to copper-rank adventurers. Of course, from what he had gathered, the guild itself still had no idea how to handle the dragon and simply decided to follow due process until King Gardemagne or the Shining Crusade 'settled' the matter.

Victor had no idea what to make of the dead cyclops' axe however. It didn't have any magical powers, and it was too heavy for anything but a giant to use. He figured he would let Vainqueur toy with it, then sell it behind the dragon's back.

The former outlaw had a more important problem to deal with. Namely, the love letters, and the maiden blushing at him when he walked through the street. Now Vainqueur had agreed to settle in Haudemer for a few days after Victor conned him into fighting the Scorchers, he could fool around again. Lynette was also quite easy on the eyes...

The bath's door opened behind him, Victor's hand moving to grab his daggers on impulse. Was it Lynette, bold enough to join him in the bath? Damn, this just kept getting better and better.

Except it wasn't a maiden, but a disheveled Henry, and fully clothed at that. "Sir Victor!" he smiled at him with enthusiasm, ignoring or uncaring about Victor's weapon. "Here you are!"

"Henry, why are you in my bath?" Victor asked the obvious question. Especially since he must have gone through the bedroom to get here.

"I couldn't wait! I've been studying your case since yesterday, and it has been bugging me since—"

The Class Scholar suddenly noticed the black sword tattoo on Victor's left shoulder and paled. "That's the mark of the Nightblades." He knew what the mark meant, and the organization which issued them.

Damn, the outlaw thought. He would rather keep that little secret to himself.

"Let's call them legitimate repossessors of private goods, and I left them when I became an adventurer." A lie. No one ever truly left the Nightblades. "And if you're smart you will hold your tongue about it."

Henry wisely dropped the matter, more interested in class discussions anyway. "I'm sorry, but it has been bothering me for a while," he said. "Why not Crusader?"

"Crusa—what?"

"The class! With his immense strength, the dragon would reap the best benefits of its stats' growth, and the self-healing would make him nigh impossible to put down! Think of the optimization potential!"

"You're seriously considering making that dragon impossible to kill," Victor said.

"Y-Yes, isn't it your job?"

Yes, but he wasn't going to do it *well*! "Look, all he cares about is money," Victor replied. "He's probably strong enough to handle anything short of legendary adventurers, so unless you propose a class that can farm gold without doing 'minion work', I'm not interested."

*Congratulations! For being perfectly in tune with your master's desires, you gained a level in [**Monster Squire**]! +10 SP, +1 STR, +1 SKI, +1 AGI, +1 INT, +1 LCK!*

*You gained the [**Minion Trainer**] Class Perk!*

Minion Trainer: *you and your minions gain fifty percent more experience when fighting side by side.*

"How is it that I just leveled up in Monster Squire?"

"Ah, you probably gain experience doing tasks for the dragon," Henry guessed. "You gained your class by serving him right? So, of course, the system will reward you if you protect his interests."

Great, Victor got levels by being a good, loyal henchman. Somebody up above laughed at him. Minion Trainer though? Did the Class expect him to go befriend more dragons? One was already enough trouble!

"That just proves my point," Victor said. "The way I see it, Vainqueur will level in the Noble class until he gets that stipend perk, and then he will delve into a new class better for moneymaking." One which hopefully will not make him even more invincible.

"Gambler then. They have an excellent luck growth to complement the [Old Money] perk, and multiple abilities that can multiply money gained from bets."

"I just can't imagine Vainqueur ever betting anything though," Victor said. "He's a dragon, a miser."

Henry thought about it, before having a eureka moment. "The Gladiator fighter class then! They gain lots of Perks that can provide tangible rewards if they impress crowds. Dragons have high strength and charisma, perfect to make full use of that class."

Victor guessed it would appeal to that dragon show-off. "Do you have documents on it?"

"Yes, of course! Do I have your permission to take notes on its evolution? I have no idea how it will synergize with a dragon." Henry lost himself in calculations. "You yourself have the [Claimed by Dice] perk, right? That means you get ten percent more chance to increase your intelligence and luck. You would make a good Spellcaster."

"I would rather not spend all my time reading scrolls and grimoires," Victor replied. "Don't get me wrong, I won't mind shooting lightning bolts, but I prefer to stick to daggers. All kinds of them, if you catch my drift."

Henry didn't get the dirty joke, making Victor sigh in disappointment. "Why not Gambler, then?"

He would have tried, if Vainqueur paid him. "Henry..."

"Yes, Sir?"

"That's a bit dirty, but... is there a class that helps getting laid?"

"For men or women? Most are gender-exclusive, except the Red Mage class."

That wasn't the answer Victor had expected. "There's more than one?" he asked, puzzled.

"Of course, there are dozens of seduction-oriented classes, and many of them have useful perks for it, like the Dark Knight's [Sinful Aura]. It's a very common question."

Damn, Henry made it sound like a respectable academic subject. And here Victor thought it was a stupid question! "I have a friend who has been... inactive... for a while, and he wants to stop up his game. Level ten, mostly rogue-like classes."

"He? Ah, too bad, the best class for seduction is the female-only Black Widow. Does he have a high charisma score?"

"As good as mine."

"Average then," Henry said, Victor sulking. "Then I would suggest the Fiendish Rake class, discovered by Ludvic Van. It has very high entry conditions though, including charisma, vitality, and agility scores of fifty each, and surviving a special demonic ritual. If he doesn't that score yet, he should build his charisma and grab a few perks in the Red Mage class. I can give you a book on it if you want."

Was everybody in this world a munchkin?

*For studiously learning about the Class System and how to improve your dating life, you receive the **[Observer]** personal perk.*

Observer: *you can instantly divine the class levels of someone you look at, as long as they are the same total level as you or lower. If the target is higher leveled than you, you can only see the total class level.*

Yes, even Victor himself. "Henry?"

"Yes, Sir?" he asked, his eyes full of hope.

"Thank you," Victor said. "Now get out of my bathroom, please."

The unfortunate implications of their current situation suddenly dawned on Henry, who hurriedly left while apologizing all the way to the door.

Victor sank back in the bath, leaving his dagger aside, and letting himself drown in pleasure.

His moment of respite lasted one minute before someone knocked.

"What?!" Victor complained as the person opened the door without his authorization.

Lynette walked in, wearing a summer, golden dress showcasing her assets. Victor instantly sank deeper in the water, only his head rising above the waters.

The innkeeper laughed at the sight. "Such modesty," she said. "Am I interrupting, Sir Victor?"

"Not at all," Victor replied, having a very nice view with the current sight angle. "What can I do for you?"

"I have a very pressing problem in my basement, which I think only you alone could solve."

Alone in the basement...

Ah.

Ahah! Finally! "I'm all ears," Victor grinned with a smile, Lynette smiling in response.

Victor sighed, as he walked into the inn's dark basement, a torch in hands. It smelled of cheese, meat, and brewery, and the bitter scent of disappointment.

Instead of a basement tryst, Lynette had sent him on a giant rat extermination mission.

Seriously? He knew he had technically just started his career, but this was adventurer hazing number one! And unpaid labor at that! The things he did for dragons and pretty faces...

Yet, Victor had been scouring the underground without finding any rat and started to wonder if Lynette had overreacted. She said food had been missing lately, but it could have been the cook or a staff member stealing...

"Remember, everything is in the heart!" a high-pitched voice said, coming from behind a crate, "We need to say it with the heart, the heart! And practice the pose!"

Or maybe not. Grabbing a dagger with his free hand and holding the torch with the other, Victor looked behind the crate and found himself facing five pairs of eyes.

There *were* monsters in the basement! Except they weren't rats. They were...

Kobolds.

Small, lizard-like humanoids the size of human children, and just as smart, kobolds had sharp claws, stunted horns, and long, slithering tails. Victor counted five of them, each with scales of different colors, namely red, blue, yellow, black, and pink. Quite the rainbow.

Victor noticed a small tunnel, dug in a wall nearby. The creatures must have dug all the way from the countryside to steal the basement's food.

"Oh my gosh, a human!" the pink kobold said upon seeing him, cowering at the sight of the much bigger Victor.

"Everyone, time for the choreography!" said the red one, bigger than the rest and seemingly the leader, "Remember, say it with the heart! He will cower before us!"

Much to Victor's amazement, each kobolds adopted a strange, ridiculous pose.

"We fight for injustice!" the red Kobold started.

"We live for mayhem!" the black one continued.

"We strike at night!" the blue added.

"We strive in discord!" the pink one shouted.

"We are..." the yellow reptile finished, before shouting in unison with his gang, "The Kobold Rangers!"

Victor stood there, too confused to respond.

"Yeah, we finally mastered the choreography," the red one chuckled happily, congratulating his team. "We floored him!"

"I still think we should add 'chaos' somewhere in the motto," the pink pointed out, "I mean, it has such a zing!"

What the hell was Victor watching right now? "I felt that blue's timing was off," the adventurer admitted. "Also, if you want to go all the way, you need a team pet, like a white alligator."

"What?" the blue kobold glared at him, "How dare you insult my talent! A human can't understand true art!"

"I never understood abstract art, no," Victor replied, not that impressed. Kobolds were no more dangerous than rats, and these ones looked like a bunch of utter idiots.

"Foolish mammal, the Apple of Knowledge showed us the truth!" the yellow one added.

"Wait," the red one said, giving a blank look at Victor, "How did he..."

"You humans are out of style!" the black one snarled, showing his tiny claws and leaping at him. "It's killin' time!"

Kobolds being as small as human children, Victor stopped him by wordlessly putting his foot on the creature's face. The monster struggled, its tiny hands unable to reach him, before calling to his teammates, "Help!"

"Wait!" the red kobold said, preventing the others from joining the 'battle' by moving in between the two groups. "He understood!"

"He understands?" the blue one repeated. "Absurd!"

"Yes, I understand what you said," Victor shrugged, before realizing that he probably shouldn't. The [Monster Kin] perk worked!

"And the smell," the red said. "Do you smell his scent?"

The black one stopped trying to reach Victor and backed down, sniffing the human's boot. "He smells like a reptile! A super reptile!"

"Ultra Reptile!" the yellow one exclaimed, sniffing Victor with such intensity the adventurer felt deeply embarrassed.

Even after a warm bath, spending days with Vainqueur had rubbed his awful smell off on him. And the dragon had complained his chief of staff stank?

Victor instantly cursed himself for internalizing that stupid job. But then again, maybe he could make use of it... "Listen to me, kobolds," the human declared with a broad gesture, "I am His Majesty King Vainqueur the Dragon's chief of staff, guide, and class manager! Cower before me!"

"A dragon's chief of staff!" Much to the human's amazement, they seemed to recognize its meaning. "A real minion chief of staff!"

"Such raw charisma..." 'Pink'—Victor decided to mentally nickname them after their scale color—had tears in her eyes. "I can almost feel it!"

"We have no choice!" Blue said, "We must sue for peace!"

"Peace!" Red repeated.

"Then, bring me this Apple of Knowledge, and I shall let you go," Victor ordered them, although he suddenly felt guilty for some reason. Like he was bullying guillible children.

"Quick!" Red ordered, the others running into the tunnels, and quickly coming back with a black and white tablet computer with a familiar logo on its back. Victor lowered himself slightly to look closer, as they showed it to him.

An Ipad?

Sweet! He could never afford one! Victor had heard items from Earth sometimes found their way to Outremonde, mostly brought by people abducted there. Where did the critters find it?

The adventurer lit the Ipad up, the screen loading with a delay, maybe due to aging. A quick glance at the desktop told him the previous owner had been one huge fan of downloading ebooks and videos; while most were hidden behind passwords, a few could be freely accessed.

Victor loaded one of the videos, showing old, silent footage of one of these ridiculous Japanese Super Sentai series. It was cheesy enough to make him cringe, but the kobolds watched with rapturous interest.

"He knows how to unleash the Apple's power," Blue muttered.

"Take us!" Pink implored Victor.

"Wait, what?" Victor asked, "Where?"

"Oh mighty chief of staff, please accept us as minions," Red asked, bowing to Victor and soon imitated by the others. "We do not have the experience, and it would be our very first minion work, but... but we are hardworking and polyvalent and... please!"

The human found them strangely cute, monstrous critters aside. After seeing their big, adorable eyes looking at him with candid hope, the adventurer couldn't help himself. "I'm willing to take you as interns," Victor said. "Unpaid interns."

Urgh, Vainqueur had rubbed off him.

"Interns! We're interns!" the black one jumped on place, before stopping in confusion, "What's an intern?"

"It's a great opportunity towards potential future career advancements," Victor deadpanned, repeating the words from his first summer internship.

"Such responsibility," the blue one said with big bright eyes, much less cynical than Victor had been in his place.

*For recruiting your first group of expendable minions, you have gained **two** levels in [**Monster Squire**]! +10 SP, +1 STR, +2 VIT, + 2 SKI, +2 AGI, +1 INT!*

*You gained the [**Monster Student**] Class Perk!*

***Monster Student**: you can now learn monster-exclusive Perks after you are taught or targeted by them. You also count as a monster for the purpose of class access criterias.*

Now, how would Victor word *that* to Lynette?

8: Murderhobos

Henry knocked on the door with impatience, a book under his arm.

He wondered who owned the house. Located in the outskirts of Haudemer, many thought it abandoned, its owner absent, and his host had indicated she only rented it for a while. Thorns and weeds had taken roots in the garden and the stone walls, while the shutters remained firmly closed. No matter the outside spookiness, he had run towards the place as soon as he read the invitation.

"Professor Henry." A charming young woman welcomed him, as she opened the door with a squeak. She was no rare beauty, keeping her long raven-hair tied with a white rose, but her dark eyes shone with a keen intellect. Most importantly, she wore the black and gold wizard robes of the Royal University of Gardemagne. "How kind of you to visit me."

"When you informed me you visited our beloved Haudemer, I couldn't pass up the opportunity," the scholar replied. "It is an honor to meet you in person, Miss Lavere."

"Please call me Lucie," she replied politely. "I may represent the Royal University, I never forgot my humble roots."

Indeed, it made her academic success all the more striking. She had published two papers, one on the effects of the Red Death plague on base stats, and another about spellcasting classes synergies. A brilliant young mind, she was apprenticed to the famous royal headmaster Nostredame, a wizard of great renown.

Henry examined her class with his Class Specialist Perk.

*[Lucie Lavere; **Scholar** 15/**Unknown Spellcaster Classes** 22]*

Unknown classes meant she had an item preventing him from clearly identifying her levels. A Perk would have hidden the information entirely. "Why hide your spellcaster classes?"

"University politics," Lucie replied calmly. "I study new fields of spellcasting yet unrecognized by the University, and I might get in trouble before I publish my thesis. Many covet my apprenticeship under Nostredame and would ruin my reputation to take it."

"To be level thirty-seven at your age... most adventurers retire at it. You are very good, miss Lavere."

"I am an apt pupil, and I learn from the best," the young woman replied with great courtesy, before inviting him inside, "Please come in."

Henry did so, finding the house's inside much more welcoming than the outside. The two stepped inside a long hallway, covered with a red carpet and lit up by fire elementals kept in glass containers above their heads. While the place lacked in decoration or a personal touch of any kind, the owner took care to maintain it in pristine condition.

The inside also looked far bigger than the outside. "A space altering spell?" Henry asked, impressed. He had never seen one.

"The true owner's doing, I must say," Lucie replied, closing the door behind them.

It must have been a spellcaster of great power. "I wonder what a scholar of your caliber is doing in Haudemer, especially in these dark times."

"Learning," Lucie replied. "One of my mentors asked me to follow her on a business trip, which of course must remain between us. She is a very private person. "

"I didn't tell anyone," Henry replied. He understood scholars of her caliber wished for anonymity, especially since Scorchers might target them for ransom. "I thought you would be interested."

He handed her his notes, which the woman began to read at a quick pace, almost a page a second. "Monster Squire," she noted. "I never heard of that class before."

"It has good, equilibrated growth for an unpromoted class, and very interesting Perks," Henry said, eager to impress the other scholar. This may be his chance to get his research published, and for him to finally obtain some recognition. "A whole unknown monster class. And the dragon, Vainqueur, gained levels."

"I saw this dragon, Vainqueur, laying in the sand outside the town. He is not the first case of an intelligent monster gaining levels, but this is certainly the first case for a dragon. Even the fabled Jade Dragon of the East never gained a class of his own."

"I wish I could study him further," Henry said. "Mayor Lynette told me the Shining Crusade would send a squadron of knights to kill him as soon as possible."

As he told her of the recent events, Lucie chuckled, amused by the passage on Vainqueur's demand of a lava bath. "I would not count on your crusaders for this task," she said, before stopping before a wooden door. "We can discuss it in my study. I believe your research has great potential."

"Thank you, hearing you say so warms my heart," Henry said, as he opened the door and walked inside the dark study.

Finally, after spending years researching classes, he was on the verge of a breakthrough. If Lucie validated his findings, the Royal University would publish his researches; he would get credited as the discoverer of a new array of Monster Classes and Perks, and his name would live on.

At first, he couldn't see everything, although strong odors assaulted his nose. The study didn't smell like paper and ink.

It smelled like rotten meat.

Then the room suddenly lit up, and Henry screamed.

It wasn't a study, it was a dungeon; a cold, dark room smelling of death, full of wooden operation tables and shelves covered with surgical tools. Two zombies hung in the middle, suspended to the ceiling by chains. Henry recognized the faces as a couple of fishermen, whom he had often seen while strolling around the docks.

The door closed behind him.

Henry turned around, expecting to face Lucie.

Instead, a knight two heads taller than Henry barred the entrance, pointing a sword at his throat. The titan of metal facing the scholar had shoulders that would rival a bull, and his heavy plate armor exuded a strong sense of menace. His horned helmet, which covered his face, made him look like a gatekeeper from Hell.

Henry instantly recognized him from a wanted poster, even before his Perk activated.

[Gustave La Muraille; **Knight** *20/***Heavy Knight** *4]*

A Scorcher leader.

"Ah, Lucie brought us a friend," another voice, pleasant, called from behind the chained zombie.

A man walked into Henry's line of sight, an elegant, black-haired man of Harmonian descent, with a pleasant face and beautiful amber eyes. He wore the white and gold garments of a priest of Mithras but proudly displayed the sinister crow symbol of the murderous god Deathjester on the upper left. He wielded a rapier around his belt, although he hadn't unsheathed it.

"Hello, my dear guest. My name is François, François Vilmain," the fallen priest said with a mirthful smirk. "I am a captain of what you call the Scorchers, alongside my comrade Gustave. I'm sure you've heard a lot of horrible tales about us, all of them true."

"What have you done to Miss Lavere?!" Henry asked, Gustave grabbing his shoulder with his free hand and maintaining right in place. Lacking any combat ability, Henry had no chance of fending off these two.

"Lucie?" Vilmain chuckled, "Her master owns the house and agreed to let us hide there, so long as we helped with her student's, shall we say, empirical research."

A necromancer. The headmaster laid in bed with Scorchers and necromancers? Henry froze, aghast, before realizing they said 'her' student, and the archmage Nostredame was a man.

"Please, take a seat, Henry," Vilmain offered, waving his hand at a wooden stool right next to the restrained zombie. Before Henry could respond, Gustave forcefully grabbed him with his free hand and forced him to sit with inhuman strength. "Let's have a chat."

"People will notice my disappearance," Henry pleaded, trying to buy time.

"Oh, don't worry about us, we have your case covered," Gustave replied.

Vilmain cleared his throat. "Contrary to what you may believe, Henry, neither me nor Gustave, or even Ogron, started as bandits. In fact, we fought for Gardemagne during most of the Century War; back then, the king granted adventurers and mercenaries a writ, allowing us to raid enemy towns in his name. Unfortunately, with the end of the war, our respectable occupation of massacring people and torching their villages is no longer politically correct."

"We were asked to retire, farm like peasants, or move on to much more dangerous monster-hunting jobs," Gustave said with disgust.

"Fortunately," Vilmain said with a light grin, "His Dark Majesty, Brandon Maure of Ishfania, offered us a very nice retirement sum and asylum, so long as we torched the countryside of Euskal to the ground and kept the crusaders busy while he retakes his fortress of Rochefronde. Which unfortunately for you, Henry, includes Haudemer. Do you understand?"

The poor scholar nodded, pissing himself. Vilmain glanced down at the soiled pants with a sneer, before continuing his story.

"But you see, we have a very big problem. Apparently, you have a dragon guarding the city, and he ate our men for breakfast. When we sent men to check on these men, he killed more of our men. Finally, the royal army is breathing down our necks, and for important reasons, we cannot skip Haudemer's destruction. The situation is not good for our financial future."

"So we caught these two," Gustave pointed at the zombies. "Who said the dragon had a master."

"Of course we had to rough them up before they gave names, namely, that this master, 'Victor,' often met with you."

"That is wrong," Gustave replied. "That we roughed them up. One of them talked when he saw you zombified the other."

"Ah, yes, but you had your Outlaw knife him dead afterward if I remember."

"It was to help him level up. I take care of my men."

"He got a level out of this commoner? Lucky beginners, they don't have to burn the midnight oil the way we do."

It was relatively easy to break into the two-digit range by killing low-level people, even up to level twenty for dedicated killers. Afterward, the increased experience requirements made it necessary to fight people who could fight back on even terms.

After this awful interlude, Vilmain focused back on Henry. "So, my friend, I am sure we can find a solution we all agree on."

"You're going to kill me anyway," Henry said. "Why would I tell you anything?"

"Of course we are going to kill you," Vilmain replied with a disturbing kind of serenity. "The only question is, do we have to rough you up first? Unlike my fellow Gustave here, I would rather make it quick and painless. I am not a savage, Henry."

"Says the priest of Deathjester," his comrade replied with a taunting tone.

"I am the holiest man there is," Vilmain protested. "I worship the god of crime, and he likes my work."

"Whatever," Gustave replied, swinging his weapon. "Do you talk, scholar, or do I cut a leg?"

"No, no, Gustave, wait," Vilmain raised a hand to appease his fellow criminal, while Henry shook in pure, unadulterated fear, "I tell you, I'm not a savage. While you are most certainly going to die so word of our presence does not spread, I'm sure we can honor last requests. If you tell us the truth, the full truth, the entire truth."

Knowing his life was done for, Henry figured out he might as well try to bargain for something. "Will you spare someone, if I speak?"

"Depends on whom," Vilmain replied. "We are going to kill that Victor fellow whatever happens. I am sorry. Professional pride."

"No, Mayor Lynette." He had had a crush on her for years, even if he never dared make a move. "Also, please do not burn my house. The research inside... they're my life's work."

"You demand much," Vilmain replied mirthfully, "Lynette, that's the innkeeper right? I heard she's very beautiful. Smart woman too. Do you like her?"

"Y-yes, I do."

"Ah, very well. If you speak, we will spare her life, and we will try to leave your home unscathed if you give us its location. No promise on that one, fires spread in wild directions sometimes. Maybe I will find a way to sell your papers to an Ishfanian scholar if they are truly so precious. Now, tell us everything."

And so, Henry spoke.

He gave them a rundown of his discussions with the dragon, including his general personality and levels; then, much to his shame, he sold out Victor, his class levels, his Perks, everything he could gather.

He would have lied if he could but Bishops like Vilmain could detect lies. "A Nightblade?" the priest of Deathjester raised an eyebrow. "Interesting."

"The Nightblades can control dragons?" Gustave asked, worried.

"Of course not," Vilmain replied. "I do wonder what a career criminal is doing protecting a village."

"He said he left them," Henry said.

"You never leave the Nightblades. Well, no, technically, you can leave them, but life leaves you first. No matter. Is he greedy, like this Vainqueur?"

"I don't think so..."

"He must have a weakness. Honor, fame, women..."

"Mayor Lynette had him do jobs for her," Henry remembered. "I noticed him glancing at her, and not at her eyes."

"Ah, yes, of course, no man can resist a chest, any kind of chest." Vilmain chuckled at his own sexist joke, while Gustave didn't. "What else?"

"I... I have no idea. He is a nice person who wants to help."

"A good man, with a kind heart? Ah, now this is interesting. Gustave, what do you think?"

The cruel knight's fingers twitched on his sword's pommel. "There is absolutely no way we can beat that dragon in a fight."

"Yeah, I didn't think so either."

"But he is dim."

"But he is dim," Vilmain nodded. "We will have to distract him before we burn this town down, recover the Apple, and flee on stolen ships afterward. As for that Victor, we can handle him easily enough. We're both over twice his level, and a kind heart is easily misled. Is that all, Henry, my friend?"

"I told you everything," the scholar replied, crying in shame at his own cowardice.

"Did he lie?" Gustave asked his partner.

"No, he is an honest man, albeit not a brave one." Vilmain shook his hand, before flashing a comforting smile at his prisoner. "You must not know it, but my friend Gustave here has three levels in Turncoat. That class's first Perk, [Falseness], hides Turncoat levels from scanning Perks, such as yours. The second is called [Traitor's Joy]. I'm sure a scholar like you knows what it does."

Henry clenched his fists in impotent shame. "You get an experience boost every time you betray a promise."

"I told you he was a savage," Vilmain said, sounding falsely sorry. "Poor Lynette."

"You said it, not me," Gustave replied, raising his sword.

"Wait," again, Vilmain raised a hand to stop his ally, "Not yet."

"What?" Gustave complained, "He's of no use to us."

"We could make use of him as an hostage, for now. Just knock him out. I swear you will have his head in time, my friend."

Gustave grumbled and struck Henry from behind with the pommel, the poor scholar's world fading to black.

9: Level Grinding

Instead of breeding, Manling Victor had adopted a full litter of new minions.

And already they proved useful. "Master Vainqueur, Master Vainqueur!" Yellow, the kobold with the best nose, pointed a claw at a bush, the dragon smelling a Scorcher manling hiding there. "I found another!"

Vainqueur let out a roar, raising the giant axe Ogron the one-eyed ogre had kindly given him...

Or rather, struggling, as he couldn't keep the axe properly aligned even while wielding it with all his clawed fingers. How did the manlings do it?

Like a rabbit, the manling ran out of the bushes, only for Black, the biggest of the new recruits, to chase after him with a spear. Vainqueur followed, causing trees to fall as he moved through the woods; he constantly struggled against the urge to run back on all four, as a good dragon should.

How did that cyclops do it? Raise the axe up, and then down.

Vainqueur tried, the upward swing sending a pine tree fly, and he struggled to aim right at the escaping food-in-waiting. "Minion!" Vainqueur shouted. "MINION!"

"Yes, yes, I'm here!" Manling Victor emerged from the woods with his dagger toothpicks, barring the escaping prey's way and forcing it to flee in another direction.

"This axe is not working!"

"Just swing it down when we have him immobilized! And remember, you meet the class criteria, but you have to impress your fans with a melee weapon strike, Your Majesty! Kill him with style, or you won't access the new class!"

Style? Like a crushing display of superiority? "Dear mammals," Vainqueur asked Dead Manling Running. "Do you know what dragons call pain?"

Kobold Red jumped from a bush, trapping the prey and forcing him to stop running. The mammal briefly turned his head behind, crying at the sight of Vainqueur's majesty.

"A birth defect!"

And then Vainqueur swept the scorcher with the axe, smashing him into a crater of blood and broken bones.

"Argh!" The aftershock sent his entrails splatter on Red's face, the poor kobold having to remove brain matter off his eyes. "I have human blood in my eyes!"

"Vainqueur, best dragon!" Black and Yellow cheered him up, as expected. "Vainqueur, best dragon!"

*By impressing a crowd of fans with your weapon prowess and moxie, you gained a level in the [**Gladiator**] Class! +30 HP, +2 STR, +1 VIT, +1 SKI, +1 CHA, +1 LCK! You gained the [**Arena Warrior**] Perk!*

*[**Arena Warrior**]: instantly gain medium proficiency in all melee weapons.*

"Ouch," minion Victor said. "Ouch, that joke hurt."

"Joke?" Vainqueur asked, finding the axe suddenly light in his hand. He played with it, but he still had troubles wielding the weapon without his claws getting in the way. His hands were made to run on all four or rip the prey to shreds, not carry a bladed stick!

"Wait, dragons really consider pain a birth defect?" his chief of staff asked him.

"Why, yes, only lesser beings feel it," Vainqueur replied plainly, before standing proud. "But not as much as I felt this new Gladiator class!"

"Vainqueur, best dragon!" Red added, late to the party. "Your Majesty is the greatest in the world!"

"Yes, yes, thank you," Vainqueur replied, pleased, "Still, Minion Victor, do I still need to use the axe to gain levels in that class? I find it impractical."

"No, just to impress fans with your battle prowesses."

Vainqueur gave the stick one last chance, grabbing the axe with his mouth and swinging it this way. "Hosh do I loosh?" he asked, trying to adopt a dominant pose, only to hit a tree with the back of the blade and nearly lose equilibrium.

The minions exchanged glances, too aware of their master's sensitivity to speak their mind. Obviously, he should stick to his dragon weapons.

He was too good for manling weapons anyway.

"Your axe sticks suck," Vainqueur said, as he spat out the weapon, which landed in the bushes nearby with a loud crash. "Now, Minion Victor, I keep slaughtering these Scorcher ruffians and yet [Old Money] does not activate with your kind."

"Yeah, I guess it is to prevent nobles from slaughtering their peasants for items. It should work with monsters though."

Vainqueur glanced at the kobolds with greed, before deciding no good dragon slaughtered their minions for items. For treachery and theft, always, but good, loyal minions were too valuable to get rid of casually.

The world already abounded with victims.

"At least he had some standard loot on him," Victor said, as he inspected the remains. "Iron daggers, and nice boots."

"Not good enough for my hoard," Vainqueur replied. A good dragon had wealth standards. "Next!"

"I don't smell another," Yellow said, smelling the air with his fellow kobolds. "Your Majesty got them all!"

"Aw... " Vainqueur sighed in disappointment. "So no more levels and no gold today?"

"We can always sell his belongings," Victor suggested. "I know you don't want to become a Merchant, but we don't need a class to sell these items. I could even use the gains to invest in better stuff."

"Invest?" Vainqueur didn't know the word.

"Yeah, you give away some gold in exchange for something else with more value."

Vainqueur's brain stopped working. "Giving away gold."

"Your Majesty," Victor cleared his throat. "For something else which has *more value*."

"Giving away gold," Vainqueur repeated, his noble mind unable to progress past that line.

"Yes, but you gain more afterward, so you don't really give it away. It's a disguised loan."

"Giving away gold," Vainqueur repeated these cursed words for the third time. "Manling Victor are you well? Are you sick? I did not know the lack of breeding could have such dangerous effects on your mental health."

The minion finally understood he had gone too far into sin. "Your Majesty cannot even *imagine* it."

"What kind of sane mind would?" Vainqueur retorted, before shuddering at the mere word. "*Giving.*"

"Yes, I suddenly realize that may have been too much for Your Majesty."

"Master Vainqueur, the chief of staff only tried to help you," Yellow pleaded. "Please forgive him."

"Buttkisser, buttkisser!" Black taunted his fellow, Red punching both of them in the shoulders. "Ouch!"

"No argument before the chief of staff!" Red said. "Remember protocol!"

"The protocol?" Manling Victor asked.

"The minion protocol," Vainqueur clarified, before realizing he never drilled his chief of staff on proper minion management.

"The chief of staff is the highest echelon of the minion pecking order, the ultimate honor a monster lord can bestow!" tiny Red explained to manling Victor. "It is the ultimate minion killing machine, the most ferocious enforcer of the most dreaded of masters! Fifty percent strength, fifty percent cunning, two hundred percent loyalty!"

"Now you're exaggerating on that last bit..." manling Victor replied with his trademark humility.

"You underestimate your importance in the food chain," Vainqueur cheered him up, "You are only beneath me in the preciousness hierarchy. You are even above princesses!"

"Nice to hear Your Majesty values me between himself and pretty faces," the minion thanked his generous master.

"Of course, princesses are precious, but you are almost an honorary part of my hoard, manling Victor. If we are to starve, we will make a sacrifice and eat the minions together."

"Your Majesty, I understood your first sentence, but you lost me with the second."

"The preciousness rating also represents your place in the food chain," Vainqueur taught him. "Each member of the chain can eat those below if they are hungry. If you and I are hungry without food available, we can eat minions as emergency rations."

"It would be an honor to feed Your Majesty!" small Yellow said.

"Wait, wait," manling Victor panicked. "Does that mean you count me as a potential meal?"

"Not unless we have no food or minions available," Vainqueur reassured him. "That will never happen. The world is full of dragon food."

Manling Victor probably understood he should focus more on recruitment from now on. He knew his previous chief of staff had hired a lot of goblins after they had that conversation. Minion Ressource was a full-time, difficult job, after all.

Speaking of minion management... "Where are the sweet Pink and Blue?" Vainqueur asked, having grown slightly paranoid since his last goblins abandoned him in his sleep.

"I sent them to deal with the local blacksmith on my behalf," Victor said. "I think the Scorchers aren't at Haudemer to flee the country. Or at least, not only. I believe they are looking for something, and so I want to be prepared."

"Something? Is it a treasure?"

"I dunno... maybe?"

"If it is not good for my hoard, it is good for nothing. Manling, explain."

"Haudemer's region is south of Euskal and north of the city of Rochefronde, which is held by crusaders but besieged by the Ishfanian and summoned fiends. By torching the countryside, the Scorchers cut the supply lines between Euskal and Rochefrond. Do you follow me so far?"

As it always happened with too many uninteresting words, Vainqueur zoned out, pretending to politely listen to what his minion had to say. "Interesting," the dragon lied.

"Blah blah... no strategic value... Brandon Maure... scorcher scorched... blah bla..."

"Interesting."

"-And Your Majesty is really listening?"

"Interesting," the dragon repeated.

"Interesting," Red the Kobold and his fellows nodded in agreement, before clenching his tiny fist. "The chief of staff trusted us with such an important mission, we will not fail him!"

"See?" Vainqueur said, "Minions solve every problem, when you raise them right. As expected from my prized chief of staff."

"One day too, I will be chief of staff," Black said.

"Me first!" Red butted head with his fellow, Vainqueur so proud of them fighting for the job already.

That would keep Victor sharp. He could already see the seeds of spirited competition germinate in the sharp glint of his treasured minion's eyes. That fear of losing one's position to an underling, Vainqueur found it so entertaining.

"Your Majesty."

"Yes, Minion Victor?"

"I earned a Perk which makes it possible for me to learn monsters' Perks, either if they teach me or if I experience them."

"Ah, so if I try incinerating you, you will breathe fire too?" Vainqueur asked, curious. "Is that what you want?"

The minion looked up at his beloved dragon master and the smoke coming out of his nostrils, then paled. "You know, Your Majesty, on second thought, I may have been too hasty," he said. "Let's forget we ever had this conversation."

"Your loss," Vainqueur shrugged. Why would anybody not want to breathe fire? "Maybe one day, should you prove the best chief of staff I ever had, I will teach you the ultimate technique of dragonfire breathing. It is the perfect weapon to kill manlings."

There, that should motivate him to work hard for Vainqueur's personal gain.

"I would rather avoid killing people myself," minion Victor declared. "If I kill a fellow human, I will meet all the criteria for a specific class, and probably level up in it. I don't want to."

"Oh? Which class?" Maybe it could apply to Vainqueur.

"Assassin. I really wouldn't feel proud of this one, even if the Scorchers are assholes who deserve to die."

"Minion, I have eaten enough of your kind to get sick of it, and I never received a level in that class," Vainqueur pointed out.

"I never did either!" Black complained.

"When did you ever kill a human?" Red asked.

"In my heart..."

"You need to fulfill a few more criteria," Victor shrugged. "And you need to kill members of your own species willingly, which I doubt you have yet."

"Well, minion, it's not as if you will need to defend me from your puny kind. Stick to my class planning and I will take care of the food."

"Your generosity truly knows no bounds, Your Majesty."

"I know," Vainqueur said, feeling on a goodness spree. "About this ruffian's belongings, Minion Victor, you are now—"

"Your treasurer and hoard manager?"

"Never!" Vainqueur roared, taking the manling aback as his golden eyes shone with wrath. "No touching my hoard!"

The kobold minions cowered behind their chief of staff, who had lost all the color on his skin. By now, Vainqueur had guessed manlings reacted this way when reminded of dragon superiority.

The greatest calamity of this age calmed himself. "No, manling Victor. I said yesterday selling is a minion's work, and that is exactly what you and the kobolds are going to do."

"So you want me to open a shop away from the frontlines?" Victor asked, slightly more enthusiastic than Vainqueur had expected.

"You already have the name," Vainqueur said, "V&V! That way, we get rid of the junk not shiny enough for my hoard, except gold and jewels, which are!"

"Your attempt to corner the value chain is truly brilliant, Your Majesty," the obsequious Manling Victor congratulated him.

"And, *and*, to keep you motivated, I will allow you to keep one," Vainqueur raised a claw once he had the minions' full attention, "One-tenth of the profits you will earn!"

"We... we are going to be paid?" Yellow almost had tears in his eyes. "Paid..."

"Indeed, you are way more generous than the King himself," said Victor.

The mere mention of this ruffian angered the dragon. "I swear to you, manling Victor," Vainqueur declared, "V&V shall never pay taxes to this criminal, ever."

"I will send royal constables to you, Your Majesty. I am sure they will agree to a tax exemption."

"No giving away money," Vainqueur insisted, shuddering at the words. "No investing. The glorious name of V&V cannot be associated with this madness. Also, sell the corpses. I am sick of eating manlings all the time."

"Selling corpses, Your Majesty?"

"Doesn't your kind hunt monsters to collect their corpses and sell their parts?" Vainqueur had seen many would-be 'dragonslayers' - he sneered inwardly at the word - wield weapons and items made of other creatures.

"Well, yes, but *monster* parts. Adventurers don't harvest bandit corpses."

"Then what do you do with them?"

Victor scratched the back of his tiny head. "We just leave them laying around for animals to eat..."

"No more *giving*, minion. You will now find a way to make money out of this waste of skin."

While Vainqueur removed some meat in between his fangs with his claw, Victor kept nodding to himself in short succession. Vainqueur wondered if he had broken his neck. "So Your Majesty wants me to open a shop where I sell junk and monster parts and corpses. Wonderful. Anything else?"

"This is a lot of work, but you are my chief of staff," Vainqueur reassured him, "You will find the time in between preparing my class progression and training the Kobolds in those you deem appropriate."

Manling Victor said no word, as he struggled under the weight of his duties. "Teach classes to the kobolds..."

"You fail to grasp my grandiose vision for V&V, Minion Victor. An adventurer party of minions, trained from the egg and working to the death to fulfill quests; shopkeepers selling junk and meat in every single one of your backward villages, filling chests with gold. Everyone working together to build the greatest hoard that shall ever be! A mountain of gold which will make your tallest castle crumble in shame at its shiny glory!"

Vainqueur narrowed his head, so his silent minions could see the fire in his eyes.

"My hoard!"

Victor made a strange smile, which Vainqueur assumed as one of absolute joy.

10: Gods and Zombies

Located on a creek near the docks, Haudemer's temple was a rather large stony church by manling standards. According to Manling Victor, due to Haudemer being a small town, the twelve 'gods'—Vainqueur couldn't help but chuckle at the word—the manlings worshipped had to share the same temple.

From what he had understood, puny species worshipped these stronger creatures the same way minions obeyed their dragon masters, with the bonus of being promised a place at their side after death. That part confused the dragon, he expected to live forever.

Vainqueur guessed the prospect of an afterlife could only appeal to races fragile enough to, well, *die*.

The inhabitants had deserted the temple's surroundings once they caught sight of Vainqueur. While he perfectly understood their inferiority complex when basking in his presence, a little awe and worship would have been nice. If they had enough of it to worship twelve non-dragons, then certainly they could spare him some adoration.

Only one manling hadn't fled, and harassed his chief of staff instead.

"Do you want salvation in a new world?" That manling looked even more ridiculous than the rest of his kind, with his black robe and a badly painted map of seas and land masses on his chest and forehead. "Wait, I can feel your Isekai levels, medium!"

"I'm a Claimed," Vainqueur's chief of staff protested, showing his dice tattoo. "And you mixed up North and South America on your map!"

"Ohoh, perfect!" Instead of being discouraged, the harasser grabbed the minion's arm. "If you sign up to the Esoteric Order of the New World, you are *guaranteed* to reincarnate on the mythical island of Japan, where every girl is a virgin!"

"Scram!" Victor tried to push the manling away away. "Get him off me!"

"Minions," Vainqueur ordered, as he was too important to deal with it. "Do the thing."

"Defend the chief of staff!" Red commanded the kobolds, the five critters jumping on the deluded cultist at once and clawing at his face.

"Argh, kobolds!" the manling cultist protested, as he tried to throw the critters off his back. "Get them off me!"

"Don't kill him, just restrain him!" Victor pleaded as the Kobolds restrained the poor fool on the ground. Vainqueur watched the scene with quiet amusement.

Those five were too adorable to end up as emergency rations. Vainqueur hoped Victor would recruit less funny minions whom he could eat without regret.

The scene did confuse the dragon though. "What was that, manling Victor?"

"It's a money scam," Victor complained. "I've lived on Earth, and it's *nothing* like he just said!"

"Why are we even here? Minion, while I understand your lesser species' need to pay homage to a higher power, but if you want to pray to someone, you should pray to me. I even answer sometimes."

"Your Majesty wanted to get rid selling off corpses and monster parts," his chief of staff pointed at the carriage behind them. "The church deals with them."

Ah, yes. In total, Vainqueur had 'collected' six manling thieves, and one manticore he accidentally cut down during his masterful practice with his axe. They also encountered goblins, fleeing on sight from him; the dragon had simply glared them down as if they weren't good enough for him, which they were.

What was he thinking back then, recruiting those cowards as minions? Manling Victor had made the right call, kobolds solved everything.

Manling Victor left the cultist to the minions, walking past the temple's opened gates and inside the whitened, majestic hall within. Vainqueur followed him soon afterward, head and neck first, carrying himself with pure draconic majesty.

Then, he failed to fit his wings through.

With a grunt, Vainqueur attempted to squeeze himself inside, but too fat after feasting, he couldn't fit. His shoulders hitting the walls made the temple tremble, but unlike the puny guildhall, the walls were strong and thick.

Manling Victor watched the sight with a blank expression, taking a sip of a water canteen while politely waiting for his master to finish his dramatic entrance. Vainqueur noticed a few other manlings inside the building watching with expectation.

"Minion Victor!" the dragon complained to his sidekick, "Tell the architects to build a bigger door!"

"Sure, Your Majesty," the chief of staff replied. "But could you avoid causing the place to fall on us poor mortals?"

As he finally realized he wouldn't get inside without collapsing the entire temple on his lackey first, Vainqueur settled on only letting his neck and head inside with a groan.

Why did the manlings have to be so small?

The temple of Haudemer was mainly composed of a great white hall, and two small wings on both sides. Each of the twelve gods of the puny races had a statue and altar inside, although not with the same degree of respect.

The dragon's share of the spotlight went to the same creature Vainqueur had acquired a statuette of, Mithras, the sun god of law and justice. It was a manling king wearing a golden crown of fire and wielding a blazing sword, whose giant marble statue had the largest altar. At his side was a statue of a blonde female manling knight with large mammaries, whom the puny races called Leone, goddess of art and nobility.

According to Manling Victor, these two ascended manlings were the titular deities of Gardemagne, and thus positioned at the center. "The architect placed the more ambiguous deities, such as the Dread Three, Sablar and Shesha, on the left," Manling Victor told his master, his tone so low Vainqueur could barely hear it, "And the 'politically correct' deities, the Moon Man, Seng, Cybele, Isengrim, and Dice on the right."

The manling glared at that Dice's statue with hatred. From what Vainqueur had gathered from the last prayers of the adventurers foolish to attack him in the past, the 'Dice Who Rolled,' was the deity of magic, weather, and luck. As per its name, it was a dice with an eye at the center of each of its twenty faces.

"Manling Victor, you do not like dice?" Unlike Victor's subdued tone, Vainqueur didn't care about respecting a quiet atmosphere, his voice booming through the hall. Nobody dared complain.

He would have eaten any who did.

"That dim creature summoned me to Outremonde without asking," the lackey replied. "And unfortunately since it first unlocked the class system, everyone worships it. It is almost as popular as Mithras."

Pff... *right*. As if dragons didn't level up first. Vainqueur refused to believe he was the first of his kind to do so.

Dice's altar looked more like a gambling table than a religious site, with a catkin priest busy playing a board game with what the dragon assumed to be two minions. Even Vainqueur's wonderful arrival hadn't made them raise their eyes off the game.

So Vainqueur loudly cleared his throat, and they briefly glanced up at his head long enough to satisfy him.

Most of the altars had at least one tiny priest nearby, with three exceptions. One tentacled squid whom the dragon recognized as the Moon Man, an ancient creature his kind fought off in the distant past; a humanoid crow wearing a harlequin costume and carrying a sharp scythe, drenched in blood; and a huge worm like those infesting the caves below Vainqueur's own lair. The manlings had utterly savaged the last statue.

"That's Sablar, the monstrous worm god of earth, time, and destruction," explained Manling Victor. Vainqueur was silently pleased he didn't have to voice his ignorance out loud. "No one worships it in Gardemagne, since it supports their enemies. People pray *against* it."

"And the others?" Vainqueur listened, just in case there was profit to be made.

"Bah, the Moon Man doesn't remember he has followers half the time, and Deathjester is the god of *crime*. Nobody worships him openly."

"How much levels is that Sablar worth?" Vainqueur asked, eager to get that stipend and free money. "We could hunt him down if there is a reward on his head."

"I don't think picking a fight with a god is a good idea, even for Your Majesty."

"Why? If it exists, I can kill it. I am a dragon, remember? I eat his wormy kind whenever they enter my cave."

"Yes, but that one is level one hundred and turned the southern continent into a desert. Also, nobody puts a bounty on a god's head."

Saddening.

Vainqueur briefly noticed Manling Lynette discussing with a priest nearby, but Victor focused on the matter at hand first, approaching the altar of Mithras.

"Greetings, faithful," the Bishop behind it said, a nice-smelling priestess of Leone at his side; unlike the unflappable priest, the woman observed Vainqueur with the appropriate degree of fear and apprehension. "Have you come to make an offering?"

"An offering?" Vainqueur asked, amused by the puny races' strange customs.

"You offer money to the Church as an offer to the god, in place of fealty," Victor explained to him the concept.

Vainqueur immediately saw an opportunity. "Minion Victor—"

"Your Majesty can't be a god," his lackey said hastily, the quickest sentence he ever uttered, "Unless he reaches level 100."

Vainqueur sulked in disappointment. When he reached that level and became a god, he would ask his minions to build him a larger temple and a bigger statue than this Mithras. No way he would share it with other gods either.

"We have six human corpses outside, and that of a Manticore," Victor told the priest. "Will the church take them?"

"We will purify the corpses so they do not rise as spontaneous undead, then burn them free of charges," said the priest of Mithras. "If you prefer another method, the priests of Isengrim and Cybele will bury them in the forest, so they can return to nature."

"For free?" Vainqueur glared down at the priest. "You will not pay me for the transportation service?"

"Why would we pay you for a public service?"

"Because we inquired *significant* expenses in the course of their deadification."

"This isn't a real word, Your Majesty," Victor said.

"Of course it is, since I said it," Vainqueur insisted.

"We do not pay people to gather corpses," the Bishop of Mithras replied, glaring back at the dragon. "If you want to be paid instead of doing the moral thing, I suggest you turn to the church of Shesha instead."

"Where?" the dragon asked immediately, his greed stronger than his anger at the animal's insolence.

Victor pointing a finger on the left-wing, at the altar of a serpentlike humanoid with the upper body of a winged woman and the lower half of a snake. As befitting of a creature that looked the most like a dragon, her statue was the most outrageous of all, made from solid gold.

"Hi there, Lynette," Manling Victor said as he approached that altar. Vainqueur greedily looked at the statue, leaving his lackey to his poor attempt at pre-breeding. "Of course you would worship the goddess of commerce."

"Yes and no, Victor," she replied. "It's more of a business deal."

"Unlike the other gods, who are fickle in their gifts, Lady Shesha trades for her miracles according to the rules of the market," said the goddess' priestess, a bellyful dwarven woman. "For an appropriate monetary gift, she provides."

"She improves the prosperity of my inn for a fee," Lynette explained.

"Really?" Manling Victor sounded strangely hopeful. "How much to be transported back to my homeworld of Earth?"

"Let me ask the goddess." The priest underwent a brief trance, feverishly waving his hands until a golden number made of light briefly flashed into sight.

...

...

Vainqueur had never seen so many zeros. "That's robbery!" Victor voiced his master's contempt.

"You get a twenty percent reduction if you take the Shesha worshipper annual subscription," the priestess tried to sucker Manling Victor, the number altered to reflect the deduction. "Thirty percent if you become a Bishop or Vestal. Donations to the Church of Shesha are also tax-deductible, so if you have time we can discuss your financial future."

"The minion has no intention of leaving his current, fulfilling job," Vainqueur answered for Victor, although he noted that being a god sounded almost as profitable as being an adventurer.

"Yeah," Victor replied with a strangely less than enthusiastic tone. "We came to get rid of seven corpses outside, six Scorchers and one manticore."

"We can buy the corpses to make fertilizer, and use the manticore's parts for leather and potions. Taking into account the value, I would give one gold piece per human corpse, and one hundred for the manticore's pelt."

"One hundred and six?" the dragon said upon adding the numbers, "I say double."

"One hundred and six," the priestess replied, eyes shining with the steely determination of the true negotiator.

So Vainqueur upped his price. "Triple!"

"Your Majesty, you are supposed to go lower in a negotiation."

"Lower is only for unassertive manlings," Vainqueur replied. "I am a dragon, I know what I am worth. As my representative, I expect you to show dominance as well, minion Victor."

"Dragon or not, the market is absolute," the priestess replied, her greed so *pure*, so *dragon-worthy* Vainqueur couldn't hold it against her. "One hundred and six."

Manling Lynette observed the scene in silence, while a hooded figure wearing heavy, hooded crimson robes, approached the group as the argument heated up.

"Excuse me, I heard your argument," a figure said with a raspy voice. Even if he couldn't see his face beneath the hood, Vainqueur noticed his corpselike white hands and the familiar smell of rot underneath. A ghoul. "Are you looking to sell fresh corpses?"

Vainqueur glanced at the undead, then at his lackey. "That's a worshiper of Camilla," the minion said, pointing at the mosquito crest on the newcomer's robes. "The Marquise of Blood, goddess of death, pestilence, and darkness. One of the Dread Three."

"The three what?"

"The Dread Three. Camilla, goddess of death, Deathjester, the god of crime, and Veran, goddess of fire and tyranny. A trio of evil adventurers who became gods together, and stayed friends since; they oppose Mithras, but people are too scared of them to ban their worship."

"I resent that evil label," the ghoul replied. "Our goddess is simply misunderstood."

"Didn't she unleash the Red Death plague that turned many people into bloodthirsty vampires?" Manling Victor asked.

"Only to prevent overpopulation, and the vampires played a critical role in defeating the Fomor during the Century War. As I said, misunderstood." The figure coughed. "Anyway, have you heard of the undead labor trade?"

"Here we go again," the priestess of Shesha said with a sigh.

"No, never," Vainqueur said.

"I did," Victor said. "They buy corpses from living relatives, turn them into mindless zombies, then put them to labor work, from mining to farming. Isn't it illegal, though?"

"The undead labor trade is a perfectly legal new industry, albeit currently limited to very few cities allowing it in their charters," the hooded figure replied. "Very few of them do, but in time, when they see the benefits of enslaving the dead for the betterment of the living, we hope more towns adopt it. Imagine, zombies laboring the fields in every town, from Midgard to Ishfania, or fearless skeletons saving helpless orphans from forest fires."

"Oh, where can I get one?" Vainqueur asked, now positively giddy.

"Your Majesty loves the dead?" Victor asked. "I never thought you would be that kind of dragon."

"Minion Victor, having undead as minions is a status symbol among dragons," Vainqueur told his chief of staff. "And they are so useful. They never run away, they do not eat, they are not tempted by a hoard, they live almost as long as dragons..."

Vainqueur's own rival, that arrogant Icefang, couldn't stop boasting about his army of dead manlings protecting his treasure when he didn't brag about his crown.

"From what I heard, Victor," the necromancer priest of Camilla told the lackey, "You fit the criteria to unlock the Necromancer class. You could make good money."

"Really?" Vainqueur glanced down at his lackey, who lowered his head. "You can raise the dead? That is wonderful!"

"I meet the criteria to take levels in that class," the lackey admitted. "But I'm not proud of it."

"Minion, you have to take levels in that class," Vainqueur insisted. "For my own good."

"I must warn you," said the priestess of Shesha. "That our goddess herself is currently unsure whether the potential long-term consequences of mass necromancy make up for the added market value."

"I assure you our use of undead labor is perfectly safe, and no matter what these bourgeois noble imperialists trying to crack down free undead enterprise will tell you, there is no proof necromantic energy negatively affects the environment." That necromancer couldn't help going on a tirade. "Sincerely, the use of mindless labor is more ethical than the animal slavery still practiced by our nation. Animals have feelings, animated corpses don't."

"Corpseling," Vainqueur interrupting, caring more about a quick buck than local politics. "How much?"

"If you sign a binding contract authorizing us to turn them into undead, we can provide fifty gold pieces per corpse and five hundred for the Manticore. Eight hundred in total."

"Deal!" Vainqueur said before Minion Victor could open his mouth.

"I will need to inspect the corpses first," the priest of Camilla said.

The necromancer left to examine the 'wares,' Manling Lynette put a hand on Victor's arm. "Victor, Your Majesty, can we talk for a second?"

Victor nodded, clearly eager to earn the female's favor. "What's the matter?"

"Henry is missing," she told them, before giving Victor a letter. "Someone ransacked his home last night, stole his researches, and left this inside."

Henry. Vainqueur struggled to remember that name, while Victor read the letter.

"One very pompous *Captain François Vilmain of Harmonia*," said the minion, "Politely offers to discuss the release of 'our common friend Henry' and an 'offering of gold' with 'His Glorious Majesty King Vainqueur Knightsbane' in exchange for the use of Haudemer's ships." Vainqueur silently appreciated that at least one manling knew the proper way to address him.

"Vilmain also offered coordinates for the meeting point and an hour this evening, and not at all sinisterly signed with blood."

"Our apothecary confirmed it to be Henry's," said Manling Lynette, who sounded worried, "Since we do not have any spellcaster powerful enough to locate him, I thought to ask the goddess Shesha, but the price she asks is great."

"If they want to buy my forgiveness and a ship, who am I to judge?" Vainqueur replied, still not remembering who this Henry was.

"Your Majesty, the meeting place is conveniently very far from Haudemer. This is clearly a trap."

"I know, minion, but what can they do? Not die?"

"Clearly not, but they could sack the city in Your Majesty's absence and escape," the manling pointed out. "If they haven't lied and killed Henry already by bleeding him dry."

Manling Lynette made a blank face, then left without a word. "W-wait, I didn't mean it!" Minion Victor called her, "That was just the worst-case scenario!"

Vainqueur figured his lackey wouldn't reproduce anytime soon.

In the end, after the corpseling found the wares to his liking, Vainqueur had Victor sign a very long contract with the church of Camilla. Basically, as the legal 'living relative' he swore on the gods he agreed to surrender the corpses to necromantic transformation.

"I just sold corpses to a necromancer for postmortem slave labor," Manling Victor complained. "That feels dirty."

"Why? There is no greater pleasure in life than watching my hoard grow!" Vainqueur decided to cheer his lackey up with his promised fee. "Corpseling, please give my chief of staff his fee of eight gold coins."

"Eight coins?" Manling Victor blinked. "I thought it was one-tenth of the sales?"

"One one-tenth," Vainqueur clarified.

Manling Victor looked up at his master, apparently not very good with math. "Like one-tenth of a tenth?"

"Yes," Vainqueur replied, "One one-tenth, as I promised. What, you want less?"

"No, I'm good," the minion said wisely. "This is already too generous from you."

"We will have the corpses reanimated and sent to the cities of Ferpuit and Minecreuse for immediate mining labor," said the necromancer, true name 'Jules Rapace' according to the contract. "Thank you for supporting our country's modernization."

*Congratulations! For ruthlessly selling your enemies' corpses to the church of Camilla, making the world a deader place, you earned the [**Deadfriend**] Personal Perk!*

*[**Deadfriend**]: mindless undead mistake you for one of their own and do not attack you, unless attacked first; +5 charisma when interacting with the undead or worshippers of Camilla.*

"Sweet, minion, I have a new Perk! You too?"

"Never before have I been more ashamed of one."

11: The Battle for Haudemer

That disloyal minion!

"You thankless traitor!" Vainqueur lambasted Minion Victor in front of the terrified kobolds, the sheer power of his voice making him fall down on the sand. "You, you... you *goblin*, how could you do this to me?!"

"I swear, Your Majesty, this is not what it looks like!"

"It is exactly what it looks like!" Vainqueur replied. "I turn my back on you for five minutes, five minutes, and you cheat on me with another dragon! And a wyvern at that!"

A horse-sized wyvern with lustrous black scales, and shiny ruby eyes that would lead any minion astray - and did - stood next to Victor. The pony to Vainqueur's pegasus, all pretty looks and nothing else. Wyverns were as dim as cattle, and couldn't even breathe fire!

Vainqueur had caught his minion riding that shameless creature's back, caressing the scales behind her horns. He felt disgusted just by remembering it.

And worse, the minion had brought an iron necklace adjusted to that flying rat's neck! The minion had intended to replace Vainqueur and then dress her up!

Of course, the treacherous minion tried to play dumb, "I was just testing the [Horn of Wyvern Summoning], I swear!"

Vainqueur was too pissed to care, "You fool, she is all pretty scales and nothing else! What, she let you ride on her back? Was it worth it?!"

"Your Majesty, I don't—"

"No Majesty, you maggot! I spend all my time being the best dragon master for you, and this is how you repay my kindness?

I thought we had committed to a special, fulfilling master-minion relationship!"

"I swear this is not what it looks like," Minion Victor repeated, even if Vainqueur had caught in the act. The wyvern looked at Vainqueur with a dumb, smug look.

Vainqueur would have eaten that filthy creature if it hadn't been cannibalism.

"And you cheat on me after I gave you custody of our first minions!" Vainqueur pointed a claw at their kobolds. "After I *promoted* you!"

"Master, chief, please stop fighting," sweet Pink cried.

"Your Majesty, I really, really don't like the wording of this conversation." Victor found the strength to rise back up, dusting sand off his cloak. "And I climbed on her back just once!"

"I know your species has a shameful fixation on dragon riding, but climbing on my back is a very special privilege. You know I can never give you that, minion. But it does not matter. What *matters*," Vainqueur stressed that word, "Is that you are a dirty, shameless master-chaser trying to replace me with a wyvern!"

"Wait, no, of course not! It's part of a plot to trick the Scorchers and get you richer, I swear!"

"Then what about this necklace?!"

"It's not a necklace, it's a ring! For you!"

Vainqueur froze in surprise. "Truly?" he asked, his greed getting the better of him. Indeed, that necklace did look like the rings he often saw on princesses' fingers...

"I hope I'm not going to regret it, but..." Victor sighed. "Here's a dragon-sized [Ring of Invisibility]. Just say 'blink' while wearing it, and you will become invisible. Remember when I sent the Kobolds on an errand? I asked the local blacksmith to craft that ring, and he was glad enough for your protection not to ask for a payment."

His... his first, dragon-sized magical item?

No, wait, that was a trick to get back in his good graces! "Why would I become invisible, when I am perfect the way I look?"

"It's a trick to use on the Scorchers, Your Majesty," the minion replied, "So you can take them by surprise."

Ah. Ah... "Like when kidnapping a princess by swooping in in front of knights?" Vainqueur asked, well-versed in that timeless strategy.

"Like princesses with knights," Victor replied with his usual strange, pitiful tone.

At long last everything made sense, much to Vainqueur's satisfaction. "I cannot believe I doubted my own chief of staff's loyalty. Why did you make me doubt you? I could have eaten you for it." Vainqueur grumbled at his manling's mishandling of the matter. "I will forgive you for this misunderstanding."

"I am forever in Your Majesty's debt."

"Of course, since I own you," Vainqueur stated the obvious. "Now, give me that ring before I change my mind."

And so, under the twilight sun, Vainqueur accepted the minion's gift of reconciliation. Manling Victor put the ring on his master's left fourth finger, while the minions clapped in happiness and the wyvern sulked in a corner.

His very first magic item!

*Congratulations! For making up with your trusted vassal and strengthening your relationship, you have gained two levels in [**Noble**]! +60 HP, +10 SP, +1 STR, +1 SKI, +1 AGI, +2 INT, +1 CHA, +2 LCK! You gained the [**Noblesse Oblige**] Perk!*

*[**Noblesse Oblige**]: You gain a temporary stat boost to all your statistics when you defend your vassals from outsiders.*

"Your Majesty just needs to say blink, and—"

"Blink!" Vainqueur's scales turned transparent. "I cannot see myself."

"Yes, Your Majesty, you have become invisible," Victor said, the kobolds petting the wyvern in the background.

"Yes, but it is one thing to imagine the world without me, and another to 'see' it," Vainqueur complained. He, after all, denied everyone the pleasure of watching him. "Now, minion, when do I get that [Stipend] Perk?"

"Soon, Your Majesty, soon..." minion Victor marked a short pause, his eyes set on the city nearby. "Mmm?"

"What is it, minion?" Vainqueur glanced at Haudemer's direction, noticing a thick white mist spreading to engulf the city whole. The dragon couldn't smell, nor hear anything within it. Strange. "An evening fog?"

"Spreading so quickly at this hour?" Victor shook his head. "No. The Scorchers returned, Sir. The town is under attack."

"The rangers are ready to strike, chief!" Red said, the kobolds adopting a brilliant fighting pose, while the wyvern croaked behind them.

"Can Your Majesty blow the fog away with his wings?" Victor asked his invisible master.

"Of course." Nothing easier for a dragon.

"Okay then, rangers, follow me, we'll scout ahead." Victor wandered into the fog, followed by the minions.

Vainqueur prepared to take flight and show the weather who was the master around here, but struggled somewhat to do so. As he flapped his wings, he ended up overdoing it and landing back on the sand within seconds.

Since he couldn't see his wings anymore, he had trouble orienting himself. The dragon had never flown 'blind' in his life.

"Minion, how do I turn it off?" Vainqueur asked, but manling Victor had already vanished into the fog, "Minion? MINION!

Victor somehow lost his way so badly, he ended up right where he wanted. He guessed these new luck points had worked out for him. While struggling to see within this dense mist, he had spent enough time at Lynette's inn to recognize its shape. Victor guessed the mayor gathered the townsfolk here when the fog began to spread, for their own protection.

A very good decision, for the inn was under siege.

A dozen men armed to the teeth with bows, swords, and axes surrounded the place while led by an armored knight and a priest. Victor instantly recognized them as Vilmain and Gustave; much to his horror, he also noticed Henry Bright, gagged and chained to a horse near Vilmain. The scholar had sword scars all over his body, and lost a lot of weight.

Thankfully, the Scorchers hadn't noticed Victor yet. "Rangers?" Victor's voice lost itself in the fog. Damn, he had lost the kobolds. He hoped they were fine; monstrous critters or not, he couldn't let them get killed by bandits.

Victor noticed Lynette and others through the inn's windows. The townsfolk had barricaded themselves inside, watching the encroaching bandit band with apprehension.

"Hello, friends," the priest announced himself. "I am Vilmain, François Vilmain. We come in peace. If you open the door and let us ransack the inn, we will let you leave unharmed!"

Victor hoped Lynette wasn't dumb enough to believe him. After a minute of waiting, without the door unlocking, it turned out she wasn't. "I will break the door," Gustave said, carrying a heavy claymore with one hand and a large shield with the other.

"No, no need for that hassle, my friend," Vilmain replied. "Since they have barricaded themselves in, I will set the place on fire with a [Fireball] and cook them alive. You and your men can kill those who try to escape."

"Not fair, you will get all the experience."

"I want my next Bowman Perk, sir," one of the archers complained to Vilmain. "I will never miss anymore with it!"

"Yes, I understand, but it will be quick, and we have to move before the dragon finds his way in." The priest turned towards Victor, apparently seeing him fine within the unnatural weather. "Well, would you look at that?"

Victor sighed, as a dozen Scorchers looked at him. He might as well try to buy time until Vainqueur could blow the fog away. "That's the [Disorienting Fog] spell, isn't it? Pretty high level spell. I didn't expect a level thirteen Bishop to have access it. The last spellcaster I saw use it was in his mid-twenties."

"Familiar spell? I would expect a *Nightblade* to know of it." Vilmain insisted on the mention of the criminal syndicate. "My class, Fell Bishop, allows me to cast powerful spells by sacrificing people to my dark god. So we nabbed a peasant on our way here. "

Disgusting.

"That's your fault by the way," Vilmain said, "We hoped you would leave the town to rescue poor Henry from us, but you didn't, you shameless, honorless fiend. Abandoning a civilian to his death? How unheroic."

"Yeah, trying to lure the brave knight away from the town you want to loot. That's Outlaw trick number one. I was almost sure you already killed him."

"Henry? No, it is always good to have an emergency sacrifice on hands, just in case. Don't give me that glare, he sold you out first."

That didn't make it right.

So that was their plan? [Disorienting Fog] reduced sound within its radius and caused people to get lost within it. They thought they could use the weather to prevent the dragon from burning the place down from above without friendly fire. Simple, but effective.

Why did they insist on sacking Haudemer instead of sensibly fleeing Vainqueur though? Victor guessed they had another motive than pillaging. "Why the hell are you even sieging that inn instead of boarding ships and escaping the country?"

"In time," Vilmain smirked, "But our employer, Brandon Maure of Ishfania, asked us to recover a certain magical apple buried under Haudemer. Once we have secured it, we will leave."

The iPad? They were after iPad? Victor thought about handing it to them, but realized they would still kill everyone afterward. These guys killed as much for easy levels as gold.

Vilmain coughed, "So, if you're a thief yourself, why not join us then? There's more money to make by joining in the pillaging than fighting us, and a man taming a dragon is one I want on my team. Also, you will live."

Yes, joining a group whose leaders had levels in *Turncoat* and *Vile* in their *name* was a brilliant idea. No way it could go wrong. That left fighting as the only option. Point for him: thanks to Vainqueur, he had powerful equipment, and the dragon would be here any second now...

Point for these two monsters: they were twice his level, and they had minions of their own.

Minions of their own? Damn, he was turning into Vainqueur.

Mmm... a wise man once said criminals were a cowardly, superstitious lot. "Allow me to make you a counteroffer." Victor revealed his [Horn of Wyvern Summoning]. "Surrender now, and I won't use this horn of dragon summoning to bring Vainqueur on your front door."

Vilmain laughed. "I have the [Eye for Treasure Perk], my friend. That is a simple trinket for wyverns, nothing that can bind a great red dragon."

"That's what the false description would lead you to believe," Victor lied. "And it worked that way until I unlocked its secret powers. How do you think I bound that dragon to my will in the first place?"

"Nonsense," Gustave said, losing patience. "Enough talk. Join or die."

While Vilmain and Gustave were too cunning to fall for it, Victor could see their minio—their men hesitate. He hoped their fear of Vainqueur outweighed their trust in their leaders.

"Your loss. Vainqueur, I summon thee!" Victor sounded the horn.

"Archers!" Gustave called, bowmen readying their weapons and preparing to shoot Victor. Meanwhile, Vilmain began to intone a spell. "At my signal—"

"Wait, above!" one of the men interrupted him.

The shadow of a winged dragon appeared above their heads, its features obscured by the fog.

"The dragon is here!" a bowman shouted, before immediately lowering his weapon in abject fear. The wyvern let out a screech through the fog. Immediately, one of the outlaws turned tail, and the rest lost their nerve.

"Wait, fall back into rank, cowards!" Gustave raised his blade, but his men had already started running away. Even Vilmain's horse fled at the wyvern's sight, dragging Henry with it. "I will have your head for this!"

"Fine!" Vilmain declared, the two criminals left to their fate. "[Summon Lesser Demo—"

With a surge of speed he didn't know he could achieve, Victor interrupted Vilmain with daggers in both hands. Reacting with lightning fast reflexes, the Fell Bishop parried one with a rapier, while Victor's other weapon slipped past his guard and stabbed him below the shoulder.

Victor sensed he may have a chance in close combat against Vilmain. The priest had more levels, but in a spellcasting, healer class.

Unfortunately, this was a two on one fight.

Gustave rushed to his ally's side, tackling Victor with his shield. Victor's [Sun Bracers] activated, empowering him with newfound strength and vitality. The blow almost tossed him to his back, but the Monster Squire managed to stay on his feet.

Without giving him a respite, Gustave swung his sword to try and bisect Victor, who dodged the strike. The Monster Squire, unable to harm his foe through his heavy armor, tried to work around him to get at Vilmain, but the cunning Gustave always blocked his path.

"[Skill Up]!" An unholy red glow surrounded Vilmain as he cast a spell, his free hand searching under his cloak. Victor guessed he looked for a potion to heal his wound.

Instead, he brought out a flintlock pistol and aimed at Victor.

Bringing a firearm to a sword fight? That cheater! Victor touched the [Firebomb Necklace] around his neck before Vilmain could pull the trigger. He had only three charges, so he better make them count. "Firebomb!"

The enchanted necklace activated, unleashing a sphere of fire with a crimson spark. The projectile hit Vilmain and interrupted him, but the flames didn't spread to his clothes. The criminal must have cast a fire-resistance spell of some kind, in case Vainqueur broke past the fog.

Vilmain fired his flintlock like a maniac, clearly not caring about hitting his ally. Victor dived to the ground, a bullet killing an unlucky watcher by flying through a window.

Gustave, ever the pragmatist, tried to strike Victor before he could rise to his feet, with the Monster Squire retaliating with another charge of his necklace. The Scorcher hid behind his shield, tanking the projectile like a champ.

Yeah, the chief of staff couldn't beat that knight on his own.

"No!" Victor cursed out loud over internalizing his new job, rising back to his feet and dashing at Vilmain. He managed to get past his accomplice's defense, moving between both Scorchers. Gustave tried to intercept him, but the wyvern, which had been circling them from above, fell upon him like a hawk. Her claws and fangs struck his armor without piercing it.

Unable to reload fast enough, Vilmain threw away his pistol and struck with his rapier. Victor deflected the blade before it could pierce his heart, but the sword hit his left flank and drew blood.

Damn, what was that greedy dragon doing? Ignoring his reservations against killing humans, Victor stabbed the bishop back. His dagger pierced him through the left eye, splattering the criminal's face with blood.

It didn't kill Vilmain, but it angered him. And behind Victor, Gustave had cut one of the wyvern's wings with his sword, pinned her to the ground with his shield, and prepared to finish the beast off.

Vilmain incanted a spell, moving his free hand against Victor's torso. Cackles of dark energy built around his fingers...

And then five Kobolds jumped out of the fog from behind, grabbing Vilmain's arms, legs, and head. "For His Majesty!" they shouted at once, biting the priest's flesh and interrupting his spell.

*Congratulations! By ambushing a stronger enemy in the middle of a fight, your Kobolds have each gained a level in the [**Outlaw**] Class!*

"The power!" Red said, stabbing Vilmain in the other eye with his tiny claws. "I can feel the power!"

"My eyes!" Vilmain screamed in agony as he struggled to get the kobolds off him. As the criminal lost his hold over his rapier, Victor dropped one of his daggers and stole the sword. He then stabbed the bishop back in the chest with his own weapon.

The Fell Bishop fell on his back with a painful gasp, the kobolds still biting and clawing at him.

"Vilmain, you weakling!" Having killed the wyvern with a swing of his sword, Gustave charged at Victor to save his ally. Distracted by the pain in his chest, the Monster Squire couldn't dodge in time and Gustave hit him with his shield.

Crack! The blow propelled Victor against the inn's walls, his left shoulder going numb after a brief moment of sharp pain.

"Chief!" Yellow attempted to defend Victor, only for Gustave to cut him in half with his sword. With another merciless swing, he struck down Blue.

The other kobolds immediately attempted to fight back, but they were no match for the knight. Gustave kicked Pink right in the face like a puppy, knocked out Red with his shield, and backhanded Black when he tried to flank him. The confrontation had lasted mere seconds.

"Can you heal yourself?" Gustave asked Vilmain, who crawled on the ground, struggling to get back up while covered up in his own blood.

"I exhausted... my special points with all the... interrupted spells." Vilmain coughed. "I will need help... to walk."

"Pity."

Without remorse, Gustave struck his own ally in the back with his blade, killing him in one blow.

"Sorry, *friend*, I wanted that new level more than I liked you." An unholy aura surrounded the treacherous knight, empowering Gustave further. Victor used the last firebomb, the necklace disintegrating with its last charge exhausted. The projectile slipped past Gustave's guard and hit him in the chest.

The knight didn't even flinch at the resulting blast.

A rumbling sound echoed through the fog. Had the citizens of the city decided to fight back against the Scorchers? Victor couldn't know, and wouldn't live long enough to. With his chest wound and a limp shoulder, he couldn't hope to dodge Gustave's sword.

"[Attack Stance]," Gustave tossed away his shield to wield his sword with both hands. The murderous aura around him increased in strength, the sheer pressure paralyzing Victor. "And now, I will take my sweet time cutting yo—"

Splat!

Gustave collapsed into a puddle of blood, crushed by an invisible behemoth.

"Minions? MINIONS! Where are you?" The knight's blood splattered Vainqueur's invisible scales. "Minion, there you are!"

For a split second, Victor couldn't find his words.

"I cannot see where I go, and I cannot turn it off! How do I turn the invisibility off?"

"You must say 'blink' again, Your Majesty..."

Vainqueur marked a short pause, then said, "Blink!" The invisibility veil suddenly lifting off the dragon. The beast took a few seconds to look at his own scales, without any hint of narcissism whatsoever. "Much better."

The great dragon expanded his wings, unleashing a powerful gust by flapping them. The wind lifted the fog and unveiled a trail of destroyed houses which Vainqueur left behind. The invisible dragon had damaged the city more than the Scorchers themselves.

At least no civilians had died.

"Ah, clear as day," Vainqueur said. "I can at long last hunt the thieves."

Victor glanced at Gustave's remains, stuck under Vainqueur's left foot. The dragon hadn't even noticed. "That won't be necessary, Your Majesty," he said, as Lynette and the townsfolk exited the inn, the danger now gone. "Except stragglers, most fled at your coming."

"I will have my stipend!" Vainqueur complained, before hunting for Scorchers, leaving blood behind with each step. "Sweet manlings, where are you? Come out, I do not bite... not always..."

"Victor, are you alright?" Lynette rushed to the Squire's side, forcing a green potion to his lips before he could answer. As Victor drank it, finding the taste sweet, he felt the pain vanish, and his shoulder could move again.

Unfortunately, the kobolds hadn't been as lucky as him, mourning their fallen comrades. "What do we do?" Black said, tears in his eyes. "Yellow... Yellow was the best minion out of us all... I should have died..."

"We sell them," Red cried. "That was what they would have wanted."

...

"Come again?" Victor asked, blinking.

"We sell them to make Master Vainqueur's hoard bigger," Pink said, Black and Red nodding with sorrow. "That way they will be part of it forever..."

Victor figured out he had experienced a strong culture clash.

*Congratulations! For fearlessly leading monsters to victory against superior opponents, you earned seven levels in [**Monster Squire**]!*

+120 HP, +70 SP, + 5 STR, + 4 VIT, + 4 SKI, +5 AGI, +6 INT, +6 CII, +7 LCK!

*You earned the [**Monster Lifeforce (Red Dragon)**], [**Monster Rider**], and [**Monster Insight**] Perks!*

*[**Monster Lifeforce (Red Dragon)**]: the blood of your dragon liege flows in your veins. You gain the additional creature Type: Dragon, which is both a blessing and a curse. You gain immunity to Drain, Paralysis, Fatigue, Insta-death, Disease, and resistance to Fire and Aging. You gain vulnerability to Frost, Fairy, and Dragonslayer.*

*[**Monster Rider**]: You can now ride monsters with medium proficiency. If the target is a minion, your proficiency increases to good.*

*[**Monster Insight**]: When you observe a monster, you gain a vision of their strengths, weaknesses, and tidbits of information.*

Seven levels at once? It almost made up for the deaths and the blood loss. A glance at the rapier he pilfered from Vilmain told him he had also gained some interesting loot out of it.

"I have no idea how to reward you, Victor," said Lynette. "You were very brave out there."

Reward?

Oh, and hell, why not. He had nothing to lose, except his dignity.

"Do you want to breed?" he asked Lynette.

12: Multiclassing

As dawn rose on Haudemer, Vainqueur allowed himself to rest on his back in front of the city's entrance.

He had spent the night hunting down the last of his walking punching bags, shoring up all the experience he could. His stomach hurt from the manling indigestion.

Congratulations! For crushing the Scorchers and stylishly stomping on the enemy leader before an adoring crowd, you earned four [Gladiator] levels!

+120 HP, + 8 STR, + 1 VIT, + 4 SKI, +4 AGI, +4 CH, +3 LCK!

You gained the [Crowd Favorite] and [Supercrit] class Perks!

[Crowd Favorite]: You gain a temporary, random boost to one of your statistics when you impress a crowd, alongside the small chance of gaining an item.

[Supercrit]: Double the chances of your physical attacks inflicting critical hits.

Small chance to get an item if he impressed his fans? Sweet! He should find his minions and try it out.

However, what did they mean by stomping on the enemy leader? Vainqueur looked under his left foot, noticing a lump of flesh stuck between two of his claws. "Strange," he commented, licking his claws to taste the sweet meat.

The dragon decided to turn invisible, so he could see if other manling parts had stuck somewhere else. "Blink." He was gone.

"Blink!" And now he wasn't! "Blink, blink, blinkblink!"

Vainqueur found turning his invisibility on and off strangely amusing. He could spend all day doing it.

However, the ruckus of horses stampeding interrupted his game. Vainqueur wondered if the bandits had come for another round of *'honorable demise by dragon.'* That would confirm his theory about manlings having a collective deathwish.

Instead, two hundred riders, clad in the finest armor and wearing the shiniest weapons, rushed towards him. Most of them wore a sun emblem emblazoned on their armor, but a few of them carried flags representing a golden lion on a red background.

Knights. Lots of manling and beastkin knights.

Maybe they had a princess he could add to his hoard?

The knights stopped in a line facing Vainqueur, who didn't even bother rising up. It wasn't like they *could* do anything to him, and he was full enough to just burn them to oblivion if they tried.

Their leader, a female manling riding a white unicorn, stood in front of the line to address him. She had these long, fashionable golden hair, the same color of Vainqueur's own beautiful eyes, and tiny blue spots for a gaze. She wore a purple hermine. "So it is true," she said with a shrieking voice whom the dragon immediately disliked. "Haudemer has been occupied by a great red dragon."

"Indeed I am," Vainqueur answered that waste of skin. "Vainqueur Knightsbane, First of his Name, Great Calamity of this Age and King of the Albain Mountains. But you may call me Your Majesty."

"There is no king of the mountains," the upstart manling replied, before answering with her own presentation. "I am duchess Aelinor of Euskal, second removed cousin of King Gard—"

"Not a princess," Vainqueur interrupted her, annoyed at her forgetting the 'Your Majesty' part.

The petulant woman glared back at him. "I beg your pardon?"

"Not a princess," Vainqueur repeated with contempt since the food was slow-minded. She didn't smell like a princess, and instead had the scent of *disappointment*. Also, he was too good to speak directly to that creature. "Minion? Minion?! MINION, GET BACK HERE! The food is talking back!"

Where was his official animal translator when Vainqueur needed him?

The manling's face turned red for some reason. "Vainqueur Knightsbane," Somehow she made his noble name sound like an insult. "Our forces and the Shining Crusade have defeated the last of the Scorchers and retaken the citadel of Rochefronde from Ishfania. Only François Vilmain and Gustave la Muraille escaped judgment, and I intend to bring them justice and flames."

Vainqueur knew nothing about Rochefronde, but according to the minion, they killed both of those manlings somewhere. "Done," the dragon replied. "Also, your flames are weaker than mine, so no need to humiliate yourself."

"Inspect the city for confirmation after we are done with him," the manling told one of the knights, before turning her attention back on the dragon, "Vainqueur Knightsbane, you are wanted for the uncalled destruction of the Woods of Gevaudan, property damage, and the devastation of the local Euskalian countryside. A century-old bounty of one hundred twenty thousand gold coins on your head has been issued again!"

Finally, the false news about his demise had been invalidated! However... "One hundred twenty thousand?" Vainqueur asked for a confirmation, disappointed, "That is all? I order you rescind it."

"Order me?" her face got even redder, almost as much as Vainqueur's own scales. "Do you deny the charges against you?"

"No, but I am worth more," Vainqueur replied, getting annoyed by the lack of a translator. Miscommunications, especially about their respective places in the order of things, clearly piled up somewhere. "I am at least worth one million gold coins, and I am being *incredibly* modest here. Tell your mammal king to correct my net worth."

"Are you insulting the god-chosen king of Gardemagne?" One of the knights raised his spear. "You vile creature, the Shining Crusade stands before you! You will burn in the fires of Lord Mithras for your pride!"

An aura of dread permeates the area, as the weight of the gods' judgment falls upon you. [Terror] ailment—

"Apologize to *me at once*," Vainqueur countered, his patience wearing thin.

*But it failed miserably! [Terror] canceled by [**Dragon Arrogance**]!*

"Apologize to you?" The noble manling's eyes snapped open in uncalled defiance. "What for?"

"This is my world. I do not remember giving any of you my royal permission to live in it. Also, you should apologize for your weakness, because I have no idea how you can live with yourself."

The manling leader twitched, and so did the knights.

*Congratulations! For browbeating the upstart food with words alone, you gained the [**Taunt**] Personal Perk.*

*[**Taunt**]: Your soul-crushing, humiliating taunts have a small chance of inflicting the [Berserk] status on their targets. You monster.*

Taunt? He was just stating the obvious.

"You are an arrogant creature," the manling lady rasped like a snake, amazed at being in the presence of a true dragon.

"I am Vainqueur Knightbane, King of the Albain Mountains, the greatest adventurer in the world!" Vainqueur boasted, showing off the adventurer plate around his neck. "I am a *god*! No, wait, I am better. I am a *dragon*! Your puny gods answer to me! They pay me to kill your kind!"

"Blasphemy!" One of the knights snarled back, Vainqueur ignoring the animal's yapping.

"Since I removed the trees around your land and protected this town from hostile manlings, I expect you to properly pay me for the service. I demand a wage of sixty-four thousand gold coins. Under the table, according to your manling reward ritual."

"You... you are asking a duchess for a bribe in front of the holiest of knights?! Have you no shame?!"

"A dragon will never pay taxes!" the dragon roared proudly.

Congratulations! For defending your noble, unjust privileges, you gained two levels in [Noble]! +30 HP, +20 SP, +2 STR, +2 SKI, +2 AGI, +2 INT, +1 CHA, +2 LCK! You gained the [Aristoradar] Class Perk!

[Aristoradar]: You immediately notice other nobles, even undercover and false ones. No more bourgeois.

"I have had enough of this," the noble lady said, raising her tiny hand. "Knights! Slay this stupid dragon!"

"You dare refuse to pay your due to your true King?" Now well and truly angered, Vainqueur rose back on his feet, the knights charging at him. He considered blowing them up with his breath, but decided to test his new Perks instead.

Raising his left, clawed finger, Vainqueur poked the first rider to reach him, crushing him and his horse at once and with enough force to cause the ground to shake beneath them. The knights stopped in horrified surprise.

Critical hit! [Crowd Favorite] activated!

Vainqueur's eyes widened in joy, as a golden nugget materialized in a flash of light right in the middle of the knight's remains.

Ah.

"Aha, yes! Finally!" Vainqueur glanced at his left finger. That was the secret to gain new items! He just had to poke these upstarts one by one! The dragon rejoiced, as the brave knights rushed at him, eager to make the dragon live up to his name.

Good.

He would poke them all.

Victor still couldn't believe it.

It *worked*!

That pickup line actually worked!

"Excalibur?" Lynette asked, her hands reaching to draw most of her bed's sheet to herself.

"Don't ask," Victor replied, resting on the left side of the bed. All the stress and tension of following an insane dragged had vanished.

That world rocked!

*Congratulations! For finally getting laid and experiencing the thrill of a short-lived fling, you gained the Perk [**Romantic**]! You gain a +5 Charisma Bonus when interacting with the opposite sex!*

"Very nice," Victor said, "Sorry for being so... upfront about it."

"Oh, no, actually, I'm very happy about it," Lynette replied, her body resting against his. "For a second, I thought you would ask gold of me."

Why did Victor had the sudden feeling he had just been shortchanged? "So, it's..."

"Just a transaction, nothing more."

Victor should have expected that from a worshipper of the goddess of commerce. "At least I got a Perk out of it."

"[Romantic]?"

Victor squinted at her. "How do you know?"

"I have the higher rank of that Perk, [Seducer]. You have to sleep with twenty different people to get it, and one hundred for the upgraded version. I am still dozens away from that one."

"D-did you sleep with me for a Perk?"

"Just a transaction," she smiled, "Nothing more."

Yeah, he had been BEEPED in more ways than one. Capitalism struck again.

As he left his 'damsel in distress' to rest and got dressed, Victor took it back. That world sucked.

Closing the bedroom door behind him, Victor found the three kobolds waiting for him outside, alongside Jules the Necromancer. By now, the inn's clients had gotten used to him bringing monsters around whenever he went.

"Chief, chief!" Red said, he and Black carrying the corpses of their fallen comrades on their back. "Sorry to interrupt your murder attempt."

Murder? Ah. These poor children. They had looked through the keyhole. Victor was too relaxed to scold them. "Hi, Jules. You're here for business?"

"Yes, yes, I need your signature for the new raw material Lord Vainqueur gathered. Your servants also informed me you were open to the idea of selling their dead companions; I commend you for your dedication to recycling."

"Since Yellow and Blue are gone, we are two members short for the choreography," Red complained. "We cannot serve His Majesty Vainqueur without one. We must look for recruits, stylish and colored..."

"Oh, could we look for a green and a white this time?" Black asked his leader. "We need brand new colors."

"And a sixth with shining silver scales," Pink squirmed. "A young, virile male."

"No yellow or blue will ever replace our fallen comrades," Red said gravely. "We shall look for new colors, and create a rainbow so we may showcase the great Vainqueur's luster!"

"About that, Jules, is there a way to bring them back to life?" Victor asked the necromancer. "Not as mindless undead, but true revival."

"True resurrection is a power far beyond my level, and that of anyone alive today," Jules replied, much to Victor's disappointment. "You may turn to the goddess Shesha, but she charges a harsh price for it. However... are you under level twenty?"

"I've just reached seventeen yesterday."

"Then it should be easy to take a level in the [Necromancer] Class, and use its starting Perk, [Animate Dead], to revive your servants as undead. After you reach level twenty, the experience penalties will make it significantly harder, so it may be now or never."

"Can't you do it yourself? I can pay if you accept magical items."

"I only raise non-intelligent undead for ethical reasons. [Animate Dead] will bring the lucky fellows back as intelligent ones, including the original soul, if you sacrifice coins or some of your items."

"Chief, no!" Red protested. "They gladly gave their life for you!"

"You saved my life," Victor replied. "I owe you that."

They had also gained class levels out of it, which complicated matters; while convincing monsters to fight more monsters sounded appealing on paper, his experience with Vainqueur made him fear the consequences. Neither did he want the critters to end up as Vainqueur's emergency rations. Maybe he would better send them on a non-dangerous errand for their safety?

While he didn't like taking a level in a dark class, Victor decided the kobolds, monsters or other, had earned a raise.

*Congratulations! For working with a necromancer to enter the death market, you gained a level in the [**Necromancer**] class! +10 SP, +1 SKI, +1 AGI, +1 INT, +1 CHA, +1 LCK!*

*You gained the [**Animate Dead**] Class Perk!*

*[**Animate Dead**]: You can revive corpses as undead with a touch. By sacrificing money or items, you can revive a living being as an intelligent undead, retaining both the original soul and class levels. The funds needed to revive someone depends on the soul's value, whom you intuitively understand.*

With a glance, Victor instantly guessed the two kobolds were worth a few hundred coins each; more than he owned. He removed his sun bracers, each worth as much, and activated the Perk.

An unholy, purple glow filled the room, turning the bracers to dust. The dark aura then moved to the broken remains of the two dead kobolds, binding them back together, and consuming the flesh.

Much to Victor's silent disturbance, the two skeletons rose back on their own, their bones having changed color to yellow and blue respectively. An unholy glow shone in their eye sockets.

Your Kobold minions have been revived as Kobones!

"Blue, Yellow?" Red asked as the undead turned at him. "Are you... alright?"

"Flesh..." Blue's voice had turned into a cavernous, terrible voice. **"Flesh..."**

What? "Has the Perk failed?" Victor frowned.

"Nah, I'm kidding chief," the Blue skeleton replied, regaining his original voice and letting out a strange chuckle. How the skeleton managed to do that without lungs was beyond Victor. "Still the same old me, except now I can see my clavicule."

"This new voice is awesome! Let me try!" Yellow chirped, his voice turning from his original one to the same cavernous echo. **"I am Ranger Yellow, and you have met your dooooooom... dooooooooom..."**

"Red, I am your father," Blue said with the same voice in a pretty good interpretation of Earl Jones. "Neat!"

"Dooooooooom..."

They took their transformation into undead skeletons pretty well. "Blue, Yellow!" Red embraced the reborn minions. "You are back!"

"Yes, and I don't feel my stomach ulcer anymore," Yellow said, returning to his normal voice. "Being undead is marvelous!"

Victor smiled at the scene. While annoying as hell, Vainqueur and the Kobolds did save his life and the city. Maybe he had been wrong to distrust them. Maybe they could do good, all of them.

Maybe he could get used to this new life...

Then a knight flew through one of the inn's windows and crashed against a wall, dashing Victor's hopes.

Victor glanced at the broken man, and took a long, deep breath. "Minions, help Jules with his business," he told the kobolds while his fingers went for his trusty canteen and he took a sip of alcohol.

When another knight flew through a second window, and a third hit the wall outside, the adventurer decided not to stop at a sip. "Well, well, well," Jules rejoiced, clapping his hands. "This association keeps getting better and better..."

"Minion?" An unpleasant voice came from outside the inn. "MINION!"

Sighing and out of alcohol to drown his sorrow, Victor calmly exited the inn, his hand on the new rapier around his belt. He had also taken Vilmain's flintlock with him as a trophy but didn't think he would make much use of it.

As expected, he found Vainqueur waiting for him right in front of the building. A good two dozen knights laid broken and defeated around town, the sight fitting the aftermath of a deadly drunken brawl. They bore the insignia of the Shining Crusade.

There died his hopes of getting rescued by a knight in shining armor.

Surprisingly though, the dragon had come back with a pile of treasures in his hands. "Minion, look at what they *gave* me!" Vainqueur proudly showed his new shinies, from gold purses to magic items.

"What happened?" Victor asked.

"I poked them," Vainqueur replied, licking his left finger.

"All of them?" Why did Victor sound so bored? The disaster had numbed him to the dragon's insanity.

"This is the critical hit finger, minion." Vainqueur showed him his left hand's index claw. "Every time I kill a manling with it before your brethren, they reward me for it!"

Yeah right. While at it, Victor decided to try his new [Monster Insight] Perk on his 'master.'

Vainqueur Knightsbane.

Elder Red Dragon (Dragon)

Vulnerable to: Frost, Fairy, and Dragonslayer.

Strong against: everything else.

Self-proclaimed 'best dragon', a great red wyrm who is more than a match for the strongest of adventurers. His immense strength is matched only by his arrogance and lack of common sense. Kind of greedy, vain, and self-absorbed, but secretly insecure about his minions leaving him.

Gee, you think? What a useless Perk. "Your Majesty, Duchess Aelinor of Euskal was supposed to lead this band of knights to Haudemer. Maybe we should check on her for the reward."

"Done," Vainqueur replied happily, "We can finally move on from this stinking town. I miss bathing in my hoard."

"Ah?" Victor raised an eyebrow, curious. "What happened, you poked her too?"

The dragon scrapped his teeth with a claw. "I ate her."

Victor's mind stopped working. "You what?"

"I ate her. Although I think she would have tasted better with that sweet poison sauce."

"You ate the quest giver." And a high-ranking noble in the kingdom.

"Do not worry for the gold, I recovered the reward first," Vainqueur 'reassured' him, before belching.

"W-why?" Victor choked. "Why did Your Majesty do that?"

"Because she was annoying, would not pay me, and wasn't a princess," Vainqueur replied angrily. "Also, she tasted like pork."

Victor looked at the dragon, words dying in his throat.

"Minion, do not look at me like that. There is more enough beastkins laying around for a barbecue if you are hungry."

13: Looking for Dungeons

How good to bathe in a bigger hoard!

Vainqueur had done far more than what he had set out to do. He hadn't doubled his treasure's size, but more than quadrupled it. While he once struggled to fully shower himself with coins, the dragon could now roll happily in gold and jewels.

All of this in less than a moon. At this rate, his cave wouldn't be enough to contain his full hoard.

"Guys, go away!" Minion Victor called outside, Vainqueur paying it no mind. "Haven't you seen the signposts? You will get killed if you get closer!"

"Is that the dragon's lair?" a shrilling voice answered, Vainqueur trying to block out the sounds.

"Yes, but you really, really don't stand a chance—" A zapping sound like that of lightning echoed in the distance. "Alright, that's it! Shoot them, minions!"

The sound of an explosion and tremors interrupted Vainqueur's joyful bath. The dragon turned to the cave's entrance, where his minions had barricaded themselves. "Manling Victor, what is happening?"

"Dragonslayers, again!" his chief of staff shouted back, another tremor causing an icicle to fall at the cave's entrance, nearly impaling one of the kobolds. "Blue, snipe the wizard!"

"I am trying, chief!" The undead minion fired an arrow with his bow of cattle bone. "I got him!"

Vainqueur was very proud of Victor's choice of learning necromancy. Not only did undead minions add to Vainqueur's prestige, but he could also now eat minions, spit out the bones, and still make use of them.

"Nailed him right between the legs!" Red gloated after firing his own arrow, before snarling. "They have a healer!"

Vainqueur grumbled, rising from his hoard to join the siege.

Since they achieved a level in [Outlaw]—which amused Vainqueur, who considered laws a manling absurdity—Victor had given each of the Kobold Rangers bows and taught them how to use them. A good idea, since this was the seventh adventurer party they sniped this week.

At first, it had been amusing and profitable, but Vainqueur had grown tired of the constant interruptions.

The dragon's head exited the cave's entrance, casting his minions in his shadow and glancing down at their targets. A foolish band of manlings, dwarves, and elves, mostly armed with these sticks Manling Victor called arquebuses or wands. Vainqueur counted fifteen of them.

Aw, they came back with greater numbers this time, as if it would help. *Adorable.*

Unfortunately, they didn't bring any pegasus riders, unlike the previous group, so no horse food tonight. Vainqueur would have loved nothing more than poke them, but his finger had grown sore from overuse.

"They are very persistent." As a magical projectile bounced off his head, the dragon considered learning magic himself. The way some sorcerers often threw lightning at him always fascinated Vainqueur. Not that it ever *worked*, but it amused him. "I thought they would give up after the first three pokings."

"The bounty on Your Majesty's head is very high," Victor replied. "And your lair's location is well-known now."

Yes, yes, such were the downsides of fame and celebrity.

The dragon let out a powerful roar, causing an avalanche; the snow rolled down the mountain, flooding the screaming manlings while leaving the cave unscathed. He knew choosing this location would prove helpful.

*Congratulations! For defending your territory and minions with the power of your noble roar alone, you have gained a level in the [**Noble**] class! +30 HP, +1 INT, +1 CHA, +1 LCK!*

Finally! Vainqueur had started to wonder if he would gain any experience out of this, and he was one level short of that sweet stipend. "There, problem solved," the dragon said. "Recover their treasure, while I return to my bath."

"Your Majesty, this can't continue," Victor said, black marks under his eyes. "They just keep coming, even at night. They ignore all warnings."

"We cannot repeat our new motto," Red complained. "And Yellow keeps ruining it when we find the time too!"

"I just say we should add 'doom' somewhere," the yellow skeleton replied, before switching to that deep voice he had grown awfully fond of. **"Doooooom."**

The echo caused a lesser avalanche, finishing off the few manlings who managed to crawl out of the snow. Vainqueur ignored them as he retreated inside his cave. "Minions, I am just as annoyed as you, but what can I do about it? I cannot forbid manlings from committing assisted suicide."

"Yeah, I have become comfortable killing idiots attacking us first as part of natural selection, but we should relocate." Manling Victor shuddered, freezing even while wearing a goatskin coat. "To a warmer mountain where adventurers won't keep finding us."

Abandon his cave? A dragon did not run! "Are you not happy to have a roof?" Vainqueur browbeat his minions. "You have food aplenty, the best sight of the continent..."

"We lack space, and I'm sick of eating mountain goats all the time," manling Victor complained, having grown bolder and angrier due to the lack of sleep. "Also, one cave soon will not be enough to hold your treasure, Your Majesty."

Vainqueur pondered the suggestion, his eyes settling on his hoard. Indeed, his cave would soon become too small, and a thief might get lucky stealing his gold while he hunted outside. While he trusted his minions, they could not handle so many robbers at once.

That, and ever since they cooked that squid, they haven't had received any requests. Maybe they should use the time off to find a new place to live.

"I still do not understand why your guildhalls become deserted every time we go there," Vainqueur grumbled.

"Your Majesty," his chief of staff coughed. "The problem with eating a quest giver is that no more people will give you quests, because they are afraid you will eat them too."

"But she refused to pay me first!" Vainqueur protested. "Before witnesses!"

"Yeah, well, she was also a high-ranking noble with lots of connections. I did send a complaint to the adventurer guild, and I heard the duchess' sister is secretly happy we hastened her inheritance, but we aren't getting work for a while."

"I cannot believe it, is that what your puny race do in this situation? Complain and laze off?"

"Your picture of my species is very flattering, Your Majesty," Victor said with his usual obsequiousness. "Usually we just clean a dungeon, kill monsters, and take their treasure."

Vainqueur's head perked up at the mention of treasures, hitting the ceiling. "Treasure?" he repeated, the kobolds cowering behind him to avoid falling icicles, "Minion, tell me everything."

The chief of staff scratched the back of his head, probably wondering where to begin. "Dungeons are dangerous areas, overflowing with monsters and holding treasures," he explained to his master. "Adventurers clearing the place can take everything they get their hands on, and even claim the dungeon if they kill all the monsters within. However, dungeons usually have a super-strong creature, a boss, keeping them."

"A monster lord," Vainqueur guessed.

"You have a term for it?"

"Monster lords are the top of the food chain," Pink chirped. "They are the strongest of the strongest, to whom minions owe obedience!"

"Dragons are always at the top," Vainqueur clarified. "Where can we find such a dungeon?"

"Most in Gardemagne have been emptied by older adventurers, but I heard of a few too dangerous for most, especially alongside the border with Ishfania. I guess Your Majesty could handle them."

"Are these dungeons large enough to hold my ever-growing hoard?" The minion nodded. Mmm... it might also be the occasion to rebuild his minion base since Manling Victor clearly couldn't breed for the life of him. "What kind of dungeons have you heard of?"

"There is the underwater city of Meropis—"

"Next!" Vainqueur immediately interrupted, having enough of watery adventures already. "Somewhere warm and on land. No wetness."

"No marsh, then? I had a pretty nice one in a marsh."

"No marshes, no swamp, no forest, no lake, no mud, no dirty, dung-smelling manling city."

His chief of staff kept nodding. "And no frost, for our sake. What about a nice, dry desert then?"

"Oh, oh, I heard of one!" Yellow butted in the conversation. "I heard of an antlion nest in the southern desert, beyond the mountains! It is very deep and very warm!"

Black shuddered. "The cacti shoot you with needles there. I still feel the pain in my butt."

"Ah yes, I remember that time we tried to practice in the sand," Blue said. "Now is the time I am happy not to feel pain anymore."

"Antlions don't carry treasure besides the remains of their victims," Manling Victor pointed out. "At best we will only get a few trinkets and what we can take by killing the beasts. The place would be big enough for the hoard, though."

Vainqueur would rather eat two cows with one bite. "Next."

"Great, great, then what about a castle in the middle of a volcano?" Manling Victor suggested. "Since Your Majesty *enjoys* lava baths as much as golden ones..."

Indeed he did. "I am listening," Vainqueur said. "How much lava are we talking about?"

"I dunno, I've never been there. But the place, the Castle of Murmurin, has a spooky reputation. From what I gathered, it was once an officer training facility for the continent's elite and the headquarter of the Ishfanian Inquisition. At the start of the Century War, Brandon Maure sent his general, the Lich Furibon, to claim the castle, turning it into a haven for fiends and waking up the volcano they had built the fortress on. The Ishfanian Inquisition did its best to fight off demons but—"

"Twenty words," Vainqueur interrupted his minion.

Victor marked a short pause. "Excuse me, Your Majesty?"

"I start zoning out after twenty uninteresting words," Vainqueur said. "I know you manlings love to blatter meaningless words, but a dragon has better things to do than listen. Twenty words, twenty-five if you push it, and gold, treasure, and money do not count."

Manling Victor let out a strange sound. "Lich occupying the castle, *bad*. Killing it, *good*. *Great* reward."

Vainqueur suddenly realized the manling may have used big words to hide his true lack of intelligence. That poor human. The dragon had probably saved his life while taking him under his wing. "What reward?"

"I heard the Ishfanian Inquisition kept most of their fortune in vast vaults underneath the castle, including unique relics. In fact, Maure ordered the attack so they couldn't be used against him. Also, Gardemagne promised that whoever cleaned up the Castle could claim the surrounding lands as their own, which doesn't mean much since they have long been deserted."

"Not really, chief," Red countered. "I think I know the place, and many kobold warrens made their home there."

"Deserted by the civilized races," Minion Victor corrected himself, before frowning. "Wait, you lived there?"

"Our original warren still does," Red nodded. "When resources grew too scarce to feed all of us, the five of us left to find a monster lord of our own. The minion job market is crowded there."

Blue nodded. "The mountain is full of demons, undead, and nasties, except for that one human village."

"There is still a village there?" Victor asked, only caring about his puny kind while Vainqueur imagined the legions of kobolds who would soon cater to his every wish. "How did it survive?"

"No idea, chief," Red replied. "The elders said that the village is 'bad moon mojo,' and everybody avoids it. We ate all the other adventurers for miles."

Which meant no more attempted robberies. "Nice, you have sold me," Vainqueur said. "Pack your belongings, minions, castles are the new caves."

"I must warn Your Majesty that the lich Furibon still occupies the castle and has wiped out every adventurer party trying to dislodge him. Gold-ranked adventurers even."

A lich... "Minion Victor, a lich is a kind of undead, right?"

"Yes—"

"I knew it!"

"They are the strongest of all undead, spellcasters who turned to the dark arts in order to prolong their life. And Furibon was a level fifty magician when he conquered the castle one hundred years ago. He is probably stronger now, he has armies of minions, and he himself is a general of Brandon Maure."

"Brandon whom?" The name sounded vaguely familiar.

"The demon king who usurped control of Ishfania one hundred years ago. Also, the employer of the Scorchers; since we caused them to disband, Gardemagne was able to retake the fortress of Rochefronde from his forces, so he's probably pissed off at us."

"I fail to see why I should care," Vainqueur replied, who feared no one. "I will poke him as I did with your puny kind."

"I'm just saying a demon king and a lich who killed just about every hero sent after them for one hundred years might present a bigger hurdle than a bunch of bandits."

Great, that would mean more treasures to grow his hoard with, and more levels. "I, Vainqueur, relish the challenge," the dragon replied, unmoved. "Pack your belongings and my hoard."

His chief of staff glanced at Vainqueur's treasure, marveling at the size. "Your Majesty," he said. "How do we transport all the gold?"

The dragon squinted, before realizing the problem.

Ah, indeed. Vainqueur's hoard had grown so much, the dragon could no longer carry it in his hands, and what his minions had in wit, they made up with a lack of brawn. They couldn't transport the entire hoard in one go.

"We could leave it behind," Manling Victor suggested. "Collapse the entrance. It would take days for adventurers to dig it out if they even try."

The idea of leaving his hoard unattended for days while robbers kept making their way to the mountaintop horrified Vainqueur. What if he came back to find some of the gold lost? After he struggled so much to grow his treasure! "Minion Victor."

"Yes, Your Majesty?"

"Find a bag. A big bag."

"A big bag? For the entire hoard?"

"A very big bag," Vainqueur clarified when his chief of staff looked at him with his big, ugly eyes. "And smaller, tiny bags for the other minions."

"Your Majesty, there is no bag big enough for your hoard."

Vainqueur took it as flattery. "Then do you have a better idea, minion? Gold does not fly."

The manling opened his mouth to say something stupid, then closed it, then looked inside his coat and brought a strange, white metal plate from underneath. The other minions whistled in awe, much to Vainqueur's confusion.

"Actually," Manling Victor said. "I think it can..."

14: The Event

The Castle of Murmurin looked better than anything Vainqueur could have imagined.

An *immense*, foreboding structure of black stone, the dungeon stood on a rock in the middle of a crater full of hot lava, the black smoke surrounding the place giving it a spooky look. The remains of a half-destroyed stone bridge linked the volcano's edge to the castle's entrance, a stone doorway more than large enough to fit Vainqueur through - unlike that stupid temple.

A ring of stone bound the castle's numerous towers and fortifications, overseen by magnificent dragon statues. The structure had one pointed tower larger than all others at the center, Vainqueur catching glimpses of shadowy forms through stained glass windows. Clouds of carrion birds and crows flocked to the roofs, hungry for manling blood, while giant worms roamed the magma below.

It had lava. It had a food reserve. It had towers.

In short, it was the perfect lair where to stash his hoard!

The land outside the castle was considerably less impressive than the building itself though. The volcano was suitably big and bordered the western sea, but the countryside was an unsightly patch of badlands and arroyos. The soil was brown, flowers and plants scarce, while under the southern horizon, Vainqueur could see the beginning of an immense red sand desert. The remaining manlings had built a small village at the foot of the mountain, while the dragon noticed a few primitive encampments near the desert's border.

Vainqueur would have preferred more than one village to supply him with cattle, but the castle made up for the poor neighborhood. "Strange," he mused to himself, with his minions providing the audience, "I can remember flying over this region two centuries ago, and it looked much greener."

Not that the great dragon cared. He was already in a good mood, and a mere glance at his flying hoard cheered him up.

Manling Victor and the minions had created an ingenious device: a flying ship.

By exhaling without igniting his breath, Vainqueur provided hot gas to fill a giant bag of made of silk, paper, and other stuff; merchants from around the Albain Mountains gave them up when the dragon asked kindly. Somehow, when powered by his marvelous breath, the enormous balloon could lift even a ship.

Working together - continuously in the case of the kobones, who never slept - the minions created a wood ship, much smaller than the balloon, and which could carry the hoard. The kobones powered wooden helixes with pedal, allowing the ship to change direction thanks to a wheel operated by Manling Victor. Vainqueur had asked that the ship's bridge be open, so he could see his hoard inside and catch any treasure flying overboard.

It had taken the minions a good week to finish the ship and sew the balloon while Vainqueur watched, but in the end, it worked out.

While Manling Victor had worked on the ship's design, the Kobolds had discussed other methods to fly the hoard, which included: using stuff called 'magnets'; strapping bird wings to chests; putting everything on throwing discs and then launching them above the mountains; and finding a magical bag which would make the hoard tiny. Vainqueur had shot down that suggestion immediately.

While the dragon had liked the winged chest idea the most, he was satisfied with the final result. No longer did he need to carry his gold the old-fashioned way! He only had to fly next to it and occasionally provide hot air.

"Good job, minion Victor," Vainqueur congratulated his chief of staff, as he flew next to the ship. "I am proud of being your master."

"Yeah, I noticed the iPad's files held schematics for planes, so I thought maybe they had information on aircrafts; and I guessed a dragon's breath had to work on some sort of gas to catch fire. We aren't going to cross the Atlantic with that airship, but it will do for short distances."

"Only our chief of staff could access the true power of the Apple of Knowledge!" Red chirped. "And it worked on its first try!"

"It flew on its first try after we crashed the eight prototypes," Manling Victor pointed out. "You know, I wouldn't have been able to design anything like this while back on Earth. The eleven Intelligence points I gained since really showed there."

Vainqueur didn't understand half of what they said, too happy to care. "Minion, you will land my hoard there after we are done with the introductions," the dragon pointed at a small, isolated valley, "Away from thieves."

"Sure," minion Victor said, glancing at the castle while keeping the ship above the crater's edge. "I'm pretty certain the owner must have seen us coming."

"Good," Vainqueur replied, hovering above the volcano's edge. "What is his name again?"

"Furibon."

"Minion, announce my presence to that Furibon."

"Is Your Majesty really, *really* sure they want to do that?" Manling Victor took a deep breath, then shouted towards the crater, his booming voice causing the crows to flee, "FURIBON! King Vainqueur Knightsbane, King of the Albain Mountains and greatest adventurer to ever live, wants to have a talk!"

"Minion, do not forget 'Great Calamity of this Age,'" Vainqueur chided his lackey. "I worked hard on earning that one." So many princesses abducted... the dragon promised himself he would grab one after moving in.

Unfortunately, the current owner teleported outside the castle before the minion could correct his mistake.

Furibon the lich was a skeleton, larger than that of most of the puny races, with a long serpentine neck and a manling-like skull. His bones seemed made of gold, the teeth of jewels, while the empty eye sockets shone with a bright, purple light. The creature wore expensive, red and purple robes like living wizards, but while it had long, thin arms, it lacked legs. Magic alone allowed it to fly.

And it had a nice crown, whom Vainqueur immediately wanted for himself. "I wonder what is his level... let's use [Observe]..." Manling Victor's eyes widened. "Fifty-eight?!"

The undead flew upward towards the dragon and his flying hoard with a speed that rivaled Vainqueur's. The lich stopped right in front of the ship's bridge. "Greetings, mortals," the lich said with a deep, frosty voice. Vainqueur noticed the air chilled out around him. "His Majesty King Vainqueur Knightsbane, and Victor Dalton, I assume?"

"Indeed, I am King Vainqueur," Vainqueur replied proudly, happy at being shown proper respect. This day just couldn't get better.

"You face Furibon, archmage of Ishfania," the undead replied, "Welcome to my humble abode. It has been so long since I have had living visitors. My creations are so... *eager* to fight."

"You know our names?" Manling Victor spoke up. "You were *expecting* us?"

"My lord and master, King Brandon Maure, warned me that you helped Gardemagne retake the fortress of Rochefronde by destroying his chosen agents, and stole the Apple of Knowledge." The creature's 'eyes' moved to examine the ship. "I see that you already peered in its forbidden knowledge."

They did what with Rochefronde? Vainqueur hadn't paid attention back then.

"Have you come to return the artifact to its rightful owner?" the lich asked, "I hope not. I would have to spare you in that case."

"As if anyone could take what belongs to me," the dragon taunted the lich with disdain.

The creature let out a deep sound which Vainqueur thought to be a laugh. "Why not play a game for it, then? You are adventurers eager to challenge my castle, are you not? The lack of victims bores me so very much; your feeble minds cannot fathom the number of trap designs I went through over the last half a century. When you are immortal and tasked with holding a crumbling ruin, you have to occupy your time somehow."

"By making death traps?" Minion Victor asked with a strange tone. "To each their hobby."

"A sarcastic mortal," the lich replied with the exact same tone, except it somehow sounded more scathing. "How original. [Black Curse]."

A black aura surrounded Manling Victor, instantly draining all colors from his skin and bringing him to his knees.

The sound the minion made though... Vainqueur had never heard such a ridiculous sound in his life, and neither did Furibon, who let out a chuckle. "Still standing? Then, let us try again. [Black Curse]."

Victor collapsed to his chest this time, almost falling overboard. "Chief!" the kobolds and kobones immediately rushed to his help.

"Why did it not make an amusing sound this time?" the lich wondered.

"Because I already... learned your monster Perk... wanna see?" Manling Victor raised a feeble hand at the lich. "[Black Curse]..."

A black aura surrounded the lich, who shrugged it off. "A [Monster Squire]. How amusing, trying to fight me with my own Perk. Maybe I should cut the greetings short and cast down this ship from the skies, and you with it."

"Stop bullying my minions," Vainqueur warned the creature, moving between the flying ship and the lich. "He is my chief of staff. To attack him without my permission is to show *me* disrespect and commit suicide by dragon."

"Oh? You wish to fight? I admit I would rather test my creations on you first, but if you wish to skip directly to a fight, I will take back the Appl—"

Bored with the conversation and eager to claim his new castle before dinner, Vainqueur fingerpoked the lich in the chest.

The blow sent him flying towards the castle, but the creature's flight stabilized before it could hit the walls. "You..." the lich fumed with cold anger. "You lizard, how dare you touch me? I will mount your head on a spike in my library!"

He survived the poke.

The lich survived the poke.

"How dare you survive the poke!" Vainqueur complained, raising two fingers. "Now I will have to use half my hand to destroy you!"

"Your Majesty, powerful undead are immune to critical hits..." Minion Victor warned, regaining enough strength to speak up normally. "Use your breath!"

"[Magic Up]," the lich rasped, shining with a crimson aura. "[Greater Fire Res—"

Vainqueur just blasted him with a quick fireball, vaporizing him at once.

He instantly regretted it.

The crown!

Congratulations! For taking a powerful lich by surprise and temporarily destroying it before your fans, you have earned a level in [Gladiator]!

+30 HP, +2 STR, +1 SKI, +1 AGI, +1 CHA, +1 LCK!

"Vainqueur, best dragon!" his minions congratulated him. "Vainqueur, Vainqueur, Vainqueur!"

"Where is the treasure?" Vainqueur asked, once the smoke settled to reveal nothing but dust. "He should have dropped a treasure."

"That's because he's not dead, Your Majesty," Manling Victor said, as he rose back to his feet.

"Of course he is. He is an undead, he was dead before I killed him."

"Your Majesty, first, Furibon is a lich. Their souls are held by a container which will allow them to revive within a few days if not destroyed."

Before Vainqueur could argue further, the lich materialized right back in front of them, powerful sorcery surrounding him. "[Greater Fire Resistance], [Magic Ward], [Stone Ward], [Accelerate], [Greater Evasion]."

"Already?" Victor squinted at the sight. "Shouldn't it take you days to recover?"

"I have a special Perk which accelerates the process. As for you, Vainqueur, I will teach you why your kind is—" The lich dodged Vainqueur's attempt to poke him by flying out of the way. "Stop this at onc—" Again, he avoided a poke. "Stop this! [Crimson Barrier]."

A shining sphere of red magical surrounded the lich, blocking Vainqueur's frustrated attempts at poking him with two fingers. "Better. King Vainqueur, I thought you would be an entertaining victim, but now I cannot wait to make a bag out of your skin."

"As if," Vainqueur replied with smug disdain. "A dragon has no weakness!"

"Is that so?" The lich flew to get a direct line of sight of Vainqueur's gold, on the ship's bridge. "Is that your hoard, King Vainqueur?"

No... "Do you not dare throw my hoard in the lava!"

"Throw that wealth in the lava?" The lich chuckled. "Do you take me for an animal, Vainqueur Knightsbane? What kind of wasteful monster would throw such a hard-won hoard into magma?"

Ah. Ah, thank the elder wyrm, that undead was a civilized fellow.

"I have a better idea in mind," the lich said, raising both hands and calling upon purple sparks of lightning.

"[Transmute Gold to Lead]!"

Before Vainqueur's mind caught on, his entire hoard turned from beautiful gold to unshiny lead with a bright flash of dark magic.

For a long, agonizing moment, the great wyrm was too shocked to compute the situation, his brain freezing inside his skull.

...

"Boss? King Vainqueur?"

...

"Your Majesty?

...

"Ohoh, I 'lived' for centuries, and I never knew dragons could make that face."

...

"Minions, turn the ballon away. Let's get the hell out of here *now*."

"But chief—"

"Turn the damn balloon away!"

...

"Well, King Vainqueur, now that I have taken what you value most, why not make a deal? Return the Apple to me at once, and I will change your gold bac—"

Vainqueur's sight turned bloody red.

Attack Up! Attack Up! ATTACK UP! Fire Power Up! Warning: [Berserk] ailment!

"RAAAAAAARGH!"

Vainqueur instantly blasted a giant fireball at the lich, a projectile big enough that the few manlings who witnessed the attack in the past mistook it for a meteor. "[Teleportation]." The lich blinked out of the way before the fires could destroy him, the projectile hitting the crater's edge and causing a large span of it to fall into the magma.

The lich reappeared nearby, observing the destruction with ominous silence. "In hindsight," he muttered to himself, "Maybe that was a mistake..."

In the ropes of berserk rage, Vainqueur blasted the entire area, castle and lich included, with fiery death. This time, Furibon was hit directly by a fireball, shattering his crimson shield and sending him flying through one of the castle's wall. One of the smaller towers collapsed on him.

Too angry to think, Vainqueur kept firing at the dungeon, melting the stone and blasting another tower into the magma. Immediately afterward a bright, yellow magical barrier surrounded the castle, shielding it from the dragon's repeated bombardment. The monsters in the magma cowered in fear.

Vainqueur furiously roared to the heavens, and the mountain trembled.

15: Just your average Hometown

Holy hell... Victor thought as he watched the fireworks from the foot of the mountain. The crater above appeared in the middle of a fiery eruption, fireballs and clouds of rancid smoke flying out while the earth trembled.

While not religious at all, the adventurer prayed to the twelve gods that Vainqueur didn't start an actual eruption while rampaging. "Guys..."

"Chief..." Red and the other kobolds cowered at the sight, hiding behind the hill of lead Vainqueur's hoard had turned into.

"I think it would be best never to mention the *event* ever again around Vainqueur." The critters all nodded at once. "He will calm down *eventually*, but when he does, we will show our beloved dragon ruler full emotional support, and carefully avoid the word 'lead' until we die. This is for everyone's own good."

Victor glanced at the mess around him; he had managed to make a semi-respectable emergency landing without Vainqueur's support in the badlands, stashing the hoard there. Not that he thought anybody wanted to steal it now.

Maybe they should consider becoming plumber adventurers? It worked out for Mario.

"Chief, what do we do?" Blue asked him, terrified and looking for guidance.

"Right now... well, you have family here, right?" The critters nodded. "Go visit them, or practice your choreography. Take some time off."

"But chief," Pink protested, "We can't abandon Master Vainqueur when he needs help!"

The ground trembled with another fiery detonation. Victor looked back at the mountain, noticing huge monsters fleeing the volcano. It appeared the local horrors had wisely decided to bolt the hell out of the region. One giant worm flew over the crater's edge, probably tossed out by Vainqueur.

How long did dragons rampage? Days? Or would he calm down if he managed to kill Furibon?

"Right," Victor said. "Look, 'Master Vainqueur' is too furious to act rational, and he isn't calming down anytime soon. Consider this a vacation. You earned it after all your good work so far."

As the kobolds and kobones kept exchanging glances, Victor suddenly realized these professional minions had no concept of a vacation. They literally lived to serve bigger creatures and didn't understand life outside it.

"Okay, look, minions, I am giving you a secret mission. Do you remember Vainqueur's glorious vision about V&V?" Merely mentioning the name gave him cancer. "You said the local minion job market is crowded, and His Majesty has a shortage of them. So, fetch us more minions."

"Chief, are..." They looked about to cry, even the undead ones. "Are you replacing us?"

"No, in fact, you are now no longer interns, nor even new minions, but *minion lieutenants*," Victor improvised. "You will be the admins serving under me, but above new minions. The *elite* of our adventurer guild."

"We... we've been promoted!" The tears quickly turned to joy, with Red outright jumping on place. "Promoted!"

"So go find more interns." Victor made a dramatic gesture. "They will be your responsibility though, so accept only the best."

"Yes, chief!" They bolted off so fast, Victor's eyes could barely follow them.

Truth to be told, Victor actually started to enjoy leading minions around. He mostly blamed it on Stockholm Syndrome and Vainqueur rubbing off on him the wrong way, but it felt nice to be obeyed, rather than obeying.

Damn, he was turning into a dragon.

That, and after that stunt with the duchess, Victor was all but trapped with Vainqueur. Without the dragon's protection, he would no longer be able to set foot in Gardemagne without being executed. More minions meant less people likely to pick a fight with him.

Now alone, Victor decided to visit the one village around, in case he could buy supplies. He was aware of the minions' warnings about the place, but he could probably handle it on his own if he was careful.

From afar, it appeared the town had less than two hundred people living there. It was a small farming community, with Victor recognizing olive, citrus, and stranger fruits orchards, even a vineyard. The large stone houses could accommodate entire extended families, reminding Victor of American ranches.

Also, he noticed that they had a lot more sheep than they should need.

Besides these details and the pervasive scent of dogs, even if he couldn't see any, the village seemed relatively normal. Victor approached it warily, and two locals immediately came to greet him.

The two looked like a couple of ranch hillbillies, one male in his late twenties and a girl a bit younger than Victor himself. Both were brown-skinned, with eyes of the same color, and similar enough that Victor assumed they must have been part of the same family.

"Hi there, traveler," the man spoke up. Powerfully built, with a mane of black hair and dirty, rancher clothes, he looked straight out of a Clint Eastwood Western. "I'm Croissant and this is my sister, Chocolatine. Welcome to Murmurin."

"Hello, handsome," said the girl, a pretty creature with semi-long coffee hair and dressed like Little Red Riding Hood, "You're an adventurer coming to hunt the dragon, right? Right?"

Victor had the strange feeling a lot of eyes were observing him. "Hunt the dragon?"

Croissant pointed a finger at the volcano. "A dragon just made its lair in our mountain and is frightening the livestock. If you could kill it, that would help us a lot."

"No, I'm a lead merchant," Victor deadpanned.

"Lead?" Croissant repeated, confused.

"Lead. I love lead. Are you all vampires?"

"What? Of course not! Vampires are vile, tasteless things! Nobody likes them!" Tasteless… odd choice of words. "Why the sudden accusations, stranger?"

"My Kobolds interns told me of bad moon mojo around here, and you're a creepy village in the middle of nowhere. I've watched movies, and I can defend myself."

Victor suddenly realized that wording made no sense, but the duo seemed to understand. More and more suspicious, the adventurer decided to use [Monster Insight] on them, just in case.

Croissant

Werewolf (Humanoid/Beast)

Strong against Moon, Beast, Madness and Fairy effects.

Weak against Silver, Manslayer, and Beastslayer effects.

Older brother of Chocolatine, and a werewolf; can turn into a giant wolf-hybrid at will, but goes berserk during the full moon.

Kind of rough around the edges, especially if you mention Gevaudan. Oh man, you are so BEEPED if you mention Gevaudan. Almost as BEEPED as if you BEEP his sister.

Chocolatine

Werewolf (Humanoid/Beast)

Strong against Moon, Beast, Madness and Fairy effects.

Weak against Silver, Manslayer, and Beastslayer effects.

Pretty little riding hood, foe to all grandmothers everywhere, and sister of Croissant. A priestess of the beast god Isengrim, she looks sweet and innocent while being anything but. Finds you very appetizing due to your big charisma boost, and wonders whether she should cook you with a stew or with pepper sauce.

"Ah, werewolves! Bad moon, of course you would be werewolves."

"Wait, are you..." Croissant trailed, before turning to his sister. "Is he one of us?"

Chocolate said a few words, apparently casting a spell on Victor. She smiled happily at once. "It's okay, brother, he's a monster, too! A Humanoid/Dragon Type!"

"Oh by the Moon Man, for a second I thought you were a homeless person nobody would miss," said Croissant, horrified. "We avoided a terrible mistake. I'm so sorry."

What the— "You were going to kill me?"

"Not *us*," Croissant shrugged. "Some of the villagers often feed strangers to the Moon Man's eldritch children, and they think the dragon is punishment for being late with the current sacrifice. I do not condone it, but we are an open-minded community, you know? I hope you can forgive us for the misunderstanding."

Of course! It made Victor feel so much better!

"Guys, it's okay!" Croissant shouted in the settlement's direction. "He's a monster, too! You can drop the disguises!"

Victor heard sighs of relief, and watched, astonished, as the locals exited their houses.

Half of them looked human enough, although [Monster Insight] informed him most of them were werewolves or shapeshifters, like Doppelgangers; the other half, not so much. Victor noticed a large family of pallid ghouls, a squid-human hybrid with a calmar-like head, a rusty steel golem, and two dozen other creatures straight out of a bestiary.

The entire village was populated with humanoid-looking monsters.

Victor blinked, as he recognized a familiar figure among them, a tall Lizardkin with sandy scales, sharp fangs, and long claws. The humanoid lizard had short back swept horns and a barbed tail, but kept most of her powerfully built body beneath brown and green traveler robes. As usual, she carried a sash full of potions and various spices, and had the Nightblades' black sword tattoo on the left side of her face. "Savoureuse?" Victor called her. "Sav, is that you?"

"Vic?" The beast took a few steps out of the crowd to get a better view of him. Besides having tanned a little, she was exactly the same as in his memories, with those warm, green reptilian eyes. "Hey, Vic!"

"Hey, Sav!" Victor waved at her. She had briefly been his friend during his brief tenure as a professional thief, showing him the tricks of the trade. "Long time to no see! What are you doing here?"

"Business." She winked at him. "We're discussing with the locals to set up a warehouse there, so the Nightblades' guildmasters sent me."

"Nice, sounds like a good vacation."

"Aha, it's good to take a break from waste collecting sometimes. Shame you left us, Vic, you were an excellent repossessor."

Ah, the old naming conventions. 'Repossession' instead of theft, 'waste-collecting' for assassination, and 'community contribution' for extortion. No wonder Victor left the criminal syndicate the second he could get away with it.

"By the way Vic, why didn't you tell me you were a dragon monster in disguise? I'm almost insulted you managed to hide it from me."

"It's a pretty recent change," Victor replied. "So what is this, a secret humanoid monster community?"

"Yes and no, we disguise as humans to avoid inquisitors and adventurers who often wander in the region," Croissant explained. "They always try to wipe us out otherwise."

"So we kill them in their sleep first," Chocolatine chirped with a sweet, happy smile that sent shivers down Victor's spine.

"We also have something of a school for mimics and other shapeshifters, so they can learn to blend in within a safe, family-friendly environment," said Croissant, before he moved to firmly shake Victor's hand. "Victor, is that it? Nice to meet you, what kind of monster are you?"

"I'm a dragon's chief of staff," Victor explained, a few of the locals whistling.

"*That* dragon's?" Croissant glanced at the volcano.

"Yeah. We came to take over the castle, but the current owner pulled a prank on my 'master,' who didn't take it well."

"Owner? Furibon? Even with no flesh anymore, he's a giant dick." Victor couldn't help but laugh at Croissant's stupid joke. The werewolf's tone implied this wasn't the first time the lich caused them trouble. "I heard he was so annoying a fomor transformed him into a cave troll, before he turned himself into a lich. He leaves us mostly alone, so we do not bother him either, but he's very open to us supplying adventurers trying to challenge him."

"I think he's bored and lonely in his castle," Chocolatine said with a conspiratorial tone.

"So, Vic, it was true what I heard?" asked Savoureuse. "You fed the Duchess of Euskal to a dragon?"

"Did you?" Chocolatine had stars in her eyes.

"I..." Well... technically he *did* bullshit Vainqueur into hunting down the Scorchers instead of the Kraken, which indirectly led to that disaster. "You could say that..."

Croissant frowned. "That's a bit over the top, no?"

"I don't understand, Vic, have you left us, or have you not left us?" asked Savoureuse. "Because feeding a noble to a dragon is very Nightbladish to me."

"I guess my current job isn't that different from the old one," Victor admitted.

"Anyway," Croissant butted in. "We're happy to welcome you to our community. How long will you stay?"

"I dunno, as long as the dragon stays here. Maybe longer." If Vainqueur did kill Furibon and managed to claim the promised reward, then they might settle in the region. "Why that question?"

"Eh, they're a small community, and they want more people to avoid inbreeding," Savoureuse replied. "They have a nice open door policy for newcomers. Isn't that right, Croissant?"

"Yeah, we're recent settlers, too. We used to live in the Woods of Gevaudan, in Gardemagne. Ah, times were good. Best hunting grounds we ever had, so much food around."

The woods of...

"But that was before some dumbass human and their pet red dragon burned it to the ground while hunting trol—"

Croissant stopped mid-sentence, then glared suspiciously at Victor.

Uh oh.

16: Cult Management

This world sucked!

The locals had bound Victor to an olive tree with heavy chains under the faint moonlight. Around twenty werewolves had gathered to observe the sacrifice, while a squid-like humanoid held the ceremony, chittering incantations while wielding a scepter. Victor guessed the Moon Man worshippers were a relative minority in the community.

Unfortunately, the majority had given Victor the silent treatment.

"Brother, is that smart?" Chocolatine asked her brother, one of the few who did argue against the adventurer's capture. "He is the dragon's chief of staff, and that one is angry already…"

"He burnt our previous home, sis," Croissant pointed out. Unlike his sister, he had shapeshifted in a monstrous, car-sized black wolf, glaring at Victor with seething hatred.

"Yes, which is why I don't want him to burn our current one."

"I'm sure Victor was just following orders," Savoureuse tried to argue with the cultists, although that wasn't the passionate defense Victor had hoped for. "Do not blame the follower, blame the leader."

Croissant sneered back. "I asked the adventurer guild after the dragon devastated our home, and they confirmed the 'human partner' led the dragon in the first place."

"But Vainqueur burned the forest on his own!" Victor protested.

"You still led him there!" Croissant snapped back.

"He burned my house!" another werewolf complained in the crowd.

"I watched all my livestock die!"

Savoureuse gave Victor a sympathetic gaze. "I'm sorry, Vic. I tried. I would have fought to release you if my life wasn't in danger."

Victor shrugged. It was more than he expected.

The Moon Man's priest finished the incantation, and a beam of light descended from the skies. With a brilliant flash, a horrible insult against nature manifested in front of Victor, a bus-sized hybrid of a dragon and a squid, with no eyes and only squirmy skin. Its countless tentacles thrashed around, tossing away some of the werewolf cultists.

The mere sight of the creature gave Victor a headache.

*Charisma check successful! [**Madness**] negated!*

The creature sounded no more happy to be here than Victor himself. "You *again*!" it shrieked with a shrilling, inhuman voice. "Why will you not *stop*?"

"Great Moon Beast!" the lead priest called, the other cultists bowing before the creature. Only Croissant, Chocolatine and Savoureuse remained still. "Your rancid glory honors us! Please, accept this sacrifice in atonement!"

The monster didn't feel grateful. At all. "I do not understand the movements of your squishy tongue, skinbag, but I swear on the Moon Man, one day I will lose my self-control, and I will drip my pseudopods in the hole you use for excrement."

"Mmm... sir," Victor told the creature. "I would like to say that I am not complicit in this."

The titan froze. "You speak r'lyehian, skinbag?"

R'lyehian? Victor figured his Perk had translated the words in the creature's native tongue. "Well, yes I can understand you just fine." The adventurer blinked. "They can't?"

"He can understand the Moon Beast without going mad?" the squid priest turned to Croissant, who shrugged his shoulders in confusion.

Victor guessed they lacked the Perk needed to discuss with the interstellar abomination. "Since you can also understand me," the human told the creature. "Words can't convey how unappetizing I am."

"Why would I eat you? You don't even have pseudopods. Eurgh… you moving gametes disgust me… your face is terrible, and you look like a cancer with these big, bulbous, disgusting… *eyes...*"

How did it even know Victor had eyes since it had none itself? "Yeah, having eyes is terrible, almost as much as being tied to a tree while being threatened with death."

"I will tell you what is terrible, gamete creature. You are minding your own business, enjoying your once in an eon vacation, before the stars are right and you must go back to work, and you are *this*," the abomination raised two tentacles, "*this* close to eating that tasty telepathic spider. Then, without warning, someone teleports you right as you have your food in your tendrils, then throws a screaming human whelp at you. And they do that. Every. Single. *Moon*! Wouldn't *you* vent a little?"

When seeing things this way… That would explain why tentacled creatures always destroyed the world when summoned.

"Yes, but…" Victor trailed, glancing at the cultists and Croissant in particular, who couldn't understand the Moon Beast's half of the conversation. "Why at *me*, and not at *them*?"

The creature sighed. "The Moon Man is… absent-minded, so we have to take care of his cults. He already has so few of them, and while *stupid*, this one is devout. I wish they could just stop summon me all the time, though. I do not know where they got the idea that the Moon Man needs live sacrifices, but the idea spread everywhere."

"I think they do that because they do not understand what you say, unlike me," Victor replied. "I can clarify your needs to them, and make them stop."

"You can make it stop?" The titan's tentacles wriggled and let out a sound that sounded dirty. "Oh, yes! *Yes*!"

"You've got to spare and free me free first, though."

"Yes, yes, anything it takes." The titan's tentacles surged towards the chains, breaking them without effort. Victor walked away from the tree, enjoying his newfound freedom, much to the amazement of the cultists, and Croissant's frustration.

None were more than the leading priest. "He... the newcomer has been chosen by the Moon Beast as its mouthpiece!"

"It says..." Victor trailed, before frowning at the Moon Beast. "Actually, what is your name?"

"Thul-Gathar, gamete skinbag."

"Thul-Gathar says moonly sacrifices are not needed to show your devotion to its progenitor."

The cultists exchanged hushed whispers. "Then how can we serve the Moon Man?" asked the chief priest.

"They're asking what they should replace the sacrifices with," Victor translated.

"Tell them they must moonwalk until they collapse of exhaustion every full moon, then to eat their own fecal matter."

"Seriously?"

"No, but that would have been funny," the Moon Beast replied. "Tell them to pray to the Moon Man for insight, then to hold a quiet, private orgy under the moonlight every full moon; narcotics are encouraged, but not necessary. Order them to stop summoning me, as I have other cults to guide."

"Thul-Gathar says that you must pray the Moon Man for insight, while..." The cult listened to him with religious, rapturous attention, making Victor uneasy. "Having a drugged orgy every full moon."

"Also, no more incest," the Moon Beast clarified. "It is very important Father's cults remain healthy and fertile. We allowed inbreeding long ago, and cults keep dying out because of it today."

"Thul-Gathar explicitly forbids incest, which is an affront to the Moon Man."

"Even cousins?" the priest asked.

"Are cousins allowed?" Victor transmitted the message.

The Moon Beast hesitated for a good minute, before coming with an answer. "Cousins are reluctantly forbidden, but in-laws are allowed in return."

"Cousins are not allowed, but since blood is the only barrier to love, thou can lay with your in-laws. Finally, your repeated summonings prevent Thul-Gathar from guiding other civilizations to glory. It says that you have reached sufficient enlightenment to manage yourselves."

"Ch'yar ul'nyar shaggornyth," the cultists said all at once.

"Yes, yes, inbred gamete people," Thul-Gathar answered dismissively, his flock unable to understand him. "Are we done?"

"Yes, I think they will behave from now on."

"Then thank you, skinbag. Show me your hand, so that I may reward you for giving me peace."

The Moon Beast touched Victor's left arm with a tentacle, the moist contact sending shivers down his spine. The shining, white mark of a full moon, the Moon Man's symbol, appeared on his skin.

*Congratulations! You were granted a blessing by a star spawn of the Moon Man! You earned the [**Claimed by the Moon Man**] Personal Perk!*

[**Claimed by the Moon Man**]: *when you level up, you have an additional 10 percent chance of gaining a Charisma point. You gain Immunity to Madness and Moon effects unless those caused by the Moon Man and his servants.*

Nice! Finally, things turned around in his favor for once!

"Tell me, gamete animal, would you like a job?" the Moon Beast offered. "You can make a good mouthpiece to address the Moon Man's flock, and I have been looking for a chief of staff to lead my minions."

A chief of staff? Here we go again. "I am already taken, sir."

"You are?" The creature hummed at Victor. "A dragon's scent? You serve a dragon?"

"Unfortunately, yes."

"Look, carbon-based mammal, dragons are prestigious, but they underpay their minions." Like it wouldn't believe. "If you serve me, you will be swimming in pearls and seashells by the next moon. As my chief of staff, you will also have unrestricted breeding privileges, including ignoring the incest restriction. You can keep your tendrils in your family."

It was official, the creature was officially trying to bribe him. Victor pondered the offer, the idea of managing a fertility cult appealing to him.

But considering how Vainqueur had reacted when he thought Victor had left him for a wyvern, and that he would be in a cranky mood for a while... "I am very flattered," said Victor. "But my dragon is very insecure about me leaving him, too, so I am not tempting his wrath. I also kind of like the other minions."

"Your funeral," the Moon Beast replied. "If you change your mind, visit me on the moon."

"But thank you, I am honored by your proposal," Victor said politely, in case the creature could hold a grudge. He turned to the cultists. "Also... what am I to do with them?"

"BEEP them." The Moon Beast vanished in another flash of light, clearly in a hurry to leave the place behind.

*Congratulations! For resisting the temptation to cheat on your dragon master with a Moon Beast, proving your faithfulness, and for serving as a bridge between monster lords and their flock, you have earned **two** levels in [**Monster Squire**]!*

+60 HP, +10SP, +1 SKI, +1 AGI, +1 INT, +1 CHA, +1 LCK!

*You earned the [**Rally Minions**] Class Perk!*

*[**Rally Minions**]: By uttering a strong authority statement, such as "Die to them, or die to me," you can increase all the stats of your minions for a short duration.*

"Nice work," Savoureuse congratulated Victor, "I didn't understand half of what it said, but you handled it like a champ."

Victor shrugged. He had the feeling he had done the best he…

Wait.

Wait, wait! Victor hadn't asked the creature if it could send him back to Earth!

"I guess I will have to eat him myself," Croissant said, showing his fangs, only for the priest of the Moon Man to block his path with his scepter.

"You will not lay a fang on a prophet of our god, Croissant!" The priest turned back to Victor. "Please, chosen Victor, what was the final revelation? What are you to do with us?"

… do not abuse your power, Victor. Do not abuse your power, don't abuse the power.

Abuse the power. "Thul-Gathar asked me to—"

Before Victor could make his unreasonable demand, a powerful shadow obscured the moonlight, followed by a familiar sound.

"MINION!"

Everyone trembled, as Vainqueur landed in the field with a loud crash, his landing blowing off dust. "Minion! There you are! Stop daydreaming, and tell me where is my hoard! Is it safe? Is it cured?"

Victor sighed, his vacation was very short-lived. He already regretted not taking the Moon Beast's offer. "I put it where you wanted, Your Majesty, but no, it is not 'cured.'"

"As I feared," Vainqueur fumed, his golden eyes falling upon the gathered villagers, the fire in his gaze making them step back. "What are they, new minions?"

"They're survivors from the Woods of Gevaudan, which Your Majesty burned."

"Yes, we are." To his credit, Croissant had enough courage to stand up to Vainqueur. "You burned our home."

"Then you will apologize to me at once, wolfling."

Croissant glared back at the dragon, aghast. "Why would we apologize to *you*?"

"If you had not survived, I would have gained more treasure," Vainqueur replied. "So your survival cost me. You will *all* apologize by becoming my new minions. Now, there is a great reward for doing as I wish. Namely, living. Any other dragon would have eaten you all for your sinful crime, and would never have taken werewolves in their service, but I am forgiving and merciful."

Victor had terrible flashbacks at the wording, which he blamed on Post Vainqueur Stress Disorder. The more Croissant listened, the more incredulous he looked. "You cannot expect—"

"I am a dragon. A dragon who never ate a wolf before, and you are starting to sound like food. Minion Victor, is that wolf food?"

"That depends," Victor looked at Croissant dead in the eyes. "Are you dragon food, Croissant?"

The wolf looked at Victor, then at Vainqueur, realized that he was twenty times smaller, then glared at Victor again. "I am starting to realize that the 'just following orders' excuse may be valid," he grumbled.

"You're goddamn right," Victor replied, a bit too happy to rub it in the wolf's face.

Croissant looked at the rest of the villagers, none of them willing to take a stand. And then, proving himself far smarter than every noble in Gardemagne, he decided to cut his losses after a glance at his sister. "I apologize to both of you," the werewolf said, forcing himself to say every word. "Just don't eat us."

"Not unless you run out of sheep," Vainqueur replied, the villagers looking at one another. The dragon lost interest in the wolf pack, turning to Victor. "Minion, I must become a wizard."

"A wizard, Your Majesty?"

"The lich does not stay dead when I kill him, and now hides in his castle like a coward. You said he hides his soul in an item, which makes it immortal."

"His phylactery, which is probably hidden in the castle, yes." Victor started realizing where the dragon was going.

"I cannot break the magical barrier protecting it nor cure my hoard, so I must become a wizard to do so," Vainqueur explained. "We must destroy the great evil that is Furibon, Minion Victor. This is no longer about wealth, minion. This is about all dragons, all hoards, present, and future. Furibon is the greatest threat to the dragon way of life since the Gold-Eating Insects."

"There are insects that eat gold?" Victor asked, wondered how that even worked.

"There *were*," Vainqueur said with an ominous tone. "I was overconfident, thinking being an adventurer was all about increasing the size of my hoard. I now realize that I was blind to the danger ahead. There are threats to all hoards hiding in the darkest corners of the world, and I must destroy them."

Victor said nothing, astonished by Vainqueur's passionate speech.

"Furibon is evil incarnate, a cruel, heartless monster who delights in taking all that brings worth to the world and turning it to *lead*. Imagine if he spreads that spell outside of this castle? Imagine a world without gold?" Vainqueur marked a short, rhetorical pause. "You cannot, manling, and neither can I! Because only a twisted monster like Furibon could imagine it! He is evil, and he has to be *stopped*. So we will break the magical barrier, clear that dungeon and destroy the lich for good. Even if it takes us a thousand years!"

They were all doomed.

Vainqueur had started behaving like a true adventurer.

17: Vainqueur's Private War

Sitting amidst an orchard and a pen whom he had emptied of its sheep, Vainqueur glared at Murmurin's volcano, a dark, fuming place even under the bright sunlight.

What kind of atrocity the lich was planning deep in his dungeon? How long before he spread knowledge of this dark, horrifying spell to the outside world? Vainqueur seethed at the thought, simmering with anger.

Although he heard Manling Victor and the new werewolves minions approach, Vainqueur didn't even bother glancing at him, entirely focused on the mountain. "Your Majesty?" minion Victor called. "Your Majesty, are you alright?"

"Where are the kobolds?" Vainqueur asked.

"I sent them to recruit new minions."

Good. More fodder to throw at the lich. "Minion Victor, you are now my military advisor," Vainqueur told him, "I would have promoted you to general, but command of this operation is too important to delegate. I will oversee the war against Furibon myself."

"The war, Your Majesty?"

"Yes, minion, *war*. This is war, against an enemy willing to cross any line into depravity. So you will gather all information about this dungeon, every trap, and every defender, every way to break this magical barrier, every way to return my hoard to normal, and then you will give me strategies to validate. You will also research ways for me to become a wizard stronger than Furibon, who is evil and must be destroyed."

"Dragons can be wizards?" Croissant asked.

"Dragons can be *anything*," Vainqueur clarified.

"I can't believe I'm saying this..." Manling Victor hesitated. "But Your Majesty's choice of taking levels in the [Wizard] class will be very suboptimal. Let alone the fact it will take you at least fifty years of study to become anywhere near Furibon's level."

"Fifty years is the length of a nap to me," Vainqueur clarified, resolute in his choice. "I told you, minion, that I would destroy that lich, even if it takes me centuries."

"Yes, but wouldn't it be faster and easier to just recruit a professional wizard? I already asked Savoureuse for her contacts, and that way I would live long enough to see the lich defeated."

"Your Lizardkin ally may be of use, and look reptilian enough to please me," Vainqueur agreed, happy the minion shared his resolve. "But I can smell she serves another monster lord, and I will not rely on another's minion to win this battle."

"You remember her name?" The minion seemed shocked. "Holy... Your Majesty is *not* fine."

"A dragon is not poor, Manling Victor," Vainqueur told his chief of staff. "My gold is sick, and so I am. Only gold and revenge against Furibon, who is evil and must be destroyed, can cure me."

"Technically sir, only your gold is 'sick,' the silver, jewels, and magical items are fine. So the hoard is not totally gone, most of your assets are just... frozen."

"A dragon's hoard must have gold in it!" Vainqueur replied angrily. "Or it is not shiny enough!"

Having no hoard worth bragging about was a fate worse than death to Vainqueur, and he refused to suffer through it.

"I'm just... you're being so intense and serious about it, Your Majesty, it's scaring me a little."

"Furibon took everything that was worth to me!" Vainqueur ranted, the strength of his booming words making Victor fall on his ass. "I am the great calamity of this age! I am the apex creature! No one mocks me and lives! My reputation will be in tatters if word of his cruelty spreads! So if I cannot blast his fortress the proper dragon way, then I will do whatever it takes to *destroy* him!"

Furibon had made Vainqueur feel like a *pauper*, and for that, he had to die. Or become deader.

Vainqueur would also learn how to break that curse of lead, in case another Furibon rose up after he had destroyed the current one.

"Your Majesty, I have thought about the problem, and if I may, I think there is an easier solution than working years on becoming a wizard." Manling Victor rose back up. "There is a spellcaster-class called [Witch Hunter], which specializes in killing spellcasters and demon worshippers, and they learn exorcisms highly effective against both. With enough levels in it and Charisma points, you should be able to break the barrier."

While Vainqueur stubbornly sought to cover his rear with magic, the idea of a class dedicated to destroying Furibon's kind appealed to him. "What has my natural charisma to do with canceling a barrier?"

"The potency of [Witch Hunter] Perks is based on Charisma, and from what I gathered Dragons have lots of it. Must be the scaly charm."

It suddenly occurred to Vainqueur that he never cared about what those points did. He stopped looking at the mountain, focusing intently on Victor.

As expected of his chief of staff, Minion Victor explained without Vainqueur having to ask. "Health Points represent your lifeforce, health, and longevity. The more of them, the longer you live and the slower you age. Special Points power magical abilities. Strength is strength, Vitality increases your constitution and endurance. Skill handles your dexterity and skillfulness; Agility represents speed and reflexes. Intelligence is intelligence. Charisma influences willpower and charm. The more you have it, the more you get laid. Finally, the more Luck, the more randomness favors you."

"So the higher the Charisma, the more willpower I have?"

"It also improves the use of certain spells and abilities. Since it represents willpower, [Witch Hunters] can use their Charisma to dispel magic or rain holy judgment on their enemies."

Vainqueur checked his current stats. "Menu."

Vainqueur Knightsbane

Level: 14 (Noble 8/Gladiator 6)

Type: Dragon.

Party: V&V.

Health Points	5,615
Special Points	1320
Strength	109
Vitality	89
Skill	20
Agility	47
Intelligence	14
Charisma	79
Luck	48

Personal Perks	Class Perks
Dragonfire Breath	Old Money
Fire Immunity	Snobbery
Red Dragon Lifeforce	Nobless Oblige
Dragon Arrogance	Aristoradar
Dragonscale	Crowd Favorite
Super Senses	Supercrit
Virgin Princess Radar	
Lesser Poison Resistance	
Deadfriend	
Taunt	

"My Charisma is seventy-nine, Minion."

"Seventy-nine?" Croissant almost choked.

So did Manling Victor. "That's three times more than me!"

"Yes, yes, minions, everybody loves me," Vainqueur replied dismissively. "It should be more than enough to break the barrier, then."

"Well, you must burn an arcane spellcaster to get the class, like a witch or another lich. Demons also work."

"I have the burning part covered," Vainqueur replied. "Fetch me a witch. Any witch. It is not enough that I destroy Furibon, who is pure evil and has to be destroyed. Anything that looks like that cursed creature will burn in the fires of my wrath!"

"Furibon Delenda Est," Minion Victor spoke a foreign language as if it made him sound more intelligent. "But we don't have many liches or spellcasters available."

"That's not true, we have a dryad drui-" Croissant put his hand on sweet Chocolatine's mouth before she could finish.

"It is easy to take levels in class before reaching level twenty, from what you manlings told me," Vainqueur said, formulating a plan at once. "I awakened the proud [Noble] class simply by learning I could take levels. Gaining access to [Witch Hunter] should be quick, even without a witch on hands to burn."

Minion Victor stayed silent for a moment, before making a face and asking, "Your Majesty, what is your intelligence stat?"

"Fourteen, and I started at nine!" Vainqueur said proudly, assuming the Manling started at one.

"I'm just scared of what Your Majesty will achieve with more points."

"Oh, I have a great idea!" said Chocolatine with a gleeful smile, after pushing her brother's hand away. "Why not summon demons as practice dummies?"

"Summon demons?" Victor turned to her, appalled.

"Yes! Since there is no witch nearby, we just summon demons! Demon witches, and you *murder* them, and we harvest the body parts."

"Chocolatine, I already told you no," Croissant told his sister. "We're not sacrificing sheep to summon demons and then kill them. This is too dangerous, even if we summon only lesser fiends."

"But we would got more meat that way! And Rolo said he wanted fertilizer for the farms..."

Vainqueur listened with attention, smelling an opportunity. "Minion Victor, could I gain [Witch Hunter] levels out of this?"

"You can gain [Witch Hunter] levels by burning demons, or people possessed by demons, yes," Victor said, scratching the back of his head in embarrassment. "You would think they had some kind of fire resistance, though, seeing where they come from."

"To your puny fire maybe, but not my dragonfire!" Vainqueur boasted.

"Some are immune to it, but we can summon those who aren't," said Chocolatine.

"Yes, but... summon demons just to kill them?" Victor grumbled, too pessimistic to see the golden opportunity. "I dunno, it sounds like prank calling Hell. No way it's not going to backfire somehow, right?"

"Minion Victor, how can you not see the potential?" Vainqueur chastised his lackey. "That way, we can both gain quick levels, minion. I kill the demons, then you revive them as undead, and then I kill them again. This will double my experience, and I gain treasure both times!"

"Your Majesty wants me to turn demons into undead so he can kill them *all over again*?"

"Also, you will also let the demons use their Perks on you whenever possible, in case you can learn them."

Minion Victor's skin turned pale. "I would rather not—"

"That's a great idea!" Croissant complimented Vainqueur's choice, Manling Victor sending him a fierce glare. The werewolf answered with a smirk.

"It's okay, Victor, I can cure you," said Chocolatine with a cheery smile. "So long as you are not dead, I cast a spell and zap, you're fine again!"

"Is your god even okay with this scheme?" Victor asked Chocolatine. "I thought Isengrim was one of the nicest deities."

"Of course he is! Commandment Seven: *you shall respect the hunt. Hunt to feed, or to thin the herd, but never for profit or pleasure, and never to extinction. Except demons and undead. Demons and undead can be hunted for pleasure, for profit, and to be made extinct.*"

"As far as divine declarations go, it's pretty direct."

"Minion, while I never felt it, I understand that pain hurts for your kind," Vainqueur reassured his lackey, "But this is *war*. War calls for sacrifices, and sweat, and tears. For the sake of my hoard, you cannot fail, and so you will do whatever it takes to become the best chief of staff you can be."

Minion Victor said nothing, lowered his eyes, then raised them back. Vainqueur noticed a change in his gaze, a gleam that wasn't there before.

The spark of a dragon's greed.

"Alright, Your Majesty, but, can I ask you a request? Can I keep the undead instead of having you destroying them again? I'm not sure you will gain experience, and I could use them as minions."

"Oh, and you can always sell them afterward for me," Vainqueur caught on. "Good idea minion."

"That's the spirit," Minion Victor said with an ominous tone.

And so, for the first time in his immortal life, Vainqueur began to train seriously.

Using a knife, Chocolatine sacrificed a lamb, then drew a circle of blood around the cattle outside the village. She began to recite incantations, the circle shining bright with unholy light. "[Summon Lesser Demon!]"

As she finished her prayer, a creature manifested inside the circle, a manling-sized goat with wings and wielding a fork. "Hell's Witch Customer Service, what can I do for you? Is it to sell your soul for magical powers, or some other..." The fiend stopped, looking up to Vainqueur. "What the Heaven is—"

Vainqueur lightly blasted him with a fireball.

The explosion tore the fiend in half, sending the remains fly a few meters away from the impact; the sacrificed sheep was entirely vaporized.

Argh, he had wasted the food! Vainqueur decided to breath lighter next time, since demons looked very fragile.

*Congratulations! Through your sheer hatred of a spellcaster, burning of a foul fiend at the stakes, and your inclination to solve every problem with fire, you earned a level in the [**Witch Hunter**] class!*

+30 HP, +10 SP, +1 VIT, +1 AGI, +1 INT, +1 CHA, +1 LCK!

*You earned the [**Spell Purge**] Class Perk!*

*[**Spell Purge**]: By exhausting one SP per second, you can radiate a field of antimagic energy which automatically cancel any spell in its range, including yours; your Charisma must be higher than the spell's effective level (Spell Tier + Main Stat Value of the Spellcaster at the time of casting) to cancel it. You can activate and deactivate Spell Purge at will.*

Vainqueur's mood improved when two treasures appeared on the spot where the fiend had fallen. [Crowd Favorite] and [Old Money] had both activated!

At this rate, he could rebuild his hoard within the month.

"I am so going to hell for this..." Victor said, as he put back both halves of the fiend together and raised it as a soulless zombie. "But it's going to be worth it."

Vainqueur suddenly realized they forgot to train his minion first. "Manling Victor, next time, you stand in the middle of the circle. Do not forget to let them use their abilities first, then get out of the way so I can burn them. Chocolatine, bring another sheep."

"Can you leave a bit more meat next time, Your Majesty?" Chocolatine asked, disappointed by the experiment's result. "I really want to cook a demon's heart with beans."

18: Job Interviews

"Wait, wait, don't kill me, don't kil—"

Vainqueur poked his hundredth demon in a row, a monstrous rat the size of a manling, crushing it between his claw and the ground below. Like an insect, the creature died without making a sound.

Nothing. No level, and no treasure.

With a growl of disappointment, Vainqueur tossed the corpse on the pile of demon meat which had yet to be turned into undead. "I am out of sheep, Your Majesty," Chocolatine informed him, who stood next to a second, bigger pile of slain cattle. "Do we move to pigs or children?"

"No," Vainqueur replied, bored to death. Even his chief of staff had asked for a break after the eightieth, and the dragon started to understand why. He couldn't take the tediousness of the process anymore.

Level grinding was no fun at all.

As if reading his master's mind, Manling Victor joined them, carrying papers under his arm. "Is Your Majesty done bullying Satan?"

"Minion, I cannot get that eleventh level of [Witch Hunter]!" Vainqueur complained while Chocolatine left to feed some demon corpses to her remaining cattle. "Is the system broken?"

"Your Majesty, I told you, the greater your level, the more you receive an experience penalty to gain a new one. Repeating the same activity over and over by killing weaker opponents is good before level twenty, but afterward, the system rewards fighting opponents who can fight back."

"So I am stuck at level ten in [Witch Hunter] until I destroy Furibon, who is evil and must be destroyed."

"Pretty much." His class manager read the documents Manling Henry had once given him on class progression. "Okay let see your new Perks so far... [Spell Purge]... [Witch Burning], your fire attacks bypass magical resistance and inflict additional holy damage, so your breath should be doubly effective against undead like Furibon. [Lesser Magic Resistance], meaning you can shrug off weaker spells. [Exorcism I] allows you to learn and cast Tier I exorcisms, and [Hunter's Resolve] gives you a bonus against attempts to control your mind."

"The Exorcism Perk does nothing," Vainqueur complained.

"Spells or spell-like effects are organized into tiers of power, from one to ten. You do not gain access to them automatically, though; the Perk only allows the owner to learn and cast them. At this point, Your Majesty is the ultimate anti-magic tank."

"What is a tank?" It sounded awesome.

"It means nobody hits harder than Your Majesty," Manling Victor flattered him, before whistling at the pile of treasures Vainqueur obtained from his training. "So the next item on your war agenda is the recruitment of new minions. Is Your Majesty sure they want to deal with it personally? You sounded okay with me recruiting the kobolds on my own."

"This is different, Minion Victor. We are not hunting weaklings, but Furibon, who is evil and must be destroyed."

"Is Your Majesty going to repeat that every time they mention him?"

"Yes, minion, because this is *war* and everyone must know!" Vainqueur sat and observed the line of applicants waiting outside the orchard, mostly kobolds, but also other unique monsters.

"In total," said Victor, "We have one hundred kobolds applicants. I also ordered Croissant to send us inhabitants with class levels above twenty, which include a troll, a dryad, and a golem. Does that cause His Majesty problems?"

"Minion, I do not discriminate. All creatures are equally inferior to me. I will always fight for the right of everyone to become my emergency food."

"Your Majesty is truly ahead of their time."

"Of course, since I am a dragon." Vainqueur turned to the applicants, clearing his throat to make an announcement. "V&V is more than an adventurer company! You are part of my treasures! Do you shine enough to be part of my hoard? Do you have what it takes to become a true minion?"

"He's looking at us!" One of the kobolds chirped to the rest of its warren, led by Red.

"Quick, lower your spine in obedience!" Red forced the animal down. "Please excuse my cousin, Your Majesty."

Ah, yes, *minion nepotism.* An insidious slippery slope leading to complete lack of discipline. However, since kobolds had been helpful and zealous so far, Vainqueur decided to examine them first. "You will be interviewed as a set," Vainqueur said, who couldn't be bothered to check every one of them individually.

"Rangers!" Red called, the Kobold rangers adopting a pose. "After the chief promoted us as minion lieutenants, we gathered every able-bodied kobold we could find!"

"Minion Victor, you promoted them on your own?"

"Uh, yes, I did. Is that a problem?"

"No, no, I am proud of your initiative. You acted like a true chief of staff." Vainqueur had so many offices to assign. "When I remember the day you begged me to become my minion, back when you were but a purposeless thief adrift, I am amazed by your growth."

The minion glanced at him with his big eyes. "Your Majesty, that is not how I remember our meeting."

"Then you know to trust my version, which is now the official one," Vainqueur focused on the new recruits. "V&V only recruits the best of the best. Are these kobolds battle-tested?"

"Not yet, Your Majesty, so we made them interns," Blue said. "Unpaid interns."

"I am so proud," Manling Victor said.

"Then they will be on probation, and the responsibility of the Kobold Rangers," Vainqueur agreed. "While they will be too weak to fight Furibon, they can help carry the treasures we find."

"You heard that?" Black turned to the other kobolds. "You are all interns!"

The kobolds cried in joy, some hugged one another, and one collapsed due to a heart attack. Vainqueur dismissed them. "Next."

"Next is the dryad and the steel golem. Apparently, they come as a set."

"No," Vainqueur decided immediately. "Steel golems are not minion material."

"What? Your Majesty, why not? They're super strong!"

"Minion Victor, have you considered the logistic?" Vainqueur chastised his chief of staff. "We cannot eat it if we are out of food."

"But he could hunt it for us, then!"

Vainqueur frowned. "Only if the dryad is fat enough for two, then."

The two candidates walked towards Vainqueur. The golem looked like an armored knight two heads taller than the average manling. Its steel armor had rusted, and it wore an old straw hat and a bag of grains. The dryad was like the rest of her kind: a tasty, green-skinned humanoid looking exactly like a manling, with fully black eyes and long black hair. She hid her legs beneath a robe of flowers and vines while leaving the top exposed. Vainqueur found her a bit too thin, but she seemed appetizing.

"You're olive-skinned," said the minion, distracted by the female's mammaries. "Like an actual olive."

The tasty dryad glared at him. "Do you have something against colored people?"

"No, no, of course not! Some of my best friends have colored scales! It's just... it's a fantasy land, I haven't seen any non-white, non-furry humanoid since I left the United States."

"United States?" The dryad's eyes widened in recognition. "Where? New York?"

Minion Victor's eyes widened. "You too were reincarnated—"

"—in that other world?" she finished the sentence at the same time, both smiling at the other. "Although not as a human. Can't complain though, this body is way better. I lucked out."

"Yeah, I heard an unlucky claimed became a slime." Since the minion seemed familiar with the creature, Vainqueur let him take over the interview. "Where do you come from?"

"Morocco, but I'm half-Spanish on my mom's side. You're a 'Murrican, aren't ya?"

"Chicago boy all the way." Minion Victor showed up his sleeve, revealing dice and moon tattoos on his skin. The dryad responded by pointing a mark on the back of her neck, representing a spiral-shaped flower. "Oh, that's the brand of Cybele right? The sex and fertility goddess?"

"Ah, yes, because that's the *only* thing people pay attention to with her. She also the goddess of forest and knowledge, you know? She's very wise and ancient."

"Sorry, I'm not too religious. Especially since people here worship a human abducting dice or a tentacled horror. Still, you sound pretty happy with your own claimer."

"I am. I was gonna die a very dumb death, and this marvelous goddess appears to me and says, 'Allison, would you like to live again and restore the land?' How could I refuse?"

"She appeared to you directly instead of just branding and throwing you aside?"

"I'm here to help Rolo with his farming project." The dryad gave the golem a pat on the back, "He had been praying to Cybele for someone to maintain him while he continues farming, and I was an auto-engineer on Earth. Golems aren't like cars, but I manage. No more nine to five desk job. Anyway, I renamed myself Lys here, because it sounds cool, but my true name is Allison. You can just call me Al."

That made too many names. Vainqueur subtracted her some points.

"Enchanted, I'm Victor," the minion replied while showing his bright teeth to the female. Unfortunately, his desire to breed led him astray. "I thought golems weren't self-aware?"

"One percent of them wake up with free-will. Rolo is one of those. Since he has a soul, he even has class levels. Sixty-seven, all [Farmer]."

"Really?" Victor blinked. "That's the highest level [Farmer] I've ever met. He has more levels than the Shining Knight!"

"Rolo refuses to take levels in anything but [Farmer]," the dryad clarified. "At least until his goal is realized."

"I, Rolo, have a dream!" the golem farmer pumped a fist. "To see the red desert green again!"

"So I remembered right, the area used to be greener," Vainqueur rejoiced.

"It was, before the Sablaris dried out the region," the golem said, its voice brimming with anger.

"The Sablawhat?" Vainqueur repeated.

"The Sablaris were a dark elf empire ruling most of the southern continent, Ishfania, and Barin," Alison said. "Cultists of Sablar the destroyer eventually took it over, hence the name; to hasten their patron's goal of universal entropy, they caused a magical cataclysm that turned their entire empire into a red desert. Brandon Maure, the bastard of a demon lord and a dark elf, then took over the ruins of Ishfania with summoned monsters."

Vainqueur noticed he could listen to long monologues without being bored now. Was it the result of new intelligence points? "Since you're from Earth too," Allison continued. "Did DiCaprio win an academy award at last?"

"Yes, but not for the Wolf of Wall Street." The dryad seemed disappointed. "I know, I think they gave him a consolation prize after that movie."

"Maybe I should move to that world's North America and open a better Hollywood then. That's *unjust*."

"That world's North America?" the minion picked up.

"You haven't looked at a full map of the Mistral continent?"

"Only that of Gardemagne's southern regions."

Noticing Manling Victor's embarrassment, tasty Allison cast a spell, vines growing out of the ground and forming a map with names whom Vainqueur didn't recognize.

"That looks like a rough map of Europe with the countries' frontiers all wrooooong..." the minion suddenly left the word hanging, as if reaching a realization. "No way..."

"Outremonde is a magical mirror of Earth," said Alison, "With pretty big differences. I mean, they have an Atlantis-like island in the Atlantic Ocean, Malta is flying, and the—"

"Minion," Vainqueur put back the interview on track, "We are here to discuss their future as meat shields, not friendly chit-chat."

"Yes, yes, Your Majesty. What is your level, Allison?"

"Twenty-four, mostly [Druid] and [Vestal]."

"Nice. You can serve as a healer while we storm the dungeon."

"Storm the dungeon?" the tasty creature frowned. "As a dryad, I cannot physically leave a mile away from my orchard without dying."

So she couldn't leave the village. That settled it. "You are both fired," Vainqueur immediately 'congratulated' the golem-dryad duo.

"You did not employ us," Alison countered.

"You are still fired. You are no longer emergency food. Now you are just food."

The two wisely decided not to linger any longer. "Before you go," Victor asked sweet Alison. "Do you want to have a drink somewhere?"

"Only if it's on you," she replied while showing her teeth, the vine map vanishing behind her.

The minion watched the two leave while looking at the female's behind. "Minion," Vainqueur sighed. "You should ask her to breed and get on with it."

The minion's face turned red. "It worked last time, but I think it's a bit too early there."

"Minion, if you want to put your eggs in a female, you need to impress her with the size of your hoard. Show her your shiny gold before asking them to breed. Females also do the same to entice males but be sure to check the size of their treasure. You do not want to let paupers take care of your eggs."

"Does Your Majesty only reproduces with the wealthy?"

"Of course not. Why would I put my eggs in another dragon? More dragons meant more competitions for my hoard later. No, minion, breeding is for creatures like you, who die all the time and must perpetuate their species before it goes extinct."

Come to think of it, since other dragons meant no more competition for hoards, and he may be paid for killing his kind... Vainqueur pondered the moral problem of hunting his own kind for money, before deciding it would wait for the destruction of Furibon.

"Also, Manling Victor, no breeding harassment between minions, that causes tensions and minion wars."

"That is why I waited until after you fired her before making a move," Manling Victor replied, before the next candidate showed up, a tall, lanky green troll with green hide and a tusked, piglike face. "This is Barnabas."

"A troll?" Vainqueur squinted. "I burned a lot of them recently."

"I noticed," the troll replied. "You killed everyone I knew when you destroyed the Woods of Gevaudan. The good thing is, I hated everyone I knew."

"What is your level, Barnabas?" Manling Victor interrogated him after clearing his throat.

"Twenty-one, [Blacksmith], [Merchant], and [Alchemist]. Mostly [Blacksmith]. I make weapons, don't wield them."

"You're hired," Vainqueur said immediately. "I promote you to my official armorer. You will work on dragon-sized items at once."

"Sure, if I can I get new raw materials." Victor pointed at the pile of items which dropped during Vainqueur's training. "That will do."

And so ended the recruitment. "That was fast," said Victor, as Barnabas immediately went to work.

"That was effective," replied Vainqueur. "Next?"

"Chocolatine and Croissant, whom you already 'recruited,' both have class levels that could help for the dungeon. Chocolatine because we need a healer, and Croissant, because we need a meat shield for the traps and I hate him. I wish we had a decent level spellcaster with us for the raid, but we'll have to make do with what we have."

"It will do, minion. It will do."

Congratulations! For recruiting a vast adventurer company meant to cater to your noble desires, you gained a level in [Noble]!

+30 HP, +10 SP, +1 VIT, +1 AGI, +1 INT, +1 CHA, +1 LCK!

You earned the [Stipend] class perk!

[Stipend]: You gain a monthly stipend of four hundred gold coins multiplied by your total level.

Vainqueur's eyes widened in pure, unbridled joy, as a huge pile of gold materialized right in front of him with a bright flash of light.

Finally!

By the elder wyrm, he had waited so long for this moment! Four hundred per level? Once Vainqueur reached level one hundred, that meant forty thousand coins a month, half a million the year! He would swim in a vast ocean of shiny gold and—

"[Transmute Gold to Lead]."

The coins turned to lead with a flash of black magic, causing Vainqueur's heart to skip a beat. He immediately glanced at the source of the disaster, sitting atop the pile of demon corpses.

Furibon! His bony finger still cackled with his foul sorcery!

"That was for blowing up my library, you dimwit lizard," said the lich, before adopting a taunting tone at Vainqueur's silent hatred, "It is true what they say... silence is *golden*."

Furibon insisted so much on the word, Vainqueur was paralyzed by fury.

"Your Majesty," Victor butted in. "Use [Spell Pur—"

Snarling with rage and reacting before his minion could finish, Vainqueur attempted to smash the lich the dragon way, but the undead teleported away while cackling. Instead, Vainqueur's hand smashed onto the pile of demons, creating a crater and causing a small quake.

"Holy Hell, Your Majesty's strength points are showing," Minion Victor complimented his master, as if it could cheer him up.

"No more waiting, Minion Victor," Vainqueur declared, his heart set on vengeance. "We raid the dungeon tomorrow!"

He already imagined the treasure that Furibon would drop.

19: Uninvited Guests

Due to his role in their new dragon overlord's administration, the locals had wisely 'gifted' Victor a large mansion overseeing the rest of Murmurin. Finally, the human's life as a homeless adventurer had reached its end, at least until they claimed Furibon's dungeon tomorrow.

And what a place it was! With three floors, a basement, and a roof, it was huge enough to welcome a lord's entire retinue. Unlike the early medieval architecture of Gardemagne's manors, the place had been built in a later time's style, with wide rooms, black wood flooring, and a central velvet stair leading to the upper floors.

Victor had heard it once belonged to a dark wizard doing experiments in the basement though, and considering the dust around, the inhabitants hadn't touched it in years. He better watch his back inside.

Victor entered the grand foyer with Savoureuse and twenty mindless, demonic skeletons in toes. "Go clean the place," he ordered his servants, "No dust must remain."

The automatons spread around as ordered. "And now I officially live in a ghost mansion," Victor told Savoureuse, as they moved to explore the ground floor while the earth trembled. "Do you think Vainqueur smashed a succubus this time?"

"I don't think Chocolatine can summon on—" Savoureuse suddenly chuckled. "Ah, I get it, smash a succubus!"

"You can't imagine how much I missed someone laughing at my lame jokes," Victor said, finding a large cozy room with an old fireplace and armchairs. "We had good times."

"It's not quite the same since you left, Vic. We're taking a wrong turn since that Lavere woman arrived."

"Wrong turn? The Nightblades are an outlaw ring. That's pretty redundant."

"Yes, but we respected the government," Savoureuse said, Victor giving her a blank stare. "Okay, sometimes we put nobles through death traps, but who doesn't? We didn't take up arms against the King, because it was bad for business. But last time I was at our headquarter in Noblecoeur, there were talks of supplying Ishfania and the Scorchers with weapons."

Well, Vainqueur shot that plan down.

Victor sat in one of the armchairs, finding it extraordinarily comfortable. "[Channel Hellfire]!" His finger fired a ray of ghastly blue flames at the fireplace, lighting up the leftover black wood.

That was the only Monster Perk he got out of this grueling training, and he earned it. He should have listened to the priests' warning of fire and brimstone in his childhood.

"Do you want an omelet?" Savoureuse asked him.

"Sure." The proposal couldn't make Victor happier since she had many levels in the Cook class. Other Nightblades had fought to the death over her meals.

The reptile sat on the ground like a chicken. "Do you want me to go to another room?" Victor asked, embarrassed.

"No, it's okay. I do it everywhere."

Victor turned his eyes away from the sight still, finding a treasure chest in a corner of the room, overflowing with gold.

Yeah, right. Just a chest.

"Treasure!" the disguised mimic barked. "Treasure!"

As if Victor would fall for it. "You know, most adventurers are wary of chests nowadays," the Monster Squire told the creature. "You should take the shape of a magic weapon, like a shiny sword, and you mustn't make a sound."

The chest apparently understood, for it repeated, "Shiny sword? Treasure?"

"Trust me, no adventurer can't resist the appeal of a big shiny sword, especially if set in a stone."

"You can understand mimics?" Savoureuse asked him, rising up to reveal a large, ostrich-like egg under her clothes. "It is very difficult to make them behave."

"I think there are frying pans in the kitchen, and yes I can," said Victor, before shouting, "Minions! Minions!"

A skeleton immediately rushed inside the room. The M-word had never felt so pleasurable. "Go get us kitchen tools," Victor ordered, the undead immediately obeying.

The squire took it back. Mindless undead slaves made his life way easier than before.

"Sword treasure!" By now, the chest had morphed into a huge, outrageous two-handed sword made of pure gold and jewels. "Sword treasure!"

"Better, but too much," Victor told it, who suddenly wondered how the mimic could talk without a mouth, "Try having a black metal edge and an elegant pommel. Don't overdo it."

"Sword treasure." The mimic followed his instructions, becoming the perfect picture of a magical sword.

"Excellent. Now you shouldn't have trouble getting food. Just don't kill anything in the village, alright?"

"Sword treasure!" The sword purred and hopped out of the room like an animal, just as the skeletal servant came back with four frying pans. "Sword Treasure."

Victor now had a pet.

On a whim, he called it Vainqueur Junior.

Congratulations! Through your teaching, Vainqueur Junior has gained a level in [Fencer]!

Really? Like that? Victor guessed [Minion Trainer] made it easy for monsters to gain class levels when following his directions. "Is this place the mimic school I heard of?"

"Yes, and I would avoid the beds if I were you."

Victor suddenly wondered if disappearances in inns were caused by disguised mimics.

"Nothing better than a warm meal after a good day of training," said Savoureuse, breaking her egg on the frying pan, before adding spice to her omelet. The skeleton stood there waiting, so Victor sent him away looking for plates and cutlery.

In total, Victor had gained six levels in Necromancer before hitting a Level glass ceiling like Vainqueur. The dragon still asked Chocolatine to summon more demons to calm himself after Furibon's last visit.

Victor still couldn't believe an ancient lich had nothing better to do with his time outside of pranking a dragon. He must be really, *really* bored in his dungeon.

"You little—" Victor heard Croissant's voice from outside the room. The werewolf soon joined them, in human shape and with a bloody hand.

"Croissant, are you alright?" asked Savoureuse in worry. "What happened?"

"I found a sword laying on the ground, and it bit my hand when I tried to grab it! Then it ran off!"

Vainqueur Junior grew up so fast. "Sad," Victor lied since he found some twisted pleasure in that jerk's pain. "Why are you here?"

"I asked Vainqueur what we should run ourselves, now that we are all his minions and that we are going to run out of sheep. He answered, textually, 'A dragon has no time for sub-minion management; I have a war to prepare for, so go to my chief of staff for directions.' Then, he had my sister summon another demon and punched it."

"So I'm basically your village's mayor now. Wonderful."

"Looks like it, pal. Also, the Moon Man's followers are at the door, waiting for your 'final revelation.'"

Victor let out a sigh. They had kept pestering him every time he wasn't with Vainqueur, who scared them to death. "I will be their prophet later."

"No hard feeling for that perk stuff, right? You brought Vainqueur here, so you kinda deserved it."

"No, no hard feelings, since you will serve as our scout tomorrow."

The werewolf blinked. "I'm what?"

"We are raiding the dungeon tomorrow. Your sister is coming too, but she's going to be fine in the rear. As a rogue class, you will scout ahead for traps."

"But I'm a [Ranger], not a trap finder! I hunt beasts, I do not disarm traps!"

"I know. I meant you will scout out traps by *triggering* them. Maybe next time, you won't try to sacrifice your future commanding officer to a cult. Just saying."

"You... you petty snake..."

"As a wise woman told me," Victor smirked at him. "I wish you would go to hell, Croissant, but I think you are already there."

Clenching his fists and fangs, the werewolf exited the room with fury in his eyes. "Merciful Isengrim, damn that dragon, damn his staff, damn them all..."

"That was very immature, Victor," Savoureuse chided him, "Even if he deserved it."

"Ah, it's fine," Victor replied. "We've both blown off steam, now we're cool."

"You look like you need a warm meal to ease you up," said Savoureuse, who finished the omelet. "Here."

"Thanks," Victor replied, as he sat back in the armchair. "What else in on the menu—"

Of course, his stats appeared when he said that word.

Victor "Minion" Dalton

Level: 26 (Outlaw 5/Monster Squire 14/Necromancer 7)

Type: Humanoid/Dragon

Party: V&V

Health Points	645
Special Points	240
Strength	24
Vitality	23
Skill	32
Agility	31

Intelligence	30
Charisma	30
Luck	29

Personal Perks	Class Perks
Claimed by Dice	Lockpick
Observer	Eye for Treasure
Deadfriend	Knife Master
Romantic	Monster Kin
Claimed by the Moon Man	Minion Trainer
Black Curse	Monster Student
Channel Hellfire (Minor)	Monster Lifeforce (Red Dragon)
	Monster Rider
	Monster Insight
	Animate Dead
	Necromancy I

Lifespell

Minion? Even his goddamn menu had started calling him that!

Still, very good stat growth so far, although he never tested the new Necromancer Perks. He was now around the same level as the late Gustave and Vilmain.

*Congratulations! Due to meeting entry requirements through your [**Monster Student**] Perk and [**Necromancer**] levels, you can convert some of your levels into promoted Monster Classes! Stats will not be affected, but Perks will.*

*You can either combine [**Monster Squire**] and [**Necromancer**] into [**Death Knight**], or [**Outlaw**] and [**Necromancer**] into [**Reaper**].*

The change will be permanent and cannot be undone; you will no longer be able to progress in the converted classes if you choose to combine them.

Interesting, Victor thought as he took a bite out of that delicious omelet. Savoureuse partook in the feast in a weird act of self-cannibalism. What were these classes?

*[**Death Knight**]: An undying warlord, commanding armies of the undead to rid the land of life itself. Specialties: All Weapons, Necromancy, and Riding. Major growths in Strength, Vitality,*

Skill and Agility. Perks affected: Monster Kin, Monster Student, Monster Lifeforce (Red Dragon), Necromancy I, Lifespell.

[Reaper]: A thief and stealer of souls who does terrible things in their quest for power. Specialties: Scythes, Necromancy, and Dark Magic. Major growths in Skill, Intelligence, Charisma, and Luck. Perks affected: Lockpick, Knife Master, Dead Divination, Lifespell.

Charming. So [Death Knight] was a pure combat class with some dash of magic thrown in, while [Reaper] was a mix of rogue and spellcaster.

It didn't take long for Victor to make a choice. He doubted he would progress further in the [Outlaw] class, making it redundant, and his [Monster Squire] class was too good to trade. Besides, Vainqueur had the pure combat niche covered.

He could definitely see the effect of the new intelligence points.

"Ever heard of the [Reaper] class?" he asked Savoureuse.

"It is usually reserved to dark fairies or psychopomps who steal souls," she explained, sitting back again to lay another egg. "I heard rumors that the god Deathjester was one, and that he killed so many people with a scythe, it turned into an artifact."

Then it was official. Time to *reap* these levels.

Choice registered! Your [Outlaw] and [Necromancer] levels have been transformed into [Reaper] levels. [Outlaw] and [Necromancer] are no longer accessible.

[Lockpick] replaced with [Skeleton Key]. [Skeleton Key]: you can unlock any lock on a successful Skill check, even

magical ones. You always count as 'invited' to any location magically protected.

[**Knife Master**] replaced with [**Scythe Lord**]. [**Scythe Lord**]: you gain perfect proficiency with scythes; scythes now count as staves for the purpose of spellcasting.

[**Dead Divination**] replaced with [**Helheim**]. [**Helheim**]: if you kill someone with a scythe, you can trap their soul in your weapon, increasing the weapon's statistics. The victim cannot be revived, reanimated, or reincarnated as long as they are trapped in the scythe. You can talk with the trapped souls and release them at will.

[**Lifespell**] replaced with [**Steal Life**]. [**Steal Life**]: when you inflict damage with a scythe, you recover HP equal to half the damage inflicted.

Victor briefly grabbed the daggers around his belt, finding that he had lost all familiarity with it. With [Knife Master] gone, he could no longer draw in the class' pool of knowledge.

"What are you going to do with all these undead servants, by the way?" Savoureuse asked him in between bites, as he used the dagger as cutlery. "I thought you found them disturbing?"

"I recently asked the goddess Shesha the price to return home, and it's terrifyingly high. I noticed you could make a killing in the undead trade," Sav chuckled at the phrasing. "So I thought I could save money to pay her the service."

"How high?" Victor told her the price, and Savoureuse almost choked on her omelet. "Vic, that is insane! Even if you take over the continent, you won't have enough gold to pay that price!"

"Yeah, but I miss my family and friends on Earth." Victor had been growing homesick long before he met Vainqueur, and the discussion with Allison only increased that.

"I know you keep saying this world sucks and you miss your old one, but you're making a life for yourself here. If you're missing on your family and friends, you can make new ones here. You also have a lot of opportunities. You are working with a dragon, and gaining levels so very fast. Who else is that lucky?"

He wouldn't call it luck, but yeah... even if the fiasco with Euskal had killed every other avenue for work. No way he could set foot in the country again without Vainqueur's protection.

Against his better judgment, his thoughts turned to Vainqueur's 'advice.' "Hey, Sav. Would you find a male with a very big hoard of gold attractive?"

"Of course. Who doesn't like someone with a lot of money they can repossess?" Unfortunately, the crafty creature immediately guessed his trail of thoughts. "So that was true? You asked Allison to breed?"

"N-no, nothing that direct," Victor defended himself. "There are steps in between. Like a drink."

"You are too good for her," said Savoureuse with a motherly tone. "I would not try to breed with her if I were you. You do not know where she has been."

"What is that supposed to mean?"

"She is a priestess of Cybele. She must have laid with half the town and called it religious service."

That... that meant...

"I knew it!"

"Victor, what you need is a well-bred, nice woman with strong family values," said the reptilian assassin for hire, without any hint of hypocrisy whatsoever. "Like Chocolatine. Not a dryad of loose morality like Allison."

Chocolatine? That psycho? She had fed some of the demons' flesh to pigs hoping they would grow fatter on it!

"My religion does not allow love triangles." Someone knocked on the room's window, Victor glancing to notice the calmar priest right behind. With a sigh, he rose from his chair and opened the window. "Yes?"

"Oh, prophet of the Moon Man!" The priest had gathered the entire congregation outside. "Please deliver unto us the final revelation!"

... don't ask them to bring you virgins, don't ask them to bring you virgins. "Bring—" Victor stopped himself, realizing that he had a unique occasion to tame a dangerous cult. Even if their master forbade human sacrifices, they might interpret his command with violence and zealousness.

"Bring?" the priest picked up.

"Bring love and friendship to all, for we are all the children of the Moon Man." That sounded less cheesy in his mind. "There. You have the final revelation."

The cultists exchanged glances. "Did Thul-Gathar meant to bring love in the figurative sense?" one werewolf asked the calmar priest.

"I believe it must have been literal. As in, you must love your neighbor as you would love your wife."

"Or maybe it meant—"

"Guys," Victor interrupted their theological debate, "On your way out, can you ask Barnabas to forge me a scythe for battle? A really cool scythe, but not a scary one. No skulls motif."

"We shall, prophet! Now, I was saying, I think it meant we must open the Full Moon Orgy to everyone—"

Victor closed the windows, leaving them to their religious debate and sliding back in his chair.

He hoped it would work well. Now that he had some free time and a belly almost full, he brought out the iPad, intent on exploring its content while eating. Savoureuse observed the Apple product with envy. "Is that..."

"You recognize it?"

"The Nightblades' leadership was looking for it." Victor glared back at her. "I wasn't sent here for it, so I'm not going to steal your stuff, Vic."

Better. While she was a friend, he had already seen it wouldn't matter if her life was at risk. Victor looked into the various file folders, finding schematics for various kinds of planes. Nothing extraordinary, but valuable in an early Renaissance world. The previous owner must have worked in aeronautics.

The name of the most encrypted, restricted folder though?

'Lockheed Martin Corporation.'

... Yeah, Victor now knew why so many people wanted it. How did it end in Haudemer, though? Could it be that since Outremonde and Earth were mirror worlds, items and people often traveled from one to the other on their own?

Come to think of it, he was centuries ahead of his time here. Valuable knowledge. Perhaps he could help improve that world and make a profit out of it, gain money by doing good.

The sound of the entry bell echoed in the room. That must have been Allison... "Better that someone alive opens the door," Victor thought out loud, rising up with the iPad under his arm. "Sav, do I smell good?"

"Better than her, Vic," the reptile hummed, "Much better than her."

The adventurer smirked as he opened the mansion's door.

"Good evening, young man." Furibon smirked back with a dark glow in his empty eyes. "You have something that belongs to my master, or so I heard."

20: The War of the Hoard

- Chronicles of the War of the Hoard, final chapter: "Furibon must die."

In a magical land, far, far away...

Murmurin is at war! In a stunning move, the foul Furibon has kidnapped Lord Victor, first among all minions. The lich's evil has swept across the land, corrupting all that is shiny. But hope remains.

Deep in his fiery forge, the great smith Barnabas forged a dragon-sized [Ring of Elemental Resistance] and a [Killer Scythe]. In them, he poured stat boosts, magical protections, and his frustration at working overtime.

A last alliance of kobolds and werewolves march against Furibon's armies, and on the slopes of a fiery mountain, they fight for the great hoard. Wielding the master ring, the good King Vainqueur leads a desperate charge, determined to end the lich once and for all.

For Furibon must die!

That was it, Vainqueur thought when he hummed the smoke and listened to the drums of war. The final battle for the dragon's way of life.

His heroic minion armies, led by the Kobold Rangers, used mobile wood bridges to reach the castle, fighting imps, and undead. Kobolds, werewolves, and undead minions fought together as one, under Vainqueur's watchful eye.

The dragon statues protecting the castle fired rays of light at Vainqueur, who circled around the castle, blasting the defenders with his breath. The dragon majestically avoided them, taking the opportunity to show off.

"Brother, I'm flying!" said Chocolatine, being held in one of Vainqueur's hands. As a good and loyal minion, she carried the scythe Barnabas crafted for Vainqueur's chief of staff.

"I'm going to throw up..." Croissant the meat shield complained in Vainqueur's other hand.

"[Spell Purge!]" Vainqueur's Perk activated, and the great dragon radiated a dark aura, causing the magical barrier around Castle Murmurin to blink out of existence. With the defenses now exposed, Vainqueur crash-landed on the statues, blowing them apart and causing the castle to shake.

He tossed the fiends defending the entrance into the lava, then released his two werewolf minions in front of the entrance. The doors were open, the darkness unwelcoming. "Croissant, go inside and trigger all the traps while I finish off the defenders," Vainqueur ordered. "Die if you must."

"Can we skip the last part?"

"Die if you must!" Vainqueur ordered, the werewolf going in while whining. This Croissant was only good as a meat shield, as his chief of staff had warned.

The mere thought filled Vainqueur with fury. That abominable lich, it wasn't enough to curse his hoard, he went the extra mile and stole his most precious henchman. He imagined Furibon heinously forcing poor Victor into minion recruitment sessions, or to bring him gold coins he could sicken.

Victor was part of Vainqueur's hoard, the best chief of staff the dragon ever had. The Manling *belonged* to him, and no one else.

But Vainqueur had come equipped. On his right left finger, his new [Ring of Elemental Resistance] would shield him against the worst of the lich's magic. This time, the evil Furibon would not escape him.

Vainqueur unleashed his breath against flying gargoyles and vicious creatures attempting to protect the entrance, his flames now shining with a bright, golden afterglow. All were vaporized instantly.

"[Fire Amp]," Chocolatine said, who cast spells on her King as he fought. "[Regen], [Strength Up]!"

Your fire attacks now inflict twenty percent more damage!

+4 Strength for ten minutes!

You recover one percent HP every ten seconds for five minute!

As he vaporized the last of the defenders, his minions climbing the castle's walls and taking them over, Vainqueur turned to the entrance, running through it with Chocolatine in tow.

Vainqueur soon found himself in a great stone hall, with two doors on each side. One had been opened, with bloodied spikes and acid arrows littering the ground. "I think my brother went this way," said Chocolatine. "Do we follow him?"

"No, Chocolatine," decided Vainqueur, who could smell his chief of staff's scent. He disabled his Spell Purge, so he could save it for later. "That would be the manling way, and playing by Furibon's rules. We will find my chief of staff the dragon way. Blink."

Vainqueur turned invisible, prepped himself up, and then solved the door problem the dragon way.

He charged the wall in front of him, powering through. The stones were no match for his strength, and parts of the ceiling collapsed behind him; roaring proudly, Vainqueur kept going, destroying wall after wall, stamping on fiends and skeletal warriors, and redesigning his future castle.

Finally, after a long charge, Vainqueur smashed his way inside a large, dark throne room, illuminated by ghostly candelabras. Six steel statues of armored manlings held next to ancient, ruined tapestries. His loyal chief of staff, bound and held hanging by chains from the barely holding ceiling, rejoiced at the sight of the wall collapsing. "Your Majesty!"

The evil Furibon waited on his sinister throne on the opposite end of the room, a paragon of evil and madness. In his dark eye sockets, Vainqueur saw no mercy, no hint of civilized intellect; only the bitterness of a pauper determined to ruin the rich and the wealthy.

"You realize I can hear you, Vainqueur Knightsbane?" the lich taunted Vainqueur, obviously lying. "You made a big hole in my wall, so you are not very discreet."

Vainqueur knew it was a trap to imbalance him, and try to make him reveal his position. Chocolatine, who had ran after her master, walked into the room while panting. She used Manling Victor's scythe as a pole against which to breath.

"I am saddened you skipped most of my traps, but at least we can have a proper confrontation." The lich dramatically extended his arms. "You have done it, King Vainqueur. After all your sacrifices and your losses, you have reached your beloved lackey."

"I can't believe I'm the damsel in distress," Manling Victor complained, ashamed of his weakness.

"At long last, I can unleash my greatest creation." As Furibon spoke, a circle of dark energy lit up in the middle of the room. "Cower before the strongest undead I have ever created, from the far reaches of Hell! The Black Beast of Murmurin!"

An undead abomination manifested in the middle of the circle; a monstrous, grotesque, hound-shaped amalgam of white, fossilized flesh stitched together. Black stone coated the upper part of the body like a cuirass, and while far smaller than Vainqueur, the creature was big enough to challenge him without looking ridiculous. The titan wriggled with unholy strength, opening its eyeless mouth and revealing ranges of venomous teeth.

"And now, both of you, fight for my entertainment!" Furibon ordered.

The undead abomination did not move. Not even an inch.

The invisibility worked!

"I said, fight for my entertainment." The lich twitched as the monster refused to move. "Is it broken? [Magic Scan]."

Words of purple light materialized in front of Furibon eyes, as he 'glanced' at his creation, and then around the room. "The [Deadfriend] Perk? You *all* have it?"

"Chocolatine, you have it too?" asked Minion Victor.

"Why, yes, how do you think I dispose of the bodies? It helps create strong bonds between the churches of Isengrim and Camilla."

"That is highly disappointing," the lich said, his empty, soulless eye sockets burning with fires that turned gold to lead. "Such a waste of good flesh. In that case, I will have 'Your Majesty' attack it first to trigger its rage. [Enthrall Monster]."

*[**Enthrall**] ailment negated by [**Hunter's Resolve**]!*

"A dragon's will is greater than yours, Furibon!" Vainqueur replied proudly, slowly tiptoeing around the corpse titan and toward the lich for a sneak attack. "I trained three days for this! *Three days*!"

"Maybe, but I too had time to prepare. [Clock Stop]!" To Vainqueur's senses, time seemed to stop for a brief instant, and when it flowed again, Furibon had covered himself with multiple colored layers of magical energy. "I see you came well-equipped, dragon, but I have more spells than you have years."

"Only a dragon will never know defeat!"

"Then let us dance like the damned." Furibon rose from his throne, his hands shining with foul sorcery, "But know that you are too late to stop us. The Apple of Knowledge already belongs to my master, Brandon Maure."

"Why would I care about a vegetable?" Vainqueur replied with arrogance. "I only eat meat!"

"Soon, you and all of Outremonde shall know iron and blood! [Ancient Met—" The dark lich stopped still. "You do not know about my master's plan?"

"I know of your plan," Vainqueur replied, furious at the depraved plot. "To infect all the world's gold with lead sickness, ending the dragon way of life forever!"

The lich tried to deny his culpability, "No, I do not... that would be amusing, but ridiculous."

"Also, Your Majesty," Manling Victor butted in. "Gold being turned to lead is not lead poisoning."

What had that poison sauce have to do with this? The lich seemed as confused as Vainqueur. "If you did not come to Murmurin to stop my liege's from laying waste to Gardemagne, then why are you here?"

"To stop your sickening scheme!" Vainqueur replied, proud to fight for the future of his hoard.

"This..." the lich let out a deep, bellowing sound. "Why did you come here in the first place? The seal below? How did you learn about it? Did that dark woman send you?"

"We know about the treasure of the Ishfanian Inquisition you keep in your vaults," Victor said. "That was part of the reason we came here. What? Aren't you keeping it?"

"You believe an ancient lich wizard would spend a hundred years holing up in a crumbling ruin to keep a stash of hidden gold?" The lich disdained the dragon way of life, firmly cementing himself as completely irredeemable. "Do you even know what is down there, waiting?"

Manling Victor fell mute.

"You do not." Furibon the Evil twitched. "Then, and this time you will answer or die, why did you come here?"

"We needed a castle where to stash His Majesty's hoard," Manling Victor answered with a pitiful tone. "Because the previous cave was too small."

As the lich's skull slowly turned to Victor, Vainqueur realized his lackey was distracting the lich for his master to deliver a sneak attack. Brilliant!

"Stash his hoard?" The undead's neck cracked. "You attacked me, tried to take my home, and killed hundreds of demons, because you needed a place where to *stash your gold*?"

"A dragon does not go to the bank!" Vainqueur boasted, having circumvented the undead titan and now with a clear line of fire. "Only a dragon can be trusted with his gold!"

"Why did you not just bury it in your *backyard*?!" the lich snarled. "But, but... what about the demons? Why did you keep summoning them, except to thin the ranks of my master's forces? Why did you create an undead army?"

"I kinda intended to sell the undead corpses for money," Victor admitted.

"With a ninety-nine one-tenth going to my hoard," Vainqueur reminded his chief of staff.

Furibon shook on his throne in envy and hatred of Vainqueur's wealth. "I spent one hundred years keeping watch over this crumbling ruin, weakening the seal, preparing traps and monsters while praying Dice that a powerful adventurer would finally challenge my monotony... and the one who does, wants a bigger cave to *stash his hoard*?"

"The biggest hoard in the world!" Vainqueur boasted as he breathed long and deep.

"You... you..." The lich scratched his skull with his bony fingers with fury. "Argh!"

*[**Taunt**] successful! You successfully applied the [**Berserk**] status to Furibon! The lich is too pissed to spellcast!*

And so, while his nemesis was distracted, Vainqueur unleashed a great fireball with a defiant roar. "Surprise attack!"

An immense, fiery projectile hit Furibon, the power of the blast destroying the throne and most of the wall behind it. The lich's robes were incinerated, his bones blown apart in two halves, with his torso flying and crashing against one of the steel statues.

*Your [**Witch Burning**] Perk was super-effective!*

Vainqueur looked at the broken bones of his defeated enemy with smug satisfaction. "Blink," the dragon revealed himself back in his full glory, freeing his chief of staff by biting the chains holding him. "Minion Victor, are you safe?"

"Yes, yes, Your Majesty, I'm fine," the lackey replied, stretching. "Thanks for saving me."

"Of course, Minion. You are the crown jewel of my hoard." The minion glanced up at Vainqueur with happy eyes, warming the dragon's heart. "You are my most precious asset and most loyal servant. I will never let you go. Ever."

The minion blinked several times in a row, overwhelmed with emotion. "Oh gods," he finally said. "You are never letting me go."

"That was quick," Chocolatine grumbled in disappointment.

"It is not over," Minion Victor said wisely.

Indeed, in the blink of an eye, the evil Furibon teleported right next to his former corpse. His body radiated dark magic, as he pointed his palm at Vainqueur. "[Ancient Meteor!]"

Before Vainqueur could react, a huge, fiery stone hit him right in the eye before exploding.

Vainqueur learned a new sensation he never experienced before, which he didn't like it at all.

You have taken damage!

Vainqueur had no idea what that sensation was, but it felt itchy and *wrong*. Like an indigestion.

"Stash your gold!" Furibon glared at Vainqueur with seething hatred, the same the dragon felt for the lich. "I could have *understood* if you attacked me on principle because I am a lich, but to *stash your gold*? I will not be expelled from this castle by home invaders!"

"Then you will die disappointed once more!" Vainqueur replied by blasting his foe with his fiery breath.

"[Clock Stop]," the lich cast. In a blink, he had teleported out of the way of the flames, and spike of ice appeared out of nowhere to fly at Vainqueur. They bounced back off his scales harmlessly. "[Elemental Resistance]? Then I will weaken your flesh, and then blast you to death! [Black Curse], [Accelerated Superflare]!"

A dark aura covered Vainqueur, who suddenly didn't feel so well, and then an explosion detonated in front of him. Once again, that strange itching, uncomfortable sensation filled his scales.

*All enhancements removed! All stats diminished by one stage! You can no longer recover HP while [**Black Curse**] is active!*

Sweet Chocolatine, who had immediately taken cover behind her invincible master, tried to support Vainqueur with spells. "[Curse Breake—]"

"[Accelerated Silence]," the lich cast, robbing sweet Chocolatine of the ability to speak before she could finish, "Out of my way, mortal! [Hasten]!"

Furibon began to move at greater speed, dodging a fireball by running around, while firing green, jagged beams of light at Vainqueur; the dragon retaliated by firing fireball after fireball, blasting walls and statues.

"Guys, stop, you're going to collapse the castle!" Manling Victor shouted, as the explosions caused debris to fall from above and Vainqueur's flames spread to the tapestries.

"Minion, do not distract me while landscaping!" Vainqueur replied, as he fruitlessly tried to smash the lich, who kept teleporting around before the dragon could put him in range of his [Spell Purge].

"Fine!" Furibon snarled, his mouth moving so fast Vainqueur could barely understand the words. "I would rather turn that castle into a crater than surrender it to that dragon!"

"Your gold-destroying plan will be stopped, Furibon!"

"I do not... you wyvern imbecile, gold is nothing compared to arcane secrets!"

Vainqueur's eyes flared with rage. The lich had gone mad. Not only did he use the cursed *W-word* to demean a true dragon, he also sprouted insane nonsense.

Vainqueur decided to fight seriously, and destroy this lich with extreme prejudice. "[Spell Purge.]" The dragon activated his Perk again, extinguishing one of the explosions as it entered his antimagic field's range.

Charisma check successful! **[Black Curse]** *lifted by:* **[Spell Purge]***!*

"You will run out of SP for that Perk before I exhaust mine, wyvern!" Furibon snarled.

It didn't matter. The lich may be a wizard with shiny spells, he would become a powerless skeleton once Vainqueur caught him in range of his [Spell Purge]; while *he* would stay an invincible dragon. He just had to catch him.

Vainqueur lunged at the lich.

The undead teleported out of the way before Vainqueur could get him in range.

The dragon roared furiously as he kept trying to trample and bite Furibon, who dodged each of his attempts. The more he did, the more Vainqueur grew furious. It was like playing catch with a frustrating goblin.

"Foolish!" Furibon taunted him, his hands cackling with unholy power. "Your brute strength is no match for my mastery of magic, Vainqueur! I have peered into the abyss of time, overcome death, and become power incarn—"

Then his own undead abomination caught the lich in its jaws from behind.

Vainqueur, who had been entirely focused on the evil Furibon, noticed his scythe-wielding lackey riding the abomination's back with Chocolatine.

"Who is a good undead dog? Who earned a bone?" Manling Victor told the abomination, who kept shaking Furibon in its jaws like a dog with a mouse, "Who earned a treat? That's you! That's you! There, throw it to your friend."

The undead hound tossed the angry lich at Vainqueur. "[Telepor—]"

Vainqueur caught the foul lich in his hand before he could cast his spell, negating it at once.

The dragon glanced down at his captive with smug satisfaction. "Good job minion," he congratulated his lackey, who earned it.

"I knew [Monster Rider] would come in handy," Minion Victor said, his monstrous mount scratching under him.

"[Teleportation]!" Furibon cursed, but nothing happened.

"Manling Victor," Vainqueur said. "You are now promoted to my royal executioner. I know you must still be reeling from the torture the lich inflicted on you, but you will pass judgment on him at once!"

"He didn't torture me. Actually he was quite chatty, in a creepy undead way. I think he *really* needed somebody to talk to after a century alone making traps, like a middle unlife crisis."

Poor minion. The pain had broken his mind, forcing him to sympathize with his abuser. Vainqueur would make sure to give him the caring needed to recover.

"Kill me," Furibon let out a furious hiss, like the wounded snake he was. "This day cannot get any worse."

"After we find your phylactery," said Manling Victor.

The lich let out a chuckle. "Do you take me for a fool? I moved it a hidden crypt on another continent when the dragon threatened to destroy my castle. I will return, and when I do, no more games. I will rain spell after spell until you are all dead."

"You know, I somewhat sympathized with you until that last part." Minion Victor glared at Furibon with the same disdain as Vainqueur, before swinging his scythe. "If I understand it, your soul returns to its phylactery when your body is destroyed, allowing you to create a new one."

"Yes, this is called immortality," Furibon replied with a patronizing tone.

"Which means that your soul inhabits your body right now. Otherwise, if your current vessel was an animated puppet, I don't see why you wouldn't abandon it right now instead of waiting for us to destroy it. Ever heard of the [Helheim] Perk?"

The lich fell silent, then finally said, "It will not work."

"Let's find out, shall we?"

"[Enhanced Teleportation]! [Teleportation]!"

Minion Victor swung the blade, cutting off the lich's skeletal head.

The lich's bones crumbled instantly, a specter of black energy escaping from them; it silently tried to flee out of the room, only for a dark force to drag him inside the scythe. Right afterward, the blade reflected Furibon's screaming face within.

"Poor choice of last words," said Manling Victor, as he swung his scythe again, Furibon's ghost silently snarling inside the blade. Chocolatine looked at the scene with gleeful eyes. "His silent screams are so sweet."

"You sealed him, minion?" Vainqueur asked, his lackey confirming with a nod.

"I think his soul will return to his phylactery if the scythe is destroyed, but for now, yes, he's sealed."

"Finally, his evil will never befoul my wealth again."

*Congratulations! For sealing the evil Furibon in your minion's weapon, and claiming the Castle of Murmurin as your dungeon, you earned a level in the ultra prestigious [**Kaiser**] class!*

+30 HP, +10 SP, +1 STR, +1 VIT, +1 SKI, +1 AGI, +1 INT, +1 CHA, +1 LCK!

*You earned the [**Dungeon Owner (Castle of Murmurin)**] class Perk!*

*[**Dungeon Owner (Castle of Murmurin)**]: you are magically tuned to your dungeon. You can instantly teleport in any place within the confines of the Castle of Murmurin at will, and you can navigate inside with perfect awareness of your path.*

Vainqueur didn't pay it much attention, his eyes instead set on the new treasure that appeared in his palm, amidst Furibon's remaining bones. A magnificent, jeweled golden crown, the most beautiful headpiece Vainqueur had ever seen.

But it was manling-sized.

"Minion Victor, you will have Barnabas forge me a dragon-sized crown, after we find a way to cure my gold."

"Actually, I think I have a solution," Victor said. "Your Majesty negated the lich's spells with [Spell Purge], so you should cancel—"

"I can cure lead sickness!" Vainqueur interrupted his lackey, overjoyed.

At long last, the hoard was saved.

And so Furibon, enemy of all that was good, was destroyed by the same obsession that fueled his bottomless evil: his hatred of gold. Once again, the forces of greed prevailed, and the dragon way of life endured.

Through the blessing of King Vainqueur's [Spell Purge], his wealth was returned to him, and so was his faithful minion. Croissant the useless, who survived every trap only to find the battle done, was mocked, and wept. A great feast was ordered. Sheep were eaten. Using their entrails, demons were summoned. They, too, were eaten.

And so peace returned to Murmurin. In the depths of his castle, King Vainqueur gathered a great hoard, one hoard to bind them all. Lord Victor alone, to atone for his capture, carried the burden of keeping the pauper Furibon sealed.

I, Pink Ranger, was tasked by King Vainqueur to write the glorious chronicles of the Great War against Furibon, who was evil and had to be destroyed. I swear my words are the truth, the official truth, from the mouth of King Vainqueur himself. May his glory shine through the ages to come.

And so, remember, always, that in the darkest times, even in face of the most sinister of evil...

The wealthy always win!

21: Emperor Vainqueur

The vaults of the castle overflowed with treasure.

Deep in the depths of the dungeon, Manling Victor had found strong, metal doors so thick and huge, five dragons could have gone through them at once. After some fiery landscaping, Vainqueur and his minions had forced their way inside, only to be welcomed with the most beautiful sight in the world: an immense underground metal vault, overflowing with hills of gold and silver coins.

Vainqueur immediately jumped into his new treasure, swimming in the gold like a shark in the water. So many baby coins imprisoned below ground by that lich, and without a good dragon to take care of them!

"Minions!" Vainqueur shouted, while vicariously showering his belly with coins. "Grow my new hoard by adding the old one to it!"

"Sure, but... what the hell is *that*?"

Vainqueur, who focused on his new shinies alone, hadn't noticed a second door on the other end of the vault. This one was made of ancient stone and sealed shut by heavy chains covered with ancient runes.

Was there a bigger vault behind it? This kept getting better and better!

"Oh, that's written in old Ishfanian." Sweet Chocolatine moved to examine inscriptions written on the stone. "'Beyond these doors, closed by the blessed Inquisition of Mithras the Eversun, is the demesne of the Archdevil Isabelle, Mistress of Blades. May these bindings never break, or Ishfania shall know Hell Unending.'"

"Of course the Ishfanian Inquisition would build a fortress over a gate to Hell," Minion Victor said. "The castle was meant to protect it from invaders coming from *inside*."

"Isabelle is Brandon Maure's mother," Croissant the Useless said. He still hadn't recovered from the traps Vainqueur sent him to scout through, with slashes and paint all over his body. "Furibon must have worked to open these doors over the century and supply his master with demonic armies to throw at Gardemagne."

"What about the seal?" Manling Victor asked. "Will it hold?"

"The bindings have weakened from lack of maintenance, but I can repair them with Squid's help..." Chocolatine's face beamed. "Oh, oh, why don't we open them ourselves? That way we can slaughter demons as they come out. More money, more meat."

Vainqueur's chief of staff didn't share her enthusiasm. "I really don't like the undertones of tricking an entire species into getting killed one at the time by entering a closed room, even demons."

"But organized slaughter is okay if it is done to fiends!" Chocolatine protested.

"No, it's not! And does Your Majesty really want to give an army of would-be robbers direct access to their hoard?"

No. That would be like the mountain, except with winged goats rather than manlings. "Wolfling Chocolatine, you will keep these doors closed," Vainqueur ordered. "You can still use sheep to lure them in your backward peasant village."

The werewolf pouted in disappointment, while minion Victor rejoiced. "Wolflings, you go fetch that squid and reinforce these doors," Vainqueur ordered. "I will not have my vault open to the paupers any longer than necessary. Kobold Rangers, go ask Troll Barnabas if my crown is ready. Manling Victor, you stay here to discuss my class planning."

The minions left with haste to attend his needs, leaving Vainqueur alone with his most beloved treasures: his hoard, and his chief of staff. "Now that the evil Furibon has been destroyed, we can focus on what truly matters to me," the dragon said, burying himself in gold until only his head was above it. "That sweet [Stipend] provides me with more gold the higher my level. Find a way to increase that amount."

"The obvious way would be to level up further, Your Majesty," Victor stated the simple solution. "Maybe a magic item or specific Perk can increase the money you receive, though."

"I leave you to find the proper solution, Manling Victor. You are my class advisor."

"Your Majesty, about magic items." His chief of staff cleared his throat. "I suggest you let the minions keep and use your non-dragon sized magical items, as you allowed me."

"Minion, Furibon is sealed forever, and the castle is mine." He had already put the crown recovered from Furibon around his finger, like a ring. "There is no need to spread my wealth around. And speaking of loaned treasure, where are the sun bracers and the fireball pendant I gave you?"

The minion fell silent for a second, embarrassed. "Well, Furibon caught me by surprise before I could equip myself..."

"You should be more wary next time, and wear my items proudly," Vainqueur chided his lackey. "It pleases me to always have my treasures in sight. It reassures and looks good on me."

"Yeah, I get it. I'm just saying, now our adventurer company is in charge of the barony, we may need a good police force, and minions with magical items will be more effective."

Vainqueur squinted at his minion. "The barony?"

"I told Your Majesty before, Gardemagne promised that whoever destroyed Furibon could lay claim to the surrounding lands, which is called a barony. I had Savoureuse send a message through a homing pigeon, so you should officially be named Baron of Murmurin once the adventurer guild is notified. And if they refuse, well, It's not like they can do anything about who owns the place. Murmurin is so far away from Gardemagne, so full of monsters, and so close to Maure's territory that not even suicidal adventurers will dare dislodge us."

"The Barking of Murmurin," Vainqueur corrected, before explaining his logic to his confused lackey. "Baron King Vainqueur. Barking Vainqueur."

The minion gave him an empty stare.

Vainqueur suddenly realized the problem with the name. "Kingron? Kingaron?" Nothing fit! "Is there a title that could include both? King of the Albain Mountains and Baron of Murmurin does not sound melodious."

"I think Emperor is above King, Your Majesty, since empires are bigger than kingdoms. So it should cover everything."

Really? And all this time he just called himself a king because he thought there was nothing above it! "Minion, I shall henceforth be known as His Majesty Vainqueur Knightsbane, First of his Name, Great Calamity of this Age, and *Emperor* of Murmurin and the Albain Mountains."

"As you wish, Your Majesty *Emperor* Vainqueur."

Vainqueur realized that never before had he loved a new word so much.

"It displeases me to spread my hoard around and out of my sight," said the dragon, "Asks Barnabas to create the minions weapons; until then, I agree to loan the kobolds weapons, so the beauty of my hoard encourages them to work, but only for a time. You alone are worthy to wield my sacred treasures in battle, Minion Victor. You are the only one I can fully trust not to lose them."

"Thank you, Your Majesty," the minion said, without any pitiful tone this time. Come to think of it, Vainqueur didn't remember him ever using such a warm voice before.

"As a celebration for my promotion to Emperor, I declare today to be the Vainqueur Day. Every year, we will rejoice over the defeat of Furibon, who was evil and had to be destroyed. A great feast of cattle will be held, and I will burn a wood puppet of Furibon before an adoring crowd while they cheer me." Maybe he would get a treasure out of it. "Also, the minions will build a statue of me in that werewolf village, so my subjects can be in awe of my emperor person. I want a bigger statue than the gods in your temples."

"Your Majesty, holidays and public works are good, but what about actual laws? I think Murmurin's inhabitants want to know how they will govern themselves now that you are the top dragon in town."

Vainqueur thought about it, and the first direction became obvious. "Minion Victor, this experience, and the cruelty of your manling king made me realize that there is no greater crime than separating a dragon from his hard-won hoard. In my magnanimity, I declare my first commandment to be: no taxes, ever."

"No taxes, ever?"

"No treasure tax of any kind will ever be levied in my empire. Taxes are evil. Instead, I will take a daily tribute of cattle in reward of my enlightened dragon leadership."

"I think Your Majesty invented tax havens way ahead of their time. What about reducing the tax on my one one-tenth fee then?"

"That is different," Vainqueur replied, incensed by the Minion's base greed. "That is not a tax since you are selling my non-shiny possessions on my behalf. The one one-tenth is a *reward.* If you want to get rich and impress females to breed with you, build yourself a hoard by working hard."

Manling Victor let out a sigh. "I guess levies and mindless undead labor will cover for public service."

"My second commandment will be: no lead. Lead is the work of Furibon and forbidden until the end of time. Everyone found smuggling lead in the lands of Emperor Vainqueur shall be eaten. Unless the lead is sickened gold, in that case, it shall be cured and added to my hoard for eternal safekeeping."

"Copper for plumbery then."

"My third commandment is," Vainqueur stared at his minion dead in the eyes, "Minion Victor, do the thing."

His lackey blinked, the honor overwhelming him. "Do the thing?"

"The non-dragon thing," Vainqueur clarified. "I have better things to do than manage the life of wolves, minions, and manlings, like counting my new coins or killing liches. I am a dragon, I do not care how minions run their lives so long as they do as I say when I demand it. So, Manling Victor, I now promote you to my Grand Dragon Vizier, and Doer of the Thing."

"So, I keep doing what I always did, doing the boring stuff while you enjoy the rewards."

"Do not abuse your privilege."

*Congratulations! By self-promoting yourself to Emperor, establishing your 'imperial authority' over the Murmurin region, and possessing enormous personal power worthy of such a title, not only did you earn a level in [**Noble**], but your Noble Class has evolved into the [**Emperor**] Class!*

***Warning**: you will lose the benefits of the [**Emperor**] Class' Perks if you cannot defend your title from challengers and doubters; you will regain these benefits only if you fend off naysayers.*

+30 HP, +10 SP, +1 AGI, +1 INT, +1 CHA, +1 LCK!

*Your [**Old Money**], [**Snobbery**], and [**Aristoradar**] Perks have changed!*

[Old Money] changed to *[**Born in the Purple**]: Your chances of gaining treasures after killing monsters are tripled.*

[Snobbery] changed to *[**For the Emperor**]: When you lead them in battle, your soldiers and vassals gain a stat and moral bonus proportional to your Charisma.*

[Aristoradar] changed to *[**Dynasty**]: You can grant a [Noble] level to others at will. You can only grant only one level per person after which, they must level up the class on their own.*

Vainqueur thought it nice that the system recognized his authority, but now that he had his sweet stipend, that class interested him less. At least the level and that [Born in the Purple] Perk would increase his monthly gains.

Thinking of gains... "Manling Victor, has this misunderstanding with your duchess' untimely demise been cleared with your species?"

"I dunno." The minion shrugged. "It should resolve itself once the news of Furibon's demise reaches them, or else it never will for anything. Your Majesty wants to go on an adventure again?"

"One with a princess," Vainqueur said. "Bragging Day will arrive soon, and I need a princess to parade as the crown jewel of my hoard."

"Your Majesty already brags all the time," Minion Victor replied. "Every day is Bragging Day."

"Yes, but not to dragons," Vainqueur said, his minion frowning when he mentioned his amazing species. "This is Bragging Day. Now that my hoard is cured of lead sickness, it has grown big enough to brag about to the rest of my kind; but a true hoard is not complete without a princess caught in the wild to showcase. I want to hold a Bragging Day here in two moons, so find me a well-paid quest with a princess."

"Is Your Majesty going to eat the princess?" the minion asked worryingly. "I know you said you wouldn't, but... if this is a special occasion..."

"Minion, I am not a savage. I will keep it until the end of the Bragging Day, then I release her so she grows into a queen, and makes more princesses. So will continue the cycle of life. I am a dragon mindful of preserving the wildlife."

"Okay good." His minion breathed in relief. "How many dragons are we talking about? No offense, but Your Majesty is already a lot for us mortals to handle."

Vainqueur thought about it long and deep. He would invite every member of his kind whom he had remained in contact with, so he could showcase his wealth in a great show of dominance.

"No more than two hundred," Vainqueur said, the minion losing all colors on his skin. "You should prepare the cattle already. It would be very miserly of me not to show my wealth by welcoming them with a great feast."

"Two... two hundred..."

"I know, so few, but we dragons enjoy our alone time too much to stay in touch," Vainqueur explained. "Most of my kindred are hunting princesses in the north, in lands so cold I freeze thinking of them."

The minions returned with both that strange squid who worshipped the ground Manling Victor walked on and Minion Barnabas. The troll struggled to carry a crown, helped by the kobolds.

The second he saw it, Vainqueur immediately fell in love with the trinket.

It was the most beautiful crown he had ever set his eyes on; a golden, dragon-sized diadem with three miniature copies of Vainqueur rising from the front of the circlet, surrounding an enormous ruby. Four ivory horns were mounted on the edges, giving it a strong, yet elegant look; it would mesh so well with his own natural horns.

"This is a [Crown of Dragon Authority], Yer Majesty," Barnabas said. "+10 Charisma, and a whole host of benefits."

"Mine!" Vainqueur's hands greedily reached for it, putting it on his head at once. The crown fit right around his black horns, and the dragon immediately looked at his reflection in his hoard's coins.

Pure perfection!

Which was him!

"I am Emperor Vainqueur Knightsbane, owner of all I see!" Vainqueur boasted, the minions falling to their knees. "Praise me! Cheer me up!"

"Vainqueur, best dragon!" "Vainqueur, best dragon!" "Vainqueur, best dragon!"

22: Minions of the Month

Victor walked out of the Castle of Murmurin—or rather, the ruins left standing—with his throat still sore from the shouting, and only one thought in mind.

"Ffffff..."

They were doomed.

Two hundred dragons! Two hundred dragons and he would brag to them how being an adventurer made him richer! How could that not backfire?!

That and Vainqueur was steadily getting smarter. He had noticed Victor had sacrificed his items, and even if the adventurer could deflect his attention, he needed to replace them as soon as possible.

The notification of his new level gains did alleviate his fears.

Congratulations! For landing the coup de grace on an ancient lich on behalf of your dragon master, and cunningly trapping the soul in your scythe, you gained two levels in [Monster Squire] and two levels in [Reaper]!

+90 HP, + 20 SP, +2 STR, + 4 VIT, +4 SKI, +4 AGI, +3 INT, +3 CHA, +3 LCK!

You gained the [Mook Promotion] and [Necromancy II] Class Perks.

[Mook Promotion]: You can cause your minions to evolve into stronger forms, if your level is higher than the evolved monster's theoretical danger rating and if hidden conditions are met. Promoted minions keep their previous class levels.

[Necromancy II]: You can learn and cast Necromancy spells up to Tier II. This replaces Necromancy I.

*By consuming the soul of a powerful lich, your [**Killer Scythe**] has been upgraded into a [**Killer Scythe+**]. +25 percent chance of inflicting critical hits.*

Holy hell, those growths... he had lucked out today. At this rate, he would catch up to the Shining Knight in no time flat.

__Warning__: You have reached the level 30 class ceiling.

*You will no longer be able to gain additional levels until you use a [**Crest**].*

You can still gain perks through special deeds, but your experience gains are set to zero.

Uh?

What, there were level ceilings? He needed to bribe the system to get into the middle class? Damn, it was just like on Earth.

For once, though, the system gave him more explanation.

*[**Crest**] are powerful but rare items which allow someone to break the level 30 class ceiling.*

*[**Heroic Crests**] are even rarer and more powerful [**Crests**], which are needed to break the level 60 class ceiling.*

Afterward, you are free to level up to 99, which will allow you to access __Valhalla__ and attempt __Apotheosis__.

Valhalla. The final challenge. Only twelve creatures survived it and walked out as the deities of Outremonde.

Still, he had no idea where to find a [Crest], or even what it looked like. Questions for later. There was something more urgent than levels or preparing for that Bragging Day.

"Furibon," Victor spoke up at his scythe, the ghastly face of the lich materializing on the blade's edge. "Furibon, are you there? Furibon! Furi?"

"What?" the lich whispered back with an irritated tone.

He could indeed understand him. "What is that deal with the iPad?" The lich's silence made him roll his eyes. "The Apple of Knowledge."

"Why would I tell you? I hate you, and everything that dragon stands for. I wish you all die."

"Thank you, you are so kind. Now as for why..." Victor gave the lich a sly, cruel smirk. "Because otherwise, I am giving up that scythe to Vainqueur, and you will spend eternity as part of his hoard. You will have to support his insanity until the end of times, watching him shower in gold in *your* castle's vaults, and sprout nonsense until you go mad."

The lich's horrified silence was golden. *"You are a monster,"* Furibon said. *"You look weak and innocent, but you are a monster."*

"Humanoid/Dragon type," Victor confirmed. "Now tell me, before I go through with it. You know I will."

Furibon let out an angry sigh but hated Vainqueur too much to refuse. *"My Master, Brandon Maure, to use your crass language... backed the wrong horse. He assisted the fomors led by King Balaur in their war with Gardemagne, so he could seize southern territories, but his side lost. Now, with the fairy lords defeated, Gardemagne has many adventurers and crusaders, and no enemy to fight."*

"So he's afraid Gardemagne will attack him next."

"Prydain and the Dark Forest, the strongholds of the remaining fomors, are too dangerous for Gardemagne to threaten, but not Ishfania. With his losses during the conflict, my master no longer has the forces to face the full might of his neighbors."

"Okay, so he's desperate to find a way to turn the tide and save his remaining territories." Using the Scorchers to distract adventurers, trying to summon reinforcements from Hell... "Let me guess, he thinks weapons from other worlds will solve his problem?"

"We always researched the technology from the world of Earth, whenever we could find it. In many ways, it completes our own magic. King Maure offered great rewards to Claimed willing to share knowledge with him, and one day that dark woman brought him one carrying the Apple of Knowledge."

That tale sounded very familiar. "Is that woman's name Lavere?"

"No. That woman's name is Melodieuse. She is poison in human form, a beautiful, deadly flower who kills on touch."

Ah. Too bad. Victor guessed not all conspiracies were connected. "So, that Claimed, who probably worked for the biggest weapon manufacturer of my world, offered his services to Brandon Maure in exchange for power and money. He basically just changed employers. Then, how did his digital notebook end up in Haudemer?"

"Digital?" The lich shrugged. *"The Claimed grew what you would call a conscience, and which I call weakness. The coward fled to Gardemagne, taking the Apple with him, and when Maure's human agents killed him around Haudemer, they found monsters had already stolen the device."*

Blessed be the Kobold Rangers.

"I could not unlock the magical passwords protecting the forbidden knowledge, but King Maure has powerful allies, including Claimed of his own. In time, the knowledge will be his, and you, no, all of Outremonde, will learn fear and fire."

Yes, yes. As far as threats went, Victor had heard better. The possibility of a demonic dictator gaining access to plane schematics *was* worrying though; Maure may not fully replicate the original designs without the necessary infrastructure, but Victor himself had created a poor man's aircraft. It could be done.

He would have to warn Gardemagne or convince Vainqueur to somehow deal with Maure before he could threaten the continent. "And the woman? What does she want? Where does she come from?"

"I do not know, I do not care. I serve my master as you do yours, I do not ask questions."

There were so many wrong things in that sentence, but the lich didn't seem to lie. Or if he did, Victor had no way to check. The squire suspected another power supported Maure from the shadows to strike at Gardemagne, but for now, he could only guess whom.

Oh well. He would send warning alongside the "imperial declarations."

The Kobolds Rangers exited the building behind him, drawing him out of his thoughts. Blue carried a sword that Victor immediately recognized.

"Treasure!" Vainqueur Junior barked.

"Did the sword talk?" Blue asked, examining it more closely.

"A mimic?" Red examined it, noticing lips on the pommel. "Why didn't it bite you?"

"Because Junior is a good mimic," Victor said, the sword purring in response, "Who is a good treasure? Who is a good treasure? That is you!"

As he observed the minions, Victor felt an instinct stirring inside him. He couldn't put his finger on why, but he had the intuition his [Mook Promotion] Perk could work on both the mimic and Red. Not on the other kobolds though; either their evolved form was stronger than him, or more likely, Red had earned more combat experience as the group's leader and thus fulfilled hidden conditions.

"Red, come here for a second, I want to try something," Victor ordered. "Blue, give me Junior."

He patted the dutiful Red on the head and took Junior from Blue's hand. The second he touched the two creatures, the Perk activated. Both of them were swallowed by a bright light and transformed as Victor watched.

Red grew into a bipedal, humanoid saurian who almost reached Victor's own height. His features changed into a cross between a raptor-like dinosaur and a kobold, with retractable blades attached to his arms. A red scarf appeared out of nowhere around his neck, and on a closer look, Victor realized it was part of the body. The way it stood, Red reminded him clearly of a reptilian version of the sentai heroes he had taken inspiration from.

"Style?" Red was almost brought to tears, as he admired his new features, especially the blades. "I have style, and I am grown!"

The mimic though...

Never before had Victor seen a more disturbing horror. The mere sight caused the kobolds to ignore Red's transformation and instead cower behind Victor.

He had to drop the sword before it could finish the metamorphosis, as it grew considerably. The misshapen entity in front of him was the size of a horse, with a main, spherical body carried by six, handed legs. The skin's texture reminded Victor of stone, and could easily camouflage as it.

The monster had a mouth big enough to swallow a man whole, sharp teeth, and a sickeningly long tongue. Finally, a beautiful, clearly magical sword sprung from the main body, like a fish's lure.

By burying itself in the ground, the creature could easily look like a sword in the stone, an Excalibur tempting the foolish. This creature was *the* next evolutionary step towards the complete decimation of adventurers.

*Kobold Red has been promoted into a **Raptor Ranger**.*

*Mimic Vainqueur Junior has been promoted into an **Excalitrap**.*

"Sword treasure!" the monstrous abomination barked with a strong, terrifying voice.

Victor Dalton. Pokemon Master, and Grand Vizier of Dragon Switzerland.

At least they would help keep the peace. Now, first order of business, buy new bracers and necklace to replace those he lost in Haudemer. He already felt bad lying to Vainqueur about them, and—

Wait.

He was feeling bad about lying to the dragon? Not actually fearing for his life for purely pragmatic reasons, but feeling *ashamed* of it?

Come to think of it, even if Vainqueur had made it clear he would never let Victor out of his service, the adventurer wondered if it was truly such a bad thing. He had become the region's regent in all but name, gained many levels, made friends, albeit difficult ones, and gained a powerful protector. Vainqueur did save him from Furibon after all, even if he would have picked a fight with the lich anyway.

Was...

Was he actually starting to *like* Vainqueur?

"I think I have Stockholm Syndrome."

23: The Shining Knight

- **1291 After Mithras, Mithras' heavenly realm**.

Death *sucked*. Not as much as she thought, though.

Kia had never been religious, and so, she expected a dark void and then nothing. Apparently though, religions were onto something.

The afterlife existed, and it looked like a greek temple made of marble, golden clouds and shining light. Whichever god ruled this place had given her a comfortable chair on which to sit, in front of a bright pyre.

"Kia Bekele."

She raised her eyes, finding that what she thought to be pillars were in fact the legs of two immense figures.

The first was a great man with marble-like skin, like a statue chiseled from the stone. The entity wore a crown of flames and carried a blazing sword, hidden below a royal mantle. It was the archetypal king, with two suns for eyes glancing down at Kia with kind benevolence. "I am Mithras, god of the sun, law, healing, and justice," he presented himself with a warm, booming voice.

"And I am Leone, goddess of glory, nobility, art, and strength." The second was a true knight in shining armor, a woman with blonde hair, glowing blue eyes, and clad in golden armor. She carried a great sword anchored in the ground with both hands on the pommel, and radiated an aura of bravery. "We are two of the twelve gods of Outremonde."

Outremonde?

"A coin has two faces, Kia," Mithras said. "Earth is but one world among many, and it has a twin. Outremonde. A world similar to yours in shape, but with dragons instead of planes, magic instead of science. A world threatened by a great blight, and in dire need of heroes."

"You died an early death on Earth before you could fulfill your destiny," Leone continued, Kia wondering if they were married or very close friends to synchronize so well. "But death is a door. It can lead you to whatever afterlife awaits, or to a new chance in Outremonde."

"Like reincarnation?" Like the novels she read online?

"If you wish," Mithras explained her options. "We can return you to Outremonde as you are now, with all that you carry. Or we can reincarnate you into the body of a man, an elf, a dwarf, or even a cat. As long as it is neither a fomor nor a dragon, you can become anything, or anyone."

"That's... oddly specific," Kia pointed out.

"Fomors have no soul and thus you cannot incarnate as one. Dragons..." Leone made a face of absolute disgust, before regaining her composure. "Dragons are forbidden. You will be granted divine blessings, and great boons, so you may forge yourself a new destiny. But great power comes with a certain obligation."

Of course, there would be a catch. Kia hadn't done anything extraordinary in life. She moved from Ethiopia to Europe with her parents, only to die a school student when her stupid boyfriend drove their car into another. Beyond some charity work in her free time, she had nothing heroic to present. "You have a mission for me."

Leone nodded. "The people of Outremonde are threatened by an ancient foe, the fairy lords of the fomor."

"They are not the little fairies of your movies. The fomors are soulless abominations, wicked witches, eaters of children, and cruel giants. They treat humans as toys or food, and create life only to enslave it. They uplifted the beastkin by giving animals the gift of intelligence, only to hunt them for sport. They are foul tyrants who once ruled Outremonde with an iron fist alongside their dragon rivals, before our fellow deity Dice came along."

"Through our support and the power of Classes, humans and other species have slowly pushed them back in the dark corner of Outremonde. But almost a century ago, one of them decided to fight back."

Mithras raise a hand, and miniature phantom pictures appeared in front of Kia, like holograms.

The scene represented a medieval city inhabited by humans and assaulted by monsters. Trolls, ogres, winged harpies and other horrors had breached fortified walls, setting the city on fire while fighting a collapsing defense of knights and magicians. It would have looked awesome if the battle wasn't horribly one-sided in the horde's favor.

A monstrous rider the size of skyscrapers rampaged around the city, crushing houses with every step. The creature, a humanoid, rode a giant lizard with spikes on its back as if it was a horse.

Was that a D&D tarrasque? Or Godzilla? And something was *riding* it?

The giant riding it looked like a monstrous, headless knight, carrying an enormous axe of flesh and bone with one hand. A floating eye of blue flames hovered where the head should have been, glaring down with malice at the small people the monster cut mercilessly.

"King Balaur, strongest and foulest of the fomors, has raised a terrible army and wages war against the Mistral continent," Mithras explained with a grim voice. "Countries have fallen to him, and now Gardemagne, the stronghold of mankind, is threatened with destruction. If he succeeds, Balaur will soak the continent with the blood of all mortals, so they may never rise again to challenge the fomors."

"Why do you not help the mortals directly?" It always bugged her why deities never seem to do so in stories, and that creature seemed like a threat big enough to warrant it. "That thing looks *nasty*."

"We would like to, and once I did," Mithras said, surprising her. "But we are not all-powerful. We are closer to your Olympians, or your Aesir. We are powerful and we cannot die, but we have our limits."

"A millennia ago, we gods agreed not to fight on Outremonde itself," Leone said. "For when we did, we caused more harm than good, with no clear winner. Another god, Sablar the World Eater, supports the fomors in his quest for universal decimation, and thus prevents us from intervening. So for now, all we can do is guide and empower mortals. We can reincarnate people from Earth, by 'claiming' their souls, and making them our champions."

"So, if I agree to fight this Balaur, I will be granted a new life and amazing powers?"

"This will be a dangerous journey, and you may very well die," Mithras said. "But know that if you die in the line of duty, you will be granted a place in our divine realm. Neither will you be alone."

"We reincarnated many other humans from your world, who had the potential to become true heroes," Leone confirmed Kia's own thoughts, "Together, you will form a great crusade and fight as one against Balaur."

They were bribing her with heaven?

Now that she knew it existed, how could she resist?

"Can I get a better body?" she asked, a bit embarrassed. Kia was black, with a nerdy look and glasses; the kind of girl who spent their time in the library without seeing the light of day. She had always had some sort of body issue over it, and so seized the chance. "I want to stay human and close to what am I, just... better-looking."

"That can be arranged," Leone said, who didn't sound surprised.

"Yes. I don't want too much change, just to be in better health, not need glasses, and have a beautiful face. I know that sounds stupid, but..."

"This is not stupid, Kia," Mithras reassured her with kindness, "In fact, you are more mature and humble than the others."

"Ah? How so?"

"Most of them ask for bigger... implements... and I shall not sully myself by giving lurid details."

"You can get a bigger chest? Is that on the table?"

The gods' stare became cold and unbearable.

"I was kidding," Kia said, who wasn't sure herself. The offer was good, and she was in no hurry to find whatever 'normal' afterlife awaited her. "I'm in."

"Thank you, Kia," said Mithras. "Shall we, Leone?"

"Beforehand, though, can I ask you a question?" The gods nodded at Kia's demand. "Why me, among all the others? What made me special?"

The deities exchanged a glance in uncomfortable silence. After long, agonizing seconds, Kia grew very nervous.

"I do not have the heart to tell her," Leone told Mithras.

The god sighed in response, glancing down at Kia. "Kia. I am the god of justice. Truth and honesty are under my purview, which means I am physically unable to lie, no matter how much I would like to spare someone's feelings. My words will be the objective truth, so please, do not take anything I say personally."

Kia prepared herself for impact.

"You are bland, and forgettable."

Kia sank deeper in her chair.

"You were largely irrelevant in your previous life, and while you died with good karma, it was more because of an absence of evil deeds than any worthwhile quality. You are, for a lack of a better word, *mediocre*, but *passable*."

Never before did Kia thought words could hurt so much.

"We have already reincarnated all the people whom you could call true hero material, but the fomors either killed them, or they are not enough on their own. We are, to use your local expressions, scraping the bottom of the barrel, and accepting anyone with remotely good karma. We hope that where quality failed, quantity will succeed. The situation is that terrible. Even if we do not expect it, you have the potential, with some boons and luck, to become a hero. It is *unlikely* but *possible*."

By now, Kia's self-esteem had been torn to shreds, and she couldn't find her words.

"But no pressure," Leone tried to reassure her, with a forced smile.

No, not at all.

"You can still become a hero, and seize the chance to grow into a legend," Mithras said, kinder than before. "Even if you fail, I will welcome you in my realm, where you could enjoy a bountiful afterlife. The choice is yours."

She liked the idea a lot less than before, but it was still better than the alternative.

Both deities raised a hand at her, and two symbols materialized on the back of each of Kia's palm as tattoos: a shining, golden sun, and a shield with a stylized pen symbol.

*Congratulations! You were granted a level in the prestigious [**Paladin**] Class!*

+1 STR, +1 VIT, +1 CHA, +1 LCK!

*You earned the [**Holy Champion**] Class Perk, and the [**Claimed by Mithras**] and [**Claimed by Leone**] Personal Perks!*

*[**Holy Champion**]: You gain advanced proficiency with Swords and Spears, all attacks you make with any weapon will inflict additional Holy Damage.*

*[**Claimed by Mithras**]: When you level up, you have an additional 10 percent chance to gain a Charisma or Strength point. You are also immune to all Fire and Holy effects, except those caused by Mithras or his servants.*

*[**Claimed by Leone**]: When you level up, you have an additional 10 percent chance to gain a Vitality or Skill point. You gain a 30 percent experience bonus whenever you finish a quest or slay a monster.*

Mediocre and passable? Kia promised herself that she would show them they were wrong.

She would show them all.

• **1301 After Mithras, three days after Emperor Vainqueur's self-coronation.**

"KIA! KIA! Get your ass out here!"

Kia awoke from her slumber with a heavy headache, the bottle of wine she drank last night on the side of her king-sized bed. The morning sun bothered her through the windows, making her groan and draw the bedsheet to herself.

She heard her butler reason with the guest on the other side of the door. "Sir Nostredame, the Shining Knight does not wish to be bothered... she doesn't feel well..."

"I'm her teammate, I've seen her in the most humiliating positions imaginable. A bad morning is tame."

Recognizing the man's voice, Kia let out a frustrated moan. "Let the sucker in..."

The door opened with a kick, and a tall, charming dark elf with dark skin and short white hair stepped in. He wore shadowy blue and gold robes brimming with magical power, alongside a host of powerful artifacts, from rings to a silver diadem. His purple eyes set on her with heavy disapproval. "Kia, what the hell, it's one in the afternoon!"

Her hands reached for the stuff laying below her bed. She grabbed her legendary sword Arondight, forged to kill the mightiest of dragons, and used it as a cane to stand out of bed. "What's the matter..."

"Kia, my gods, are you *drunk*?" He closed the door behind before opening the window with telekinesis, letting fresh air inside.

"No, I just had... a little too much wine last night... gimme a sec..." She put a hand on her chest. "[Cure]."

The hangover ended with an aura of green light, and Kia could think properly again. "Better," she said, standing straight and smirking at her old teammate, "Hi, Kevin."

"It's Nostredame!" her friend lambasted her. "How many times did I tell you to use my hero name?"

Kia remembered, but still teased him. Like many other Claimed, Kevin had chosen a new, fantasy-sounding name upon arriving in Outremonde. Since they were thick as thieves, he let her get away with it for the same reason she was comfortable letting him in her room while she only wore white lingerie.

Kia moved towards her bedroom's two-meters high mirror, adjusting her hair. When the gods reincarnated her, they altered her appearance to the point she forgot her old one. Her new body in that strange world resembled the model Liya Kebede, with shoulder-long black hair, lustrous dark skin, and piercing eyes. She had lost some muscle and gained fat since she started living in the vineyard, but she still looked more like an amazon than a fragile flower.

Most lusted at her on sight, to the point of making her uncomfortable, but Kevin didn't. That nerd only loved magic and math, to the point that he asked to become a dark elf because it would make his Intelligence growth better. "The butler told me you drank all the time," Kevin scolded her. "I know we had epic, messy parties back in the day, but drinking alone isn't like you."

"I don't have anything better to do," Kia admitted.

Two years ago, two hundred experienced adventurers in the sixty level range and above fought King Balaur at the Golden Fields, Kia among them, in an epic battle for the continent's future. Each of them had the best equipment, including artifacts, preparation time, and a well-oiled strategy.

By the time Kia landed the final blow, they were down to eleven.

But at long last, with their leader dead, the fomors fell into infighting, their horde scattering, and the stragglers easy picking for adventurers. While generals like Mag Mell successfully retreated to their homeland of Prydain, the war was over. Mortal life would endure.

Kia, as one of the greatest heroines of Gardemagne, was granted the title of Shining Knight and noble lands. Including a vineyard estate where she spent most of her free time nowadays. Kevin, meanwhile, had become the headmaster of Gardemagne's royal academy and an advisor to the king.

And it bored her to death.

Kia had now reached beyond level sixty, and almost nothing could threaten her anymore. Well, some powerful monsters could, but after that legendary battle with King Balaur, everything felt like a let-down. Instead of going on epic quests, she spent her days making speeches or courted by nobles wishing to marry the Heroine of the Golden Fields. Even one of Gardemagne's princes had gotten to it.

'Back in the day,' as Kevin said. Kia felt like these cranky old people ranting about the 'good old times,' and she *hated* it.

Her eyes trailed to her bright, green starmetal armor and shields standing in a corner. Maybe she could go back on the road as a solo hero, fighting the fomors in Prydain, or exploring the western continent?

"Do you want a drink?" Kia offered her friend, as he snapped his fingers, causing a table covered with paper to appear, alongside chairs.

"No thanks," he said, sitting and inviting her to do the same. "I came for business, actually."

He did? Kia was suddenly all ears since business usually involved the fomors or Brandon Maure. "The King finally decided to invade Ishfania?"

"Not yet, and we have a new fox in the hen house. A great red dragon appeared in the south and caused a lot of turmoil there. He has been identified as Vainqueur Knightsbane, an elder red wyrm who terrorized Midgard before it was destroyed by Balaur and then assimilated by Gardemagne. He was presumed dead during the Century War, but so far, reports and divinations agree that this is the real deal."

An elder red wyrm. Like a fomor, one would need a party in the fifties to kill it. Kia could probably take it down solo, so bringing the entire party was overkill. "How dangerous?" she asked, her hopeful tone surprising her. "The name sounds familiar. I think I heard stories about him."

"He's pretty much the archetypal dragon in Outremonde, at least in the southern lands. He was considered the greatest calamity of the age, before King Balaur came along, and earned the Knightsbane nickname because he killed every hero who challenged him."

"I figured. The king wants me to deal with it?" It would change her mind and distract her for a bit.

"Actually, it's… it's more complicated than that. I don't know how to say it with a straight face but… He has a human partner, and they…" Kia frowned, as her friend struggled to find his words. He eventually gave her a short letter. "Just read."

Kia proceeded to, and the more she read, the more confused she was. "*Emperor* Vainqueur Knightsbane? V&V adventurer company?"

"The dragon wants to be paid with lands and gold for destroying one of Maure's generals, the lich Furibon."

"What do you mean, the dragon wants to be *paid*?" She quickly figured it out. "Don't tell me…"

"The adventurer guild recognized Vainqueur Knightsbane and his human partner as an adventurer company, plates included. With Furibon's destruction, they should be upgraded to gold-rank, but after the Euskal fiasco, they will probably settle on the politically safer iron or bronze."

The Euskal fiasco? What did she miss last night? "A dragon. A dragon adventurer."

"With class levels."

Dragons could get class levels? She thought they were like the fomors, soulless, and thus unable to access the system, even after being informed of its existence. "How did this happen? Start from the beginning."

"The human partner is Victor Dalton. He is a Claimed of Dice, who ended up joining the Nightblades shortly after arriving in

Outremonde. He took levels in the [Outlaw] class and had a short—"

"Dalton," Kia interrupted him. "His family name is *Dalton*, and he started as an *Outlaw*?"

"Yes, he was predisposed for evil. Imagine if his name had been Dick Dalton." Kia couldn't help but chuckle. "Anyway, he worked for the Nightblades syndicate in Noblecoeur before leaving to become an adventurer. He was hired by the Marquise of Carabas through the Albain chapter of the adventurer guild to recover a rapier, which led him to Vainqueur's lair. We do not know what happened there, but three things were certain afterward: Vainqueur returned, Dalton had become his accomplice, and they forced the local guild to declare them an official adventurer company."

"Is Dalton—"

"He doesn't control the dragon as far as I can tell, but my apprentice, whom I sent to investigate, told me he accessed a Monster Class called [Monster Squire]. I suspect he sold his soul to the dragon in exchange for power." The archwizard presented her two piles of paper. "I have two radically different versions of the events that followed, both plausible and with nothing in between. I do not know what to make of them."

"Tell me," Kia asked. "The more information we have, the better we can deal with them."

"The first version is mostly based on the testimony of the nobles and their retinues," Kevin warned. "Dalton and Vainqueur first moved to Carabas to wreak 'revenge' on the marquise, burning her lands and threatening her into surrendering a tribute of gold and food. The marquise tried to have the dragon poisoned, but he shrugged it off, and Dalton blackmailed them for items."

Well, that escalated quickly. Kia guessed that dragons and outlaws remained monsters, no matter what they called themselves.

"The two then occupied the town of Haudemer, on the west coast. Our spies tell us they sought to recover an artifact hidden by a Claimed who escaped Brandon Maure's clutches, the Apple of Knowledge. After the duo devastated the countryside, recruiting savage monsters along the way, the Scorchers fought them over the artifact and were massacred. After the carnage, Dalton…" Her friend paused. "Do you really want me to give you the ugly details?"

Kia nodded, a dark look on her face.

"He… Dalton ordered one of the women to *breed* with him."

Kia tightened her hold over her sword, thinking how she would castrate that criminal with it.

"Duchess Aelinor arrived with knights and crusaders to free Haudemer, but Vainqueur crushed them. Then, when she refused to pay him a tribute of gold, he ate the duchess alive. Dalton, who had already sold corpses to necromancers, began to raise monsters from the dead as undead slaves, and together they slew a dozen adventurer groups sent after them. They then moved to Murmurin, conquering it for themselves."

So these two were a duo of villains, the likes of which Gardemagne hadn't seen since the end of the war. A human criminal and a savage dragon, who somehow managed to draw the worst out of the other.

Kia knew these were bad news, and that she shouldn't feel joy over it, but she once again brimmed at the call of a righteous quest. "What about the other version?"

"Well… I interrogated the local guild manager, especially about her experience with Victor, and she said: *'he is an idiot, and I wish him to suffer for bringing that dragon to my guildhall, but he is no villain. Just an idiot.'* The Count of Provencal said the arson was the result of a monster-extermination request that the dragon interpreted a bit too zealously, and that Victor saved his life by covering up the poisoning incident. As for Haudemer, they left a mixed memory to the locals, who say they saved them from the Scorchers at the cost of unnecessary property damage."

"But what about the woman Dalton forced himself on?" Kia asked, appalled. "What about the undead business? The duchess' murder?"

"The victim of the *breeding* insists this was consensual and that, I quote, 'eight out of ten, not the best I had, but I would gladly do it again.' The undead deal was apparently a completely legal operation under the new Undead Labor Laws. While Dalton handled the paperwork, the dragon was the main pusher according to witnesses, for purely venal reasons. Finally, Dalton explained through letters that the duchess refused to pay Vainqueur for the Scorchers' demise, and it escalated into a fight. Aelinor's successor, Justine De Sade, officially recognized that version and didn't press charges."

Kia digested the news in silence. Indeed, there was little middle ground between the two versions. "So they are either fiendish villains or destructive idiots."

"Or both."

"Show me a map of that 'empire of Murmurin'." Her friend showed a spot between Gardemagne and Ishfania's western frontier, bordering the sea. He circled a small area, making Kia laugh. "They call *that* an empire? You can't even fit Delaware inside!"

"What do you have against Delaware?" Kevin protested, since he came from there. "It's a dragon, Kia. Common sense doesn't apply to them. Remember that Black Wyrm in the swamps?"

Kia still shuddered at it. That dragon had abducted a dozen of noble ladies so it could 'raise princesses in captivity.' "Would that not help Gardemagne?" she asked her more politically-minded friend. "The dragon is right between the kingdom and Ishfania, and already declared war on Maure by taking over that area."

"In theory it does help us, but a dragon with class levels is something to watch out for. Dragons warred with the fomors for control of Outremonde until the fairies bribed them with gold. So far that wyrm asked to be paid in return for services rendered, but imagine if he realizes he can bully towns into giving him gold? And while a controversial figure, Victor worked with the Nightblades. He's a criminal."

Kia pondered the problem. Her gut told her these two were closer to amoral mercenaries than dangerous calamities, but she couldn't know before checking up first. "You said they claimed that region. They did it as an adventurer state?"

Her friend confirmed with a nod. Since Outremonde's lands were more than sixty percent unexplored, monster-ruled wilderness, Gardemagne allowed adventurer companies to claim areas which they conquered. In theory, they worked as tributary states, but in practice, the company ruled their territory as its leaders saw fit. Gardemagne's ancestor, the Mithraic Empire, started as one such state.

Eventually, the kingdom fully absorbed these areas by making adventurers official nobles, but no adventurer state ever had a dragon at its head. Especially one calling himself emperor. Rebellious adventurers were usually crushed, but they weren't castle-destroying behemoths. "What does the King say about it?"

"His current stance is to ignore the dragon. Since duchess De Sade declined to press charges for her sister's death, and the beast destroyed Furibon, King Roland froze the bounty on Vainqueur's head. Better to let the wyrm play noble, he says, so long as he follows the guild's procedures and limits his aggression to the kingdom's enemies. Since everyone who picked a fight with Vainqueur died, and Murmurin is a monster-infested desert nobody wants, that seems reasonable."

"But you don't share his opinion."

"I'm wary of letting power get to a dragon's head since they are egomaniacs at best. Lucie already proposed to move to Murmurin to check on them, alongside a representative of the adventurer guild." Kia knew that by that, he truly meant a long-term spy of the kingdom. "Since you are looking for excitement..."

"I could check up on them, and take them down if needed."

Within an hour, Kia took her armor out of storage, and her gryphon out of his stable.

24: The Meat is Life

"You call that a castle?" Vainqueur complained as he bathed in the lava around his new lair, "I demand at least seven towers! Work harder!"

"Yes, Emperor Vainqueur!" the kobolds shouted back, while Vainqueur briefly closed his eyes in satisfaction at the name. The minions had built a large bridge to carry raw material from the mountain to the castle, rebuilding the towers the dragon had destroyed during the War of the Hoard.

The hyena-like humanoid called gnolls carried most of the black stones making up the castle, the males doing most of the work under the supervision of their females. Vainqueur found their spotted fur and their clothes funny to look at.

As it turned out, the encampments south belonged to gnoll tribes who lived in fear of the dread Furibon, who allowed them to live and keep their gold so long as they obeyed him. Most had fled the region when Vainqueur warred against the lich, but the few who didn't came to Murmurin looking for work. After condemning them for knowingly serving that cruel undead, Vainqueur forgave them and accepted them in his service.

The gnolls had proven lazy and cowardly though, unlike the zealous kobolds; they stopped working when Vainqueur wasn't looking or picked fights with the other minions. The dragon had to eat twenty troublemakers before they started behaving.

"Also, the highest tower must have a crown!" Vainqueur ordered the minions. "A stone crown!" If it could give him more charisma, then surely, it would make his castle more beautiful.

"Your Majesty?" Vainqueur turned towards the bridge, seeing manling Victor riding that undead beast, with the corpseling and necromancer Jules Rapace on the back. Barnabas had dressed his chief of staff strangely, granting him a cowled, tattered mantle and dark boots. "I see you're enjoying the new accommodations."

"The temperature is just right, minion," Vainqueur said, although he was careful not to let his crown too close lest it melt. The dragon felt some sympathy for his chief of staff, whose lack of immunity to fire prevented him from partaking in the bath.

"Emperor Vainqueur," Jules the corpseling saluted the dragon with great deference. "How good to see you again. Words cannot properly express my gratitude."

"A dragon does not turn away good minions," Vainqueur said. Especially those he could digest, unlike that steel golem. "You should have asked to join V&V back in that backward village, instead of waiting so long. I know a true dragon may intimidate your kind, but I am an equal opportunity master."

"I didn't know Your Majesty would go this far back then. How could I resist the call of a country lacking Gardemagne's heavy taxation on undead labor, and open to the idea of mass zombification? I feel a great corpse boom will soon start, and that the Empire of Murmurin may kickstart the undeathstrial revolution I dream of."

"Interesting," Vainqueur replied, trying to calculate how much funds they could gain from that business. "Now, for the important matter. My hoard was treacherously attacked by Furibon, who was evil enough to attack innocent, defenseless gold. It almost died of sickness."

"I had him read the book, Your Majesty," said manling Victor. "We used mimics to print it en mass."

"It is a national best-seller," Vainqueur boasted. Everyone should learn of his great deeds, and how he saved the world's gold from the lich. "My hoard must learn to defend itself, especially if I am on an adventure and not present to protect it. Minion Victor said you could help."

"I can indeed imbue your hoard with the ability for self-defense," Jules the corpseling said.

"Then show me."

Manling Victor and Jules climbed down from the mount, with the chief of staff giving a purse full of gold to his corpseling minion. Vainqueur watched the scene closely.

Spilling gold on the bridge, corpseling Jules cast a spell on it. "[Animate Golem]."

To Vainqueur's marvel, the coins combined into a vaguely humanoid shape, a tiny, shiny engine of destruction. "This is the miniature version, but Jules can make golems the size of Your Majesty," Manling Victor said.

"They will obey Your Majesty's orders, and attack anyone trying to pilfer your treasure without authorization," Jules said. "I may add alarm spells to the underground vault, to warn you of intruders no matter the distance."

"You shall do so, Corpseling, and you shall be rewarded for your good deed. You shall be moved between Manling Victor and the other minions in my emergency ration priority list. You are now equal to the Kobold Rangers in the food chain."

"Your Majesty's generosity honors me," the corpseling replied with a deep bow.

"Minion Victor informed me I would not be able to gain levels beyond thirty," Vainqueur asked. "Why is that?"

"The 'why' is a mystery, but people need to use items called Crests to gain additional levels. This may be the system's way to test if users are ready for greater challenges beyond mere experience progression."

Vainqueur promised himself to have a word with the dragons who created this system when he found them. "Where can they be found?"

"Crests are heavily regulated by adventurer guilds and governments," Jules explained. "The Gardemagnian Guild confiscate all Crests they can and issue them only with the King's authorization. This allows them to control the levels of people, and reduce the number of dangerous criminals."

"I sent a request, but I doubt it will lead anywhere," Victor said.

"Otherwise, I believe Your Majesty will have to find one by conquering dungeons, fulfilling quests, or buy one on the black market."

Vainqueur frowned. "Corpseling, repeat the last sentence."

"Since Crests often find their ways through the government's grasp, Your Majesty could buy one the Black Market for a sizeable sum."

Yes, that was indeed the word he used. *Buying.* Even thinking of it made Vainqueur sick. "So I must destroy more Furibons to earn a Crest," he said, refusing to entertain the other possibilities.

"Your Majesty may also contact the fomors if they are desperate," Jules said. "The fomor Mag Mell created artificial items called Dark Crests, which break the level ceiling, but come with dangerous side-effects."

The fomors? Those upstart fairies who pretended they had created the world when obviously dragons did it first? Vainqueur despised them as much as he did the lich. "Could a quest with a princess yield a Crest?"

"I'm afraid I cannot say. Crests are generated by the system without warning."

"Minion Victor, we will try to fetch a Crest while hunting princesses."

"Princess*es*?" Manling Victor picked up. "With an s?"

"I need three princesses now," Vainqueur confirmed with a serious tone.

"What?" Manling Victor once again proved terrible at math. "Three princesses? Why?"

"Because my hated rival Icefang has caught twins," Vainqueur said, the mere thought of that frost dragon outdoing him driving him mad. "I will not be overshadowed at my own Bragging Day, so I will have *three* princesses to parade."

Manling Victor put a hand on his face for some reason, before sighing, "Unfortunately, Brandon Maure has no daughter, so we can't kidnap her."

"Minion, it is not kidnapping, it is capture. A true dragon has enough class not to kidnap baby princesses." Also, Vainqueur heard they cried all the time.

"Your Majesty, quests with one princess are rare, let alone three of them."

"Minion, you are my grand dragon vizier, my second-in-command, and the warden of Furibon," the dragon reminded his minion. "I push you hard because I know you will rise to the occasion."

Manling Victor stared blankly at his beloved master, awed by the positive reinforcement. "Hm, thanks, Your Majesty."

"You are welcome, minion," Vainqueur replied, "If needed, we will capture these princesses separately instead of as a set. Also, we have a quest specialist in town. Ask her."

After his coronation, the adventurer guild had finally cleared that mess with Vainqueur's last noble meal, with a guildhall manager settling in Murmurin and granting them iron plates to replace the copper.

The manlings had sent Manling Charlene, whose skin was constantly red, and her mood always foul.

Vainqueur didn't know the reason, but this should make her more open to breeding with Manling Victor, which was why he encouraged his minion to spend time with her. The dragon was losing patience with his chief minion's inability to sire a new litter of minions, the only black spot on his otherwise perfect record.

"Charlene is never in a good mood when she sees me," Manling Victor said. "Also, while I am all for chasing princesses, we have a much more urgent matter to deal with. Namely, the *food*."

"Have you not already started solving this problem?" Vainqueur climbed out of the lava, peeking over the crater's edge with his head. "Look at how greener it is!"

While the lands right next to the volcano were somewhat fertile, the region was too dry to feed Vainqueur's guests for Bragging Day. So Minion Victor, ever the perfect Doer of the Thing, organized a great greening project with the added minion workforce. Gnolls dug canals from the sea and towards Murmurin, while kobolds gathered trees which provided shade for grass; Rolo the steel golem had taught them how to use devices called spades, which could also be used to mine gold.

Vainqueur almost regretted firing him.

"Rolo and Allison plant trees, while the minions build irrigation canals or pits to draw water from the mountain's underground sources," Manling Victor said. "According to Rolo, we need magical plants which thrive on sandy soil and will remove the salt from saltwater. We also experimented with seawater greenhouses for agriculture—"

"Minion," Vainqueur interrupted him. "Twenty-five is not fifty. Try to make shorter sentences."

The manling blinked. "How did you count them? Anyway, what I mean to say is, based on Your Majesty's average diet, and accounting for excesses, we need at least *two hundred and fifty tons of meat* for Bragging Day, and that is a conservative estimation."

Corpseling Jules counted in his head. "So, roughly two thousand and five hundred well-fed sheep, or four hundred cows, per day."

"Sheeps, with a s," Vainqueur corrected him.

The corpseling didn't understand Vainqueur, which reminded the dragon why he needed a translator with animals. "Your Majesty, the plural of sheep is sheep."

"Of course not," Vainqueur replied, educating the minion. "How else could you tell one sheep from many? This would be confusing."

"Your Majesty, I insist—"

"I am a dragon. You will say sheeps, or you will be sheep."

Jules said nothing, with Manling Victor putting a hand on his back and shaking his head. "Still, Your Majesty," the chief of staff said. "We don't have the means to feed our own minion population, let alone so many dragons."

"Minions, you fail to notice the perfectly good rations building my castle," Vainqueur said, eying the gnolls and the werewolves. Only the kobolds, he couldn't bear to sacrifice and would have to hide from his kindred. "Also, that way, it means less mouths to feed."

"I would rather not," Manling Victor said.

"Then summon fiends. They are plentiful if rancid and bitter."

"At this rate, I think we will depopulate Hell faster than Heaven ever did. Your Majesty, we need more resources, more food, than we can provide right now. I'm using everything we have, even having Jules scour the countryside to revive decades old corpses as undead labor, and two moons is still too short a time window."

"Well, Victor, since you use seawater greenhousing, you must accumulate a lot of salt, do you not?" corpseling Jules said, "It is highly sought after, especially to slow down zombie degradation. I can use my contacts with Gardemagne to exchange them for fresh meat."

"And you shall be granted a one one-tenth commission," Vainqueur encouraged the corpseling.

"I've also been toying with other activities to build funds," Manling Victor crossed his arms, "Since Your Majesty forbids taxes, and keeps the underground vaults, they could keep deposits safe from thieves for a cut."

Vainqueur glanced at his minion with a knowing look. "No manling in their right mind would try to steal from a dragon, is that what you imply?"

"I didn't know Your Majesty was alive!" the minion protested.

Vainqueur considered the proposition. Protecting the hoards of the world appealed to him, but on the other hand, it went against his dragon instinct to keep those of others without seizing them as his own. It sounded a lot like being a banker, which was a manling absurdity. "Are we that desperate for meat?" he asked his chief of staff.

"Yes. Yes, we *are*."

Vainqueur didn't believe it. They were desperate for meat to feed both his guests and the minions. If they sacrificed the latter, they would satisfy the former.

However, he could see that Manling Victor was desperate to save as many of them as possible; and Vainqueur had grown attached to a few of them, especially the Kobold Rangers.

After the torture he suffered from Furibon and his hard work, Vainqueur decided to indulge his chief of staff. He would make a sacrifice for Bragging Day. "Then no hoard shall be left defenseless in my empire. Minions and hoarders may send me their treasures if they fear for their safety, and I shall protect them from the Furibons of the world."

*Congratulations! For showing a sliver of true nobility and understanding a true leader often puts his minions' well-being first, you have gained a level in [**Kaiser**].*

+30 HP, +10 SP, +1 STR, +1 SKI, +1 VIT, +1 INT, +1 CHA!

A *sliver* of nobility?

"Well, now we are officially dragon Switzerland," Manling Victor said, although Vainqueur didn't understand the last word.

"I also declare that all creatures dying within my service will be reanimated to work as sentient undead, as were the Kobold Rangers," Vainqueur decided. "No need for death to end their fulfilling jobs. They shall serve me in death, as well as in life."

"I do not raise thinking undead for ethical reasons, and Your Majesty will need size—"

"I will take care of that," Manling Victor said, putting a hand on Jules' shoulder. "But can I get an exception, Your Majesty?"

"Minion, you will not die on my watch unless we run out of other minions and I starve," Vainqueur said, before remembering the fragile manlings could die of old age.

"While I will not do the deed, I can ask a less ethical colleague to bring you back as a thinking undead, Victor," corpseling Jules proposed, although his chief of staff didn't seem so keen on the idea, "A vampire, or a ghoul? Perhaps even a lich, if you are ready to make a live sacrifice to Camil—"

"No lich!" Vainqueur snarled, making the crater tremble. "Minion, I forbid you from becoming a lich!"

"I would rather live longer as a living creature, than forever as an undead," said Victor.

But come to think of it, Manling Victor was indeed mortal and fragile. Vainqueur had already almost lost him to Furibon. They would need to solve that problem as soon as possible before he suffered a tragic minion death. "Manling Victor, how long do Manlings live?"

"I dunno, eighty years?" Vainqueur laughed at the paltry number, the minion frowning. "Some of us reach one hundred!"

"You can calculate your longevity with your Health Point, Victor," said Jules, "Take your maximum Health Points, then divide it by six; if you have aging resistance, you can double it, as you age two times slower. Other elements increase longevity or outright grant immunity to aging, such as the 'Claimed by Sablar' perk or the Undead Type."

The minion did the calculation, as did Vainqueur. "Two hundred forty-five?" was the number his chief of staff came up with. "I can live up to two hundred forty-five?"

"And I shall live to two thousand years," Vainqueur boasted, before realizing the problem. "A dragon *can* die of old age?"

"There is little chance for anyone to die of old age," said the corpseling. "According to my research, you have a fifty to sixty percent chance of dying by violence in Outremonde, either in battle or from depredation, and twenty percent to sickness."

"That will not be a problem for us," Vainqueur replied with confidence, but he found the number worrying. Two hundred and a half was very short. "Minion."

"Yes?"

"Find a way to become immortal. You still have too much work to do."

25: The Regent

"Hi, Charlene." Victor waved at the poor office manager, as he rode through the town square while on top of his new mount, the Black Beast of Murmurin. "What's up?"

The guild manager glared back at him. Her 'office' was composed of a board, a desk, and a chair in the middle of the town's square, gnolls and kobolds often checking the few requests available.

Murmurin had grown thrice-fold since the 'War of the Hoard', with minions building more houses or tents to accommodate newcomers. A giant stone statue of Vainqueur stood in the middle of the town, with Vainqueur Junior buried underground right next to it, ready to ambush anyone trying to pull the false sword.

They had been forced to equip the locals with axes and spears, or otherwise, Junior became jealous and tried to eliminate the competition. Even Victor's rapier had suffered his envious wrath.

Since he reaped most benefits by wielding a scythe, Victor gave Red Ranger the musket which he stole from Vilmain. The raptor had proven himself an incredibly deadly shot, gaining [Gunslinger] levels at a pace that surprised even the chief of staff. The Kobold Rangers had become the official sheriffs of Murmurin, keeping the monsters in line. In fact, they had even started taking requests from Charlene as official members of V&V, chasing rogue monsters who didn't submit to the 'Emperor's' authority.

They had a pretty effective strategy too. The weaker rangers ganged up on and exhausted the troublemaker, and then Red swooped in to deliver a finishing blow.

Kobolds being kobolds, they surrendered their gains to Vainqueur all the time.

"I hate you," Charlene told him, clearly not happy to be here. Since she was the most familiar with V&V, having named them, the higher-ups had transferred her to Murmurin instead of someone else. "I hate you and that dragon so much."

"No need to be snappy," Victor replied. "I'm still sore about that iron plate. Our company destroyed an ancient lich who killed gold-plated adventurers, and we're not even bronze?"

"They took the politically safe path with your company. I wonder *why*."

Since civilized species feared Vainqueur, only other monsters and unsavory characters had started moving into Murmurin. Which meant only monsters or close enough creatures like Jules the ghoul made up the company, and with his new Perk, even Victor counted as one now.

They were the first fully-inclusive monster adventurer company.

"Also, just feel thankful I let you keep your adventurer fee behind Vainqueur's back," he told Charlene. "No tax, so spoke the Emperor."

"I wouldn't even be here if you hadn't told that dragon about classes and levels."

"If it had been anyone else getting that rapier, Vainqueur would have destroyed the nearby villages in his fury," Victor pointed out, before glancing at the board. "We're looking for princess-oriented quests. With three princesses, and which would make Brandon Maure's life miserable if possible. Do you have any?"

She gave him the 'are you serious' look, then twitched upon realizing he wasn't. She stared at him blankly, then turned around, seized an isolated request on the board, then gave it to him.

'The Demon King's Captive

Rank: Gold.

Giver: King Roland Gardemagne.

Brandon Maure is a fiend infamous for collecting foreign beauties as trophies. Imperial princesses from the fallen Sablaris empire, noble ladies from the Harmonian League... and the king's own niece, Princess Merveille, abducted as a child during the war and kept as a political hostage. The King offers a boon to the rescuer of Merveille, so long as it is within the bounds of reason.'

"A harem? Maure kidnaps women as brides?"

"No, of course not. He sacrifices them to demons for power." Yeah, somehow that made it sound better. "Maure has captive princesses kept in his capital of Mauria, so if you want to die to the demon king, please consider picking it up."

Like the salt of the earth, Croissant joined them, aiming for Victor, but his eyes getting sidetracked upon catching sight of Charlene. "Oh," Croissant looked at the office manager like an appetizing meal. "Vic, you didn't tell me you knew such a pretty woman."

The guild manager smiled, slightly charmed. "Thank you."

"I love mature women with lots of meat on them." Victor shuddered at the wording, while Croissant put an arm on the guild's counter. "What's your name, pretty one?"

"Charlene."

"I'm Croissant. I run this town."

"He *did*," Victor clarified, the werewolf glaring at him. This just encouraged the adventurer. "Now he's run *over*."

"Did they ruin your life too?" Charlene asked Croissant, giving him a sympathetic look.

"Like you wouldn't believe." The werewolf returned to his flirting. "Why don't I give you a tour of the place, especially the spots the dragon doesn't know about yet?"

Charlene's mood improved tremendously. "This town may not be so bad after all."

Yep, they would end up together. Although Victor still wondered if Croissant intended to eat her or flirt; maybe even both. "Before I vomit on Charlene's counter, why are you here Croissant?"

"Savoureuse has brought a newcomer and is waiting for you at the town's entrance, and Sis and Allison have a problem with a summoned demon who won't let himself get killed at the temple. This' gonna sound strange, but that woman outside creeps me out more than the demon."

Victor would have loved to say this was the weirdest problem he had to deal with in Murmurin, but it wasn't. At all. He sighed, then had his monster walk to the town's entrance.

He found Savoureuse talking with a woman his age whose raven hair was tied with a white flower; she wore some kind of university uniform, and felt, for lack of a better word, off-putting.

"Hey, Vic!" Savoureuse waved at him. "How are you? I hope work isn't stressful."

"Not as stressful as getting kidnapped by a lich while you watched," Victor replied with heavy sarcasm.

"Yes, but my life was in danger," Savoureuse said. "I could not help."

Yeah, right. Why was he friends with her again? For the food, he decided. And maybe the Crests, if she could smuggle one as he asked her to. If only Furibon had left one behind, but he had sent all of those found in the region to Brandon Maure to empowering his soldiers.

His eyes settled on the newcomer. "And who might you be?"

"Remember the woman I told you about?" Savoureuse asked, slightly embarrassed. "This is her."

"My name is Lucie Lavere, of the Royal University of Gardemagne," the newcomer said with a formal, professional posture. "I heard a lot about you and your master, Lord Victor."

"Oh? From whom?" According to Savoureuse, this woman belonged to the Nightblades, and so she was bad news.

"Many, but especially my new friend Henry. Since the debacle with the Scorchers, I keep an eye on him so he does not get into trouble."

Somehow, her tone implied something sinister... which it probably was. "Are you here to keep an eye on us too?" Victor asked, suspicious.

"Depends. Are you going to meddle with the wrong crowd?"

The conversation had taken a sharp turn towards the tense. He could play the game too. "Not unless you do it first."

"I will not." She smiled at him, but behind the smirk, there were sharp teeth. "I choose my friends carefully, and I think you may be a trustworthy, reliable fellow."

He immediately used [Monster Insight] on her.

Lucie Sinistra Lavere

Alchemical Vampire (Undead/Humanoid)

Strong against Sunlight, Moon, Alchemy, Darkness, Unholy, Blood, Frost, Necromancy, Drain, Insta-Death, Mind-Control, Disease, Poison, Fatigue, Sleep, and Beast (Boss Undead, huh?).

Weak against Holy, Fire, Life, Berserk, Manslayer, and Deadslayer.

The archmage Nostredame's prized student and top spy. Secretly a deadly monster lord and the criminal mastermind behind the Nightblades syndicate. She's Evil with a capital E, MUCH stronger than anyone in Murmurin except Vainqueur, and currently reading your thoughts with creepy undead mind-reading. She knows you know.

In short, thou art BLEEPed.

"Interesting Perk that you have," the woman said, amused.

"How the hell can you walk under the sun?" Victor asked, his hand reaching for his scythe while Savoureuse watched, disturbed.

"Fairy flowers, gifted from one of my teachers," she replied, caressing the flower in her hair with her fingers. "I am repaying the favor by carrying some politically-minded tasks."

"Savoureuse told me you asked the Nightblades to support the Scorchers," Victor put the two and two together, growing more and more uneasy. "You are the one who handed Henry to Gustave and Vilmain. Are you working for Ishfania?"

"Sometimes. Sometimes, I work for Gardemagne. Nostredame asked me to report on your new 'empire.'" The name amused her as much as it did Vic. "But do not worry, I have no intention of bothering you. Unlike that lich in your scythe, I am not stupid enough to pick a fight with a dragon."

'In hindsight, I would not recommend it, no,' Furibon whispered from in the scythe, annoyed.

"I have come for Nightblade business alone. We are looking for a warehouse that could serve as a relay for our black market endeavors. If you agree to leave us alone, so will I. I will even turn a blind eye to your desertion. You know the usual punishment."

"Are you threatening me?" Victor wasn't amused. "No repossession here, or waste disposal, or Vainqueur will have you killed."

"Certainly," Lavere said. "Who in their right mind would try stealing from a dragon?"

Victor glanced away.

"You were." The vampire chuckled. "Oh my, how far you have gone since then. You have even learned necromancy. Perhaps I could even give you... private lessons."

Was she flirting or threatening him? Victor couldn't tell and didn't want to. In any case, she was creeping him out like nobody else ever did.

"As a token of good faith, I will tell you a secret," Lavere said. "After you took out Furibon, Brandon Maure has decided to get off his throne and come for you personally. Expect an ambush in the near future."

Well, that made attacking him in his capital a preemptive counterattack then. "Sav, give her the official history of Murmurin, 'The War of the Hoard.' It has been transcribed from our emperor's mouth to paper by our scribe, Pink Ranger, and then duplicated by mimic printing presses."

Creatures capable of transforming in nearly any items had turned out surprisingly useful, once Victor could provide them directions. He would order one of them to keep an eye on that woman while she stayed in town.

"It won't work," Lavere replied, reading his mind, before taking her leave with Savoureuse. "See you soon, *Vic*."

Victor rode to the village's main temple a lot less confident than before.

The temple the gods Isengrim and Cybele shared wasn't a temple as much as a druidic circle, ten olive trees circling two statues of the deities. Isengrim was represented as a white deer whose horns ended in blades, with the goddess Cybele was an incredibly beautiful woman, with flowers for hair, vines for a dress, and horns of wood.

Victor climbed down his undead ride, who Allison had forbidden inside the area, and walked inside the circle. He found his fellow earthling and Chocolatine keeping watch over a huge prisoner.

The priests had trapped a demon in a circle of runes, a huge, bipedal, insectoid monster with ice plates for an exoskeleton and sapphires for eyes. The creature looked big and nasty enough to tear Victor in half with its two pincers. He immediately used [Monster Insight] on the fiend.

Malfaisant

Bug Demon (Demon/Insect)

Strong against Unholy, Frost, Water, Physical, Disease, Poison, Critical Hits, Petrify, Bug, and Swarms.

Weak against Fire, Holy, Demonslayer, and Bugslayer.

An ice demon with unconventional ideas and a greedy streak that rivals dragons. Local manager of one of Hell's corporations, Infercorp, which is a completely legitimate business mindful of post-mortem customer safety. Has come to investigate the 'demon slaughterhouse.'

"Vic, there you are." Allison glared at Chocolatine. "She summoned that thing in the temple, and now I cannot give offerings to my goddess properly."

"It was an accident!" the young werewolf retorted. "I intended to summon an imp like always, but a major demon came through instead!"

"Three hundred lesser fiends went missing after using your summoning line, and my superiors sent me to investigate," the demon rasped with a smarmy voice, glancing at Victor. "Are you the legitimate authority? The Grand Dragon Vizier Victor Dalton?"

"Lord Victor for short." He was sick of his full, pompous title. "Malfaisant, is it? Your kindred had... how to say it, dragon accidents, and then were recycled."

"I do not follow."

Victor pointed at animated demon skeletons building up a house next to the druidic circle, the bug fiend looking at them, then at Victor, then back at the undead. "You killed my kind, to raise them as mindless slaves?"

Victor cringed at the wording but nodded, as the demon's cold eyes peered into his soul. "You mortals say Hell is other people, but they are wrong. Hell is people like *you*."

The fact it came from a goddamn demon made it all the more shameful.

"Which is to say, Hell *needs* people like you." The demon's tone turned admirative, much to Victor's confusion. "People who *care* about the *bottom line*. About profit. Mortals who are ready to sully their hand for *their* greater good."

"Wait, you're not mad?"

"Please, Lord Victor, call me Malfy," the demon replied with a charming voice. "No, I am not mad. In fact, I misjudged you. I feared that you were cunning demon hunters, but you have the trappings of a good business partner. Let's make a deal."

"So I can keep summoning demons for more food?" Chocolatine asked, hopeful.

"Not in the temple!" Allison chided her. "And no!"

"But we have more carnivores than meat! We cannot sustain our ecological niche without sacrifices!"

Her argument surprised Victor, who found it rather well-thought out. Not that the demon cared. "I will reroute the summoning channel to send you victims of corporate downsizing and violent layoffs. By having you deal with the severance package, we can cut corners on our execution costs and you get free labor. Everybody wins."

Victor wanted to be horrified at the sheer callousness, before realizing he should have expected something like that from a hellspawn.

"Lord Victor, since you seem interested in economically developing your region, I have *fantastic* opportunities for you. Succubus brothels, casinos..."

"You are seriously asking me for *Hell's* permission to invest there?" Victor asked, dumbfounded.

"Taking over the mortal world by force? Treacherously twisting the terms of Faustian bargains? It damages our PR, and Angels have a killer marketing department. If we want to improve our shareholders' soul dividends, we must offer clear deals where mortals are so happy with our customer service, that they convince their friends and families to sell their souls too. 'Buying souls by doing good business.' That's my motto."

Victor had more urgent matters to deal with than vague corporate promises. Also, **Hell**. "We picked a fight with the local Demon King's forces."

"Brandon Maure? His mother runs a demon corporation different from ours. We often cooperate on joint-ventures on Outremonde, but there is no love lost between us."

That made it better, but just barely. "If you want to come, you have to bring food, do whatever labor we ask of you, and respect the law, which includes no lead. In return, you won't pay taxes."

"No taxes?" The demon's head perked up. "This is way better than I thought. I will gladly use my control swarm ability to assist with food production. Part of the revenue from our ventures will also find their way to your pockets, alongside VIP privileges."

"Are you bribing me in public?"

"No, of course not, I donate to the community."

Yes, a bribe. Victor would keep one one-tenth for himself and send the rest to Vainqueur, to avoid trouble.

"I would expect a demon to stay in Ishfania," Allison said, doubtful.

"'King' Maure imposed a heavy tax in order to fund 'the inevitable war of annihilation against Gardemagne.' Now, human sacrifices and slave gladiator combats, I can get behind. But losing two-thirds of my hard-won savings? Never!"

Charming. "Is he telling the truth?" Victor asked Chocolatine.

"It's a circle of demon binding, he is forced to," the werewolf said, before joining her hands. "Please, please, say yes."

Victor rolled his eyes, before considering it. They needed food and money that much, and he had already stepped as low as selling corpses for money. On the other hand, he was wary to give a demon a permanent residency in Murmurin, even one promising to behave.

"Okay, at least for the demon downsizing," he decided, Malfy letting out a happy sound and Chocolatine smirking with cruelty. "But summon demons outside the town next time. For the... investments... I need to consider it more thoughtfully."

"I will return to Hell and come back with a proposal from management. Thank you for your trust." Malfy vanished in a cloud of white smoke, the circle following afterward.

"Thank you, Vic," Allison congratulated him. "I don't know what I would do without you. You just ooze authority now."

"I'm still trying to get the Earl Jones tone right," Victor joked, "Like 'You have failed me for the last time.'"

"You sound like Tim Curry, more creepy than awesome."

"Okay, I'll try again. 'The emperor is not as forgiving as I am.'" Which was true.

"No, seriously," she laughed at his performance. "Stop, it sounds ridiculous."

Victor had quite a fun time hanging out with Allison, talking about Earth, about their respective experiences, and life in general. She wasn't that different from him; she died a stupid death by causing an explosion while tinkering with a car's fuel reserve and adapted to the new world in spite of being surrounded by monsters.

She liked gardening and was very passionate about making the desert green again. Her partner, Rolo, couldn't be bothered to do anything but gathering seeds and disdained everything else. Much like a certain other creature...

He could definitely feel a connection brewing. "Hey, Allison..." Victor plucked up his courage. "Would you like to have that drink tonight?"

"I'm kind of fully booked with the orgy, but we can try tomorrow. Is tomorrow okay?"

That wasn't the answer Victor expected. "You are *breeding* with other people?"

"What? No." She looked at him strangely. "I am a vestal of the goddess of pleasure, and the Moon Man cult is organizing an orgy. Since our cults are friendly, I have been asked to help with protective spells."

"And you... you participate?"

"Vic, this is an orgy for *werewolves*. During the *full moon*."

His brain betrayed him and provided him with a mental picture. It felt like an ice shower. "I'm sorry, I need to go out," he blurted out, struggling to breathe. "I need air."

"We are outside Vic... Vic?" Allison called him, as he fled the druidic ring. "Vic, what's up?"

Victor's mind blocked out her words, as the picture wouldn't leave his mind. Goddammit, now he would need to drown himself in work to forget! He climbed on the back of his ride, ready to return to the castle when he noticed Chocolatine following him outside. "Yes?"

"So, mm, Victor, about that orgy..." Chocolatine gave him a cheery smile.

"Do you want to breed?"

Victor gave her a blank, empty stare that should have made her drop dead. She took it as encouragement. "It's okay, I'm on the pill. No full moon transformation. We can put that Monster Rider Perk to gooooood use."

Okay, that was too many details, too soon. She skipped a *lot* of steps. "I didn't know you saw me that way..." said the adventurer, unsure how to answer without her slicing his throat in his sleep.

"I didn't either until you killed that lich with your scythe," she swooned, putting her hands on her cheeks, "The way you rode that undead beast and trapped his soul for eternal torment... and the way you showed that demon who was the boss..."

Victor suddenly realized that his monster-oriented Perks combined with his increased charisma meant monsters may see him as quite the catch. All that time he had failed at pursuing human women when he should have asked out werewolves instead.

On one hand, she was cute, and somewhat nice when demons and undead weren't involved; but on the other hand, she was *Chocolatine*. And the crazy gleam in her eyes...

...

No. *Definitely* not. "I'm sorry, but, I don't want to ruin our friendship," Victor lied, leaving her crestfallen.

No way he would BEEP her except to save the human race.

Even Victor had standards.

26: Dragon Profiling

Sand. Sand. Sand.

Walking cactus!

Oh, it was dead.

Sand. Sand. Sand…

Vainqueur forced himself not to fall asleep out of boredom in the middle of the flight. He was sick of this endless desert, carrying his chief of staff in one hand, and a big, goatskin bag for princesses in the other. "Why am I flying invisible again?" the dragon asked his minion, who had insisted Vainqueur use his 'Blinkblink' ring. "And why didn't we bring the other minions?"

"Because otherwise Brandon Maure will have us shot on sight, and my [Cowl of the Reaper] grants me some camouflage." The minion sounded tired, and just as bored as his master. "It's better to travel light."

"Minion, I meant why I should care if that fiend notices?"

"Because we are on a princess rescue mission, which means we need to be discreet. Otherwise, Maure will evacuate them elsewhere, and we may not know where this time."

At long last, Vainqueur finally noticed their destination when he squinted his eyes at the horizon.

A rock the size of the Albain mountains' tallest peak floated above the desert, a fortress-city built from red, bloody bricks; greenish stones below the flying structure released a whirlwind of swirling sandstorms keeping the city afloat. Vainqueur noticed a few flying creatures patrolling the skies near it, each of whom would make for passable snacks.

Instead of rejoicing at finally reaching their destination, Manling Victor let out a heavy, crushed sigh.

"Minion, why are you so down?" Manling Victor also sounded a lot less enthusiastic about this adventure than Vainqueur thought he would. Come to think of it, he hadn't argued about Vainqueur bringing a princess bag, while the minion usually worried about everything. "Have you bred yet?"

"No. I tried." The minion sighed, crestfallen. "But as it turns out, Allison likes girls..."

The dryad? "Minion, I am not that strict about minion harassment. You have my imperial permission to bestow your eggs on Manling Charlene, for example."

"I'm pretty sure Croissant got there first."

"Then eat him." Vainqueur would have sworn the minion looked up at his master in confusion, but he couldn't tell with the cowl. "You are a chief of staff, he is below you in the food chain. If he bothers you, eat him. I have never devoured a werewolf before, but they must taste like a cerberus, strong and thick."

"Your Majesty has eaten cerberi?"

"When I fought the fomors as a young wyrm with the rest of dragonkind. They kept sending monsters like cerberi to die to me back in those days." Eventually, the fairy lords paid Vainqueur and his kin a large tribute of gold as an apology for falsely claiming to have created the world first.

Speaking of food, what was that scent in the wind? "I can sense we are being followed." Vainqueur hummed the air. "It smells like a big bird, with a manling on its back."

"Huh? We should be wary, it could be one of Maure's men—"

"[Solar Judgment!]"

A beam of light hit Vainqueur in the back by surprise, the blast making him crash into the dry sand below.

[Solar Judgment] *bypassed your* *[Fire Immunity]! You have taken heavy damage!*

Once again, he felt that itchy sensation... "Minion, I do not feel well in my back," Vainqueur said, opening his palm to find his chief of staff safe and sound. "What is this?"

"I think that it is pain, Your Majesty!"

Pain? Of course not, only mammals suffered from it.

Vainqueur glanced up at the one responsible for his back itches, a manling knight in heavy green armor. The treacherous creature rode the back of a golden lion, with the head, wings, and talons of an eagle.

A griffon! And an adult, meaty one at that!

"I doubted your guilt until I scanned your classes, Victor. [Monster Squire] and [Reaper]!" The knight pointed a shining blade at Vainqueur, who could tell it was a cursed fairy work meant to kill dragons. According to the voice, the knight was a female manling. "The unholy scion of a thief of souls and a necromancer, with a dash of scum! And your perks! [Helheim], [Channel Hellfire]! You reek of evil!"

"That armor..." the minion trailed, as the dust settled. "Holy shit, level sixty-six?"

"I am Kia Bekele, the Shining Knight of Gardemagne! Prepare to die, miscreants!"

Annoyed at the greenish knight not announcing his imperial name next, Vainqueur just blasted the bird out the skies with a fireball.

"[Bravewind!]" Much to the dragon's surprise, the bird and its rider flew out of the way of his flames, carried by strong winds. They dived down as Vainqueur kept trying to blast them, moving at speeds that even the dragon had a hard time following. Before he knew what hit him, the knight slashed at Vainqueur between the neck and the shoulder, cutting a scale.

*[**Arondight**] inflicted doubly effective [Fairy] [Dragonslayer] damage!*

Like that damn lich, the knight and her flying cattle retreated before the dragon could poke them. Manling Victor tried to assist his master by blasting bluish hellfire at their foe, but she flew out of range and made a circle in the skies. Vainqueur suddenly wondered how she could notice him while invisible, with a glance telling him the sand on his body revealed his position.

Above, the knight moved to dive back, shining under the sunlight.

That female manling was eager to make Vainqueur live up to his name. "Minion, stay there," Vainqueur ordered his manling, putting him on the ground with the princess bag. "I will take flight and deal with this flying snack personally."

"Your Majesty, she's the strongest adventurer in Mistral, and the slayer of King Balaur! Don't underestimate her!"

"Balaur?" For once, this made Vainqueur pause. "The fomor?"

A mere manling riding a flying cow took down *Balaur*, the *second* greatest calamity of this age? When?

"[Spell Purge]!" Vainqueur snarled, revealing himself in his full draconic glory as his Perk negated his ring's invisibility. "Fear my wrath, manling knight! You face Emperor Vainqueur Knightsbane, First of his name, Great Calamity of this Age,

Emperor of Murmurin and the Albain Mountains, and Slayer of Furibon!"

"I know about the lich," the knight said, raising her blade. "I would say thanks since we never got around to killing him before, but—"

"You knew about Furibon?" Vainqueur glared at the knight, suddenly outraged. "And you did *nothing*? Do you know what he was doing in that dungeon? Do you *know*?"

The knight paused, halting her descent. "Excuse me?"

"I am sure he must have sacrificed hundreds of baby princesses to prepare that dread, foul, evil spell! He was about to release it on the world before *I* stopped him! Do you know what he made me suffer through? The bloody war I had to fight? The sacrifices I had to make? Do you *know*?"

"Uh, no, I—"

"You would, if you were cultured enough to read *The War of the Hoard*!" Vainqueur kept ranting. "My minion was abducted and tortured by Furibon! The lich stole his vegetable and forced him to eat baby coins!"

"Your Majesty, maybe you are exaggerating there..."

"My minion risked his life to seal that foul lich's soul away!" Vainqueur ignored his chief of staff and kept shaming the knight, who had lowered her sword. "We had to fight a horde of three hundred demons until he could become strong enough to imprison that depraved monster!"

"I, I..." The knight struggled to find her words when faced with her obvious incompetence. "I'm... I'm sorry, I didn't know..."

"I am sick and tired of you manlings' speciesism!" Vainqueur vented off. "I am being the best dragon adventurer to your backward species, and you deny me my rightful payments when I solve your problems! You even send thieves after my hoard, even after I worked hard to save the one true way of life from Furibon!"

"Your Majesty always says all species are equally inferior to dragons," Manling Victor reminded his master.

"Which is a *fact*, not a silly superstition!" Vainqueur replied, the knight now silent as her griffon looked up at her in confusion. "And your species' attitude has done nothing to change my opinion! *I* saved everything good in the world from Furibon!"

"Also, attacking us after using a magical scan, just because I have monster classes and Vainqueur is a dragon?" Minion Victor shouted at the knight. "It's called racial profiling!"

"It's... it's not!" the knight protested feebly. "Two secs. [Enhanced Karma Scan]."

"You are doing it again!" Victor accused her, as light words appearing in front of her helmet while she looked at both Vainqueur and his lackey.

"No, I'm not!" she protested, the words quickly vanishing. "Okay, I have checked your karma, with both of you being neutral, with the dragon very much oriented towards chaotic and Dalton tending towards good."

"Dalton?" Vainqueur squinted at his minion.

"That's my family name," the manling said, Vainqueur realizing he never even considered his lackey may have one. "Also, neutral... isn't that a polite name for bland?"

"Enough talk!" Vainqueur extended his wings. "I will kill you, Knight Kia, and eat your flying cattle for your treacherous attack."

"I, uh... I don't think it will be necessary for us to fight, I jumped the gun," the knight said, casting a spell. "Sorry, [Rain of Healing]."

A shower of golden powder fell on Vainqueur and his lackey, with the dragon attempting to grab the gold on instinct; the powder vanished on touch but made his back stop itching.

You have recovered all your HP!

"I deeply apologize," the knight said, although she stayed at a respectable distance. "I mistook for villains, instead of the goodish mercenary type. I can't believe I never imagined you would be that kind of heroes."

"It happens all the time," Manling Victor said with surprising warmth.

"Minion, you will reproduce with someone else," Vainqueur lambasted him for his skewed priorities, the minion lowering his head in shame while the knight recoiled. "She attacked me, and she will pay me a tribute as apology. I demand no less than five griffins as reparation."

"Your Majesty, I do not think that is a good idea. She must be almost as strong as you, and we have princesses to save."

"Minion, a true dragon has no equal," Vainqueur replied, unwilling to let it slide. Even if she had killed Balaur, he was only the second greatest calamity behind the dragon. Vainqueur had *earned* that title.

"Princesses to save?" The knight interrupted. "Princess Merveille? You intended to go to Mauria and rescue Princess Merveille?"

"Her and all the other princesses Maure captured," Manling Victor spoke up.

"And you... and you will keep them for yourself?" asked the Shining Knight, her hold over her sword wavering.

"Of course not, do you take me for one of these horrible humanophiles?" Vainqueur shuddered in disgust. "I will release them back in the wild once I am done, and your Manling King has granted me the promised boon for their rescue."

"About it, Your Majesty hasn't told me how much they intended to ask for," Manling Victor pointed out.

That was because Vainqueur had an idea for a special gift. If that manling king proved unable to deliver, then the dragon wouldn't ask anything less than one million coins or a hundred thousand jewels, to add to his current hoard.

"Okay, we are on the same page." The knight had her griffon land on the ground in front of Vainqueur. "I deeply apologize for my uncalled attack, but I'm not giving up my griffon. However, if you agree, I could make it up by helping you in your quest."

Vainqueur squinted at the griffon, who glared back at him. "I am listening," he said, in case that knight could be helpful in carrying his princesses to Murmurin.

"First, I have to ask, do you intend to fight Maure yourselves? Because I can't support it."

"Why? Because it would be dangerous?" Minion Victor asked.

"What? No, it would be *amazing*, and I insist on coming along." The manling sounded positively giddy. "I've been trying to convince my party for months to kick that foppish demon bastard's ass, and they always delay. Same with the lich. If we had known he worked a foul magic which threatened the world..."

"Your feeble mind cannot imagine the depth of Furibon's depravity," Vainqueur said grimly. "He was pure evil, the kind that existed for itself. He was unliving *lead*."

"For a dragon to say that... I'm not going to ask for the gory details. Is that his soul in the scythe?" The knight looked up at the Manling Victor's weapon, "I see... you took that cursed Reaper class because it was the only way to defeat the lich. It must have been a difficult choice."

"You could say that..."

The green knight removed her helmet, and Vainqueur squinted, for it was the first time he saw a manling with skin so dark and hair that did not look ugly. Manling Victor stood in place speechless, while his master wasn't impressed. She didn't smell like a princess.

"I'm Kia. Kia Bekele. Sorry to have shot you out of the sky." She put a hand through her hair. "You both have a terrible reputation."

"Canihaveyourautograph?" Manling Victor spoke so fast that even Vainqueur's imperial ears had trouble understanding him. The female manling laughed warmly, amused. "You're the Shining Knight, the greatest paladin in the world! Are you really a Claimed?"

"I am. Came from Ethiopia, although I stayed some time in the United Kingdom." The knight seemed to struggle to find her words, obviously as poor as Manling Victor at pre-breeding conversations. "And you, Victor, where do you come from? Can I call you Victor?"

"Sure! I'm Ame—"

"Manling," Vainqueur let out smoke by his nostrils, annoyed at the knight ignoring him. "How will you make up for the crime of striking the Emperor of Murmurin and the Albain Mountains?"

The knight sheathed her blade and opened her empty palm, a blue, shining, egg-shaped stone materializing within it. "It's an [Agarthan Warp Stone], a one-use item that can teleport you and anyone close back to any place you visited. It even bypasses protections against teleportation effects, such as the barriers protecting the city of Mauria."

"My [Eye for Treasure] tells me this is the genuine article, Your Majesty," said the minion.

"I always carry two of them, just in case," the knight said. "You can use one to transport everyone back to a safer place, safe from Maure."

Oh, and that way Vainqueur wouldn't have to burn fat flying back home! Perfect. "As Emperor of Murmurin and the Albain Mountains, I accept this tribute, and forgive you for your sinful offense against my person. Any other dragon would have killed you for your insolence, but I am generous and magnanimous."

The two manlings exchanged glances. "Dragons," they both said at once before Victor frowned. "You met another?"

"I fought one with my old party. Blightswamp, I think that was her name."

"That pauper living in the boonies?" Vainqueur sneered. "She doesn't even have a cave in her swamp!"

"She had a tar pit before we dislodged her. I don't know where she fled afterward."

She ran from manlings? *Manlings*? And to think he invited her to his own Bragging Day, what was Vainqueur thinking?

It made his celebration all the more important. As far as Vainqueur knew, he was the only one protecting the honor of dragonkind against hordes of liches and peasants. He had to put pride back in the heart of his kin.

"Also, Nostredame's intel woman told me you had lost the Apple of Knowledge to Brandon Maure," the knight asked Minion Victor. "From what I understood, it's an iPad?"

"From a Lockheed Martin engineer," the minion said, the knight frowning. "With schematics to match."

"Alright, it is indeed time to kick Maure's ass. Do not underestimate him. He is eccentric, but nobody survived a duel with him, and he possesses one of the most optimized Fighter Class combinations in the world."

Vainqueur shrugged with contempt. "He is an elf. Elves are cattle, they eat *grass*. I will devour him and then get the princesses."

"Still, don't underestimate him." She turned to the flying rock. "Shall we go?"

27: The Demon King

Vainqueur had to give it to the elves. Unlike the manlings, they kept their lairs clean.

Their flying city was a treat for the eyes, with shiny white stone and marble statues which Vainqueur thought would look great on his hoard. He promised himself to return for groceries after recovering his princesses.

Gargoyles with forks patrolled the city's ramparts, unable to see Vainqueur nor the cattle-riding knight. She too had turned transparent, although the dragon could smell her just fine. "The invisibility will trick lesser fiends, but neither Maure nor his elite guard," Kia the knight whispered. "I wonder why the city is so lightly defended, though. It's usually so full of demons our spies can't even approach it."

"I can smell many fiends nearby," Vainqueur said, humming and looking for his meal. The flight had made him hungry, and he had gotten used to demon flesh. He flew toward the source of the scent, some kind of flying port, with a great metal bird nesting in the middle.

...

That was a big, *big* metal bird.

Many, many times bigger than Vainqueur himself, with great iron wings and iron spikes under them. Demons manned strange devices on its back, which looked like bigger versions of the musket weapon Red the Kobold carried with him. The bird had only one eye made of glass, with fiends and elves hitting it with hammers.

As usual for his puny race, his chief of staff was deeply intimidated by the animal's size. "Holy hell, they broke the iPad's passwords. They built a *bombardier.*"

"It's not a bombardier, it's a flying fortress," the knight said, just as terrified. "It's bigger than the *Titanic*! Do you think it's functional? It looks rough and archaic."

"Dunno, but we've got to destroy it before it takes off."

Only manlings could worry about a bird. Vainqueur would burn and cook the fiends inside, the same way he prepared his training diet. He lazily opened his mouth to rain death on the big fat bird...

Then his [Virgin Princess Radar] activated.

Vainqueur immediately turned his head towards the source of the signal, in the middle of the city. "A princess!" His eyes widened in giddiness. "A princess maiden!"

"Your Majesty, what the—"

Vainqueur, overtaken by his dragon instincts, ignored the metal bird and flew straight towards the princess' location, knocking both the knight's griffon and gargoyles out of the skies. The fiends noticed him as he caused a building to fall after hitting it, immediately sounding horns and bells.

"Knightsbane?" Kia the Manling called Vainqueur from the sky port, who heard but didn't listen. "Knightsbane, Dalton, where are you going?"

"Princess!" the dragon shouted back.

He flew over the elven city, with his wings blowing off houses and fiends off until he found what he was looking for: a massive, circular arena of red brick in the very center of the flying city. Hundreds of elves and fiends had gathered in the stands with food and drinks.

The dragon immediately recognized the princess, chained to a marble pillar in the middle of the sandy ground of the arena.

That creature was the most beautiful pet Vainqueur had ever set his eyes on, a cute animal with pretty green hair fur which would compliment his gold perfectly. Her skin was so pure it reminded Vainqueur of cow's milk, and the fiends had dressed her like a present.

There were other two princesses bound next to her, two elves, but Vainqueur didn't care half as much; they didn't smell like virginal maidens. The one at the center, though, that was the one he wanted, the crown jewel of his Bragging Day! The others would complement her, as he put them on display atop a mountain of gold.

"Today, fiends and elves, we gathered for the ritual of the demon corrida!" A tall, bulky red fiend shouted from atop the stands, the crowd cheering at his words, "In order to gain Hell's favor in the destruction of Gardemagne, three, yes, *three* noble ladies shall be sacrificed today before the fights! The ghastly deed shall be done by our esteemed king's guest, the beautiful, the poisonous... Melodieuse!"

The elves and fiends cheered, as a purple-haired manling materialized in front of the princesses. A pretty creature with long, deep purple hair arranged in a tress, with bloody, red-rimmed eyes; she wore a queenly black dress, made of the fur of warbeasts and fiends both. The woman's sight bothered Vainqueur, although the dragon couldn't tell why.

"Witness the sacrifices!" the speaker continued. "Princess Merveille, niece of our hated nemesis, King Roland Gardemagne! The oracle of Appol—"

"MINE!" Vainqueur landed in the arena with a loud sound, blowing off a large cloud of dust around himself. "MINE, MINE, MINE!"

While the audience fell silent, and the purple-haired manling looked up at his face, Vainqueur turned to the captive princesses, showing them his princess bag.

"Get in the bag!" The princess maidens looked around them in fear and confusion. "I said, get in the princess bag!"

"Your Majesty, you are invisible, and they are chained!"

"[Null Magic]."

Vainqueur's invisibility vanished, and he could feel the power of his other trinkets negated as well. The crowd panicked at his sight, while the princesses shuddered in fear. The dragon ignored all of them, glancing at the source of the attack.

"[Crystal Prison.]" At the strange manling's command, barriers of purple crystal grew around the princesses, trapping them within like bugs in amber. The dragon instantly recognized the substance as cursed fairywork. "Knightsbane, you have come to delay our ambitions?"

The thing looked like a noble princess but smelled anything but. She smelled like the deadly flowers of the Dark Forest, of death, and putrid miasma.

Not a manling.

A *fomor*.

Vainqueur exchanged a glance with the fairy, and her soulless eyes confirmed his suspicions. A tense, hateful silence fell between them, neither willing to make the first move; the dragon dropped the princess bag and his chief of staff, ready to smash that abomination at the first sign of hostility. Their species may have made peace, but her mere presence infuriated the dragon.

"Your Majesty?" His chief of staff, unaware of the woman's nature, looked back and forth between them. "Who is she? I can't read her with any of my Perks, and she feels *wrong*."

"Minion, hide behind me," Vainqueur said, extending his claws and preparing to fight to that creature's death if needed. "Fairykind hunts manlings for their fur."

"Ohoh, viewers, a surprise challenger stormed in! Vainqueur Knightsbane, 'Emperor'," the fiend commentator laughed, and so did the crowd, much to Vainqueur's confusion, "of Murmurin and the Albain Mountains, self-proclaimed great calamity of the age!"

"Self-proclaimed nothing!" Vainqueur contested the lie.

"In the other corner, the demonic superstar, the invincible champion, the undefeated king of Ishfania... the fabulous Brandon Maure!"

An elf stepped into the arena through a door built into the stone wall itself, as thin and fragile as the rest of his kind. His skin was light purple, almost greyish, with silver eyes and short hair of the same color. He wore a gold-plated, shiny cloth that covered his whole body except for his exposed chest, and a horned, silvery diadem around his head. The dead meat walking carried a blade with one hand and a red cloth with the other.

The crowd cheered at the elf's coming, who raised his red cloth at them. Openings in the arena's walls unleashed streams of fire and white smoke above. "Maure, best demon!" The cattle audience chanted. "Maure, best demon! Maure, best demon!"

The elf, who smelled like brimstone, smirked at Manling Victor. "Ah, the mere sight of Brandon Maure's perfect body has made you fall for him. Brandon Maure gets this reaction all the time."

"Actually, I was just very surprised by the *traje de luces* outfit—"

"There is no need to deny your lustful feelings for Brandon Maure's sublime body," the demon king cut off the chief of staff with a smug look which Vainqueur immediately despised."None can resist Brandon Maure, and he welcomes all admirers. For beauty has a lover, and it is Brandon Maure."

Elves. Always the arrogant cattle.

That fomor however... Vainqueur kept his eyes focused on the fairy, in case she went for a sneak attack. He didn't even move to smash the arrogant cattle, unwilling to give that sworn foe of dragonkind any opening.

"You, V&V, have slighted Maure for months," the elf said while walking to the fomor's side. "You slew his human minions, stole his precious apple, destroyed his court magician, and ruined a century of demon summoning work. Now you want to take his hard-won sacrifices from him? Brandon Maure truly wants to know: what has he done to you to deserve this?"

"You exist in my world," Vainqueur replied as a matter of fact, his eyes still on the witch. "I am Emperor. I do as I want."

"You, Vainqueur, are no Emperor. Murmurin is a daughter of Ishfania, and Ishfania has only one king. The king who stands before you!"

*Warning: your [**Emperor**] title is contested by Brandon Maure!*

*If you do not assert your rightful authority, your [**Emperor**] class perks will be nulled!*

"Contest? What is there to contest?" Vainqueur snarled. He should not even have to defend his title, since its validity was obvious!

"What do you intend to do with that bombardier?" Manling Victor asked, still more preoccupied with the metal bird than the challenge to his master's authority. "How did you even build it so fast?"

"Maure had the Iron Eagle built months ago, but his minions lacked the knowledge for the finishing touches. As for what he will do with it, earthlings have a word for it, if Brandon Maure remembers. Something with carpets."

"Carpet bombing," the fomor said, her voice without warmth.

"Yes, carpet bombing. Brandon Maure will carpet bomb the monkey farms of Gardemagne until only rubble and dead apes remain. He will also make a short detour to raze these stinking Haudemer and Murmurin villages."

"W-why?" Manling Victor asked. "What is the point?"

"To starve my guests by destroying the cattle," Vainqueur explained.

"Because Brandon Maure has many qualities. Beautiful. Perfect. Generous. But *forgiving,* is not among them."

Vainqueur's chief of staff readied his scythe. "Not on my watch," he said, prepared to defend his master's honor and food supply.

"Maure cares nothing for monkey props." The arrogant elf turned to look at the minion's scythe. "And if you wish to survive with all your ears attached to your body, you shall release Maure's lich servant at once."

Furibon? That monstrous elf wanted to break the seal keeping Furibon prisoner! "I will not let you release that evil on the world, fiend!" Vainqueur declared, preparing to blast these two with fire and flames, fomor-dragon peace or not.

"Maure's will shall be fulfilled." The fiendish elf turned to the fomor witch. "Melodieuse, please do Brandon Maure a favor, and clear his arena of peons."

"As you wish, princeling."

Vainqueur immediately blasted the spot where the fomor stood with a fireball, but she teleported out of the path the same way the frustrating Furibon did.

"[Hellzone]." Before he could react, she raised a hand, and the very fabric of space collapsed around Vainqueur and Victor; a rift showcasing a world of fire and brimstones superposing over the arena. The mirage lasted only an instant, but his chief of staff vanished with it.

Luck check successful, but your minion has been banished to Hell.

"My chief of staff!" Vainqueur wrathfully extended his wings, to showcase his dominance to the fomor. "Bring him back at once! I am not clearing a dungeon again!"

"Only a true winner makes demands, dragon!" Brandon Maure replied while a beam of light fell straight from the heavens, hitting the area where the iron bird was nested. The elf looked in this direction with an angry snarl. "The Iron Eagle! They have brought reinforcements!"

"Not for long." The fomor witch glanced at the source of the light, then vanished in a veil of darkness, leaving nothing behind.

"I will show you your place, grass-eater!" Vainqueur snarled, intending to eat that walking cattle, put the princesses in the bag, and then force that witch to release his chief of staff. He would find the time to rampage somewhere in the middle. "Your feeble spells will do nothing to me!"

"Only the weak rely on magic to win their fights! A true warrior just needs his muleta and his espada! You, Vainqueur, Brandon Maure challenges you! One on one, champion against dragon!"

"Vainqueur Knightsbane does not back away from a fight!"

*You accepted Maure's **[Demon Corrida]** challenge!*

The audience will empower or weaken the fighters depending on their performance!

"Then, Vainqueur, Brandon Maure swears it on his honor as a [Matador]..." The elf swung his blade. "Today, you shall learn the bitter taste of defeat!"

28: First Blood

As it turned out, Charlene had been right. Victor did end up in Hell after all.

It was a horrible place, but not for the reasons Victor had expected.

Hell was a fiery, brimstone cave, like the religions of Earth foretold; but they had moved away from burning souls and into new, more inventive forms of punishment. On one side, Victor noticed row after row of captive humans bound to chairs in front of a large mirror, forced to watch some kind of horribly acted, medieval reality TV show. On the other side, other damned souls fashioned tiny, hand-held mirrors reminding the adventurer of mobile phones' screens, while being whipped by imps.

Victor would have loved nothing more than free those poor souls from their eternal torment, had he not been surrounded by insectoid fiends. Three dozen of the creatures looking like thinner, moth-like cousins of Malfy pointed sharp, poisoned spears at him.

One figure, however, differed from the others and looked at Victor with pupilless blue eyes. A hybrid creature between a woman and an insect with greyish skin, she had two large, golden moth wings with a skull motif growing out of her back. A black, skintight dress covered her entire body, except for sharp claws where the fingers ended, and a mink-jacket like ring of white fur around the neck. She was eerily beautiful and elegant, in a creepy ice queen sort of way. Only two horn-like antennae growing out of her long, silver hair betrayed her demonic nature.

Her face looked a bit too much like Brandon Maure's to Victor's liking, though.

"A new sacrifice." Much to Victor's amazement, the female demon sounded remarkably soft-spoken. "You are not a virgin maiden."

"Neither have I been mistaken for one," the adventurer replied, tightening his hold on his scythe with one hand and looking under his cowl for the Agarthan Warp Stone with the other. He had no idea if it could teleport him out of Hell, but he saw no other escape route.

The bug fiends raised their blades against his chin and his hands, stopping him dead in his tracks.

However, the demoness leader raised an eyebrow at him, more confused than anything. "You can understand High Infernal?"

He wasn't supposed to? Thank the twelve gods for that Perk, maybe he could talk his way out the way he did with the Moon Beast. Victor immediately used Monster Insight on the fiends' leader, desperate for a morsel of information.

Isabelle Maure

Archdevil of Vanity and Mindless Entertainment (Demon/Insect)

Strong against: Light, Darkness, Drain, Mind-Control effects, Insta-death, all negative status effects, Frost, Lightning, Unholy, Fire, Acid, Screens.

Weak against: Holy, Wind, Demonslayer, and Bugslayer.

The mistress of blades, and one of Hell's corporate overlords. The fiendish mind who invented procrastination, gladiator fights, and Outremonde's equivalent of reality TV. Owns many businesses dedicated to enslaving souls through the power of screens, such as Infernal Cable and Helltube, but secretly regrets sacrificing her golden years for her career.

Uh oh. "You smell of dragon, and is that a soul I see trapped in your scythe?" The demoness asked, her eyes set on Victor's scythe. "Furibon? Is that you?"

"Kill him, Your Highness!" Furibon shouted from inside the scythe, Victor doing his best to keep his poker face. *"This is an enemy of King Maure!"*

"What is he trying to say?" the demoness asked. "I can see his teeth move on the scythe's edge, but I cannot hear a word of it."

"He is complaining about his old master executing him for screwing up opening a Hellgate," Victor lied through his teeth.

"Ah, so this is what happened. I was wondering why the portal had been reinforced without warning. I had an army of thirty thousand fiends waiting behind it."

"And you are...?" Victor trailed off, although he already knew and Furibon kept screaming without being heard.

"Archdevil Isabelle Maure, Mistress of Blades, Chief Demonic Executive of Maure Hellcorporated."

"The mother of Brandon?"

"Oh, you know my Braniño?" Her delicate face showed some worry. "How is he? Has he conquered Gardemagne yet? The gate was supposed to open from his side but never did, I worried so much."

"Wait, he didn't inform you?" Victor sweated internally, thankful for Maure's carelessness.

"He never visits and only calls when he needs something. 'Mother, Brandon wants a new demon horse', or 'Mother, Brandon needs more infernal power!' I know I birthed him in the first place so I could expand into the overplane, but a little affection would not hurt. I am not a cold-hearted hellspawn all the time."

"Parenting is a thankless job," Victor replied, half trying to be nice and half trying to talk his way out of an early grave. "What about his dad? Maybe you could ask him for support."

"Oh, I drained him of life while we conceived Brandon," she said, sending shivers down the adventurer's spine. "He wanted a child to perpetuate his inbred, infertile bloodline, and I wanted an agent on Outremonde. A win-win. Unfortunately, elves are frail with few health points, so he died halfway through. A shame. Braniño inherited his good looks. Have you had children, Mister…"

"Victor," Victor blurted out, but thankfully the name didn't ring a bell to the woman. Brandon Maure *really* didn't call his mother often. "A werewolf chick asked me to breed, but I had to refuse. She was crazy."

"Werewolves," Isabelle Maure sneered with elitist disgust. "You did well, they have fleas. So, Victor, you are my son's new executioner? How did you end up in Hell, Mr. Victor?"

"I'm a chief of staff, actually. That Melodieuse woman sent me here with a spell." Technically true, and so far the charade had kept him alive. If Victor survived this, he promised himself to take levels in a Charisma-oriented class.

"I told Braniño he shouldn't listen to that woman," the demoness said with a frown as if Victor confirmed a previous opinion. "Nothing good can come out of dealing with fairies, I told him. What we fiends do for business, they do for pleasure."

Victor guessed what this Melodieuse was, and decided to avoid her at all costs. He was thankful she sent him there instead of killing him on the spot.

"I will correct this mistake," Isabelle said, the bugs lowering their weapons.

"I am most thankful, ma'am. My master is waiting for me though, so I shouldn't be away for too long."

"My ungrateful son will wait," she replied with a tone that brooked no disobedience. "Thank me by indulging me over imp brewed coffee. I want you to tell me everything Braniño has been up to. Then you will be killed."

"With pleasure..." The last words suddenly registered. "What?"

"Then you will be killed," she repeated flatly. "I will be correcting Melodieuse's mistake and make sure you die this time."

"But... but..."

"I can understand what the lich says, Victor Dalton. I was playing dumb partly because I wanted to see if you were trustworthy, and partly because I enjoy playing with my dinner." She smirked at him, and behind the lips, there were sharp teeth. "If you tell me everything about Braniño, I *may* make it painless. Since you ruined a century of efforts on that gate, you better be entertaining."

"Oh, I will have a hell of a time watching this," Furibon rejoiced.

Victor's hands moved to grab the Agarthan Warp Stone, but two bug soldiers caught his arm and restrained him, SWAT-style. "Take him to the tea room, and prepare the spice for the seasoning," Isabelle asked.

"Halt!" A new voice came up. "This is a violation of our rights."

Malfy? Victor recognized the voice, as the fiendish manager walked into sight, backed by two similar, thinner bugs clad in suit and ties.

"Infercorp?" Isabelle Maure didn't hide her surprise, as her soldiers pointed their weapons at the newcomers. "What the Heaven are you doing here?"

"Protecting our client." The bug in a suit handed a huge paper file to a surprised Isabelle. "As per our procedures, Victor

Dalton here present is protected by our Faustian Associate Protection Program. He is a true mortal partner of Infercorp on Outremonde, and thus protected by our non-competition clause."

"Give me that." Isabelle grabbed the file and read it, her frown deepening. "Murmurin? But it is part of my market!"

"It *was*, now it's *ours*," Malfy replied, before turning to Victor. "Mr. Victor, fancy meeting seeing you here. You've come under a lot earlier than I thought."

"Hi, Malfy," Victor replied, still sore as the demon soldiers kept him restrained. "What's up?"

"It's Vice-President of Mortal Market Development Malfaisant now. The shareholders loved the new Murmurin project so much, they promoted me after they chocolatined my predecessor. You can still call me Malfy though, Mr. Victor."

"Any violence against our client will be seen as an act of corporate warfare, and we will have to send the imp ninjas," the bug in a suit, clearly a lawyer of some kind, argued to a livid Isabelle Maure. "We ask that, for the sake of our mutual investments, you will abandon all pursuits against Mr. Dalton."

"Of course, since you now understand the benefits of having friends in low places, I expect you to approve our construction project in return," Malfy whispered to Victor.

"Which project?"

"The one you will find on your desk tomorrow morning."

*Congratulations! For pulling off a Houdini on Isabelle Maure and getting a crash course on corporate impunity, you have earned the [**Get out of Hell Card**] personal Perk!*

*[**Get out of Hell Card**]: As long as you maintain favor with infernal powers, true Demon-Types affiliated with Hell cannot*

use direct violence against you, although they may still scheme or use proxies. If you use violence against a Demon-Type affiliated with Hell, you will lose this Perk.

"Is this a common thing?" Victor asked, curious, as the bugs reluctantly released him.

"Yes," Malfy told Victor. "We have made sure that rich people get away with *everything* since you mortals invented capitalism."

Vainqueur opened the battle with his secret weapon.

The poke!

Furiously raising his index finger, Vainqueur attempted to poke the elf in the face. Moving with incredible speed for his feeble kind, Brandon Maure dodged the strike by leaping above the hand and landing on his arm.

Before Vainqueur knew what hit him, Brandon Maure dashed on the arm, jumped, and struck him in the neck with his blade. "[Estocade]!" he shouted as his blade grazed Vainqueur's neck, unable to pierce the scales.

*Insta-death negated by [**Dragonscale**]!*

Vainqueur roared and threw the grass-eater off of him, raising his hands to crush the creature. Maure landed on the ground, and the fiend dodged the dragon's attempts at squashing him like a bug. "You shall not land a single hit on Maure's perfect skin, Vainqueur! [Death or Glory!]"

Brandon Maure's Agility, Skill and Strength have increased, but his Vitality has drastically decreased!

The elf began to move with greater speed, faster than a fly or even the evil Furibon. He danced around Vainqueur's limbs, nailing the dragon's ankles with his blade. The dragon felt some itches on his legs, growing more and more annoyed with every second the grass-eater stayed alive.

"Come back here!" Vainqueur attempted to smash the elf, who leaped atop the fairy crystals holding the princesses. The dragon carefully aimed, humming and preparing to unleash a stream of fire at the elf without harming his new treasures.

"[Faena Muleta!]" Brandon Maure rose his strange red cloth in front of Vainqueur. The dragon's eyes fixated on the red cloth, finding it strangely mesmerizing. For a reason that escaped him, his flames died in his throat.

Intelligence check failed!

Your strength has increased, but you can only use physical attacks against Brandon Maure!

What? Vainqueur hummed again, but he could only unleash hot air out of his mouth. The elf had cast a spell on him! "[Spell Purge!]"

"This is no magic trick, Vainqueur!" Maure raised his blade and red cloth piece in a stylish pause. "This is all Brandon Maure!" The crowd cheered at his words, singing his name the same way the kobolds usually cheered Vainqueur.

*The love of his fans has empowered Brandon Maure! His blade will now deal [**Dragonslayer**] damage!*

"[Airblade!]" The very winds swirled around Maure's sword. And quick like the wind, he leaped off the crystal and struck Vainqueur between the eyes.

This time, the sword didn't make his scales itch.

This time, it felt *much* worse.

Vainqueur let out a frustrated growl, moving his hands to scratch the elf off his head. The damn insect backflipped before the dragon's claws tore him apart. Brandon Maure sliced the air in the middle of his fall, unleashing cutting blades of wind at the great calamity. Each strike hitting his scales made his body itch worse and worse.

Vainqueur tried to blast the upstart with fire, but yet again, it didn't work. Neither could he take his eyes off that cursed piece of cloth. It infuriated him so much, all he could think was to charge at it like a bull.

And so he did, his horns and crown first while snarling. They smashed the arena's walls, collapsing them alongside a good chunk of the stands, with the audience fleeing towards higher areas. Yet, his majestic attack failed to even hit Brandon Maure, who raced below Vainqueur, slashing him on his soft belly.

As if the terrible itching wasn't humiliating enough, the elf kept taunting him. "You are a bull, Vainqueur! All strength, no skill! You are no emperor, but a beast who should have stayed in its cave!"

Argh, this creature was as frustrating as Furibon! But like the lich, the dragon only had to hit him once. Vainqueur just needed to take the grass-eater by surprise to catch it.

"Blink!" Much to his displeasure, the dragon did not turn invisible. That fairy's attack had broken his magical items.

"Magic? I should have expected that from a feeble dragon!" The insect taunted him, standing within the reach of Vainqueur's hand and yet unharmed. "While you savage beasts ate cows in your caves, we elves ruled the greatest empire in the world!"

"We made the world first!" Vainqueur snarled back. "I had more power as an egg than your entire inbred species!"

"You crass beast, while in diapers, Brandon Maure was stranglings manling monkeys with his mere han—"

While the elf was busy ranting, Vainqueur grabbed some of the arena's sand and threw it at him.

Surprised, the elf took the sand right in the eyes, while the crowd fell silent. "Maure's eyes!" The elf started crying, as his kind usually did, while Vainqueur opened his mouth. "Maure has sand in his eyes!"

Chomp!

Vainqueur swallowed Brandon Maure whole like a snack and gulped. Finally, he had caught the frustrating cattle.

The audience came out of its silence to boo at him.

The crowd condemns your dirty fighting! All stats decreased!

Vainqueur didn't care. He had won. Now, he would enjoy his reward, put the princesses in the princess bag, and then find his chief of staff...

Wait. His stomach started to feel... feel sick...

A sharp, horrible feeling made him throw up Brandon Maure at a wall like a projectile, raising a cloud of dust.

You have lost a quarter of your HP.

What... what was this feeling? It was beyond itching, beyond...

Beyond painful.

For the first time in his thousand year long life, Vainqueur realized dragons *could* feel pain.

The elf rose out of the dust, but he was no longer an elf. The walking cattle had transformed into a white and golden humanoid moth, with jet black wings and a mouthless face. A red wing grew below his left arm, replacing the cloth, and the sword now shone like the sun. With a swirling movement, he cast Vainqueur's saliva off of him, sparkles on his skin.

"A true Matador's pride is unbreakable!" the bug buzzed, with the demons' cheers becoming deafening.

The crowd's electric enthusiasm raised all of Brandon Maure's stats!

"[All or Nothing!]" As the moth raised his sword of light for a new strike, Vainqueur let out a defiant roar, rose on his two back legs, and prepared to firebomb this bug once and for all.

His eyes set on the crimson wing, and his fiery breath turned to hot air.

Faster than Vainqueur's eyes could follow, the moth dashed at him and sliced the dragon's chest. The emperor's world briefly turned white from the pain, and he collapsed on his back with a loud sound, blowing off dust all over the arena.

Massive damage!

You have lost half your HP!

What... what happened? Vainqueur tried to get back up, but his chest hurt worse than anything he had ever imagined. The crowd turned uproarious, cheering the demon king's name.

He... he was being *matched*? By an *elf*?

They eat *grass*!

"You are no emperor, Vainqueur! Thou art a beast, fit only to have your horns cut!" The moth raised his blade, as the crowd acclaimed him. Items and jewels materialized around the dirty creature, with a furious Vainqueur realizing that the fiend had activated his own [Crowd Favorite] Perk. "Brandon Maure rules supreme!"

"Brandon, best demon! Brandon, best demon! Brandon, best demon!"

Vainqueur raised his head, feeling something warm on his belly. A shining, beautiful golden liquid flowed on his scales from the place where the bug had cut him.

It looked like dragon blood.

His blood.

Vainqueur could bleed?

A text notification added insult to injury.

*Warning: You failed to properly defend your [**Emperor**] title by steamrolling Brandon Maure.*

*All of the [**Emperor**] class perks are ineffective until you regain your honor.*

"And now, Vainqueur, know that Brandon Maure will slaughter all your fans after you are done," the moth declared. "Then, he shall claim all your treasures as his own!"

...

No!

Vainqueur had to win.

For the *hoard*.

Giving up when faced with a true challenge was what a *manling* would do. Vainqueur was a *dragon*. The apex species, a supreme beast of legends, the greatest calamity of this age! Dragons never gave up, because, in the end, they always win!

*[**Dragon Arrogance**] triggered! All debuffs removed!*

Roused by his pride and his pure love for his treasure, the great calamity forced himself back up on all four, much to Brandon Maure's surprise.

"I will not fall!" Vainqueur roared with defiance. "For my hoard!"

"You, Vainqueur, are a worthy, well-bred, noble beast!" the moth said, adopting a wary fighting stance. "Your guts honors this arena! It will be an honor for Maure to kill you!"

Charisma check successful!

*By impressing the cruel crowds of Ishfania with your fighting spirit, you earned the [**Bravo Bull**] personal Perk!*

*[**Bravo Bull**]: When your health is critical, your strength is greatly raised.*

The elf thought the dragon a beast who couldn't think, and maybe Vainqueur couldn't win with strength alone. But he had *fourteen* in intelligence, and even Manling Victor started at *one*. If he couldn't crush his prey with strength alone, he would outsmart it.

Vainqueur couldn't take off his eyes from the moth's red wing as he paraded; he couldn't even close his eyes. So long as he couldn't breathe fire, he was at a disadvantage. He couldn't hit that Maure cattle with physical attacks, but he could only use them against him.

Vainqueur suddenly realized the key flaw in that [Faena Muleta] Perk.

He extended his wings and unleashed a strong gust of wind at Brandon Maure. The demon elf protected his face with his crimson wing, vanishing from the dragon's sight behind a veil of sand.

Vainqueur couldn't target the *moth elf* with his fire.

The Perk didn't say anything about incinerating the *stage*.

And so did the dragon unleashed fireballs all over the arena, unable to see that cursed crimson wing nor its owner; he carefully avoided the crystallized princesses, but blasted the rest of the battlefield into ashes. Hopefully, he hit the grasshopper.

Your flames are inflicting heavy Holy damage to Brandon Maure!

While the moth couldn't use that cursed Perk on him, Vainqueur turned to the true source of the bug's power.

His minions.

Without giving the spectators a warning, Vainqueur chomped at the stands, eating a good dozen dark elves and fiends by surprise. The cattle's cheers turned to screams, and they ran off in panic as Vainqueur kept on chewing more of them.

These fiends tasted like spice!

Within seconds, the crowd dispersed, fiends flying away, dark elves stepping on one another, others jumping over the stands' ledge…

*You interrupted the [**Demon Corrida**]! All stat changes have been canceled!*

By feasting on the spicy thralls of Brandon Maure, you recovered some HP!

"[Sandstorm]!" The winds swirled around the arena, a rising sandstorm extinguishing the flames while the moth elf walked into sight. It looked furious, and much to Vainqueur's delight, bleeding and burned at the wings. "Maure's fans! What kind of beast attacks an audience of loving demon supporters?!"

"The dragon kind!" Vainqueur boasted, proud of his tactic's success. "No more minions to support you, grasshopper!"

"You only delay your inevitable defeat, Vainqueur! Cheering fans or not, Maure will triumph!"

Vainqueur roared to the heavens, extending his wings and facing the moth elf in a show of dominance. The moth raised both his sword and crimson wing, ready to finish the fight.

Then Manling Victor teleported between them with a cloud of rancid smoke.

"Huh? That's less damage than I imagined." In stark contrast with both fighters, Vainqueur's chief of staff looked unharmed. "Your Majesty? Damn, you look savaged!"

"Minion, you are back!" Vainqueur rejoiced, although he kept his focus on that cursed moth elf.

"Dalton?" the moth elf raised a blade at Vainqueur's lackey. "Thou have escaped Hell?"

"As expected of my chief of staff!" Vainqueur boasted. "I trained him well."

"Braniño?" Minion Victor waved a hand at the moth while holding his scythe with the other. The annoyed visage of Furibon reflected on the blade's polished surface. "I almost didn't recognize you for a second."

The demon king of Ishfania made a short pause. "How do you know that nickname?"

"That's what your mother called you. Why, is it forbidden?"

Much to Vainqueur's displeasure, the moth lost interest in the fight and pointed his blade at Manling Victor. However, before the dragon could blast him with flames, the bug also paraded his red wing in his foe's direction. "What have you done to my mother, ruffian?"

"Nothing. My infernal lawyers saved my hide, and apparently I have full immunity from fiends. Your mother did insist on sending me back there herself for some reason."

The bug's eyes narrowed dangerously. "Brandon Maure knows why. He's half-fiend, and he loves piñata."

The minion blinked, before adopting a defensive stance. "Wait, wait—"

Vainqueur attempted to squash the bug with his hand before he could attack, but even slowed down from the loss of his stat boosts, the creature moved faster than the dragon.

In the blink of an eye, the moth elf closed the gap between his minion and himself, before stabbing Manling Victor through the chest.

Vainqueur's vision turned red.

29: Heaven's Door

"The pain..." Vainqueur's chief of staff complained as Brandon Maure gored him through the chest with his blade, before smirking. "Thanks."

The Demon King raised his head. "Indeed, there is no greater pleasure than dying by the blade of Brandon—"

"No, thanks for getting close..." The minion grabbed Maure with his free hand. "Black Curse!"

A black aura surrounded Brandon Maure, instantly draining him of his vibrancy and strength.

All of Brandon Maure's enhancements have been removed, and all his stats reduced by one stage!

*Brandon Maure can no longer recover HP while [**Black Curse**] remains active!*

"What have you done?" Brandon Maure stumbled with his sword, while Manling Victor collapsed on his knees with a gaping chest wound. "Maure no longer feels amazing..."

Enraged, and only able to use physical attacks, Vainqueur raised a fist and lunged to hit Brandon Maure with a roar. The moth moved to dodge but reacted slower than before; he couldn't run away this time.

"NO TOUCHING MY HOARD!"

And so Vainqueur punched him.

The dragon's enormous fist hit Brandon Maure with such furious strength, that it made the arena tremble and caused a blast of wind on impact. The sheer might of the blow shattered the bones in the fiend's body, and sent him flying. Maure went through the flames, the arena's wall, and then through the stands without stopping.

An entire part of the arena collapsed after the blow, Manling Victor watching on with a terrified look.

Vainqueur, meanwhile, managed to calm himself upon realizing what happened.

"I hit him!" the dragon gloated. "I finally hit the moth!"

You punched Brandon in the face! By punching a major demon lord into temporarily 'retreating', you gained a level in [Gladiator] and a level in [Kaiser]!

+60 HP, +3 STR, +1 VIT, +1 SKI, +1 AGI, +1 INT, +2 CHA, +2 LCK

You earned the [Victory Fist] and [Summon Herald (Victor Dalton)] class Perks.

[Victory Fist]: You gain advanced proficiency in unarmed combat; your physical attacks can now harm even intangible opponents as if they were tangible.

[Summon Herald (Victor Dalton)]: At will, you can summon your monster herald and trusty chief of staff Victor to your side; this is a teleportation effect. If an effect should prevent teleportation, you can ignore it with a successful Charisma Check.

Warning: You have reached the level 30 class ceiling. You will no longer be able to gain additional levels until you use a [Crest]. You can still gain perks through special deeds, but your experience gains are set to zero.

"I wasn't sure if that perk could work on him... but I'm glad it did..." His beloved minion coughed up blood. "I need a healing potion..."

"Later, minion." The notification said, 'temporary retreating,' and he hadn't regained his rightful Emperor title. "The moth yet lives!"

"Yeah, I figured it wouldn't be easy..." Victor glanced around the arena, a hand on his bleeding chest and using the scythe to stand up straight, his eyes settling on the crystals. "The princesses..."

"These fairy crystals curse on touch with their magic," Vainqueur explained, the fomors having fashioned that damn spell to annoy the dragon race. He grabbed back his princess bag and activated his now favorite perk. "[Spell Purge]."

Charisma Check partially successful! **[Fairy Crystal]** *weakened by* **[Spell Purge]**!

Vainqueur grabbed the crystallized princesses, the touch of the crystal freezing slightly on touch, and put them in his grocery bag. "Now, minion, let us find the elf moth." With luck, he would drop a Crest for Vainqueur to use.

He smelled Knight Kia and her flying cattle coming, circling the arena. Her griffin was burned around the wings. "You have Merveille?" the knight asked. "Good, let's use the Agarthan Warp Stone and get away, quick!"

Get away? From whom? "Not without my Crest, the moth's head, and a tribute of cattle, Knight Kia."

"Have you destroyed the plane?" Victor asked her.

"I damaged a wing, but that woman... she's an archmage of some sort and she packs a punch. Then Brandon Maure teleported there and ordered the plane launched! They staffed it with an army!" Noticing Manling Victor's wound, she cast a spell on him at once, "[Greater Healing]."

A golden light enveloped his chief of staff, the chest wound closing. Victor let out a sigh of relief, and so did his master; he had worried his chief of staff would die from the blood loss like his fragile kind usually did.

Still furious, Vainqueur prepared to take flight and hunt the moth when the stench of fairykind filled his nostrils. Flying through sorcery like Furibon, that woman, Melodieuse, descended from the skies, glaring down at them.

"I tire of you, Claimed," the fomor said to the manlings, before turning her attention to Vainqueur. "Leave, dragon. You have no business interfering. Take your slaves with you, and I will order the princeling to let you rule Murmurin unchallenged."

The dragon finally recognized the smell. The fomor Mag Mell's. Was she that fairy in disguise, or another of its spawns? No matter. "I fear no one, and especially not a grass-eater! Go back to your forest, fairy!"

"Then perish. [Call the Hunt]." A torrent of purple smoke surrounded the fairy, and four monstrous, elephant-sized black hounds made of dark shadows materialized around her. The creatures let out roars as they landed among the arena's ruins, charging at the dragon and Manling Victor.

Fairy hounds. Warbeasts the fomors once created to fight dragons, and whom Vainqueur slew by the dozens in his younger days.

The first of them lunged at the dragon, who backhanded it away against the very last of the arena's walls with his free hand, collapsing it on the abomination. Much to Vainqueur's astonishment, his body reacted on its own, finding more entertaining, better ways to punch and poke the beasts as they came into range.

One of the beasts attacked Manling Victor, who blocked the jaws with his scythe before they could snap him in half. Knight Kia immediately rushed to help him, summoning her Solar Judgment on the creature; a beam of light hit the fairy hound in the back, vaporizing half of its body.

The fomor engaged Knight Kia in an aerial battle, raining down fiery stones and sharp spears of ice while the flyer dodged every one of them. The knight quickly closed the gap between them and tried to slash the creature in half, only for Melodieuse to quickly catch the sword with her hand, not bulging.

"[Darkest Fe—]" Melodieuse summoned a spell, only for Knight Kia to punch her in the face with her free hand. It didn't harm the fairy, but it did distract her enough for the knight to free her sword and put back distance between them.

"She is delaying us!" Knight Kia shouted, before invocating Solar Judgment on the fomor, blasting her with light. Vainqueur heard a deep, powerful sound approaching. "Use the stone!"

Retreating?

Never! A true dragon does not run, because he cannot die!

Vainqueur ignored her, as one of the hounds he poked to death collapsed into smoke, leaving behind a pile of gold. The dragon immediately pulverized a second one with a fireball, eager for more treasure. "Minion!" he called to Manling Victor, who had managed to fend off his own opponent with his scythe. "Quick, grab my gold!"

"Your Majesty, I think we should listen to Kia!"

"Minion, a true Emperor does not run!" Vainqueur replied as he finished off the last of the fairy hounds with a stomp, and a cloud's shadow began to cover the area. "What should I fear?"

Manling Victor raised a finger at the skies, Vainqueur following it.

The giant metal bird flew high above the arena, casting it in its immense shadow. Strange, spear-shaped iron talons pointed at them, while the left wing let out some smoke. "Vainqueur!" The voice of the moth elf came from the iron bird, the dragon noticing him through the beast's window eye. "You have slighted Brandon Maure long enough!"

Sweet, the moth had come back to die. "I will slight you as long as you do not recognize me by my title!" the dragon roared, extending his wings proudly...

Then a magical circle appeared beneath Vainqueur's feet. "What is this?" he wondered, glaring at the fomor witch in case she intended to attack with it.

"Death," the fomor witch replied, dusting off her burnt robes before vanishing with a veil of darkness. One of the spear talons fell from the bird, then flew straight at Vainqueur, propelled by strong winds.

"Vainqueur, Victor, flee!" Knight Kia immediately grabbed a stone from under her armor with her free hand, vanishing alongside the griffon.

"Holy sh—" Manling Victor immediately ducked behind his master, who also put the princess bag behind him for safekeeping.

Before Vainqueur could react, the spear hit him in the face, detonating on contact with a blast of sharp, blinding light; the explosion unleashed a blast of compressed wind in all directions, blowing off stones, dusting the flames, and making the dragon collapse to the side.

His *entire body* itched.

*You have taken massive damage from the Wind Spear! Critical health, [**Dizzy**] ailment!*

*You are below a **fourth** of your health!*

*[**Bravo Bull**] activated!*

Vainqueur rose back up, a surge of strength helping him do so, but he had trouble standing straight. His head hurt, and the world blurred. "Minion, I do not feel well," Vainqueur admitted, feeling like throwing up his dinner. "I feel sick..."

"He *survived*?" The moth sounded very angry above. "How the Heaven did he survive a weapon made for *castles*?!"

"I am..." Vainqueur forgot his next words, stumbling on his boast, "Unforgettable..."

"Carpet him!"

Four, maybe five more magical circles appeared below Vainqueur, and more spear talons fell from the iron eagle.

"Okay, we're done!" Manling Victor said, whom Vainqueur's body had shielded alongside the princess bag. "Hoard, hoard, hoard!"

As the spears flew towards them, the world changed; in the blink of an eye, Vainqueur was back in his hoard, surrounded by his precious jewels and coins.

"It worked." Victor collapsed on the gold, and for once, Vainqueur did not complain about him touching his hoard. He was too exhausted to chastise him. The Agarthan Warp Stone in his chief of staff's hand turned to dust. "By the gods, that was close..."

"I'm not feeling well..." Vainqueur collapsed on his hoard, the warmth of the gold soothing him. His eyes moved to the princess bag, damaged but the content intact, his eyelids falling... "I'm not... I'm not well..."

"We almost died, your Majesty," Manling Victor said something stupid. "I would settle on feeling *not well* rather than *dead.*"

"Nonsense, death is... death is a birth defect... only mammals suffer from it, like pain..."

But he did feel pain. If Vainqueur could suffer, then... maybe he could die too?

No. No, it was impossible. Vainqueur was the biggest and strongest of his kind. He could not suffer from a disability, unless every other dragon had it.

Unless... unless...

The horrible truth dawned upon Vainqueur, like a revelation from the Elder Wyrm itself. The darkest possible conspiracy theory among dragonkind, proven!

Death...

Death was *not* a disability!

Congratulations! For figuring out that yes, dragons are mortal, you earned +1 INT point.

"My entire culture is built on a lie!" As if the day could not get worse, Vainqueur realized his chief of staff had only his scythe on him. "Minion, have you grabbed my gold?"

His chief of staff glanced back in silence, and Vainqueur twitched.

Victor collapsed on his bed with his clothes on, more tired than ever. That plan did not work. At all.

They almost *died*!

Vainqueur almost died. *Vainqueur*! Brandon Maure was alive and vengeful, his magitech plane functional. If they hadn't pissed him enough to develop a grudge, then taking his princesses and punching him did.

He had to prepare Murmurin for war because his gut told him Maure would make that promised detour to bomb the region, and very soon. He had ordered the Kobold Rangers and Jules to sound the alarm at the first sign of a giant bird in the skies, and he hoped Kia would warn Gardemagne.

"No one can save you," Furibon taunted him from within his weapon. *"You can no longer take levels, and my master commands the most powerful weapon in the world. You shall all die, so very soon."*

As his mind worked furiously on methods to protect his charges, Furibon's words made Victor turn to the lich's soul. "You can help."

"What?"

"Even if we can't level up without Crests, I can learn Necromancy spells, and Vainqueur can learn Exorcisms," Victor pointed out. "You're an archmage, you must know many of them." He would also ask Jules for training tips.

"Teaching you and that dragon magic? Never!"

Annoyed, Victor shook the scythe like a dog with a treat, Furibon's soul hitting the blade's limits while he did, much to his annoyance. *"This will not—"* The adventurer swung harder. *"Okay, okay, stop swinging me! Only you! I do not know any Exorcisms, and I do not want to be around that dragon!"*

Good. Victor gave the lich a respite. "We begin tomorrow," he said, his eyelids heavy.

Before he could sleep, a bright, soothing light lit up in the room. Victor immediately raised his head, worrying Maure had teleported an assassin to him.

Instead, he found an angel at his bedside.

"Mister Dalton," the heavenly beauty said, her voice soothing him. The creature took the shape of a blonde, eerily beautiful woman, with shining green eyes, large silver wings, and a magnificent white dress. "I am the angel Miel. I have come to save your soul."

"Am... am I dying?" Victor asked, horrified. Was Maure's blade wound cursed?

"No, but you almost did," the angel replied. "Every year, hundreds of thousands of neutral-aligned, unclaimed mortal souls end up in Hell by accident. You escaped once, but you may not be so lucky next time."

"Are you saying I will go to Hell if I die now?" The angel nodded. Victor would have loved to say he was surprised, but after everything he did, it didn't. "But I've been Claimed by two gods, shouldn't I go to them after death?"

Not that he wanted to go to Dice, but he could settle for the Moon Man.

"You do not worship them, and those deities are chaotic," the angel replied. "You will find no salvation with them. No, Mister Dalton. The only way to avoid damnation is to take the proper Karma Insurance. It is not too late for you."

...

Oh, come on.

"By insuring your karma, giving us some of your Special Points every month and all of them when you die, you can avoid eternal torment," the angel continued her sales pitch. "Please consider taking our 'Hellfire Protection Plan', or else you will be tortured forever when you die. We angels *care* about your safety."

"Or at least you care about my SP." Victor squinted at her.

"We use them to send guardian angels to orphans and heal the sick," the angel defended herself. "If you do not give us SP, you are committing a *sin*."

Was she trying to *guilt-trip* him? Victor started to understand what Malfy had said by angels having killer marketing. Then again... "What are your insurance plans?"

The angel blinked. "You are interested?"

"What, wasn't it the point to sell them to me?"

"You are my first client, and the higher-ups said you were a very difficult case." She smiled at him, like a telemarketer. "They think Redemption Chasing is a dirty job, and that you would never see the light."

Had he such a terrible reputation upstairs? "Look, I already have very pushy offers from below, so give me a rundown."

"Yes. First, we have the 'Halo Health Insur—"

"MINION!"

In a blink, Victor landed in Vainqueur's vault, his back against the gold and the angel nowhere to be found.

"Ah, minion." Vainqueur glanced down at the surprised Victor. The dragon pointed at the crystalized princesses, whom he had put atop his hoard like candles. "First, I cannot break these crystals no matter how hard I punch them. Find a way to free my princesses."

"H-how did you teleport me there?"

"I summoned you," Vainqueur replied as if the answer was obvious.

"You can do that? *How*?"

"I call 'Minion' and you show up," the dragon replied, as a matter of fact. "Now, anytime I need you, I no longer have to find you. You can fulfill my requests without wasting time."

As the implications dawned on him, Victor wanted to scream, but his voice died in his throat.

"Secondly, after much thinking, I have come to accept that," Vainqueur seemed to practically force himself to speak the next words, "that death is *not* a birth defect."

"Yes, Your Majesty, death comes to all of us," Victor replied to Vainqueur, unsure what to make of the dragon's reaction. He had said it with the solemnity of someone discovering the Earth hadn't been flat all along. "Except maybe the gods."

'They can,' Furibon replied from within the scythe. *'They just do not stay dead. How do you think someone had the idea of lichdom?'*

Better not mention that idea. A dracolich would solve the meat problem, but also cause new, bigger problems.

"Which makes reaching level 100 all the more important," Vainqueur declared. "You will find two Crests, so that I may blow up that giant bird, eat that grasshopper, and never die."

"*Two* Crests?" Victor frowned.

"Yes, for the two of us," Vainqueur clarified, his tone similar to one talking to a stupid child. "Minion Victor, I told you to become immortal. Do not make me repeat myself."

Victor would still take the angel insurance.

Just in case.

30: The Chocolatine Factory

It was offering day, and so Chocolatine decided to bake three cakes: one for her god, one for her crush, and one for her brother.

Humming to herself as she dressed, Chocolatine explored her and her brother's farm looking for the pantry. She kept a lot of demon flesh salted and fresh, and an imp in an iron birdcage. The demon looked at her with his big eyes. "Kill me," the fiend pleaded. "Send me back to Hell, you crazy wolf."

"Maybe later," Chocolatine replied cheerfully, looking inside the cage. "I need eggs." Savoureuse had given her one of her own, but it wasn't enough for three cakes.

The imp looked inside the straw that worked as his nest, giving her four black eggs. "Only four?" Chocolatine complained, putting the eggs in a basket. "That's twice less than last week!"

"I'm hungry," the imp complained.

"But I give you meat all the time!"

"Demon meat! I would rather starve than eat my kindred!"

Chocolatine rolled her eyes. Damning souls and working for a lich was fine, but *cannibalism* wasn't? What was the logic behind that? "I will give you a homeless inquisitor if I find one, but they are getting rarer. Or a gnoll. Do you imps eat gnolls?"

The imp nodded with energy, Chocolatine making a mental note to ask Jules for leftovers. She put the sugar, baking powder, and some of the strawberries Rolo gave her last week into her basket, then moved to the pens outside her ranch to milk her cow, Raisin, harvesting three bottles. She took a second to oversee the pigs' pen; unlike that prickly imp, they gladly accepted demon meat, growing fatter and gaining tiny horns. With further animal husbandry, she would create a new breed of demon pigs who could sustain the village.

People thought her odd, but that was because she cared. As a priestess of Isengrim, it was her role to maintain the balance of nature, and a village full of carnivorous monsters presented unique problems she had to solve. One day, she would find a way to make the community sustainable, even if she had to keep importing food from Hell.

The vestal then went to the kitchen to bake, finding blood-splatters everywhere, even the oven. "I forgot to clean?" she asked herself out loud. Bah, she would do it tonight. Nothing better than the smell of sheep blood to get pumped while cooking.

After an hour of steady work, she finished the three strawberry cakes, the most beautiful she had ever made. Each of them, she shaped like a heart; the symbol, not the organ. She tried once, it didn't take.

*Congratulations! For creating delicious cakes with love while using morally dubious ingredients, you gained a new level in [**Monster Patissier**]!*

+30 HP, +1 AGI, +1 SKI, +1 CHA, +1 LCK!

Another level in that class? At this rate, she would hit level thirty in no time!

Croissant entered the kitchen just as she finished, lured by the lovely smell. "Good morning, sis."

"Good morning, brother." Chocolatine gave him his present inside a lunch bag. "Here is Charlene's cake, with extra flavor."

"Thank you, sis. You are sure there will be no secondary effects? The last cake bit me."

"I told you, it was a Birthday Mimic, not my cake!" Since her Victor mass-promoted every monster he could find in order to prepare Murmurin for war, Chocolatine had no end of trouble with those shapeshifters. "None of my desserts killed anyone yet!"

Croissant gave her 'the stare,' but took the cake anyway. "Why three of them?" he asked, noticing the other two lunch bags she prepared, "One is for Isengrim, but the other?"

"It's for my crush," Chocolatine replied, without mentioning the name. She knew her brother couldn't stand her Victor since he politically emasculated him.

"When are you going to tell me who it is?"

"So you make him run away like the last one?"

"I didn't chase him, I ate him," Croissant defended himself. "According to the taste, you were too good for him."

"You're not eating my new crush, brother." Of course, she knew her Victor would laugh it off, but her brother's overprotectiveness annoyed her. "How would you react if I ate Charlene?"

"Touché," Croissant admitted. "At least promise me it's not a gnoll this time."

"No, he's way cleaner," Chocolatine chirped happily, taking the two lunch bags and leaving the house with her brother. "He is strong, charming, and forceful."

"Eh, you can present him to me once you've caught him." Croissant shrugged, as they separated, him going to Charlene's office and her to the temple. "Maybe we'll get along."

She doubted it.

Chocolatine cheerfully reached the temple she shared with Allison, finding the dryad praying her goddess with Rolo. The golem had brought a sheep, asking Cybele to bless it. "[Multiply

Cattle]." Rolo touched the sheep and activated his Perk, the animal dividing into two, then four, then eight.

Chocolatine waved at the two, then attended her deity's needs. She placed the cake in front of Isengrim's deer statue, knelt, and spoke the prayer. "God of the Hunt, Lord of the Beasts, I offer you my sacrifice. I ask you for your blessing. You are the great white deer who roams the summer woods, the bringer of spring. Oh, Isengrim, please accept my gift."

With the prayer, she sent a few of her SP to her god, and the cake vanished from the altar. Her lord had accepted the offering.

"Chocolatine, my favorite vestal, your cake tastes delicious!" The deer statue's eyes shone, the god Isengrim speaking through with his youthful, cheerful voice. *"You have done well maintaining the natural equilibrium in Murmurin, ousting the lich Furibon from power, and hastening the extinction of demonkind. I am proud of you, keep up the good work!"*

"Thank you, my lord," Chocolatine nodded. "Can I ask for your guidance, oh Isengrim?"

"Of course. What is troubling you, my child?"

"There is a boy I want to breed with, but he will not. How do I breed with him?"

"Is that that Victor whose name you keep repeating in your prayers?" Chocolatine nodded ardently. *"Is he married?"*

"No." If that was the problem, Chocolatine would have solved it long ago. She had lots of poison in her pantry. "He is single, although he does not like it."

"Have you offered to lay with him during the mating season?"

"Yes, I did, but he said he didn't want to break our friendship."

"While I am the god of the hunt, that kind eludes me. I will ask my friend Cybele, goddess of love, on advice on your behalf.

Otherwise, try perfume. The sweeter the smell, the greater your chances of catching your prey unaware."

"Thank you, great Isengrim!"

"Good luck, Chocolatine!"

The priestess ended her prayers, the light leaving out the statue's eyes. She found out that Allison and Rolo had finished her own prayers. "Choc, are you available this evening?" the dryad asked her. "We need anti-vermin spells to help protect the culture from depredation."

"With pleasure." She owed the dryad one. When her Victor tried to make a move on her, proving that the 'friendship' could be overcome, Allison had said that she liked girls—which was true, but she liked boys just as much—to fend him off. The sisterhood resisted! "Do you think we could feed a big city, after the dragons are gone?"

"Ten thousand, if we finish the irrigation canals," Rolo replied. "With judicious use of my, and Allison's [Grow Plant] Perks, we could hasten the landscaping."

"You wish to invite more settlers," Allison guessed.

"Cousins from other tribes," Chocolatine nodded, pumped by Rolo's answer. "I thought about it while in Gevaudan: why do civilized species hate us werewolves, monsters, and predators?"

"Because you eat them," Rolo replied.

"Because we eat them, and we eat them because we lack enough meat; to retaliate, the humans and their kin chase us away from the cities which could sustain our hunger, and the cycle continues! Mimics, vampires, and others adapted by infiltrating civilization, but that is not enough! We need trade, import! By creating a city of monsters which can sustain itself, we can inspire our kindred to imitate us, and 'civilized' species that we can feed in harmony! Maybe even trade!"

"You meant live," Allison picked up. "Live in harmony, not feed."

"Yes, same thing," Chocolatine replied cheerfully, as the two worshippers of Cybele exchanged a glance.

Her service done, the vestal carried the last cake with her to the new building in the north part of Murmurin. Bug fiends under Malfy's direction had constructed a large, ivory-draped, six-floor building there, the tallest next to Emperor Vainqueur's own statue. Chocolatine didn't particularly like the rounded architecture—which the fiends called 'modern and trendy,' but the place stood out.

She found a crowd of monsters gathered in front of it, including the Kobold Rangers, and Malfy himself. A ribbon kept the doors closed, her Victor ready to cut it with his scythe while riding the Black Beast of Murmurin.

The voice of Malfy, enhanced by a spell, resonated, the monsters focusing on him. "Welcome to the grand opening Nethermart, the first fiendish magic item shop in all of Outremonde, open to all monsters and mortals! If you cannot pay with coins, you can keep a tab with us for the low, low price of your soul as collateral! And to celebrate the coming war with Maure, we offer a thirty percent sale on weapons! An axe in every home!"

The crowd of undead, kobolds, gnolls and other monsters cheered as one.

"The Emperor couldn't bear to watch his minions buying stuff with the money he pays them, so he sent me to inaugurate it in his stead!" Victor said, raising his scythe. "In his name, I declare the Nethermart open!"

He narrowed his weapon and cut the ribbon. The monsters immediately rushed to the gates, with Malfy the fiend barely having the time to move out of the way.

Only Chocolatine, Malfy, and Victor remained outside. She immediately worked on her crush. "Vic!" She approached him with a leap. "What a coincidence, I was looking for you!"

"Oh, really?" He didn't sound half as enthusiastic as her. Had she overdone it? "What for?"

"I know you are super exhausted with preparing the Bragging Day, so I prepared you lunch." She offered him the cake, but his free hand didn't reach for it. Instead, the Doer of the Thing appraised the gift with wariness.

"Is it poisoned?" Victor asked.

"Of course not!" Chocolatine replied, offended. "If I wanted to kill, I would eat you, and eating poisoned food is unhealthy."

"That is reassuring," Victor replied, before taking the lunch. "Thanks, Chocolatine."

Her crush started opening the lunchbox, whistling upon seeing the cake. It was working, it was working, it was working...

Then Victor popped out of existence with the cake before he could take a bite, leaving his undead mount behind.

"Unfortunately, that is happening more and more," said Malfy, moving to shake 'hands' with the astonished priestess. "Chocolatine, how beautiful you are today. Thanks for coming to our opening day."

"You're welcome, Malfy. You are my best import source." The werewolf shook the fiend's pincer, regaining her cheery disposition once the bitter disappointment and shock had passed. Unlike other followers of Isengrim, she didn't hate fiends and undead; they were just easy, bountiful prey whose hunt her god condoned. "You look so happy, too!"

"Nethermart's share value is through the roof on Soulwell Street. Thanks to the goodwill gained from our current partnership, we will make a killing on the soul stock exchange."

"Nice," Chocolatine said, although she had no idea what he meant. She glanced around, in case someone was listening, asked him for advice. "You sell everything?"

"Almost. Following the mysterious mass disappearance of swords in the region, we no longer sell those."

Junior strikes again. "Do you have love potions?"

The bug looked at her with what Chocolatine took for disapproval. "We no longer sell love potions. They are unethical, and the equivalent of slipping someone a roofie. We respect our clients' free-will, which is the cornerstone of our bottom-line."

Chocolatine pouted. "But you come from Hell! Shouldn't you offer that kind of solution?"

"We are no longer called Hell," Malfy replied. "After decades of benchmarking studies, our Corporate Overlords identified the name as no longer politically-correct. We have now been rebranded as *Happyland*."

"Happyland?" Chocolatine raised an eyebrow. "It sounds like a fair."

"Exactly the reaction our marketing department looks for. We expect mortals to assimilate the new branding within fifty years, correlating with an increase in soul revenue. I insist that, in spite of what the name would imply, *Happyland* does not sell mind-control devices."

Why couldn't she find an easy solution? "May I ask who is the victim?" Malfy asked, curious.

"Vic."

"Ah, Mr. Victor? I understand the cake part better." The bug let out a sound of interest. "You would be such a good influence on his ethics. Can I offer you my help?"

"You will?" The bug nodded. "Great! Any idea on how to catch him?"

"I believe the quickest solution would be assassinating your rivals for Mr. Victor's affection."

"I can't kill half the world's population!" Chocolatine protested. "It is impractical, and against my religion."

The fiend summoned a pen and a paper, while the first clients exited the Nethermart with weapons, potions, and other items. "Let me ask you, what relationship status are you hoping for? Shotgun wedding? Deadly mantis coupling? Cat and mouse relationship? The more details the better tailored my solution."

"No wedding." Chocolatine hadn't thought that far ahead. "I just want him to break into my temple, tie me up with ropes to my god's statue, then say 'time to *desecrate* this holy place,' and—"

"I do not imagine Mr. Victor in that kind of situation without severe use of mind-control," Malfy interrupted her, scribbling notes. "Which I cannot endorse."

"I just want him to use his [Monster Rider] Perk on me at least once a week." Her brother's overprotectiveness had left her frustrated and starved.

"That Perk can apply to this kind of situation? Thank you for the information, I will tell the Succubus Department." Malfy took notes. "So no marriage? What you want is a purely physical relationship?"

"I would like some foreplay, tension, excitement..."

"Yes, but no tying down. Good. As a demon, I cannot, in good conscience, support marriage." The bug considered the matter. "We at Nethermart sell magical items which can increase your charisma, but Mr. Victor may lose interest upon reaching the naked part of the process. A more rewarding, longer-lasting method would be refashioning you."

"Refashioning?"

"Before I became manager, I was a damnation coach for the Succubus Pickup Scene. We had fall from grace down to a science. Thankfully, Mr. Victor is, what we call in Happyland, a 'good-hearted lecher,' one of the easiest marks. We have many protocols for him."

"Protocols?" Chocolatine frowned. "You were planning to seduce him?"

"We fiends have been subject to libel-filled PR campaigns from angels since our arrival in Outremonde. Unfortunately, Mr. Victor has been influenced by this heavenly propaganda, which slows down our progress in Murmurin; I even discovered he agreed to a Karma insurance plan with them, which means Heaven tries to enter *our* market." The fiend shook with anger, before calming himself. "We will launch a holistic lobbying campaign aimed at nudging Mr. Victor, and through him, the Emperor, towards a complete paradigm shift on the subject of Happyland."

Chocolatine did not understand half of the fiend's buzzwords, but she got the gist of it. "You have a plan."

"Yes, I recommend opening the seduction with Redemption Signaling."

Chocolatine listened in with rapturous attention, the fiend explaining himself with a professional tone.

"It is a technique where you send mixed messages to the mortal target about the possibility of redemption. The idea is to qualify yourself as a PRT, or 'potential redemption target,' and then his heroic instincts will kick in. Mortals are suckers for broken birds. Now, you have to maintain a careful balance, like *'I steal, but I fight worse people,' 'I'm not bad, I just don't follow the rules,'* or *'it is not my fault I am like this, blame society.'*"

"And it *works*?"

"All the time. It would have been even better if we could make a 'cat burglar' motif work with you. The core of the strategy is to make the target believe they can change you, that you could 'go straight' with a special person's love, which they will believe to be themselves. Play hard to get so the mortal believes he has to work for it, and they will fall into the trap."

"It sounds very manipulative though," Chocolatine pointed out.

"Do you want him or not? Then show him signs of the wounded heart beneath your... predatory... exterior, look vulnerable when he thinks you do not know he is watching, and over time, he will get attached." The fiend handed her over the paper note. "Here is a script for you to follow."

Chocolatine read it with great attention, her eyes widening as she went on. He even had a tree chart for each possible answer.

Could she really be desperate enough to follow his advice?

...

"And what happens if you are nice for real?" Chocolatine asked, finding that option nowhere in the chart. "Not pretending."

"I do not understand," Malfy replied. "You mean a double-layer trap? I would not recommend it, only an expert can pull that off."

She would give it a go.

31: Dragon Guests

"You are certain, Manling Victor?" Vainqueur asked, upon looking at the strawberry cake, which his lackey had moved in front of the fairy crystals. "This seems like a waste of good food."

"Positive," his Doer of the Thing said. "Come on, try."

"[Lesser Demonbane]!" Vainqueur cast the exorcism spell with his finger, a ray of light hitting the cake. While the food remained unharmed, a dark, crimson aura escaped it, letting out a terrible scream.

You have exorcised: Demon Strawberry Cake.

"It worked, Manling Victor!" His very first spell! "I am a wizard!"

The dragon had spent days in his cave, practicing the spells that Corpseling Jules taught him. Since Vainqueur never bothered to learn how to read manling language, he had the corpseling teach him how to read scrolls and grimoires.

The dragon picked it up very quickly. Vainqueur could have sworn it took him years to learn to speak his minions' primitive tongue, centuries ago.

"It should work well against Brandon Maure," his lackey said. "His enhancements make him dangerous, but if Your Majesty hits his demonslayer weakness with exorcisms, they should dispel them."

"Then I eat him," Vainqueur nodded in agreement.

"My turn then..." The minion raised his scythe like a staff. "[Death Candle]."

A tiny spirit made of bluish, ghostly flames appeared above the cake, like a candle. It stared at Manling Victor with two yellow spots of eyes without a word. "Nice. I can use the scythe to spellcast. Must be that [Scythe Lord] perk."

"Minion, my guests cannot eat ghosts," Vainqueur pointed out, the flame spirit looking at him next. "You should learn to summon demons, like tasty Malfy."

"One tier at a time, Your Majesty."

"Have you found a way to break the fairy crystal curse?" Vainqueur asked, looking at his beautiful trapped maidens. "While they make for great decoration, we dragons prefer talking, singing princesses to stuffed ones."

"Unfortunately, nobody in Murmurin has powerful enough magic to shatter them. Malfy said his company may have the necessary tools, but he must ask his executives. Charlene also informed me King Roland Gardemagne will come personally to, I quote, *'Recover his niece, meet with the self-proclaimed Emperor of Murmurin, and grant unto him a boon for his service.'* I think he will bring stronger sorcerers with him, maybe Kia."

"Self-proclaimed nothing!" Vainqueur contested angrily. "I am Emperor!"

*Your [**Emperor**] Class is no longer recognized.*

"Of course it is!"

*Your [**Emperor**] Class will be unrecognized until you defeat: Brandon Maure.*

"Minion, when is that moth supposed to attack us?" Vainqueur narrowed his eyes, eager for payback.

"He already should have," Manling Victor replied. "Kia must have damaged his flying fortress enough to delay him. I promoted every able-bodied minion I could find, asked everyone to prepare for a siege, bought weapons from Malfy—"

"Bought?" Vainqueur glared at his minion, horrified. His lackey couldn't be desperate enough to embezzle his treasure!

"With my own money," Victor reassured his master, although it still shocked the dragon. "All of this to say, I wouldn't worry about Maure coming. The only question is, *when,* and with how many soldiers."

"How many steaks," the dragon corrected him. Vainqueur almost wished for that moth to come on his Bragging Day, so he could stylishly smash him before his brethren. Almost.

Someone frantically struck the vault's doorbell, causing Vainqueur and Victor to look at the gate. "Open!" The spells set by his spellcaster minions causing the vault's door to widen and reveal the Kobold Rangers.

"Birds, Your Majesty!" Red the Kobold said, panicked. "Big birds in the sky!"

"Bird*s*?" Manling Victor panicked. "Maure has a *fleet*?"

"More than one!" Blue panicked as well. "Half a dozen with great wings and breathing smoke!"

"Minion, those are not iron birds," Vainqueur clarified, energized. "*They* are here! Prepare the appetizers!"

Manling Victor started to panic. "But, but, but they should have arrived tomorrow!"

"Ah, yes, I forgot to inform you that, unlike your kind, dragons are smart enough to be early when a feast is involved, so they can eat the best parts ahead of the competition."

"Is Your Majesty subtly implying my kind is mentally challenged?" Manling Victor tried to defend his kind's nonexistent honor. "We humans have ten intelligence on average, more than most species."

Pfft, no way, Vainqueur started at nine.

...

Nine.

The average manling started at ten?

...

"Menu," Vainqueur spoke up, his voice ice cold. "Show me my original intelligence score, before I gained the Class system."

Pre-class INT score: 8.

...

"Your Majesty? Why are you twitching? You're scaring me."

"Menu," Vainqueur repeated, this time his voice more ominous. "What is my *correct* score?"

Pre-class INT score: 8.

"No, it is not! What is my true score?"

Pre-class INT score: Square Root 64.

"Better," Vainqueur said, happy with the higher number. "We will welcome the first guests at once, so that I may smugly showcase my superior might and unrivaled intellect. Kobolds!"

"Yes, Your Majesty?"

"Tell the other minions to prepare the snacks. Hurry!" The kobolds scampered off, Vainqueur closing the door's vault behind them. "Minion Victor, remember what I told you. You shall second all of my boasts, not speak unless addressed by a dragon first, and you will repeat that I am good, smart, and wealthy every time I am mentioned."

"Your Majesty, I have been meaning to ask, could we please avoid mentioning classes and levels?"

"Minion, I have rediscovered this ancient dragon system," Vainqueur reminded his Doer of the Thing. "Why *wouldn't* I brag about it?"

"Because other dragons will compete with you over treasure if they learn to access it."

Oh, he was worried about his master's safety and long-term dominance. Adorable. "Good, that will keep me sharp," Vainqueur replied, embracing the challenge. "It would do no good for my reputation if I was the strongest of my kind because they are all weak; does anyone boasts about being the best manling? Or the best troll? No, because nobody wants to be the best manling. Everyone wants to be the best *dragon* because dragons are *awesome*."

"But your greed—"

"Minion, while there is nothing greater than my hoard, I will brag fairly. Silence invites accusations of fraud, and I shall prove that I earned my wealth. Finally, without this system, I would not have had the power to cure the curse of the evil Furibon, who had to be destroyed. Other dragons must know in case the lich is ever released from his seal."

Manling Victor put his hand on his face. "I knew this day would come..."

"Of course, I told you," Vainqueur replied, before making use of that [Dungeon Owner] Perk of his. With a thought, he teleported atop the highest of his castle's tower, under the bright sun.

Vainqueur glanced at his territory, finding that his minions had finished refurbishing the castle as he commanded, even adding a stone crown to the tallest tower. Perfect.

"MINION!" Vainqueur summoned his chief of staff at his side, before giving a majestuous roar as his manling almost fell from the tower.

Above, six dragons answered with roars of their own, the flock descending to nest on the various towers' roofs; the minions staffing the castle stopped briefly to look at them through the windows, and Vainqueur didn't chastise them for it. Being in his company was already an honor, more of his kind was an overdose to their senses.

His first guests were, as he expected, his close family, among them his favorite cousin, the brown wind dragon Genialissime. A clutch of three dragonlings the size of poneys followed him, the children he had gained custody of after mating with Blightswamp. Each of them was black like their mother, but Vainqueur hoped they had inherited the father's intellect. He also noticed his niece, the red dragon Jolie, all grown up.

Unfortunately, there was one exception: a white, frost dragon with icicle spikes growing out of his back, smugly staring at Vainqueur with smug blue eyes. "Icefang," Vainqueur said in the old dragon tongue, glaring at his hated rival. That smug lizard had grown almost as big as the great red dragon. "Still unable to breed?"

"Vainqueur, still poor?" Icefang replied with a jab of his own, flying above the castle without bothering to land, a very foppish manoeuver. "And it is *Great King* Icefang now!"

"I was never poor!"

"Compared to me, you are!"

"Your hoard is made of silver!" Vainqueur contested, refusing to be upstaged on his big day. "It does not count! It does not shine enough!"

"Wealth knows no limits!" Icefang shouted back. "I hope for you that you can back up your boasts, for I will count every coin!"

"Then you will count until the end of time!"

Besides the natural rivalry between red and frost dragons—since the reds were obviously bigger and wealthier—Icefang had made it his life's purpose to upstage Vainqueur as the greatest of all dragons, spending all his time while awake gathering a bigger hoard, beautiful princesses, and the finest of minions. He always failed, and a fifty-years nap had only worsened his bitterness.

Vainqueur would show him the true meaning of rich.

"Uncle Vainqueur!" Vainqueur's niece Jolie landed on a tower near his own. She had grown into a small but elegant red dragon, bigger than an elephant. "Happy Bragging Day!"

"Jolie, you have grown bigger!" Vainqueur saluted his niece, as he did his cousin. "Good to see you too, Genialissime!"

"How could I miss my dear cousin's Bragging Day?" the wind dragon replied happily, his clutch of dragonlings landing on their father's back. "Children, I present you your first cousin once removed, Vainqueur Knightsbane. Vainqueur, this is Courageux, Sage, and Fort."

"Money?" one of the dragonlings, Courageux, asked, with his father's big eyes.

"How much?" replied his sister Sage, while the third tried to speak the word 'gold.'

"Oh, they are saying their first words!" Vainqueur rejoiced, Genialissime nodding with paternal pride. "They have your eyes."

"Thank you, but we must discuss an important subject." Genialissime scowled. "A great enemy is in our midst."

"The evil Furibon," Vainqueur replied grimly.

"Your minion messengers told us of the Goldslayer Furibon, and his insane scheme to turn the world's gold to lead," Icefang said. "Where is he?"

"I defeated Furibon, and my lackey, Victor," Vainqueur put his hand behind the shy Manling Victor's back, pushing him at the forefront, "sealed his twisted soul inside his scythe. Manling Victor, show them!"

Manling Victor, anxious at so many dragons looking up at him, raised his weapon, showcasing the dark soul kept within. "Manling Victor does a great service to dragonkind, keeping this depraved lead-lover sealed," Genialissime declared. "I propose that no dragon eats Manling Victor until he dies fulfilling his sacred duty."

"For as long as the Evil Furibon remains sealed, I welcome this motion," Icefang said.

"Uh, thanks..." the manling said, taking a step back as the dragons' eyes turned intense.

Genialissime whistled. "Vainqueur, your chief of staff can speak and understand dragon?"

"I taught him well," Vainqueur boasted. He knew Manling Victor would reflect well on him!

"That is because Your Majesty is good, smart, and wealthy," his lackey confirmed. "Not necessarily in that order."

"Anyone can teach draconic," Icefang replied. "Nothing to brag about. The dragon language is pure and simple, even the lesser species can learn it!"

"Are you implying that dragon speech is on the same level as the manlings' backward language, Icefang?" Genialissime replied, offended. "Teaching a member of the lesser races our complex and noble language demands extraordinary effort, and that primitive humanoid speaks like a native!"

"While I am proud that my *unparalleled* genius spilled onto my chief of staff, how do you find that less bragworthy than defeating the evil Furibon?" Vainqueur asked, incensed they did not cheer his great victory.

"You cannot boast about it," Icefang replied. "Since according to your own *War of the Hoard*, which my own chief of staff found poorly written, by the way, Manling Victor delivered the final blow and sealed the evil Furibon. You could not have destroyed the lich for good on your own, so it does not count."

"I agree, unfortunately," said Genialissime. "The boast goes to Manling Victor alone."

"But he is my minion!" Vainqueur protested. "I chose him, prepared him! When I found him he was but a homeless thief! I made him the best chief of staff in the world!"

"You can boast about your great choice of minion, which is bragworthy, but it would not be fair to claim the death of Furibon as your own, Vainqueur," Genialissime said. "I am sorry, cousin, I cannot give you full points for this boast."

"This is an indignity!" Vainqueur replied angrily. "I will not stand by this! Look at the castle I claimed from the lich! See the towers? See the lava?"

"Mmm... seven towers." Icefang hesitated, even he admiring the architecture. "Good. It is a very good castle."

"It is the greatest castle in the world, brimming with my dragon majesty! Hundreds of undead minions built it!"

"But can it *fly*?" Icefang nitpicked, ignored by the others.

"Uncle Vainqueur, you have undead minions?" Jolie blinked in awe.

"Hundreds of them!" Vainqueur boasted, the dragons amazed by this status symbol. "Those I do not eat, I raise!"

"Uh, you eat still minion meat?" Jolie complained, less enthusiastic than before. "Should you brag about it?"

"My niece is a cattletarian," Vainqueur told his confused chief of staff with a sigh. "She only eats non-speaking animals and cattle."

He found that dragon movement ridiculous since every creature had the fundamental right to be eaten by him. Discriminating made them no better than manlings.

Also, he had heard that she let her minions ride on her back, which he found socially offending. He hoped that her teenage rebellion phase wouldn't last another century.

"Manlings and other sentient beings have souls, like us," Jolie said, most of the other dragons rolling their eyes or snickering. "Yes, eating them and abducting their princesses is morally wrong."

"Except elves," Vainqueur told his chief of staff. "Elves are fine."

"While I applaud your stand on not eating my kind, why not extend that mercy to elves?" Manling Victor asked. "They're people too."

"Your chief of staff is badly trained, Vainqueur," Icefang said. "He speaks out of turn."

"No, it is fine, I will explain cattletarianism to him, too!" Jolie replied, before turning to Manling Victor and speaking with a teacher-like tone. "Manling Victor, elves are not people. They are *elves*. They eat grass like cows, and they make the best princesses."

"Have you released the one I caught for your first Bragging Day back into the wild?" Vainqueur asked his niece, who dutifully nodded. "Good. Every dragon must be mindful of preserving the wildlife."

"Princesses are an endangered species in the north due to wanton dragon overhunting," Icefang lamented. "I wish more of my kind was environment-conscious."

"Blightswamp has been trying to find a way to preserve them by raising them in captivity," Genialissime said. "However, she has yet to find the way noble ladies evolve into princesses. She thinks they need knights to undergo the metamorphosis."

"Princessness only happens in the wild," Icefang replied with contempt. "Also, where is the sport in raising princesses at home? The hunt is half the pleasure."

While he despised Icefang, Vainqueur could not agree more. He had considered using his [Dynasty] Perk to create nobles and then princesses, before realizing it would dilute the value of wild maidens.

Sensing the spotlight getting away from where it belonged—on Vainqueur—the Emperor of Murmurin made a bold move. "While tomorrow shall be my true Bragging Day, before all my other guests, as a reward for your quick arrival, I shall present you a sneak peek of my magnificent hoard!"

"Ohoh, that should be amusing," Icefang said. "I'm sure you can't even bathe in it!"

32: Demon Feast

Much to Vainqueur's satisfaction, when Icefang looked upon his magnificent hoard, the frost dragon's eyes widened as if he had suffered from a stroke.

"So huge and deep!" Jolie walked on the hoard, amazed by its depth, its warmth, its texture... its shininess. As a kingly gesture, Vainqueur let his family touch his treasure, so they could *feel* his wealth.

"It's so warm and golden!" Genialissime added. "It's... it's the biggest hoard I have ever seen!"

"Indeed!" Vainqueur boasted with a quiet, smug voice. "Can you feel the warmth? The richness? The perfect mesh of jewels, gold, and princesses?"

"How did *you* accumulate that much gold?" Icefang asked, ever resentful. "Your treasure could barely fill a cave one hundred years ago!"

"It is because I discovered a great, ancient secret," Vainqueur kept boasting. "A system designed to make dragons even richer! By dragons, for dragons!"

"Twelve gods, please forgive me..." Manling Victor muttered to himself in a corner, while the dragons examined every inch of Vainqueur's hoard, looking for a fake setup. "I tried. I'm so sorry..."

"An ancient secret?" Jolie turned to her uncle with stars in her eyes, and so did his small first cousins once removed.

"A great sorcery, if somewhat faulty." Vainqueur decided not to mention the intelligence score errors nor his problems with the Emperor Class, before raising his index finger. "Which allows me to summon treasure by poking manlings to death!"

"This is gibberish," Icefang contested, and even Genialissime seemed puzzled. "What next, the moon is not a planet, and death is not a birth defect?"

Vainqueur realized that too many revelations at once may be too much to stomach for his kind, and so reluctantly, kept the dark secret of dragon mortality to himself. The world was not ready yet. "It is the truth," Vainqueur defended his greatest discovery. "By taking levels in the amazing Noble Class, I now earn a stipend of shiny gold every month!"

"What?!" All the dragons' eyes turned at him.

"I knew I was right to take that insurance plan..." Manling Victor muttered. "Thank the gods I did."

His dragon master ignored him and proudly showed his guests the iron plate around his neck, and began to boast eagerly, "I, Vainqueur, am the greatest adventurer in the world! The manlings worship the ground I walk on when I do not fly! They pay me to kill their kind, and so do their gods!"

"This plate made you rich?" Icefang looked at it with greed.

"Oh, look, princesses!" Jolie noticed the trapped maidens in the fairy crystals, suddenly more interested in them than the secret of gold farming. "Two elves, so beautiful... and a human. Uncle Vainqueur, that one is not ethical."

"They are stuffed!" Icefang complained. "They cannot dance nor sing! It is *indragon*!"

"Yes, feel jealous of my wealth and treasures," Vainqueur taunted his rival. He opened his mouth to gloat further when his castle trembled, and a shrieking sound erupted.

"The magical alarm," Manling Victor said, panicked. "Maure!"

"No, that is my vault's alarm!" Vainqueur glanced and smelled around, looking for an uninvited guest, and found none. He immediately glared at Icefang. "A thief! A thief in my hoard!"

"Vainqueur, I respect myself too much to steal your gold on your own Bragging Day," Icefang sneered back. "And silver is better, purer."

"No, it is not," Vainqueur replied to that heretic.

"Mayhaps this caused the sound?" Genialissime asked, pointing a claw at the second set of doors in the vault. Vainqueur squinted at them.

Indeed, the gate to Hell did shine strangely.

At once, without much warning, the chains holding the doorway closed broke. As the gates opened, a burst of sulfuric smoke entered the vault, alongside dozens of imps, fiends, and bug-like monsters. All of them carried weapons and wore armor, walking as an ordered regiment on Vainqueur's hoard.

"The seals broke?" Manling Victor raised his scythe. "But Choc and the others reinforced them! Unless..."

"Vainqueur, your illegal occupation of King Maure's property ends here!" A huge, tasty fiend that looked like a mix between a cow, a bat, and a humanoid stepped through the gates. "We, Maure Hellcorporated, shall take back our market share!"

The sight of these paupers desecrating his treasure room briefly paralyzed Vainqueur with fury, before he understood the situation. "Ah, good thinking, Manling Victor," the dragon told his confused chief of staff. "Excellent idea to bring appetizers for the early guests."

"Is that the buffet?" Genialissime said with a cheerful expression, humming at the sulfuric smell. "Nice, they smell spicy."

The fiendish leader suddenly realized that he faced seven hungry dragons of various sizes, and his troops took a step back.

"I thought you, Vainqueur, would be stingy on the food, but I am pleasantly surprised," Icefang said, glimpsing at the humanoid cattle with hunger. "He's a bit skinny around the edges, but it will make for a passable snack."

"A talking cow?" Jolie looked at the fiendish captain with interested eyes. "A new kind of cattle? It's grey enough not to count for my regime! Dibs on the cattle!"

The fiend's eyes widened in panic. "Retreat!" the cattle shouted to its troops. "It's a trap! IT'S A TRAP!"

The gold coins below the fiend moved on their own, taking the shape of a manling-like creature, which immediately restrained it from behind. Vainqueur knew he was right to give his hoard self-defense classes.

And then...

Chomp!

Jolie swallowed the cattle fiend whole, and the other adult dragons rushed for the gate with hunger. The fiends tried to run away back to Hell through the gate, only for them to get frozen by Icefang's chilling breath or stopped by the hoard as Genialissime closed in.

And so the feast began.

Vainqueur watched with quiet joy as he saw his niece and cousins catch the food and devour it with ravenous energy. Genialissime's children, too young to hunt alone, worked together to bite a screaming demon's legs and drag him to a corner; even his bitter rival enjoyed the appetizer, showing classy table manners by snapping fiends in half before eating them like sticks.

"Holy Hell..." Victor stared at the scene, horrified, putting a hand on his mouth. "It's... it's... savage..."

"Manling Victor, you've seen me feast for months," Vainqueur replied, delighting at the scene. His guests were fed, and the thieves punished. Win-win!

"There are more behind that door!" Jolie shouted, her mouth drenched in fiendish blood, as she put her neck through the gate. "Spicy!"

"Safari time!" Genialissime rejoiced, moving through the gate with the others in tow.

Vainqueur was slightly bothered that they would ignore his wealth for the food, but couldn't blame them. They had flown for miles and burned a lot of fat to come here. "Good work, minion. Your quick thinking showcased the true depth of my wealth and the bountifulness of my domain."

"Your Majesty, this wasn't my doing," the manling replied. "I believe the seals were sabotaged from our side, which means Maure not only has agents in Murmurin. This may be the opening salvo of a full invasion."

Vainqueur's eyes flared with fury. "The moth attacks us on my big day?!"

The castle trembled, and all magical alarms went off with strident sounds. The enraged Vainqueur immediately activated his [Dungeon Owner] Perk and teleported outside, on the roof.

The dragon found his castle under siege by a flock of gargoyles and spearmen riding wyverns, who fought his kobold and undead minions on the fortifications. That damn metal eagle flew high above the southern desert, followed by a large flock of flying beasts.

On the ground, a black mass, the moth's land army, spread out of the sandy lands and into his dominion. That was a *lot* of fiends and elf cattle, more than Vainqueur had ever seen gathered in one place. They were crossing the canals his minions had built, and rushed towards Murmurin with pillage on their minds.

"You will not ruin my big day!" Vainqueur incinerated the nearest gargoyles and wyvern-riders with his holy breath, their corpses falling into the lava below. His mere presence emboldened the minions, who shot arrows and spears at the invaders. The dragon took flight, hunting down the panicked air force with claws and flame.

Two circles of light materialized on the castle's ramparts, and Vainqueur instantly realized what that meant. "Not my castle!" the dragon snarled, flying above the crater, as the distant iron eagle fired two projectiles at his lair.

Vainqueur hit one with a fireball, causing it to detonate harmlessly above the crater, but the other slipped past his guard and reached his lair.

A magical barrier, the very same which Furibon had hidden behind during the War of the Hoard, stopped the weapon before it could hit the castle. A powerful burst of compressed wind blasted both minions and invaders in all directions, making the crater tremble; yet the barrier resisted.

Manling Victor rushed out of the castle's gates, riding the Black Beast of Murmurin and followed by a group of undead led by Corpseling Jules. "I had Jules activate Furibon's old defenses," Manling Victor explained as he glanced up at his master. "How many enemies?"

"All of the food in this backward desert," Vainqueur replied, unable to count.

"The entire Ishfanian army is attacking us?" Manling Victor panicked. "Your Majesty made Maure mad when you punched him."

"The foolish moth knows my emperorness is the greatest threat to his authority," Vainqueur replied.

*Your [**Emperor**] Class is not recognized.*

"Yes, it is!" Vainqueur insisted.

"They're going to Murmurin?"

"The moth is trying to take back my hard-won empire, break the seal keeping Furibon imprisoned, and ruin my big day!" Vainqueur snarled, imparting on his lackey the seriousness of the situation.

"I think he wants to wipe us out then continue to invade Gardemagne, as he planned. He must be stopped right there."

"Yes!" The dragon cared about one thing and one thing only. "We will defend my hoard and my castle, even if we have to burn every single elf out there. The coins must be protected."

"If that magical barrier can resist one of their 'wind spears,' then their air force shouldn't have what it takes to break it," Manling Victor pointed out, before turning to Jules. "You can hold the castle by yourself?"

"If I can maintain the magical protections and raise the dead as they fall, I believe we will have enough forces to," Jules said. "But if they take the village and climb the mountain, their mages may either disable the barrier or, more likely, wake up the volcano to sink the castle."

Vainqueur froze. That would destroy his hoard!

"We must stop their troops at Murmurin," said Manling Victor, showing his worth as a military advisor. "Your Majesty, the other minions and I can defend the castle and the town, but none of us can fly nor defeat Maure himself. He's probably commanding the attack from the eagle's bridge. If we take him down, the army will fall back."

"Minion, that is an iron bird, not a bridge," Vainqueur replied, before glaring at the iron fortress. Everyone counted on him to save the world. It was his moment in the spotlight. "Minion, will I gain a Crest if I kill that moth?"

"If not, I don't know what it will take."

Vainqueur nodded, extending his wings. "Minion Victor, I promote you from my military advisor to Minion General. You will win this minion war against the moth in time before my guests arrive, and you shall protect my hoard with your life."

"I will try—"

"No, you will," Vainqueur coached him. "Manling Victor, you found me when you tried to steal from my hoard, do you remember?"

"Every day of my life."

"Then you must understand how much I trust you to entrust its safety to you," Vainqueur continued, the manling's eyes widening at the honor. "I do this because I trust you. You are my prized chief of staff, and this is my big day. You *cannot* fail."

His lackey said nothing, then returned Vainqueur's words with a sharp, thankful nod. "Alright, Your Majesty, I will. We all count on you to win this."

"Of course," he replied, as Jules cast a spell and briefly disabled the barrier, allowing them out. "Dragons always win."

And with those wise words, Vainqueur flew out of the crater, invigorated by both his minions' cheers and his own burning desire for payback. Manling Victor rode with kobones towards Murmurin, while Jules set the barrier up again before invaders could slip through.

Five wyvern riders attempted to intercept Vainqueur as he rushed towards the iron eagle, but he shot them down with fireballs without slowing down. The moth may have challenged him on the ground through trickery, but Vainqueur ruled the skies.

Flying at greater speed than he ever did before, which he attributed to his stat gains, Vainqueur reached the iron eagle, blasting through the air force protecting it. The strange musket-like weapons on the fortress' back turned towards him.

"Vainqueur!" Brandon Maure, transformed into his demonic moth form and wielding his blade, flew out of the iron eagle alongside a flock of demons. "You have slighted Brandon Maure long enough! Today you die!"

"One of us will!" Vainqueur roared and engaged the flying fortress in battle.

33: The Monsters of Murmurin

When Victor reached Murmurin, he found the village under siege. The Ishfanian scouts had reached it first.

Thankfully, all the training and drilling had borne fruit. Everyone in the V&V Adventurer Company was armed, and the citizens had set barricades south of the village, where the bulk of the army came from. Allison and Rolo had summoned a thick, dense barrier of thorns and blackberries around the village to delay the invaders, entangling soldiers with plants.

Rushing on the back of the Black Beast from the north, Victor rode to the town square, where the minions fought off dozens of invaders around Vainqueur's statue. Most of the enemies were armored elf soldiers with tridents or cursed bows while huge gargoyles served as their heavy hitters.

Thanks to the weapons crafted by Barnabas or bought from Malfy—both of whom participated in the battle—the gnolls, kobolds, and undead held their own against their opponents, swarming them at the numbers of three against one. The werewolves, fully transformed and led by Croissant, handled the stronger gargoyles.

Vainqueur Junior, too, had joined the melee, grabbing elves with his hands and swallowing them whole. Other mimics, shaped like chests, swords, and cakes, followed its lead, feasting on the elves like wolves among sheep.

The sight of everyone working together warmed Victor's heart a little.

The strangest of the attackers were ethereal, demon-shaped living shadows; they cast lightning spells at gnolls and kobolds, killing one with each strike. Red and the Rangers attempted to shoot them with arrows and musket bullets, but they phased through them. Only Chocolatine, who kept her human form, and the priest of the Moon Man managed to hit them with light spells.

"Chief!" Red rejoiced at Victor's arrival. "Our weapons can't hit the shadows!"

But Chocolatine's spells could. As incorporeal beings, they were probably only vulnerable to magic... or to specific abilities. Victor used his [Monster Insight] on the closest shadow monster.

Sombreux

Shadow Fiend (Demon)

Strong against: Unholy, Darkness, Frost, Physical, all status effects.

Weak against: Demonslayer, Holy, Light, Necromancy, Magical effects.

A veteran of three downsizings. Immune to physical attacks as a bodiless soul; doesn't know you eat them for breakfast or would have fled. Hopes killing everyone in Murmurin will earn him a promotion to Financial Affairs.

"You must be the Infercorp representative," the shadow fiend hissed at Victor. "Genocide Choc!"

"You're half-right," Victor replied. "No fiend from Hell can hit me, from what I heard."

"But we aren't from Hell," the demon said with a smug, amused tone. "We're from Happyland."

*Your [**Get out of Hell Card**] Perk has been canceled, because, duh, demons.*

Son of a... Trusting his [Monster Insight], Victor charged at the shadow fiend, and cut it with his weapon. The shadowy monster laughed it off, only to find itself dragged into the scythe by surprise.

*Critical hit! [**Helheim**] and [**Steal Life**] activated!*

Aha! His Helheim perk worked well against incorporeal beings!

Victor felt the lifeforce of the creature move into him, reducing his fatigue, while the fiend's soul joined Furibon's in the scythe. *"A roommate,"* the lich said, with a tone that sounded both irritated, and strangely happy. *"Finally, some company to talk to."*

By the end, he would have a *lot* of it. "I'm always here," Victor pointed out.

"Good company."

Victor, like a mounted grim reaper, struck down any soldier or fiend he could, receiving notifications of critical hits with half of his strikes. Months before, he doubted he could kill so many enemies so casually; hell, he would have probably fled while using the chaos of the battle. Surviving Vainqueur's antics had made him braver.

A fearsome monster looking like a fiend covered in bone spikes engaged Victor in combat, parrying his scythe with a shield and trying to drag him off his mount with a spine-whip. His Black Beast mount attempted to crush the attacker, but the agile fiend leaped backward. Victor prepared to target him with a necromancy spell, while his foe swung his whip threateningly.

Then the monster gargled blood, as a reptilian hand pierced his back and went through the chest. The corpse collapsed, revealing Savoureuse in full assassin mode, her claws sharp and bloodied. "Sav!" The sight rejoiced Victor. "You haven't run away?"

"I couldn't!" she replied, causing him to facepalm with his free hand. "Fairy beasts coming from the north cut my retreat!"

Fairy beasts? "Melodieuse," Victor cursed, as he cut down a gargoyle's head before it could drag him off his mount. If she came from the north, then the entire village was now surrounded.

Rolo and Allison joined the fray as well, with the iron golem hitting a gargoyle with a shovel. "[Sheepinize]."

With the word, the giant gargoyle turned into a black sheep, which Rolo kindly moved out of his way. "Farmers can do that?" Victor asked, astonished.

"At level fifty-one," Rolo replied, raising his shovel threateningly at fiends. "You will all become Rolo's sheep!"

"Sheeps, Rolo," Allison replied, summon giant flytraps to catch the gargoyles. "Here, it's *sheeps*."

Victor suddenly realized he didn't want to learn where most of the sheep in Murmurin came from. Pink, who unlike the other rangers didn't fire projectiles at the fiends, began to sing, "*Arise, children of the dragon, the day of glory has arrived!*"

[Bardic Song] *has raised your Strength by one stage.*

"Bardic Song?" Victor blinked, as he cut down an elf bowman before he could shoot him off his mount. "Pink, you took levels in [Bard]?!"

"Since I wrote *The War of the Hoard*!" Pink shouted back, before returning to her singing. "*To arms, minions! Form your battalions, let's march, let's march! Let cattle blood fertilize our crops!*"

Encouraged by Pink's bloodthirsty anthem, Victor and the other minions backed the remaining scouts against a house's walls and slaughtered them, with only the shadow demons managing to scamper off from the slaughter.

"Meat treasure!" Vainqueur Junior gargled, as he spat out the remains of a half-digested elf.

"What is the situation?" Victor asked Red, looking at their forces. Most of the minions had survived, but they had lost dozens to the initial strike, their corpses littering on the ground. Hundreds more minions and citizens gathered at the town square, waiting for instructions. His [Mook Promotion] Perk told him many could be promoted, having gained experience from the battle.

"We pushed back the scouts, but a lot more will come!" Red said, his claws shaking as he held his musket close. "Thousands!"

"Too many!" Croissant said, Charlene by his side. She looked *very* bothered by her boyfriend's wolfish appearance but stood with him wielding a spear. "We've got to evacuate!"

"They've already encircled us!" Savoureuse replied.

"And they have cavalry," Allison, who herself couldn't leave the village, pointed out with a cool head. "They will catch up to us if we try to flee."

"Charlene," Victor turned to the one human in the group. "Have you informed Gardemagne?" Since the King was due to visit them soon with his retinue, they could warn him in time to mobilize an army and stop Maure's.

"I sent messenger pigeons, but archers shot most of them," she replied, clearly fearing for her life. "I have no idea if any of them got through, and it will take them hours to send an army."

They were on their own.

As everyone looked at him, Victor realized it fell on him to organize the defense. "We can't win a prolonged battle against their overwhelming numbers," he admitted. Especially since those were just the scouts, and the bulk of the army was running at them. "All we can do is delay until Vainqueur takes down the flying fortress and causes the army's rout."

"The Emperor has taken the field?" Blue raised his undead skull at the skies, ablaze with flames.

"To lead us to victory!" Victor raised his scythe, bringing hope back in the minions' heart. "The Emperor is fighting for the great hoard as we speak! Which is his *gold*, but also *us*! If these paupers take the village, they will steal our lives, our sheep, and our coins! Will we run away, tails between our legs? No! We will send them back to the nowhere from which they came! Remember how we won the *War of the Hoard*? We bested them once, and we will do it again! For we are *V&V*! We are mighty! We are the hoard!"

That was complete, desperate improvisation based on cartoon speeches he watched on Earth, but it worked. "We are the hoard!" the minions cheered, while the sanest citizens such as Allison or Charlene tentatively raising their hands in support. "We are the hoard!"

"They will meet their doooooooom!" Yellow the Kobone couldn't help himself.

"For my local monopoly!" Malfy added his own battle cry.

"Follow my command, and we shall prevail!" Victor shouted. "For the hoard!"

*[**Rally Minion**] activated! All minions' stats raised by one stage!*

Victor immediately singled out the minions whom he could promote, namely ten gnolls and all the Kobold Rangers save for Red himself. "Come here," he said, before touching and causing them to evolve in quick succession. "You are hereby given a pay raise!"

As they evolved, the gnolls grew from tiny to a three meters tall, monstrous, and emaciated gnoll humanoids, with a skull-like face and ashen skin. Their eyes turned red, simmering with bestial fury.

Pink and Black, the living half of the Kobold Rangers, turned into pink and black colored copies of Red, albeit with Pink having a more effeminate figure. Blue and Yellow changed into skeletal versions of their kindred, with a black, beating heart in their chests; Blue's bones turned deep blue, and Yellow's golden.

Your Gnolls evolved into **Tomb Gnolls.**

Kobold Pink Ranger and Kobold Black Ranger evolved into **Raptor Rangers.**

Kobone Blue Ranger and Kobone Yellow Ranger evolved into **Kobloods.**

"We are all grown, and color assorted!" Blue rejoiced.

Victor immediately began to distribute orders. "Allison, keep entangling the enemy. Rangers, set the thorns on fire once enough soldiers are trapped. Shoot anyone who breaks through with arrows and bullets. Malfy, cover the skies with insects, so they can't shoot arrows at us. We must create such chaos, that they will not be able to avoid friendly fire. Pink, keep singing. You, the squid priest, and Chocolatine—"

"Yeeees?" The werewolf's head perked up at her name being called, which made him shiver.

"You focus on buffing the werewolves and ashen gnolls with spells or healing the wounded unless confronted by shadow fiends, in which case you toast them." She seemed to enjoy the wording a bit too much. "Rolo, Junior, Sav, we will fortify the north with the new troops. Everyone else hit and run; ambush, isolate, swarm, then retreat behind flames and thorns. Bleed them dry for every inch of ground."

"What new troops, Vic?" Savoureuse asked, anxious.

"These ones: [Animate Dead]," Victor activated his Perk, raising the dead from both sides as zombies. Since he didn't sacrifice any gold, he only created non-sentient monsters, but they would make for nice meat shields and supplement the heavy hitters.

As Malfy summoned an enormous swarm of hungry locusts and Allison began to grow thorn trenches, Victor turned to Red the Kobold. "You are in charge. Remember, ambush and retreat, like in Haudemer."

"Yes, chief!" The rangers made a pose. "We will protect the hoard with our lives!"

Congratulations! For showing your valor leading an army of minions against overwhelming odds in the name of your dragon master, your [Monster Squire] Class has been promoted to [Monster Knight (Red Dragon)]!

Your [Rally Minion] and [Mook Promotion] Class Perks have been strengthened!

Huh? Nice...

Or so he thought until his whole body began to itch and burn. Within *seconds*, jet black wings almost identical to Vainqueur's own grew out of Victor's back and through his cloak, while a crimson, reptilian tail sprung out of his pants.

Victor remained immobile on his mount for several seconds, uncomfortable with both the new sensations and the stares he received from the other minions. Furibon laughed like a maniac from inside his scythe.

"Shut up!" the wielder complained. He could swing his new tail as if he had grown up with it, but...

Goddamnit, he was turning into a mini-Vainqueur! How gross!

No matter. He would worry about it later. He ordered his mount to dash north, followed by his undead thralls and the other minions.

...

As it turned out, riding a beast while having a tail was *incredibly* uncomfortable.

The makeshift group quickly reached the sheep pens north of the village, where five fairy hounds like those which they had fought in Ishfania had broken in, stepping on the food they gathered for the dragon guests. Melodieuse, riding the back of a horned, black pegasus, oversaw them from above, alongside three giant, monstrous crows and an escort of wyvern riders.

"My flock!" Rolo went berserk at the sight of his sheep trampled down, his rusted body heating up; moving faster than Victor's own mount, the golem broke past the fence like an unstoppable juggernaut. Following him, the Reaper cut a fairy hound's flesh as it attempted to lunge at him, both the beast and the squire's own ride circling one another. Savoureuse hid among the panicked sheep, waiting for her chance for a sneak attack.

The fairy birds dived on them like birds of prey, one of them catching Savoureuse by surprise and trying to drag her up. Junior grabbed some of the sheep trying to flee the battle, then launched them at the crow as improvised projectiles, forcing the crow to release its captive. Then the mimic grabbed the sword working as its lure and used it to slice the neck of a fairy hound reaching for him. "Sword!" Junior snarled, showing surprising swordsmanship.

Above them, Melodieuse began to sing a spell. Victor, still struggling against butt pain, attempted to blast her by channeling a blast of Hellfire from his fingertips, but she immediately summoned a purple barrier around herself and her mount.

Her wyvern-rider bodyguards began to bombard them with a volley of arrows, with Victor incinerating the projectiles before they could hit him. Rolo just shrugged them off, busy manhandling a fairy hound and beating the hell out of it with his shovel. The arrows hit Junior, making it moan in pain, while Savoureuse dodged everything.

"[Death Candle]," Victor spellcast, summoning small will-o' wisps from the remains of the sheep. He sent them to swarm the wyvern riders, halting the attack. Meanwhile, the undead he had created finally joined the fight, swarming a fairy hound like the horde of zombies they were. The beast collapsed under the weight of dozens of walking corpses.

Well, that was going way better than expected! Maybe they could handle—

"[Crimson Lightning]."

As Melodieuse uttered these words, a powerful red bolt of lightning hit Victor and his mount. The black beast of Murmurin was felled in one blow, while its rider ejected from its back and crashed on the dirt, losing his grip over his scythe along the way.

You have taken massive damage! Critical health!

"Ohoh," Furibon cackled inside his scythe, as Victor struggled to get up. *"Will your luck finally run out?"*

Victor raised his head from the dust, finding a fairy hound opening its jaws in hunger, ready to devour him. A shadowy giant bird descended to feast on him as well.

No.

It was way, way bigger than the birds, or a wyvern rider.

The fairy hound barely had the time to look up at incoming death, before the giant flyer landed on it, its sheer strength scattering a cloud of dust and sheep in all directions.

When Victor regained his sight, he found himself staring into the yellow eyes of a green dragon almost as big as Vainqueur, albeit more crocodilian than lizard-like.

"You smell like a chief of staff, and you look dragon enough to be halfway civilized," the green dragon said with a foppish, arrogant tone. The surprise sight of the ancient reptile caused the beasts and wyvern-riders to halt their assault. "Tell me, minion of Vainqueur, is this the welcome buffet? I was told there would a sweet poison sauce, which tastes good with cows and pigs, for the fashionably early."

"Yes!" Victor replied, realizing the opportunity offered to him. He pointed a finger at the fairy beasts. "But the fomors are trying to spoil the food!"

"The fairies feel acting mischievous again? Haven't they learned the food chain the first time we ate their cattle?" The dragon turned to the skies and roared. "Vainqueur brought us elves and tasty birds for snacks!"

"Dibs on the elves!" A red dragon smaller than Vainqueur roared back as it descended from above, picking a wyvern rider like a hawk attacking a dove. Melodieuse immediately cast a spell, strengthening her barrier, but her escort wasn't so lucky.

Soon, an entire flock of dragons descended from the heavens, most going south to pick on Ishfania's army, but four dived to prey on the wyverns and the fairy birds. The green dragon left Victor to feast on the fairy hounds and the sheep without discrimination, turning the battle into a one-sided feasting slaughter.

Melodieuse looked down on the disaster, leaving her escort to die while slipping closer to Victor with a hateful gaze. "The hellgate has fallen," she said. "My plans for Gardemagne wasted. You ruined *everything*."

"It was you all along," Victor realized, as his hands reached for his scythe. "The Apple, the Scorchers, Maure's invasion... you set it all up!"

"None of this would have happened without you," Melodieuse glared back at him. "You taught Vainqueur the secrets of this cursed class system, and now our rightful quest to take back Outremonde will become harder than ever before."

"Taught? You're exaggerating there."

"It does not matter. More of the lizards will follow his lead. But you will not live long enough to see it. [Darkest Fear]."

A dark aura swallowed Victor before he could retaliate, draining him of his life and vitality. An irrational fear of death seized him, as he looked at it from above.

*HP and SP reduced to one! [**Terror**] ailment! [**Necrophobia**] ailment!*

"Any last words?" Melodieuse asked Victor with fake politeness. He noticed Savoureuse make a dash to rescue him, but she was too far away to make a difference.

Victor used [Monster Insight], trying to decipher any weakness that woman may have.

???

Damn! "Can't we... talk it out?"

Charisma check...

Failed!

"We just did, manling," Melodieuse raised her hand. "[Death Spike]."

As sharp, pointy ice spears rose from below Victor, he realized that *maybe* he should have taken a better insurance plan.

34: The Bitter Day of Brandon Maure

Like he did back in that flying elf farm, Brandon Maure showed Vainqueur his cursed red wing, while his flying troops swarmed the dragon. "[Faena Muleta]."

Intelligence Check successful!

Vainqueur answered the moth's pitiful display with a stream of holy flames.

See? He was smart!

The demon king, while surprised by the failure of his previous tactic, successfully flew out of the way. His slower lackeys, the dragon incinerated. Their ashes fell in a gray rain.

The Iron Eagle approached while Vainqueur pursued the moth in the skies, the musket-like weapons on its back, firing harpoons at him. The dragon dodged them artfully, only for Brandon Maure to intercept him with his sword in the middle of his manoeuver, grazing his scales with the tip of his blade.

*[**Dragonslayer**] effect bypassed your defense!*

"Let see if you are strong without your enhancements!" Vainqueur prepared his secret weapon. "Lesser Demonbane!" His spell hit Brandon Maure in the face, much to the dragon's delight.

"My charm is greater than yours, grasshopper!" Vainqueur boasted.

"But Maure remembers how you denied him the joy of single combat last time!" Maure snarled, his movements more sluggish and less confident than before. "MINION! Come defend your king! [Summon Torero Fiend]!"

A powerful devil nearly as big as Vainqueur himself, with simmering, burning ash for skin, popped up next to the demon king. The spicy monster's dragonlike wings extended, and it flew at the dragon with its sharp claws extended. He shot a shadowy ball of energy at Vainqueur while moving to engage him in close combat.

"[Spell Purge!]" As Vainqueur activated his perk, the spell vanished upon reaching his marvelous scales. The monstrous devil reached him a second afterward, Vainqueur catching his fists with his hands.

While the creature was strong, the dragon was better and pushed him back, still holding the demon's hands captive. He attempted to bite the tasty fiend's face off, but it lowered its head before Vainqueur's jaws could close in on him.

The moth, ever the cowardly elf, retreated. He landed on the Eagle's back and activated a Perk of his own, pointing his blade at Vainqueur. "[Picador]!"

While his speed didn't diminish, Vainqueur felt his reaction time slow down, his attention reduced. It was as if he had gotten drunk on eating dwarves again.

Focusing on the moth's minion first, Vainqueur breathed holy flames right in the face of the giant devil; the fiend let out a snarl of rage as he proved as weak to dragonfire as anything else. Vainqueur rotated on himself, throwing the demon towards the clouds below before chasing after the Iron Eagle.

"Harpoons!" Maure ordered to a fiend operating one of the bird's muskets; the weapon instantly fired pointed, chained spears at the dragon. While he couldn't evade the harpoon in time due to that cursed [Picador] Perk, Vainqueur did something better.

He caught the harpoon with both hands.

Then he pulled it towards him, tearing the musket off the Eagle's back and its fiendish operator with it.

Empowered by the knowledge granted by the Class System, Vainqueur swung the chain like a flail and threw it at the flying fortress. The musket's wreckage impacted on the metal bird, but Brandon Maure managed to dodge the attack.

"Coward!" Vainqueur accused the moth, targeting the eagle's back with fireballs. His flames blasted off metal plates and destroyed the demon-operated muskets, but failed to hit his true target, who raced towards the front part of the metal bird. "Stop running and fight!"

"Maure no longer plays!" the demon king replied, before barking orders to the metal bird. "Launch the Wind Spear! Blow him off!"

The iron bird launched three projectiles at Vainqueur, the explosive needles making circles in the skies as magical circles appeared on the dragon's scales.

Unable to dodge, Vainqueur destroyed one with his fiery breath, then a second; the explosions made the Iron Eagle flinch, and spread the smoke in all directions.

Before he could destroy the third one though, Maure's summoned devil rose back from above the clouds, then rammed Vainqueur from behind, grabbing his throat with his strong arms. "Get off me, you cattl—"

"[Mando Bull]!" Brandon Maure said, pointing his blade at Vainqueur from a safe distance.

Skill check failed! Strength and Agility reduced by one stage each!

The fiend on the dragon's back choked him, preventing Vainqueur from destroying the third wind spear as it approached. With a surge of skill, the dragon moved to use the fiend on his back as a shield, the projectile hitting that frustrating minion first.

The massive explosion that resulted killed the fiend and made Vainqueur's entire body itch, one wing in even worse shape than the other. The sheer power of the detonation sent the dragon falling straight through the clouds, struggling to fly.

*You have fallen below twenty percent HP! **Critical Health**!*

[Bravo Bull] activated! You regained your lost strength!

Reenergized, Vainqueur managed to stabilize in the middle of a cloud, somewhat. One of his wings had gotten weaker than the other, he couldn't fly straight, and the moth's Perks still weakened him.

The dragon considered his options. Brute strength hadn't worked, but the dragon was more than fire breath and physical force.

He was *smart.*

Vainqueur deactivated Spell Purge, then used his blinkblink ring to become invisible while the cloud still shrouded him. Struggling against the itching and the pain, Vainqueur managed to catch up to the Iron Eagle, flying discreetly above its back. The moth glanced overboard, looking for Vainqueur's corpse.

"Is he dead?" Maure rejoiced, as he began to bark more orders. "Carpet the ground to be sure, and that ugly village with it!"

"SURPRISE ATTACK!" Vainqueur shouted as he blasted the moth with a fireball. The explosion destroyed a large part of the flying fortress' back and sent the Demon King to crash on the left wing of the bird. Half his body had been burnt to a crisp.

Vainqueur landed on the wing while dispelling his invisibility, as Brandon Maure rose back up. "You... you... how dare you attack Maure while invisible!"

"I am smart enough not to give you a chance to run around this time!" Vainqueur said, slightly insecure about his intelligence score and eager to showcase it. The tactic had worked on Furibon, and it proved its effectiveness again. "Not so strong when you cannot hide behind your minions, are you, moth?"

Cornered and unable to fly away with a burned wing, Brandon Maure swung his sword and prepared to stand his ground. "[Airblad-]"

But the dragon was faster, and didn't give his foe any respite.

"[Lesser Demonbane]!" Vainqueur cast his spell, the exorcism weakening the fiend before it could finish enhancing himself.

The dragon then breathed his mighty dragonfire at Maure, and weakened by the previous attack, the moth couldn't dodge. Vainqueur's flames melted his flesh and the metal underneath both, causing an explosion below the wing.

The demon king stood out of the flames as an emaciated, burnt husk. "If it is any consolation," Vainqueur taunted the furious elf. "You never stood a chance against me, grass-eater. You were doomed the moment you threatened my minions."

A voice came out of the Iron Eagle, enhanced by a spell. "Your Highness, the dragon damaged the engine! We have to make an emergency landing!"

"Crash the Iron Eagle in the volcano's crater!" Maure ordered, forced to use his sword to stand. "Destroy the dragon's castle and his hoard with it!"

The voice coming from the iron bird sounded as horrified as Vainqueur himself. "My liege, with all the wind spears onboard, Mount Murmurin will erupt! The entire region will be wiped out!"

"Yes!" Brandon Maure replied. "Rochefronde, Vainqueur, Murmurin, annihilate them all!"

"But our troops—"

"I DON'T CARE!" the demon king snarled, dropping speaking in the third person for the first time. "I WANT ALL OF THEM DEAD!"

Warning! [Berserk] status applied.

"It is not over, Vainqueur!" the elf ranted, showing off his blade. "Brandon Maure still has resources, and friends in low places! He will come back—"

Furious, and now faster than ever, Vainqueur poked the moth mid-rant, squashing him like the bug he was.

His mighty hand made the metal bird shake as it hit.

When he raised his finger again, he could only see a bloody smear on the metal.

*Congratulations! You regained your [**Emperor**] title with style!*

Your Perks have been restored!

The dragon let out a furious roar, and breathed a torrent of flames towards the skies, ready to rampage across the land in celebration.

Or he would have, had the Iron Eagle not been diving straight toward his volcano.

"My hoard!" Fear for the survival of his coins stripped him of his anger, his mind now fully focused on saving his gold.

Vainqueur flew under the Iron Eagle's wing and pushed with both hands against its underside. Grabbing the flying fortress by its underside, the dragon used all his strength to push it up and redirect the bird away from his volcano. He struggled against his wounds from the Wind Spear, against the pain in his wing, against the heaviness of the metal bird.

Vainqueur was a dragon. The strongest! He could do it!

He thought of the coins in his hoard, waiting for his return, of the princesses he would expose, of all his minions cheering him up on the ground. They gave him strength.

Using all of his bottomless might, Vainqueur managed to force the fortress up, making it miss the crater by mere inches; then, he pushed it towards the badlands and arroyos away from the mountain.

The dragon, finally out of strength, finally let the bird go, struggling for breath.

The bird kept going and then crashed in a remote valley; the same one where Manling Victor stashed his hoard when Furibon sickened it.

The collision unleashed an incredibly powerful blast of wind which blew dust all over the region. A cloud of sand expanded in all directions.

"I won!" Vainqueur rejoiced, exhausted and his wounded wing starting to let him down. "I won!"

Then the cloud of dust reached him, covering him in dust and sending sand in his eyes. "Argh!" The dragon let out a snarl of frustration as he scratched his eyelids to remove it.

Flawless victory!

*For defeating Brandon Maure and ending the threat of the Iron Eagle, you earned a [**Crest**].*

A light fell from the heavens in front of Vainqueur, a golden, shield-like item descending from the skies and floating right in front of him. It was one of the most beautiful devices he had ever seen, covered with colored gemstones; something worthy of his hoard.

Vainqueur let out single a tear at the scene; whether because of its beauty or the sand in his eyes, he didn't know.

*Use [**Crest**] to break the Class ceiling?*

"Yes!" No sooner did the dragon speak, the item and the light surrounding it vanished at once.

Crest used! You can now progress up to level 60!

*For using a [**Crest**], you gained the [**Crested**] Personal Perk.*

*[**Crested**]: You moved up from ordinary adventurer to folktale hero. You can now access more prestigious classes.*

Sweet! All was well in the world.

Vainqueur, exhausted, struggled to fly back to Murmurin to burn the remaining minions of the moth. Instead, he found his early guests hunting down the fleeing elves and fiends in a good old safari hunt.

The dragon was briefly worried his big day was ruined, but his kindred looked very happy with the free food. Vainqueur let out a sigh of relief, his pride safe.

Such an easy battle. Nothing like the War of the Hoard; and his Bragging Day was safe. Truly this couldn't get better.

"Minion, where are you? I have been crested!"

But no one answered.

"MINION!"

His lackey didn't teleport to his side.

"Minion?" Vainqueur repeated, now worryingly, but yet no one answered. "Minion?"

The seed of doubt worming itself in his mind, Vainqueur searched for his prized lackey. He watched his minions, led by the Kobold Rangers, fight off stragglers while Sweet Chocolatine captured imps in fishnets. The minions cheered Vainqueur as he flew over them, as they should. He didn't land to ask them, for, with his damaged wing, he knew he couldn't fly again after landing.

The dragon went north, towards the sheeps' pens, finding his dragon guests feasting on his pantry. Corpseling Jules and Rolo the golem tended to his chief of staff, laying in the dirt and surrounded by other crying minions, from Malfy the fiend to that reptilian Savoureuse. Vainqueur graciously landed nearby, covering the minions with dust.

"Ah... ah... ah minion, here you are," Vainqueur said while catching his breath. He immediately noticed that his lackey had grown wings and a tail, just like his master! What a faithful chief of staff. Vainqueur didn't have the heart to chastise him for failing to win the minion war before his guests arrived.

"Your Majesty?" Jules the Necromancer looked up at him, and at his weak wing. "Is Brandon Maure—"

"The moth is dead!" Vainqueur boasted. "I smashed him, his bird, and his pride! I received a crest from it, just as you said, Manling Victor!"

His chief of staff didn't answer. Malfy the fiend exchanged a glance with the other minions, with Victor's pet mimic letting out a sad moan, then spoke up, "Your Majesty, I am afraid Lord Victor cannot answer."

"Of course he can, I trained him to," Vainqueur replied, looking down to wake his minion from his nap. "Manling Victor now is not the time to sleep! My guests have arrived..."

Then Vainqueur noticed the ice spike through his lackey's chest and his empty white eyes.

Manling Victor was...

...

He was *dead*?

The dragon saw red. "Who *dared* do this?!" Vainqueur roared, his mere voice making the minions tremble in fear.

"The killer, that fairy, teleported away after I tried eating her." A green dragon resting on his back, his belly full, let out a belch. "Vainqueur, your sheeps taste delicious, so soft..."

Vainqueur would have thanked him if he wasn't *livid*.

"Minion, I ordered you to become immortal!" Vainqueur chastised his dead lackey, before turning to that pile of scrap of a golem. "You, tinman, you are my minion now. Fetch me Chocolatine, a healer, even that dryad if needed!"

"Nobody can cure death, Yer Majesty," Rolo the Golem replied.

"You can!" Vainqueur said, turning to Corpseling Jules. "Raise him like the kobolds!"

"I would like to, but we cannot reanimate him, Your Majesty," Jules replied. "His killer applied the [Necrophobia] status to Victor before murdering him. He cannot be reanimated, not even as an undead until it is dispelled."

"I cannot even claim his soul and incarnate him as a fiend," Malfy said.

"Then get away, bugling," Vainqueur said, as he put his hand on Manling Victor's remains and activated his favorite Perk. "[Spell Purge]!"

Charisma check failed!

*You could not dispel the [**Necrophobia**] status.*

Charisma check failed? How could it be? Vainqueur was the most charismatic dragon in the world, the destroyer of Furibon! How could he fail a check?!

Yet... yet he had only weakened the crystal curse that fairy placed on his princesses. Not dispelled, weakened. Her sorcery was beyond even the evil Furibon's. Vainqueur glanced around at the thought, thankfully finding the scythe near Manling Victor. That witch didn't have time to break the seal keeping that evil contained.

The reality of the situation slowly dawned on Vainqueur.

Manling Victor, his most prized, loyal chief of staff, class advisor, Vizier, and Doer of the Thing, was gone.

The dragon remained still, trying to process what to do next, while his minions tried to cheer him up. "Your Majesty—"

"I refuse to accept this!" Vainqueur cut him off brashly. "Find a way to raise him!"

"Why the rush, Vainqueur?" his dragon guest asked, more surprised than anything. "It's just a manling. A dragon-shaped, well-trained manling, but a manling all the same."

"Manling Victor is worth more than any minion," Vainqueur replied. He could find any new minion, but he could never find a second Manling Victor. "He is the crown jewel of my hoard. My Bragging Day cannot be complete without him."

"Your Majesty," Jules began. "There is a... a last option to raise him, but... you will need to make a great sacrifice."

"Anything to save my favorite minion," Vainqueur said, glancing down at the corpse with genuine sadness. "Anything for my manling."

35: BFF

"I'm sorry, but you can't get into Heaven right now."

Sitting on a chair in the middle of an endless, white expanse, Victor glared at Miel. The angel winced behind her ivory desk, the enormous pile of paper representing his case sitting on it. "But you said I would get in Heaven if I died in the line of duty against the forces of Hell!"

"That would be if you had taken the Heaven+ Plan, instead of the Standard Karma Insurance."

"I didn't know I would die in *weeks*!"

Also, death hurt like Hell.

At least Brandon Maure died, from what Miel told him. Vainqueur's guests, proving almost as dangerous as him, had eaten their way to victory both on Outremonde and Hell.

"Unfortunately, you *also* died protecting a village of monsters where demons buy souls openly and most citizens have an evil or chaotic karma," the angel replied, embarrassed. "I will do everything I can so we accept you into Heaven on merit since you were instrumental in the bankruptcy of Maure Hellcorporated, but you may have to wait months in limbo. The fact you died a virgin on Earth might help convince my superiors of your hidden saintliness."

Could it? Because he did his best on Outremonde to catch up on that front.

Months sitting in a chair? Victor *loathed* bureaucracy. "What about the lower place?"

Miel made a frustrated face, but searched in the papers and gave them to him. "As my client, I will tell you the other offer, but I strongly advise against it," she said, Victor reading the document. "Infercorp made a request that you be reincarnated as a demon mortal consultant... however, since they lack the power to dispel the [Necrophobia] status your murderer put you under, they cannot reincarnate you into a new shape. Your soul will end in Hell as it is now: helpless."

"Like those Isabelle Maure tortured last time I visited?"

"I do not recommend it."

Curse that fairy. Victor understood why Vainqueur couldn't stand the fomors. "Have I no other option?"

"Two deities have a claim to your soul, namely Dice and the Moon Man." The angel hesitated to speak again. "We also received a surprise third afterlife proposal from Camilla, the goddess of death, for, I quote, *'exemplary service to the undeathstrial revolution and continued friendliness towards the church'.*"

At this point, Victor might as well entertain the various offers. He hated Dice for abducting him to Outremonde, but Camilla was a goddess with a dangerous reputation. He would rather try the chaotic deities first. "Okay, what do the first two offer?"

"I will send a request for a meeting." Miel wrote on a parchment with a feather, the paper vanishing at once. "Thankfully, the Moon Man should be in one of his 'good' phases. No rampage."

No sooner did she say that, that an entity materialized next to them with a rumbling noise. Victor had to look up to see the full, titanic creature.

The other creature was an enormous version of Thul-Gathar, a monstrous moon beast over sixty feet-tall; a titan far bigger than even Vainqueur. It wore old, tattered yellow robes over its body, leaving only the tentacled, squid-like head and hands exposed. It also used a sorcerous, pine-sized cane to walk.

"Is this an appointment? Did I forget it?" Much to Victor's surprise, the Moon Man sounded more like his elderly grandfather than an abomination from outer space. More worryingly, it spoke in the human's head through telepathy, rather than through words.

"Hello, Mr. Moon Man," Miel said with a cheeky smile. "I am Miel, a junior angel insurance counselor. My client here, Victor Dalton, is the prophet of your Murmurin cult; your spawn Thul-Gathar claimed him on your behalf."

"I have a prophet?" The Moon Man sounded confused. "I have a *religion*?"

When Thul-Gathar complained about his patron deity being absent-minded, he wasn't kidding. "Don't you hear the prayers of your followers?" Victor asked.

"I hear voices often, but prayers?" The ancient abomination shook its head. "Cats and dogs rule your Earth. You think they are enemies, but they have a secret pact. The pets in presidents' houses? They *are* the presidents. Kennedy's dog Charlie ordered him assassinated when he threatened to reveal the truth."

Victor blinked. "Excuse me?"

"Mmm?" The giant squid replied. "Yes?"

"What did you say about dogs and cats?"

"That you should eat them after cuddling?" The deity touched its tentacles with its hand as if it were a beard. "I am getting old, so my memory is not all there."

"He is the god of madness," Miel whispered to Victor. "*He's* not all there."

"Sometimes I feel like I am becoming a star, with a burning core and ionized breath," the Moon Man continued. "Can you feel my gravity?"

The more he heard, the more Victor doubted that god could even provide him an afterlife at all.

Something fell on Miel's desk with a weak sound, causing Victor to look at it.

He found himself facing a twenty-faced dice, surging with magical power. Each of its faces had living, multi-colored eyes located inside or next to the numbers. All of them watched back at Victor with expectation.

"Roll me," the dice asked with a kid's voice.

...

"Roll me!" the god Dice insisted like a child. "For your afterlife! Roll me!"

Victor stared blankly at the dice, while the Moon Man looked at it with curiosity. Miel winced, embarrassed by the scene.

That... that *thing* was a god?

The one who brought him to Outremonde at that!

Eventually, with nothing better to do, Victor grabbed Dice and rolled it. The dice eventually landed on its 'tenth' face. "Ten!" said the god of magic. "Average afterlife! Reincarnated as a part-timer in Japan!"

"That doesn't make any sense!" Victor complained.

"I am a god!" the dice boasted back. "I don't have to make sense!"

"Chaotic deities," Miel said with a forced laugh, clearly uncomfortable with the situation.

Victor knew he should have worshipped Allison's pleasure goddess, Cybele.

Reincarnation in Japan tempted him; even if it sounded somewhat terrible, he could probably find his way back to the United States and his family in time. Would they recognize him though? For all he knew, he could be reincarnated as an entirely new person.

Another look at Dice trying to roll by itself on the desk made him change his mind. He wanted to rant at that creature for bringing him to Outremonde, but he couldn't muster the energy at the sight of its stupidity.

"I think I will wait for Heav—"

A new figure popped up with a golden glow next to him before he could finish his sentence.

The newcomer had the upper body of a golden-scaled, graceful winged woman, and the lower half of a green serpent. Snakes made up her hair, and she carried a bag full of paper scrolls on her back. Her slithering eyes sized up Victor like a ruthless merchant examining a product.

The human instantly recognized the goddess.

"Oh, Miss Shesha!" The angel sounded giddy at the goddess' sight. "What a surprise!"

"Miel, good to see you again." The goddess of commerce immediately turned to Victor, clearly all-business and much saner than her competition. "Victor Dalton, this is your lucky day."

"You're betting on my soul too?" Damn, Victor had become more popular in death than he ever was in life. At least she looked like an actual, dignified deity.

"Better. Mortals paid me a generous 'church donation' for your revival on Outremonde."

The human blinked. Didn't she charge a huge amount of money for that service? Who could have paid for it? Victor briefly thought of Vainqueur, before realizing that the dragon would never part ways with any coin. No, the villagers of Murmurin had probably pooled their funds to revive him.

"Wait, what about the [Necrophobia] status?" Victor asked.

"I am a goddess. While the caster's level approaches the divine, overcoming it is trivial." The goddess gave him a cunning smirk. "Now, my services are expensive. Since I have a result obligation, I will not cash my reward in if you refuse to return. Between us, if you do accept, I will grant you a free Perk."

"Are you bribing me in front of witnesses?"

"No, no, I am sweetening a deal. It has been a while since someone could afford a resurrection."

Victor was sure he had been there before.

"As the goddess of commerce, I am very interested in what you and your dragon associate are doing on Outremonde. While I am... conflicted... about your undead and demonic ventures, a tax-free commercial zone appeals to me. Hopefully, we will discuss investment terms after your return to the living."

Classic merchant, wording the request by implying he already accepted.

Victor hesitated. The other options weren't all that good, but returning to Outremonde meant continuing his life as a minion, with all that it entailed.

But...

Victor thought back about what Savoureuse told him, before the fight with Furibon. That he had the opportunity to make a good life in that new world instead of trying to chase after the past.

Victor would never admit it out loud, but he had grown attached to Outremonde, and the people he met there. Even that crazy dragon.

Especially that dragon.

"Will I still get into Heaven if I return?" he asked Miel.

"You will have to take a new insurance plan," Miel flashed a smile at him, which he didn't find innocent at all. "A better one this time."

That settled it.

"Excellent choice," Shesha said, happy with the transaction. She touched his left arm with her cold fingers, a tattoo representing a coin with a snake symbol on it materializing on his skin.

*Congratulations! You earned the [**Claimed by Shesha**] Personal Perk.*

*[**Claimed by Shesha**]: When you level up, you have an additional 10 percent chance to gain a Charisma or Intelligence point. Merchants, bankers, and entrepreneurs always see you as a trustworthy partner and will give you a 20 percent discount.*

"As dragons dance, so do Earth and Outremonde," the Moon Man said. "The golden path is paved with fairy blood."

"What?" Victor asked.

"I said, return home, and do your prophet work," the Moon Man replied, as confused as Victor himself. "I think..."

Shesha snapped her fingers, a luxurious private jet materializing out of the nothingness right next to the Moon Man. "I am the goddess of commerce," Shesha told an astonished Victor. "Trains are out of fashion, and I have *taste*."

The door of the private afterlife jet opened, and Victor walked inside. Miel waved at him. "Come back soon!" the angel said.

Yeah, right.

While death had been painful, resurrection felt like waking up from a happy sleep.

No sooner did Victor open his eyes, that he found Chocolatine's visage approaching to kiss him up close.

"Argh!" Victor jumped in surprise, the startled priestess backing away. It was a trap!

"You see, Chocolatine, I told you he wouldn't need CPR," said Allison. Victor realizing most of the minions and Murmurin's important inhabitants, from Charlene to Croissant, had gathered around him in a circle. Malfy carried his scythe. "Welcome back, buddy."

"Chief!" Pink Ranger cried at the scene. "You are alive!"

As his eyes acclimated to the light, Victor realized he had been revived deep inside the vault. The gate to Hell was closed, with Vainqueur's guests sitting in front of it, bellies full, shocked, and silent.

"You pooled your money to fund my revival?" Victor guessed.

"We all did—" Croissant began.

"No, *we* did, even Savoureuse," Allison replied, glaring at the werewolf. "Vainqueur forced *you* to."

"But it was nowhere near enough to satisfy the goddess' greed, Victor," Jules Rapace admitted. "She demanded a price too high."

Then who paid for the difference?

"How could a dragon..." Icefang said, his gaze empty and distant. "Why would *any* dragon?"

Victor slowly rose up and glanced around.

Most of Vainqueur's hoard had gone missing, with a large, empty hole in the middle. Only a few thousand gold pieces, random magic items, and the crystallized princesses remained. Vainqueur himself was whining in a corner, more saddened than Victor had ever seen him.

...

Holy hell.

"My hoard," Vainqueur whined his hands on his eyes. "My sweet hoard..."

Victor struggled to find his words, staring blankly at the hole, then back at his dragon master.

"I think we should leave you two alone," Allison said, glancing at the others. Malfy handed Victor the scythe, and the chief of staff absentmindedly took it, his mind working on autopilot. Even the dragons followed their example, leaving the old duo alone in the emptied vault.

"Why?" Victor finally asked, Vainqueur looking at his chief of staff with *destroyed* eyes. He only had that word on his mind. "Why? This is your Bragging Day!"

"You are the crown jewel of my hoard..." Vainqueur regained some of his composure, forcing himself to adopt a proud dragon face in spite of being clearly shaken. "If it hadn't been for you, I would never have gathered it in the first place. You were worth more. With you gone, what was there to brag about?"

That very instant, Victor realized he would never leave Vainqueur, no matter what.

He no longer wanted to.

"You know,.." Victor trailed off. "You have become a lot more than a 'master,' Your Majesty. You have become a friend."

"What is a friend, some kind of minion?"

"That means I will stick to you no matter what, even if I'm released from service."

"You better, Minion Victor, because I forbid you from sleeping until you have reimbursed your debt to me, which is..." Vainqueur took a long breath. "*Twelve million, five hundred forty-five thousand, one hundred thirty-three* gold coins! Which is added to the life debt you owe me for raising you as my prized chief of staff!"

Twelve million in debt? Damn, it was his student loan all over again. "Okay," Victor replied, strangely at peace with it. "I will find a way, Your Majesty."

"Then you will work until we both become gods, and order this greedy goddess to reimburse me in full for this vastly overpriced service!"

"Sure," Victor replied, as Vainqueur kept ranting and venting off, the dragon regaining his previous proud demeanor. He could settle on becoming god of minions everywhere.

It paid well, and from what he had gathered, he wouldn't be worse off than the others.

After he finished cursing Shesha, the gods, and merchants in general, Vainqueur calmed himself. "Minion Victor."

"Yes, Your Majesty?"

"As you wish, I promote you to my first and only 'friend'," Vainqueur declared, in his own, greedy way. "You better prove yourself worthy of that honor."

"I hope so," Victor replied, before correcting himself. "I will."

"*I want to puke,*" Furibon finally spoke up from inside his scythe. "*Watching you gave me diabetes.*"

36: Bragging Day

It was a starry night, and Vainqueur would soon make his bragging speech.

His gluttonous guests had gathered in Murmurin's town square for the main feast, after yesterday's elf appetizers. Dragons rested and talked, either on the ground or on nests made of the minions' houses, as Vainqueur's lackeys supplied them with a near-limitless supply of sheep, cattle, and cooked fiends.

Without a hoard to show—the thought alone broke Vainqueur's heart, although he was too dignified to cry—the Emperor of Murmurin had ordered half his minions to serve the meals to distract the dragons, and the other half to recover *anything* that could pass for treasure.

Thankfully, the moth's army had left gifts behind after dying or retreating, including inside the wreckage of their metal bird. Shiny weapons, glittering armor, and the cattle money the moth's minions had been paid with...

There was a startling lack of swords, though. Vainqueur had expected the mimic retriever to bring at least one of them.

His remaining minions, those who had survived the battle, had done their best, gathering a large pile of treasure right next to his statue. It was a good hoard, but nothing like the perfect, golden marvel he sacrificed to that greedy goddess. He could brag about it, but it wouldn't cement his status as the greatest dragon of all.

Thankfully, he had kept the crystallized princesses on top. They somewhat made up for the rest, and Icefang was livid at his twin princess record being upstaged.

"That was all we could find, Your Majesty," his flying Grand Vizier said, throwing his scythe and every magical item on top of the hoard as a token of fealty. The other minions had done the same, returning all their magical items to the great hoard, as the cycle of life demanded.

"Where are the items I lent to you?" Vainqueur asked, finding a few of them missing.

"I, uh." Victor scratched the back of his head. "To be honest, I kinda lost them."

Vainqueur immediately guessed what happened. "That fairy thief!" the dragon enraged. "Not only did she rob you of your life, but she also looted your corpse afterward!"

"No, no, I—"

"Only I am allowed to profit from my minions' remains!" Vainqueur ranted. "By robbing you, she robbed me! I vow it on your head, Manling Victor, one day I shall cook that fairy and eat her for dinner!"

"Why are you vowing on my head?" Manling Victor complained. "I already lost it once."

"Exactly, since you will never lose it ever again," Vainqueur gave his favorite minion a knowing look. "This guarantees my prophecy shall come to pass."

"This is your Bragging Day. I am not contesting your logic."

"Yes, that is why it is called *logic*," Vainqueur replied.

"Also, King Roland, Kia, and Gardemagne's royal retinue have arrived to recover Princess Merveille," Manling Victor explained. "They kinda panicked when they noticed the dragons feasting and the dead demons littering the road, but then they calmed down after Charlene told them you killed Maure. The king wasn't even surprised, from what she told me."

Clearly, that manling King was an intelligent fellow. "I shall deign to treat them as my guests, in time for my bragging speech," Vainqueur said, magnanimous, as his kobold minions brought him a cart of cooked beef with creamy poison sauce.

A group of thirty manling knights on horses made their way to him, led by Manling Charlene. It reminded Vainqueur of that time he ate the duchess of Euskal, except these manlings seemed civilized enough not to attack.

"His Majesty, King Roland Gardemagne," one of the knights exclaimed, a tall, meaty old bearded manling riding on a white horse at the forefront. This manling went shirtless, with a long ermine cloak whom Vainqueur had to admit would look good on his hoard; he wore a diamond crown on his head and a two-handed golden axe on his back. Knight Kia rode her griffon on his right, and some kind of black elf flew by his own magic on his left.

Knight Kia glanced the piled up weapons, the destroyed houses, and the smoking remains of the Iron Eagle with a dejected look. "I missed the big battle," she said, sounding incredibly disappointed. "I *missed* the *big battle*."

"Yeah, it really would have helped if you had shown up," said Manling Victor, as he landed clumsily on the ground. Since his pet's destruction, he had been forced to learn to fly to get around and hadn't quite mastered this great dragon skill.

"Vic?" Kia recognized his chief of staff. "What the hell happened to you? Is that a tail coming out of your pants?"

"Puberty," Manling Victor replied, the dark elf letting out a laugh and Knight Kia having a chuckle. "Also, it's 'what the Happyland' now."

"It has lost its zing," the dark elf replied.

"My Grand Vizier has been Vainqueurized," Vainqueur said, sighing as gazes turned to him. Did he have to teach them everything? "It is a verb which means to become awesome. I Vainqueurized that village, we Vainqueurized the world, it was Vainqueurizing, this meal was Vainqueurlicious... it goes with everything, as my name should."

"Is Vainqueurspeech going to be our national language?" Manling Victor asked with his usual strange tone. By now, his master had grown used to it.

"I am considering it, but the road toward civilizing your kind is long and paved with ordeals," Vainqueur replied.

The manling King, who had been carefully observing the scene, finally spoke up. "Emperor Vainqueur," he said, the way he sized Vainqueur up reminding the dragon of a lion sizing up a rival. "I have been hearing about you for a while, and you do not disappoint. You are exactly as I imagined you."

"Yes, the most powerful of emperors stand before you," Vainqueur asserted his title, in case the Class System once again bothered him. "The Emperor of Murmurin, and the Albain Mountains."

"And Ishfania, from what I understand," Manling King Roland replied. "You have done a great service to Gardemagne in felling the Demon King before he could bomb our cities. This act of friendship shall not go unrewarded."

"Fifteen million," Vainqueur replied, the manlings frowning in confusion. "The bounty you put on my head does not represent my net worth, which I find insulting. Thus I ask that you increase it to reflect it."

"That isn't the number Your Majesty gave me yesterday," his Grand Vizier pointed out.

"Shush, Manling Victor," Vainqueur hushed his chief of staff.

"Were you not informed?" Manling Roland asked. "I froze your bounty a month ago. I asked that no adventurer of Gardemagne go after your head."

"Aw, but that was free experience and treasures!" Vainqueur complained.

"Your Majesty, we left the previous hideout because they kept bothering us," Manling Victor reminded him. "Also, I'm pretty sure we've made many enemies who will love to go after our heads."

Manling King Roland cleared out his throat. "Bounties are for enemies, and I would like to come as a friend."

"Only Manling Victor earned that title," Vainqueur chastised the upstart, the statement taking back the various manlings.

"Then, as a good neighbor," King Roland replied. "I have no quarrel with you, so long as you return my niece to me."

"I, Vainqueur, unlike you robbers, do not tax or infringe on my minions' private property," Vainqueur replied smugly. "I shall release your princess back into the wild after tonight. But you better grant me my promised boon."

"Of course," King Roland replied, proving himself a civilized fellow, unlike that tasteless duchess. "What do you want? Lands, honors, knighthood—"

"NO TAXES!"

Vainqueur's roar made some of the guests raise their eyes from their meals to look at him. "No taxes?" King Roland frowned.

"I will not pay a dime of the treasure I burned fat to earn!" Vainqueur declared. "I want all my quests to be robbery-exempted! No guild fee, no tax, no nothing! Ever!"

"Deal," the king immediately agreed, as if expecting the dragon to change his mind if he didn't seize the opportunity. "V&V will be forever exempt from all fees usually applied to adventurer companies."

"But, but..." Manling Charlene made a face. "How will I sustain the local chapter?"

"The Kingdom will fund it," King Roland replied dismissively. "It is paramount that we keep good relationships with the new Ishfanian government."

"The new government?" Manling Victor picked up.

"With its army destroyed and Maure dead, Ishfania is gone as a nation. While a demon-infested desert, it possesses resources. Enough of them that nations like the Eversun Empire, Barin, or even Prydain may try to claim it. I would rather avoid a new Century War and fill the vacuum as soon as possible."

"But *I* squashed that moth!" Vainqueur protested. "*I* saved the great hoard from him!"

"Exactly and thus I propose a treaty," the King said. "Gardemagne will recognize your claim as Emperor of Ishfania, making it an official adventurer state; you will still enjoy all the benefits of the Adventurer Guild and rule your territory as you wish. In exchange, I ask for a solemn vow that our countries never to take arms against the other and fight united against outside threats. A mutual protection pact."

"Oh, and I will never lose access to my Emperor class!" Vainqueur realized. "Brilliant! I accept this tribute!"

The manling king nodded with dignity, then turning to his archmage. "Nostredame, a map of the continent, and a pen."

The dark elf conjured the tools with a snap of his fingers, the manling king tracing a line across it. "This is the Albain Mountains. They shall serve as the frontier between your dominion, and Gardemagne."

"But the mountains are mine," Vainqueur insisted. "Emperor of Murmurin, Ishfania, and the Albain Mountains."

The king looked up at the dragon, then at the ruins of the Iron Eagle, then back at Vainqueur. "So long as we keep ownership of the powerstone mines we opened already."

"I, Vainqueur, am too wealthy to lower myself to claiming your hoards for myself," the dragon tried to sound generous.

"Then I assent to your request," the King replied, circling a large swath of land on the map. "All of this is yours."

"Vainqueur Knightsbane," the dragon began to voice his new title out loud and rejoiced. "First of His Name, Great Calamity of the Age, Defender of the Hoard, *and* Emperor of Murmurin, Ishfania, and the Albain Mountains."

"Your Majesty," Knight Kia began.

"Yes?" both Vainqueur and King Roland said at once, the dragon being disappointed when the knight turned to her fellow Manling.

"I immediately ask to be transferred as the ambassador to the Empire of Murmurin."

"What?" For the first time, the Manling King seemed shocked. "Lady Kia, what is the meaning of this?"

"Kia, what the hell?" the dark elf echoed the king's sentiment, as the various knights present exchanged whispers.

"There are still remnants of Maure's army out there," Kia replied. "And Melodieuse escaped justice."

"But Kia..."

"I *missed* the *big battle*!" Knight Kia cut her ally off. "No more!"

The King examined her, before nodding. "Very well," he replied. "You are the hero of the Golden Fields. If you believe you can defend Gardemagne from abroad, I shall not stop you."

"Thank you my liege," the knight nodded, before turning to Vainqueur. "That is if the Emperor accepts me."

"I must consult my chief of staff." Vainqueur narrowed his head towards his favorite lackey, speaking to him very, very lowly, "Manling Victor?"

"Yes?" his manling whispered.

"Have you bred yet?"

His manling's face told him that, no, he hadn't. The dragon realized his hopeless lackey would *never* reproduce without help, and so took the matter into his own claws.

"I agree, Knight Kia," Vainqueur said out loud. "Since my Empire's capital village is under renovations, you shall be granted a room in Manling Victor's quarters. Our chiefs of staff will thus practice close minion diplomacy, Manling Roland."

"Yes!" Knight Kia pumped her fist. "Thanks, I won't let you down."

"I assume we are done," King Roland said, turning to his elf wizard. "Can you free my niece from that prison?"

"The caster's level surpasses mine, but with my artifacts and my optimized Perks, this will be trivial, Your Majesty."

"You shall release my princesses after the celebration," Vainqueur said, before extending a hand towards the buffet. "Now, eat! My minions shall see that you have your share of sheep!"

"With pleasure, Emperor Vainqueur," Manling King Roland said, as he and his retinue unhorsed, kobolds leading them to their future meals.

Wait.

If Vainqueur had waited for that cattle wizard to dispel Manling Victor's [Necrophobia] status, then Corpseling Jules or tasty Malfy could have revived him for a cheaper price.

By arriving late, that uneducated King cost him money!

For the sake of his audience, Vainqueur managed to keep a straight face but raged inwardly.

"Did you just set me up with Kia?" Manling Victor asked Vainqueur once the guests out of earshot, unaware of the great injury done to his master.

"Minion husbandry is a long-honored dragon tradition," Vainqueur replied, hoping Manling Victor's offspring would inherit his wings and tail. "If only he had come early, I might have called your robber king halfway civilized."

"He kinda short-changed us," Manling Victor said, ever the pessimist. "He dumped the responsibility of cleaning up a demon-infested country on you, secured a dragon ally, and kept all the benefits of the Albain Mountains without having to spare troops to defend them from Maure anymore. Also, I'm sure Charlene will keep an eye on us on his behalf, if she wasn't before."

"But no more taxes," Vainqueur pointed out the truly important matter.

"But no more taxes," Manling Victor replied with a sigh.

Anyway, it was time.

Vainqueur glanced at his guests and minions, and upon seeing all of them present, let out a mighty roar. All eyes turned to him, and the great dragon cleared his throat. Manling Victor, ever faithful, supported his master with a nod.

"Brothers and sisters, manlings and minions," Vainqueur began. "It with great pride that I gathered you, so that you may marvel at the tasty bounties of my domain, my immeasurable wealth, and my three, yes, *three* princesses."

"The princesses aren't dancing," Icefang immediately replied. "Six out of ten!"

"I say eight," Genialissime countered. "Because Vainqueur has two spares, which is bragworthy."

"Three princesses in one place magnify their princessness," the black wyrm, Blightswamp, agreed with a scientific tone. "Also, the fact Vainqueur caught three from different species proves my theory that princessness is a contagious condition."

"But they aren't triplets!" Icefang nitpicked. "And the food is the only thing to brag about! Look at his paltry hoard!"

Vainqueur ignored his rival, although he noticed the dragons weren't very impressed by his treasure.

Here goes nothing.

"Certainly, you must have heard rumors that I gathered a greater, golden hoard," Vainqueur continued, waving a hand at Manling Victor. "And that I sacrificed it all to revive my greatest treasure, my prized, dragonized chief of staff."

The dragons whispered between them, as Victor knelt in gratefulness. "Vainqueur best dragon!" the minions cheered. "Vainqueur best dragon!"

Although pleased, Vainqueur silenced them with a look. He waited for his audience to calm down, then spoke up again.

"The rumors are true."

When in doubt, be awesome.

"Yes, you heard that right! I, Vainqueur, have grown a hoard so big, that I can afford to *spend* it!"

His radical declaration drew gasps from the audience, as he proceeded to turn this disaster into a triumph.

"That's how rich I am!" Vainqueur kept boasting. "I am so wealthy, that I could spend *twelve million gold coins* on reviving *one* minion!"

"Heresy!" Icefang screamed, the other guests speechless at his brazen words. "A dragon does not spend his hoard!"

"That is a poor dragon's response!" Vainqueur retorted, his rival fuming at the insult. "A truly wealthy dragon should be so rich, that twelve million coins are no more precious than one!"

"Then where is the rest?" One of the dragon guests asked.

"Look around you!" Vainqueur extended a hand towards his marvelous lands. "This is my hoard! I, Vainqueur, have founded an empire on the enlightened dragon principles! A country where no minions ever leave my service, even in death, where demons can trade souls without paying taxes to manlings! An empire where greed is law!"

"You use mass undead labor?" Knight Kia blinked, before noticing Malfy and turning red. "You trade souls with *demons*?!"

"It's... not as bad as you think..." Manling Victor winced, while Knight Kia's jaw clenched.

Vainqueur ignored them, showcasing the audience the iron plate around his neck. "I have become an adventurer! The weak and fragile manlings, afraid of trolls and fairies, have paid me tributes of gold, and given me their hoards to defend!"

"Vainqueur, you have become a banker?" Genialissime was aghast. "But that is minion work!"

"I am no banker," Vainqueur replied. "I am the Defender of the Hoard! Of all hoards! I slew the dread Furibon during the First War of the Hoard, and then the Moth King during the Second! I uncovered the ancient dragon system, gaining the power to protect the dragon way of life from those who would turn it to lead!"

"Ridiculous!" Icefang rolled his eyes. "A 'system' which grants you power and money? If it is easy enough for you to access it, why haven't I? Because it doesn't exist, and I will prove it right now!"

"No, no!" Manling Nostredame began to panic, Vainqueur worrying if new moths had come to ruin his moment again. "The only requirement to take the first level is awareness of the system, and meeting the stat criteria for beginner classes! The only reason they haven't—"

"Vainqueur, if this 'system' exists, then may it appear before me this instant!"

Icefang stopped ranting, seemingly glancing at an invisible text in front of him.

Everyone fell silent at his reaction, Vainqueur smugly smirking in triumph.

"I... I have seen a message..." The frost dragon squinted. *"Congratulations! Through your bitter resentment and dragon ego, you gained a level in 'Noble.'* Noble? I am a *king*!"

"Oh? So if I say that I can become a wizard, I will be?" Genialissime blinked, apparently receiving a message of his own. He pointed a claw at a house, unleashing a bolt at it, much to everyone's amazement.

"It worked." Genialissime rejoiced. "It worked!"

"Me too!" a red dragon spoke up, unleashing a feeble spell with a word. "I am a wizard!"

"Oh, this is fun!" another guest said, the skin of the non-dragon guests turning white for a reason Vainqueur couldn't grasp. "I need to improve my cooking, so I want to be a cook!"

"Can it make me a better minion manager?" Jolie asked. "Mine keep escaping!"

"Sage," Blightswamp told one of her dragonlings. "You can become a princess! A dragon princess!"

"Princess!" her daughter replied.

Almost immediately, Vainqueur's guests took to the game and began to declare themselves sorcerers, knights, and nobles. Only that idiot Blightswamp failed to replicate true princessness, which was beyond even the system's power.

"This... this is all true!" Icefang's eyes widened, as he turned to Manling Roland. "Manling King!"

"Yes?" The King of Gardemagne had watched the display with far more stoicism than the rest of his fearful kind.

"Hand me a plate!" Icefang ordered with a haughty tone. "It is a great honor for you, that a dragon of my caliber deigns to answer your species' requests, but I will gladly do it for your gold and silver!"

"Silver!" Vainqueur chuckled.

"Silver is shiny enough for a hoard!" Icefang replied angrily, before brazenly stealing his rival's catchphrase. "I am a dragon, and I am now, an adventurer!"

"Me too!" Jolie added, "I want to go on an adventure and find a minion that I can love as much as Uncle!"

"I wonder if the manlings can pay me for the privilege of me not attacking them," a dragon said. "That way, I get richer without effort. Passive revenues!"

"Oh, great idea, but I like getting rewarded for eating food better!"

The manling King said nothing while his minions paled and panicked. Instead, he simply turned to Manling Charlene. "You there."

"Y-yes, Your Majesty?"

"You deal with this," the king ordered. "Do as the dragons say. If they want to create their own adventurer companies under the auspices of Gardemagne, the guild shall oblige. We have enough would-be Maures and unclaimed rewards in the world; dragons willing to take care of them are welcome, so long as they do not eat quest givers."

At Manling Charlene's stony face, Friend Victor exploded into laughter, held his chest, and then rolled on the ground.

"Indeed, Manling Victor!" Vainqueur rejoiced as much as his chief of staff, as the feast was drowned in buzzing, animate discussions. "Like Grandrake invented princess hunting, I, Vainqueur, inspired a new era of dragon adventuring!"

He would brag about his visionary thinking until the end of times!

"We are doomed," Manling Victor replied, crying in the middle of his laugh. "So *doomed*, it becomes art!"

Epilogue

"Bye Vainqueur!" one of his last dragon guests said, flying away under the midday sun. "Amazing Bragging Day!"

"Of course, it was mine!" Vainqueur replied, which left his close family as the only remaining dragons. "Aww, you're leaving?"

"I do not want to leave my hoard unattended for long," Genialissime replied, his mate Blightswamp at his side. "You know how many greedy ratlings live near my place. You avoid eating them for a year, and then they forget the food chain."

"Uncle Vainqueur, Uncle Vainqueur!" Jolie could scarcely stay in place. "Can I make my lair nearby? I want to become a great adventurer just like you!"

"Jolie, there is a big flying city full of tasty elves and demons which now belongs to me," Vainqueur replied, happy to have company. "I will gladly let you settle there!"

"Great!" Jolie squealed in happiness. "I will bring my hoard there!"

"It was the best Bragging Day of the century," Genialissime congratulated Vainqueur. "I cannot wait to test my new magical powers on my cattle!"

"Just wait for my new one next century!" Vainqueur said although he wouldn't stop boasting about his great discoveries anytime soon.

"This system's discovery means so much for my princess studies!" Blightswamp said, carrying Genialissime's offspring on her back. "If nobles can evolve into emperors, then this may be the process that allows noble ladies to become princesses! If I can figure out how it works…"

"Honey, I think some of nature's mysteries are best left unanswered," Genialissime replied, apparently in a philosophical mood.

The loss of his three princesses had left Vainqueur in a sad mood in contrast. After the elf wizard released them from their crystals, they had screamed at the sight of two hundred dragons. It had taken twenty minutes for Manling King Roland to calm them down. Vainqueur had offered the manlings to take one of his princess bags to carry them home, but they instead used horses to carry them away. The dragon blamed it on a culture clash.

Vainqueur waved a hand at his family, as they flew towards the skies, officially ending his party on a satisfying note.

*Congratulations! For being recognized as Emperor by a powerful head of state, achieving full dominion over Ishfania's monsters, and inspiring newfound respect as a Monster Lord, you earned a level in [**Emperor**] and two levels in [**Kaiser**]!*

*You gained the [**Imperial Authority**] and [**Malefic Secrecy**] Class Perk!*

+60 HP, +10 SP, +3 STR, +3 VIT, +2 SKI, +2 AGI, +2 INT, +3 CHA, +2 LCK!

*[**Imperial Authority**]: reduce enemy's evasion by twenty percent.*

*[**Malefic Secrecy**]: divination spells and Perk trying to ascertain information about you automatically fail, unless they succeed on an opposed Charisma check.*

Vainqueur rejoiced at the news. The [Crest] had worked!

Of course, like after every Bragging Day, the entire area looked like the aftermath of a volcanic disaster. There wasn't a house unturned, or a sheep left alive. "Minions!" Vainqueur ordered, the Kobold Rangers, gnolls, mimics and other servants rushing to his side. "The party is over!"

"Your Majesty," Kobold Red bowed, imitated by the others. "How can we serve?"

"Where is Manling Victor?" Vainqueur asked, ready to summon his trusty sidekick to his side.

"I think I saw the chief with a girl," Bony Blue replied. "But all humanoids look the same, so I cannot tell which one."

Ah! Finally!

Vainqueur resisted the urge to summon his minion, at least until he had bestowed his eggs upon a worthy stock. This would be his only day off this year. "Then you, Kobold Rangers, shall be in charge of leading the minions for the following missions."

"The Kobold Rangers live to serve, Your Dragon Majesty!" The rangers adopted a pose, Junior the Mimic letting out a happy bark behind them.

Vainqueur immediately began to distribute orders. "Ranger Red, fetch me Manling Charlene and ask her for quests! The holiday is over, now it is time for work! My vaults must overflow with gold again! Ranger Pink, you shall write a new chronicle of the 'War of the Hoard', narrating the defeat of the Moth King Maure. It shall be called *'The Return of the Dragon,'* and it shall be distributed to every home, so everyone can learn of my great deeds."

"No work of mine will ever do justice to Your Majesty's deeds, but I will do my best!"

"Ranger Black, fetch me Corpseling Jules and have him raise every minion fallen in the line of duty. If death will not end Manling Victor's service, then I shall not deny this pleasure to my other lackeys. The rest of you..."

Vainqueur pointed a claw at the ravaged village. "Clean this up!"

"Yes, Your Majesty!" they sang together, before immediately scampering to work.

Vainqueur observed his minions do their merry work, dragging away corpses and repairing the houses. His eyes turned to his volcano, then to the desert which now belonged to him. How much treasure slumbered beneath the sands? How many coins cried alone, hoping for him to carry them away to his vault? His adventures made him realize he had always thought small, before meeting Manling Victor. Now, he had to see big.

Soon, the entire country would be his golden hoard. Everyone would know his name, and the false news of his death would be at long last forgotten!

Come to think of it, Vainqueur had never punished the thieves who dared lie about killing him. With his Bragging Day done, he could finally focus on finding them.

Then he would eat them, and take their cattle.

"Ugh..." Victor woke up, his eyelids were heavy. His sworn enemy, natural light, assaulted him relentlessly. "My head..."

He had tried his best to drink himself into oblivion after last night's disaster. Due to his Red Dragon Lifeforce, he had needed a lot of alcohol for it to stick, but he had managed to overcome it.

Victor managed to open his eyes, his mind foggy. His back and neck hurt like hell, and his eyes struggled to become accustomed to the lighting.

What happened? He remembered the dragons' mass discovery of the system, Kia getting angry at him for the whole 'Soul Nethermart' thing, teaching Beer Pong to Sav and Jules, asking Allison how he could convert to Cybele, the gnoll bum fight, comforting Charlene after Croissant drunkenly admitted that he fed her cakes to fatten her for dinner...

Victor's eyes snapped open.

His eyes acclimated to the light, and Victor realized he was in an unknown, dirty bedroom, sharing a bed with someone else. The owner didn't keep the room clean, and he could see fleas hopping on the ground.

Werewolves had fleas.

The seed of doubt worming itself in his heart, Victor slowly raised the blanket to peek at who slept underneath.

Please gods, anyone but Chocolatine. Kia, Allison, Isabelle Maure, even Pink Ranger; *anyone* but *her.*

Thankfully, it wasn't Chocolatine.

"My head..." Apparently, Charlene had drunk as much as he did. "Urgh..."

Victor sighed in relief, before realizing that he comforted her in more ways than one.

He glanced at the bedside, finding a fully clothed Croissant snoring on the ground with a bottle in one hand, and Victor's scythe in the other. *"He used me to scratch his back,"* Furibon complained, sounding broken. *"To scratch his back..."*

Victor blinked at the sight; his eyes moved to Charlene, then back to Croissant, and finally back to Charlene, who returned his gaze.

"That's awkward," Victor said.

Charlene glanced at Croissant with an angry sneer. "He tried to fatten me for dinner," she said, "Serves him right."

He had forgotten how petty she could be when revengeful. "So, um..."

"I still don't like you." Charlene thought over it. "You're *good*, but I still don't like you."

Figure. "Then why?"

"You screwed me over with the dragons."

"No, but yes?"

"So I screwed you."

...

Okay.

His life was weird.

Someone knocked on the door, with Charlene immediately hiding beneath the blanket and faking sleep; the chief of staff putting on some pants just as an impatient Allison entered the room. "Ah, Vic, you are done," Allison said, upon glimpsing at the sleeping form in the bed. "First, let me say that I am so very happy you took my lessons about the worship of Cybele to heart."

"Yeah, I figured out I should worry about my afterlife as soon as possible."

"Second, I..." She paused upon noticing Croissant sleeping on the ground, and fell silent.

"Not even remotely what it looks like," Victor insisted.

Allison said nothing, and then showed him a casket. "I brought you ice and healing potions for the breeding line outside. I hope we have enough."

"The breeding line?" Had he heard right? His head was heavy.

"Yes, the line outside the house."

What the Happyland did he do last night? Still in the throes of the hangover, Victor looked through the bedroom's window. A line of people, mostly women of all ages, waited in front of the house.

More than a hundred! "How did this happen?"

"Yes, you kinda made it loud that you wanted to breed last night, the village is depopulated, and you are the second most powerful person in the 'empire,'" Allison rolled her eyes at the word. "You do the math."

No way. It was too good to be true, so it wasn't. There had to be a trap.

He examined the line in detail, and it confirmed his fear.

Most were werewolves in human form, but half of them weren't human-looking at all. Furry gnolls, kobolds, mimics, festering ghouls... "How many?" Victor asked, worried.

"Since you told them you met their god, who made you his prophet and ordered the banishment of household pets, the entire cult of the Moon Man wants a piece of your genes. Add some gnolls and kobolds, the fact that the mimics seem obsessed with seeing your *'sword treasure'*..."

At that moment, Victor realized that there could be 'too much of a good thing.'

A terrible idea crossed his mind. "Who is the first in line?" he asked.

Allison's smile didn't reach her eyes.

No.

Oh please gods, no...

"Viiiiiiiiic..." *her* voice came from behind the door.

Victor immediately attempted to jump through the window and escape.

Much like Vainqueur in Haudemer, his new dragon wings prevented him from passing through.

"This world sucks!" he complained, desperately struggling to squeeze through.

"In your case," Allison said, before pushing on his back to help him escape, "Maybe in more ways than one."

"You foolish fiend!" Kia pointed her sword at that cursed building. "Why should I not bring down this place?"

"This is a free trade area, and Happyland has invested with the full support of the Emperor," the bug fiend Malfaisant replied, he and other demons protecting the Nethermart. "Our presence here is perfectly legal!"

"It is unethical!" the knight complained, disgusted. "I am not cleaning Ishfania of Maure's fiends just to let others take it over!"

"Miss Kia, this is the perfectly normal result of a free-market economy," the fiend replied with a hint of smugness. "Nature abhors a vacuum. We are only answering the market's needs."

"So will we." A pillar of light fell from the heavens, a golden-haired angel materializing next to Kia herself.

"Miel?" Kia recognized that angel, from the time she ended up in Heaven back when she had just started her adventurer career. "Hi Miel, have you finished your internship?"

"Good morning, Miss Kia. Indeed, I am now a full-fledged heaven counselor. I must inform you that you should upgrade your subscription to Heaven+. For your sake."

Angels. Meaning well, but pushy.

"Look at that," the bug fiend's tone turned venomous. "A redemption chaser. Let me guess, your subscriptions are down again, and you have come to learn from the *better* multiplanar company?"

"Those are donations, and they are up!" Miel replied, the mere sight of the fiend angering her. "In fact, I have come to prospect new cli—new believers!"

"Prospect?! This is our market! We took it from Maure Hellcorporated, now it's our turn to establish a monopoly!"

"Since it is a 'free market economy', as you slimy sales demon said, the higher-ups want to invest there," Miel replied, showing the fiend a contract. "I have received the authorization of the Grand Vizier himself!"

"You... You will not steal our market share!" Malfaisant protested, much to Kia's joy.

"The goddess, Shesha, also voiced her intention to invest in the new Ishfania, as did the Church of the Dread Three," the angel replied. "If you fear our competition, then wait until *they* arrive."

Malfaisant turned to his fiend bodyguards. "Inform the shareholders," he ordered. "And cut our prices the way the Emperor cuts his foes!"

"Is this what I think it is?" Kia asked, seeing the big picture rearing its ugly head.

"A land ruled by, and for, greedy monsters, with no taxes, no regulations, and total freedom of religion." Miel nodded. "Ishfania will become a haven for chaotic mortals and non-humans in a very short time. Now that Mr. Dalton has opened the market after breaking Maure's monopoly, we in Heaven can finally bring light to all."

Having seen Heaven and its practices, Kia rolled her eyes when Miel didn't look. They were better than the alternative, but...

"Since I cannot harm that fiend the paladin way without voiding my diplomatic immunity, I'm going to Mauria," the knight decided. "Maure still has followers who need to be kicked out downstairs."

"You have the ear of the Emperor and his Grand Vizier, so we hope that you will convince them to take the right path." Miel gave Kia a wink similar to those in advertising. "Everyone needs a shoulder angel."

Urgh, politics again.

Not that Kia complained since she had a feeling things would turn out to be very interesting...

"All of the dragons present developed a class of their own."

The temperature dropped heavily at her words. The red-eyed, carnivorous trees of the Dark Forest observed her with hunger, ready to tear her limb from limb at their master's command.

Lucie Lavere, leader of the Nightblades and vampire criminal mastermind, kept her cool and continued her report.

"I destroyed the bindings of the Hellgate as you asked, but the dragons tore through Maure's army, leaving it in shambles. Vainqueur has claimed Ishfania as his own, with Gardemagne's support. Most of his guests followed his example, and decided to become adventurers."

"Why did you not assassinate the dragon's main minions before the attack?" her mistress pointed out, her voice betraying a hint of anger. The situation had gotten far out of hand.

"You didn't ask," Lucie replied. "You ordered me to destroy the seals. No more no less. Besides, it did not stick."

In the end, Lucie was a mercenary, and she had some laundered gold stashed at Vainqueur's castle. You do not mess with your bank.

Lucie's mistress, the fomor Mell Odieuse—who went by the name Melodieuse when falsely claiming humanity—rested on her throne of black, cursed wood, her face one of stone. Her eyes stared through Lucie, while her fingers tightened on the Apple of Knowledge. Not *at*, but *through*, as if she was a ghost.

Eyes were the windows of the soul. But Mell Odieuse had none. Her eyes promised neither pity nor praise; they promised only annihilation. Lucie believed that if pure, distilled evil existed in the world, then it must have looked exactly like that woman.

Lucie worked for the dark woman so she could walk under the sun and learn her ancient magic, but had no reason to be overzealous. She knew that the fomors hated all other life, and the criminal wasn't stupid enough to think she would somehow be spared once her usefulness had ended.

The fairy joined her fingers, thoughtful. "This has gone too far," she said. "I wanted to avoid involving the dragons, but it can no longer be helped."

Lucie said nothing, waiting for her mistress to elaborate. As usual, she didn't, keeping her cards close to her chest.

"You are dismissed," Mell Odieuse declared. "Keep an eye on Vainqueur and Gardemagne, until I have further need of your... other services."

That was how Mell Odieuse worked, fostering chaos in the shadows without involving herself directly. She had empowered Maure with knowledge, hoping he and Gardemagne would slaughter one another, leaving only the fomor victorious. In a way, she had solved the Ishfania problem, by making a bigger one.

"My teacher," Lucie nodded and began to recite a teleport spell. Before vanishing, she caught a glimpse of Mell Odieuse glancing at the immense, stone gate behind her throne, the greatest, most secret treasure of the fomors.

The gate to that strange world called Earth...

Bonus 1: The Great Calamity

- 1198 After Mithras, One hundred years before Manling Victor's ill-attempted robbery; the day Vainqueur Knightsbane became known as the Red Terror of Midgard.

Colognenburg, biggest western city of the Midgard Republic.

Vainqueur Knightsbane, First of His Name and Great Calamity of the Age, woke up with a terrible headache amidst ruins, fire, and devastation.

The great dragon didn't feel so well, his eyelids so heavy he could barely open them. Moving was a struggle, and he forced himself to stand up on his legs. His eyes slowly acclimated to the smoke, until he could see his surroundings.

Vainqueur was in the middle of a vast crater, amidst what appeared to be the ruins of a large manling city. Flames, most probably his, had ravaged its districts and reduced most of them to cinders. A large castle was still ablaze in the middle of the destruction, its towers turned into candles. The dragon was alone with the sound of wood burning, the area empty of life.

Where was he? He didn't recognize this place. Had he destroyed it? Why?

Ugh, and he felt sick in the stomach...

Ugh...

Vainqueur spat out something caught in his throat and examined it.

It looked like half-digested knight's armor, with a broken sword of some kind.

Huh? He didn't remember eating a knight since last year.

Come to think of it, what had he done last night? A fog obscured his memories, and his head hurt just trying to remember. What had he eaten to suffer like this?

Finding no food among the ruins to enlighten him, Vainqueur widened his wings and took flight, struggling to raise himself up. He was slowly getting better, especially after breathing some fresh air, but he had rarely felt so terrible.

As he flew over the city's ramparts, Vainqueur realized he hadn't destroyed one city. He had set the entire countryside ablaze in a straight line for miles. Over time, he recognized the area as a coastal region far, far west of his lair, which he only rarely visited.

The sheer scale of the chaos he left behind surprised the dragon. He usually only rampaged like this when he caught a thief stealing from his—

His hoard!

Suddenly reinvigorated, Vainqueur flew straight towards his lair, the furious movement of his wings causing trees to fall beneath him as he went. Within one hour, he reached his home, hoping his precious were safe.

The dragon had made his lair in a cave under a grass hill, in the middle of a valley the manlings had given him when he ordered them to. His goblin minions had built a small village of their own around the area, with wood and mud. They bred almost as fast as Vainqueur ate them when he ran out of cattle, feeding off the vegetables the dragon disdained.

Vainqueur landed in front of his cave, finding three greenish, childlike goblins sleeping on the job. The mere sight of these slackers infuriated him, and he landed right in front of them, the aftershock sending them flying against the cave's walls. "Minions!" he roared, making the area tremble. "My hoard!"

"Y-Your Majesty?" One of the goblins urinated on himself at the sight. "What is the matter?"

"Where is my hoard?! Is it safe?" Vainqueur moved his head inside his cave, afraid for his gold's safety.

Thankfully, he found his hoard inside, as perfect and shining as ever. The sight relieved him.

"Your M-Majesty?" one of the goblins struggled to find his words, as Vainqueur removed his head from the cave and looked down on him. "W-What is it?"

"Minion, has a thief tried to steal from me recently?"

"Y-Yes, but—"

That was it! "Minion, I do not remember what I did last night," Vainqueur said. "Tell me what happened."

"What I last remember?"

"Yes, before the last thing you remember is my stomach."

"N-No need to go that far, Your Majesty... What I remember..."

- The day before, Red Dragon Hill...

Vainqueur Knightsbane woke up to the tune of goblins whispering in the dark, and of coins falling down from his hoard.

"I say we should run away... he ate half of us last month when he ran out of cows..."

"But if we run, he will track and eat *all* of us."

"Then we wait for the long winter, yes, when he hibernates, and then—"

"Minions, what are you blabbering about?" Vainqueur said, moaning as he woke up, his eyes acclimated to the darkness. His goblin minions were discussing at the entrance of his cave. From the light, it was morning, and he was hungry.

"N-nothing, Your Majesty!" the goblin replied, the others cowering behind him. Each of them looked the same, tiny, greenish humanoids who could barely serve as snacks. "We caught a thief for you, that is all!"

They did? Such good, loyal guards he had. "Is he fat?"

"No, he's a ratling, thin and nimble."

Pity. Vainqueur would have loved a fat and meaty breakfast, like a dwarf. The dragon roused himself, walking towards his minions and causing the cave to tremble with every step. "Where is my chief of staff?"

"I, I am Your Majesty," one of the goblins said.

He was? Vainqueur squinted at the minion, who looked like every other goblin under the sun. The dragon needed a way to identify him from among the others, like a red cloak or iron teeth. "Minion."

"Yes, Your Majesty?"

"First, become more remarkable. I might get confused about your place in the food chain otherwise." The chief of staff had already recruited a lot of goblins when Vainqueur informed him of the concept. "Next, bring me that thief, and my grocery bag. I am hungry."

"The grocery bag?"

"The big bag," Vainqueur elaborated, annoyed by the minion's incompetence. "You have not forgotten to sew it back, have you? Because I am hungry, and if I cannot do my groceries, I will eat at home."

Understanding the message, the goblins bolted out of the cave, with Vainqueur simply moving his head outside. The goblins soon climbed the hill towards his cave, keeping the thief restrained with ropes, and carrying a big, dragon-sized cowskin bag. The thief was a ratling, a strange hybrid between a rat and manling, with the ugliness of both and the tastiness of neither.

The animal did show Vainqueur the respect the dragon expected upon seeing him, groveling in front of him. "Great Vainqueur Knightbane! How majestuous you are!"

"It is Knightsbane, not Knightbane!" Vainqueur roared, the goblins kneeling in obedience at his reaction. "I can tell the difference!"

"F-Forgive my mistake, my king." The ratling lowered his spine so much, Vainqueur half expected him to eat grass like a sheep. "I, I am but a humble traveler…"

"Is that what your kind call thieves now?" Vainqueur accused him.

"I did not come to steal from you, oh great Vainqueur Knightsbane… I came to gaze upon the size of your hoard, and of your magnificence… to see if you were—"

"As big as the tales said," Vainqueur finished, the thief blinked. "I heard that one before. Three times. Find a new one."

The ratling gulped. "The tales of Your Majesty do you little justice, Your Majesty… your claws are sharp as spears, your breath a hurricane…"

The dragon's eyelids narrowed in disappointment.

"Five times I have heard this," Vainqueur said. "Now you will see the inside of my bowels, which should be a first for you."

"W-wait!"

Vainqueur chomped the thief and swallowed him whole. Like every ratling, it tasted like dung and garbage, so much that the dragon almost vomited.

Sometimes, Vainqueur wondered why the lesser species thought trying to steal from him was a good idea. The matter bugged him so much, he promised himself he would ask the next one trying, unless the food wised up.

"That was all?" Vainqueur asked, puzzled. While he would have been annoyed at a thief, the fact they had caught him before he touched his hoard made the incident a mere afterthought. Nothing to rampage over. "What happened next?"

"Then you left for groceries, Your Majesty... w-with the big bag... and you didn't come back."

By now, Vainqueur was confused. He wasn't hungry, so he had found the food he sought back then. What could have angered him so much? Also, he didn't have the grocery bag with him when he woke up.

More and more puzzled, Vainqueur flew away without a word, the wind from his wings throwing the goblin on his back. He decided to check his usual grocery places, in case it jogged his memory.

The dragon quickly reached his favorite farmlands, finding the remains of barns and pens. Some sheep eating grass fled at his coming, and Vainqueur noticed his own footprint in the middle of a broken fence.

Clearly he had done his groceries before being interrupted. By what? Vainqueur circled above the area, observing every detail, smelling the air...

Suddenly, among the smell of manlings and cattle, he noticed the stinking, horrible scent of a fairy.

Yes, he remembered.

"Little Wyrm has lost her sheep, And can't tell where to find them, Leave them alone, and they'll come home..."

Vainqueur sung to himself, as he ripped off the roof of a barn, manling whelps screaming and running away on horses. He found cows, pigs, and sheep inside, making sounds at his arrival.

Let the shopping spree begin.

With one hand, the dragon cheerfully seized a cow, then put it in the bag. Then he seized two pigs and wondered if he should take the sheep with him. He would burn some fat returning home, and he wouldn't mind a snack in the middle of the road.

"Vainqueur Knightsbane..." His ears picked up his name spoken in elder draconic, and his nose the smell of a fairy. Vainqueur instantly turned towards the source, hate and disdain in his eyes.

Springing from the dirt behind him, a fomor stared back.

This abominable, sworn foe of dragonkind was two times smaller than Vainqueur; a deformed centaur with the lower body of a spider, and the upper half was humanoid. The torso was disproportionately larger than the lower half, covered with an insect-like armor; the left arm was a centipede with sharp blades for mandibles, the left one a crimson hand. Eight multicolored eyes looked at Vainqueur from the creature's head, with a row of pointed teeth underneath.

"I am Mag Mell," the fairy presented himself with a chittering voice, although Vainqueur already knew the creature. That fairy had created half the beasts the fairy lords sent against dragons during the war, from trolls to werewolves. "Father of monsters."

"I am Vainqueur Knightsbane," he replied. "I can do everything you do, but better."

The formor hissed at the dragon's rebuke, a chilling cold filling the air.

"Have you come to glare at me?" Vainqueur said at the creature with disdain. "Or to die?"

"Others will die," the fomor replied, his voice low and heavy. "All the New Folk who pollute our lands will die. Such is the word of our champion, Mighty King Balaur."

"Balaur?" That overmighty dullahan? Vainqueur snorted. "I could eat him whole in one bite."

"That was long ago, and this is now. He has grown, and so has his hatred. He is the strongest of all fomors."

"Not as strong as me," Vainqueur replied with pride. "The strongest of your kind would still be no match for the weakest of dragonkind!"

"Yet many of you we killed, in the dark days."

"They suffered from birth defects!" Vainqueur defended his kind's honor. "It doesn't count."

"Only us fomors are forever," Mag Mell replied, having no answer to Vainqueur's implacable logic. "You are the greatest of dragonkind. The great calamity of this age, or so you pretend."

"I pretend nothing. I *am*."

"Then, my King has an offer for you. Fight at his side, and paint this green land red."

"Why would a fomor ask for a dragon's help?"

"Soon, we shall wage a great war. A great Wild Hunt we gather, a horde of millions. We will spill the blood of the mortals until we have slain the last of them. Then, we shall take our war to their nest, that world they call Earth. Outremonde shall be ours again, as it was during the old days. A quiet land, where the Old Folk rules."

"I have always ruled, and I still do," Vainqueur replied, looking down on the fairy with condescension. "It is your kind who has grown weak enough to get defeated by manlings."

"Other dragons have died to them too."

"Handicapped dragons!"

"The mortal are vermin, and the magic they use a disease. Diseases are cured, and the vermin which carry it, silenced. We will hunt them into their houses, and cradle their children to sleep until Outremonde is pure again. There will be a great reward for joining in this carnage, Vainqueur. A tribute of fairy gold and mortal flesh."

"Why would I exterminate my favorite food? If I kill all the puny races, where will I find coins and princesses? Have you thought of the logistics, fairy? Do you think?"

"We can raise gold from the air, and shape slaves from the dirt. With one hand, we create life; with the other, we take it."

"I would rather eat coins than trust a fomor!" The dragon extended his wings. "Begone, fairy, before I devour you. Vainqueur Knightsbane is no one's pet."

"Then, on this day of the solstice, mark the words of Mag Mell. In time, the New Folk, too, will come for you and your kind."

The abominable fairy cursed in its archaic language, becoming one with the earth and vanishing from Vainqueur's sight. The dragon delighted then returned to his shopping—

Wait, solstice?

"The solstice is today?" Vainqueur panicked. "I forgot!"

Quick, he needed a princess! Any princess!

Vainqueur tried to remember what was so important about the solstice, but his memory remained foggy.

Had the fomor cast a spell on him? Why would he need a princess? Not that he wouldn't mind getting one, but his own Bragging Day and the Princess Hunting Season were far, far away.

Vainqueur left his shopping barn to try and retrace his way, finding the ruins of isolated elfling castles nearby. The dragon could recognize the melted stone he left behind anywhere, and the more he saw, the more his memory slowly came back...

When he reached a half-collapsed castle with three towers, Vainqueur had a new flashback.

Finally!

He had to destroy three castles, but he found an elfling princess with golden hair. Just the way *she* would love it.

Having barged inside their throne room by collapsing the castle's walls, Vainqueur seized the screaming princess and prepared to put her in the grocery bag with the cows. Guards and maids had run away at his coming... with one exception.

An elfling wearing crimson armor and a cloak pointed a rusty toothpick at him. "Vainqueur!" Much to Vainqueur's surprise, this elfling spoke in draconic with a somewhat good accent. "At long last, we meet again!"

"Elfling, while it pleases me that your kind is starting to learn the one true language," Vainqueur replied in his own tongue. "I am too busy today to help you commit suicide. Fall on your sword on your own."

"You will not ignore me, villain. I'm fifty-seven!" Pfft, Vainqueur was already bigger than their puny houses at that age. Not impressed. "I am Oersted, of Colognenburg!"

Colowhat? "Whom?"

"Oersted."

"Yes, whom?" Vainqueur repeated to the stupid animal.

"Oersted!" The elfling insisted, apparently too dim to understand Vainqueur's words even in his own tongue. And here people wondered why dragons needed minion translators. "You burned my city fifteen years ago!"

He did? Vainqueur observed the elfling closely, trying to identify him, but... nope. "Which one?"

The elfling shook. "You do not remember."

"Elfling, if you are here to bore me to death, stop right there. I am immortal, but my patience is not. Either get to the heart of the matter or get lost."

"In the west, near the sea! There is a white, chalk cliff nearby."

A chalk cliff? Ah! "Yes, I remember!" Vainqueur said, the elfling's head perking up. "That is the city with the big clock?"

"We don't have a clocktower. Our water clock was destroyed fifty years ago to put out a fire caused by a drag—" The elfling froze, before glaring at Vainqueur. "You burned our city *twice*?!"

"Your villages all look the same," Vainqueur replied. "How do you expect me to remember every place I visited for groceries? After a time they all start blurring together."

"G-groceries?"

"You think I overturn your villages because I like it? Frankly, it would be much easier if you left your cattle and princesses on display for me to take. I have better things to do than rip off your fragile roofs or collapse your towers; which I deeply regret every time I do." Towers were beautiful, like mountains.

"You... you monster! Why? Why can't you leave us in peace?"

"I allow you people to live in my world, is that not enough? I am good and generous, but do not ask too much."

"You... you..." The elfling knight finished shaking, putting both hands on the rusty pommel of his blade. "This is the thousand years old Sword of Leone! I spent years looking for it, investing all my skills in swordsmanship until I could find and master this blade! By it, you shall meet your fate."

Huh? That toothpick looked very old and fragile. "What is that supposed to do?"

"To kill you!"

With a surge of speed whom Vainqueur had to admit surprised him, the knight charged at him and hit him in the chest with his tiny blade.

The sword broke against Vainqueur's scales.

The elfling knight looked at his broken blade, almost as disappointed as the dragon himself.

"But... but, this is the thousand years old sword of Leone! It shouldn't break!" Vainqueur rolled his eyes at the sight of this crying animal. *Elves.* Sometimes, he wondered what was up with humanoids and their obsession with old, outdated swords.

After all, if they were *that* precious and powerful, why would *anyone* leave them in some cave in the middle of nowhere?

Still, understanding he wouldn't be free until he helped the suicidal elf, the dragon ate him whole in one bite while he was still crying over his broken weapon.

He put the screaming princess in the grocery bag and flew away towards the great river region.

The great river region?

Ah, he was visiting family. Why bring a princess though? To brag?

Vainqueur flew towards the great river crossing through the immense continent, witnessing river serpents and turtle monsters swimming in the current below. As he approached his cousins' territories, he ended up finding one in a compromising situation, right on the riverbank.

His favorite cousin, Genialissime, was a wind dragon, a beautiful beast with silvery feathers over his scales; like most of dragonkind, he was much smaller than Vainqueur but still big enough to eat manlings whole.

The black wyrm, Blightswamp, laid next to him, with Genialissime having put a paw on her belly. While Vainqueur's cousin seemed awake, she was in a deep, restful sleep. Still, an outsider couldn't mistake the sight for what it was.

They had *bred*?

"Vainqueur?" Genialissime raised his head to look at him, sounding tired. "You sobered up?"

Sobered up? "You bred with Blightswamp," Vainqueur said, disgusted. He knew Genialissime liked breeding, but the elder wyrm knew where she had been. She lived in a *marsh*! "Blightswamp."

"It… wasn't as bad as you think. Also, this is your fault."

Vainqueur glared back. "How is it my fault that you cannot keep your eggs home?"

"You hurt her self-esteem, I had to give her a wing to cry on."

What? "Look, Genialissime, I do not remember anything from yesterday," he admitted. "You seem to, however."

"It does not surprise me. You were in a *terrible* mood yesterday." His cousin shuddered, making Vainqueur worry about what he had done. "Do you remember what day it is?"

"The day after the solstice?"

Genialissime sighed, frustrating Vainqueur. "And who was to have her Bragging Day on the solstice?"

Bragging Day… Solstice…

"Ah, yes I remember," Vainqueur said, his memory coming back to him. "It was Jolie's first Bragging Day!"

"Uncle Vainqueur, Uncle Vainqueur!" His adorable, tiny spitfire of a niece squealed at seeing him land in front of her cave, near the riverbank. Much to Vainqueur's annoyance, he noticed half a dozen dragons had arrived before him. "You came!"

"How could I miss my sweet niece's first Bragging Day!" Vainqueur nuzzled his adorable kin. She was a red dragon barely the size of a big horse, who had learned to fly very recently. "I brought you a present!"

"A present?" She looked up at him with big, cute eyes. "Is it a minion? Uncle Grognon gave me my first minion too, a catkin kitten! Is it another?"

"No, even better!" Vainqueur searched inside his grocery bag, ignoring the pigs and bringing out his elfling captive, who kept whining and shivering. "A princess!"

"A princess!" Jolie began to cry in joy, as he looked at her present. "My first princess?!"

"She makes a whining sound when you squeeze her," Vainqueur told his niece how to use the princess doll. "Be wary of knights trying to steal her away."

"Oh, can I dress her up? Can I dress her up?"

"Any way you want, my sweet firedrake."

Vainqueur put the princess doll on Jolie's hoard, inside the cave. It was a tiny hoard, of copper coins and treasures she had managed to scrape together as a young wyrm, but every dragon present would give her positive reinforcement for her first Bragging Day. She would have all the time to work hard for her fame when she was all grown up.

"I will feed her fishes!" Jolie said, grabbing the princess by the robe with her mouth and lifting her up. "Totheriver!"

Ah, this reminded Vainqueur of his first Bragging Day, after he paid back the gold debt he owed to his parent for bringing him into the world. He watched his niece fondly, hoping she would grow almost as big as him in a few centuries.

"Hey, Vainqueur!" The red dragon turned his immense head towards the newcomer, Genialissime. "Long time no see!"

"Genialissime!" Vainqueur saluted his cousin. "How are you?"

"Great! I think I will organize a Bragging Day in ten years or so, after the new Princess Hunt Season." He glanced at Jolie's hoard. "I am so proud of her, gathering a hoard at her age..."

"Yes, especially since her father had a birth disability." Vainqueur's brother had been killed by elflings, whom the red dragon had helped commit assisted suicide afterward. "I hope she hasn't inherited it."

"Yeah, being killable sucks as an illness. I can't believe so many of us developed it the last ten centuries. It's like a plague the puny races carry with them." Genialissime glanced at the various invites, especially a black female wyrm. "Hey, Vainqueur, there is a new dwarf city nearby. Blightswamp and I discussed it, and we think we will crash the place after Jolie is done bragging about her hoard."

"The Bragging Day hasn't even begun, and you are already preparing the afterday feast?"

"That is a good question. A better question is, will you follow us?"

Mmmm... "I always get drunk when I eat dwarves, even if they are fat and tasty. I never find the way back to my lair afterward."

"Come on, just eat a few. I will stop your excessive consumption, as your afterday handler."

... why not? He hadn't eaten dwarves in a long while.

How bad could it be?

"I became drunk on eating dwarves?"

"You ate three dwarves, and then you couldn't stop! You became crazy violent, you burned everything!" Genialissime frowned. "And when Blightswamp and I tried to restrain you, you called her by the W-word."

The dragon looked at his cousin, horrified. "I called her a *wyvern*?"

"Yes, yes, you did. She was mad, but thankfully I'm fertile." Genialissime shook his head. "You have a serious dwarf intolerance, Vainqueur."

"Oh, by the elder wyrm, I am so sorry," Vainqueur said, horrified he had called a true dragon, even one who lived in a swamp, a *wyvern*. "And Jolie? Did she have a good Bragging Day?"

"Ah? Ah, yes, she had a fun first Bragging Day, regaling us with the tales of her adventures hunting copper coins in the wild. I think she really likes the princess you brought her. She kept parading her by the robe to everyone. It's a very shy princess though, she kept crying all the time."

Vainqueur would have loved to find a better princess, but he had been running out of time. Still, he was happy his niece had enjoyed his present. "Do you know where I left my grocery bag?" the red dragon asked. That was the last unresolved mystery.

"I think you burned it during your rampage."

Argh, he would have to order his goblin minions to sew him another! Vainqueur disliked eating the food surrounded by manling peasants' dung.

Come to think of it, seeing the deserted region after his rampage, Vainqueur had probably scared the food away for miles. He would have to fly for hours to find a manling shopping barn now, and maybe days to catch a princess.

Vainqueur decided that he would migrate south, to a more populated area with food close. He had heard the Albain Mountains were nice. Frosty, but tall enough for him; the climb would also discourage thieves, with no ratling to try to take his treasures from him.

Vainqueur Knightsbane, First of his Name, Great Calamity of this Age, and King of the Albain Mountain. It sounded great.

He promised himself never to eat dwarves again though.

Bonus 2: Tales of the Kobold Rangers

Three days before Bragging Day...

• **My Immortal Dragon, Chapter 2: "The Dragon's Desire"**

"Your Majesty?" Victor asked, his body slippery and sultry from the gold shower.

"You know what I want, Minion," After watching him swim in his golden hoard, he could barely restrain himself. "You are the shining jewel of my hoard..."

Victor blushed, his white skin glittering like silver in response. Truth to be told, he had never dared voice his feelings for his great, wealthy master.

"Bragging Day is tomorrow, and I need to... treat myself," Vainqueur's voice was heavy with desire. "Lay on the gold."

"Pink, what are you writing?"

Writing in Nethermart's cozy drink shop, Pink jumped out of her seat; she accidentally dropped her beer cup on the ground, much to the imp barista's annoyance.

The other Rangers looked at her in confusion. "Pink, you're late for the training, and Red is getting mad," Black said, frowning at her as she whistled. "Now you're acting suspiciously."

"She's hiding the text behind her back!" Yellow said, trying to circle her.

"No!" Pink turned to face Yellow, only for Blue to use the opportunity to grab her scroll from behind. "Give it back!"

"Is this the sequel of the *War of the Hoard*?" Blue immediately opened the scroll. "Sweet!"

"No, don't read it!" Pink attempted to reclaim the paper, but Yellow and Black restrained her. "It's not meant for publication!"

Her comrade didn't listen and suffered for it. The more the kobone read, the more he shook, the crimson light in his empty eye sockets faltering. "Oh, gods..." Blue dropped the document in horror. "I feel fear. I am undead, and I feel fear!"

"Pink, what have you done?" Black released the bard, who immediately recovered her scroll.

"I... I just had a plot lizard that wouldn't leave," Pink said, sheepish and ashamed. She never expected anyone but her to read it.

"What do lizards have to do with... with *this*?" Although usually the most aloof member of the group, Blue kept shaking in dread. "How could you write the Emperor and Lord Victor like that?"

"But they are obviously made to be together!" Pink complained. "Emperor Vainqueur, Lord Victor, and the Hoard!"

She couldn't help it since she had started taking levels in [Bard] after writing the *War of the Hoard*. The signs were there! Chocolatine, Allison, Lynette, they were all false leads which the good Emperor Vainqueur had to eat to win his minion's heart! Why couldn't anyone else see it?

"Ugh, one of your V&V 'fanfics' again?" Black rolled his eyes. "How many has it been? You haven't even finished your *'Bad to the Bone'* Vainqueur and Furibon story."

"I'm ChocoVic all the way," Blue said.

"And I'm a VainquHoard!" Yellow declared, fist bumping Blue over compatible fan followings, "And now I want to read Pink's story out of morbid curiosity."

"No!" Pink kept the scroll behind her back. "No reading my unfinished works! Please!"

"Guys, stop bullying Pink!" The voice of Red Ranger made the kobolds and kobones behave, their tall, powerful leader walking into sight with the musket and rapier Lord Victor provided him. "Why are you taking so long?"

"It's nothing, Red!" Pink lied.

"Pink was getting drunk writing a fanfic again!" Yellow mercilessly betrayed her, Pink kicking him in the leg's bone. It hurt her more than him. "Ahah! I don't feel pain anymore!"

"Traitor!"

Red sighed. "Pink, you can write what you want, and I am proud that you can." Few kobolds could even read or write. "But drinking beer before our rehearsal? What am I supposed to think?"

"I need to get alcohol to proceed with my writing sometimes," Pink admitted. Some of her ideas were so dark, so deep, so *artistic*, that she couldn't bring them out without help. "When Emperor Vainqueur asked me to write about the... the *lead event*, I had to get drunk before I could commit it to paper."

"We all know how traumatizing the *Event* was," Red said with sympathy. "That is why we must train hard. So this kind of senseless atrocity can never happen again on our watch. Remember what Lord Victor said. We are the *elite* of the minions!"

"Minion lieutenants!" Black pumped a fist.

"We are His Majesty's shield!" Red reminded them, his words brimming with charisma. "The Hoard's last line of defense! The last line to hold! We... are the Kobold Rangers!"

"Kobold Rangers!" the group shouted, the imp barista ignoring them as he served a drink to Barnabas the troll.

Pink remembered that fateful day, when they stole the Apple of Knowledge from that human. The second they had laid their eyes upon the ancient techniques of the Tokusatsu clan held within, of these brave warriors fighting paupers with style, the Kobolds had understood what they had missed in life.

On their own, Kobolds were weak, small, and unremarkable. Most died before they hit ten winters. But by learning the ancient techniques held within the Apple, and reviving the Tokusatsu clan's traditions, Red had argued that they could become more than mere Kobolds: they could become legends whom their kind would celebrate in tales for centuries! They may die anytime, but their legacy would live on forever!

And so they became the Kobold Rangers, the elite warriors of the Murmurin Empire.

"His glorious Majesty, Emperor Vainqueur's Bragging Day will happen soon!" Red reminded them. "For the sake of the Emperor, we cannot embarrass him. Our dancing and motto must be perfectly executed. And… and…"

"And?" Pink frowned, sensing her leader's troubled mind. "What is stressing you out so much?"

"Rolo has a quest for us," Red continued. "A very dangerous quest. A monster is feasting on the vegetables. If this continues, the livestock will starve, and His Majesty's Bragging Day Feast will be ruined!"

"Who would dare launch such a treacherous attack?" Black spat on the ground. "The elves?"

"Worse," Red replied ominously. "A *rabbit*."

A rabbit. The ancestral nemesis of koboldkind; they fought those mammal vermin over burrows since the dawn of time. The brave fathers of the Rangers' warren had managed to fend off one of their invasions before Pink was born.

Now, it was her turn to defend the burrow of Murmurin against those hungry monsters.

"And not any rabbit," Red added, turning away with a dark look on his face. "A Black Rabbit."

The Rangers gasped and exchanged worried looks.

A Black Rabbit. A rabbit who gained magical powers by becoming a dark prince among its filthy, verminous kind. It could summon armies of rodents, grow to enormous sizes, and cast spells from its horn.

Black Rabbits were blights upon the land, devastating all in their path. Countless kobold martyrs had fallen to them.

"If we do not kill him, entire cultures will fall to its hunger," Red said. "Rolo is convinced he will attack by twilight."

"Can we... can we defeat him?" Yellow joined his hands in a silent prayer. "One of them killed my father with its horn."

"For His Majesty, I am not afraid to die again!" Blue replied with empty bravado, his voice breaking.

"If it comes to it, and we cannot defeat the Black Rabbit on our own..." Red trailed off, turning to Pink. "We will have to summon the Mimiczord with your song."

"But she cannot control it!" Black protested. "Once called, there will be blood!"

Red slapped some sense into him. "Get a hold of yourself, you coward! There is no greater honor than dying, so that His Majesty may be fed!"

"I..." Black scratched his cheek. "I am sorry, I... I let fear control me."

"It is okay to be afraid in the face of such evil," Red consoled his friend. "But so long as we are together, you can rely on us. That is what being a Kobold Ranger is all about."

Black nodded firmly, imitated by the others. "Let's repeat the motto," Red said, happy with the group's resolve. "We fight for the hoard!"

"We are made of gold!" Black continued.

"We strike from the shadows!" Blue added.

"We strive for His Majesty!" Pink shouted, the drink shop's clients glaring at their magnificent display.

"Prepare to meet your dooom!" Yellow said, going off-script with his deep, undead voice.

"Yes, that is rig—Yellow!" Red stopped in the middle of the motto, everyone else groaning, "You've gone off-script again!"

"I'm sorry, it's too hard to resist!" Yellow replied. "I... I will say it right next time!"

Red sighed. "Second attempt!"

The beast arrived under the twilight sun.

Never before had Pink seen such a monstrous being. The incarnation of Hell had fur that was as black as night, with big vicious eyes; his enormous ears reminded the Bard of twin pillars of darkness. While as tall as any other rabbit, the ground shook under the immense power of its back legs. A single, golden horn shone in the middle of the monster's forehead, surging with magical power.

The Kobold Rangers established a defensive perimeter, Rolo's fields of carrots and lettuces behind them. Yellow and Pink carried bows, while Black and Blue had switched to spears. Red remained at the forefront, musket, and rapier in hand.

Pink knew this would be a dangerous fight. All of them had levels in [Outlaw], but only Pink and Red had delved into other, combat-oriented classes. And this... this... this was a legendary beast, far more terrifying than Gustave the Scorcher, who killed Blue and Yellow in the past.

"Food?" the black beast uttered with a guttural, dark voice.

Pink's [Bard] mind filled out the words left unsaid, translating the monster's black speech into true epic dialogue.

"Kobolds?" (You dare stand between me and my sweet pleasure, kobolds?)

"Yes, we Kobolds Rangers shall defend His Majesty's pantry from you!" Red shouted back. "You shall not pass!"

"Hungry!" (Do not get in my way! All those who do will be eaten!)

"You. Shall. Not. PASS!" Red repeated.

"Rabbits!" (Then only death will remain! Come to me, my loyal soldiers! [**Summon Rabbit Horde**]!)

The Black Rabbit let out a vivid screech, a cloud of dust surrounding him. A swarm of white rabbits crawled out of the earth, an army summoned from the farthest reaches of Hell itself. At their master's command, the rodents charged as one with a great rumble.

"Defend the fence!" Red commanded, firing with his musket at the incoming swarm, imitated by Yellow. A rain of bullets and arrows felled the first wave of rabbits, while Blue and Black readied their weapons to kill those who managed to break past them. "Pink, sing!"

Pink did so, singing the praise of the good Emperor Vainqueur during the War of the Hoard. "*Minions, remember Furibon! Take your swords, and rise, and fight! Fight for the Hoard! The wicked will perish in the king's flames!*"

*[**Bardic Song**] raised all of your teammates' strength!*

Empowered by her words, the Rangers held the line, Black and Blue impaling every rabbit that threatened to get past them. More kept coming from the burrows, waves, and waves of hungry beasts; Red and Yellow ran out of projectiles and joined the melee, the kobone fighting with its bare claws.

The Black Rabbit oversaw the slaughter with his cold dark eyes, before raising his horn to the heavens. Electricity surged from it, as he pointed it at the Rangers while the weaker rodents distracted them. "Black!" Pink warned her ally, as the horn pointed at him, firing a thunderbolt. "Watch out!"

But even the Black Ranger couldn't out outrun lightning. He barely had the time to look at the monster, before the bolt hit him in the chest and sent him crashing against the fence, defeated.

"You beast!" Yellow snarled, breaking the formation and rushing at the Black Rabbit.

"Wait!" Red shouted his rapier red with rabbit blood. "This is what he wants!"

The last of his dread servants defeated, the Black Rabbit's horn shone bright, the monster's size increasing. Within seconds, he had become as big as a cart, walking on his back legs.

The mammalian titan let out a roar and impaled Yellow Ranger with his horn, like a bull with a manling. The kobone was propelled to the side, his spine breaking in half upon crashing. The dread mammal then stepped towards the remaining rangers, his greedy, malevolent eyes set on the vegetables.

Panicking, Pink kept singing while she raised her bow, firing an arrow at the monster. The projectiles bounced off his fur.

Blue let out a maddened war shout at he charged with Red, weapons raised. The Black Rabbit easily kicked Blue aside with one of his enormous legs, but Red managed to graze his skin with his rapier. He barely dodged a lightning strike from the beast's horn, needling the beast's ankles with his weapon.

"Fight for the hoard!" the bard kept cheering her friend, as he managed to halt the beast's progress. *"You can win! You can do it!"*

But the Black Rabbit, infuriated by their resistance, turned to Pink, his horn surging with the power of thunder.

"Pink!" Red jumped in the way, the lightning bolt hitting him instead of his teammate. He collapsed on the ground, trying to rise back up, only for the Black Rabbit to stomp on him. Crushed under the beast's weight, the leader of the Kobold Rangers stayed down.

"Summon... it..." Yellow, struggling to put back his bones together, implored Pink. The Black Rabbit left the defeated Red behind, ignoring the last of the Rangers as he walked towards the fence. "Summon the Mimiczord!"

Here goes nothing.

"Behold! What a shiny sword!" Pink sung, as loud as she could. *"What a shining blade this is, trapped in stone!"*

The Black Rabbit stepped on the fence, crushing it beneath his leg. He prepared to feast on the vegetables, when a shriek interrupted him.

The dreaded Excalitrap, Vainqueur Junior, rushed into sight, its bloodthirst roused by Pink's words. The mimic rivaled the attacker in size.

"Sword?" the mimic said, Pink's mind translating the word into a full dialogue. (I am the only true sword treasure! Where are the challengers?)

"Him!" Pink pointed a finger at the Black Rabbit's horn.

As she hoped, Junior mistook him for a sword, furiously leaping between the garden and the evil beast. One of the mimic's many hands grabbed the sword lure on its back, swinging it like a true swordsman.

"Sword death!" (You will suffer the agony of a thousand deaths by my sword!)

"Rabbit!" the monster replied. (A rabbit prince fears nothing! A rabbit is fear!)

The Black Rabbit attempted to impale Junior the same way he did with the Rangers, but the mimic parried with his blade. Then, with a push, it forced the beast behind the fence.

Pink watched on, amazed, as Junior fought the monster evenly. Sword met horn in a dance of damnation. Every time the monstrous mammal attempted to cast lightning upon his foe, the mimic interrupted him with a well-placed thrust.

"Strong," the Black Rabbit screeched. (I did not expect to fight such a powerful foe. How delightful.)

"Sword strike!" (It shall take but a single stroke of my sword to put you down!)

"Horn!" (My horn will bathe in your unworthy blood!)

With a brutal swing, Junior pushed the beast back, both enemies facing each other under the sun. The mimic proudly raised its blade, swirling flames surrounding it. "[**Elemental Saber: Fire**]!"

Junior's Sword will now inflict additional Fire Damage!

One of the fabled [Fencer] Perks... Pink had never seen it in action. Would it prevail against the beast, though?

"[**Holy Horn**]!" the Black Rabbit replied, its horn growing longer, until its length matched that of Junior's blade.

The Black Rabbit's horn will now inflict additional Holy Damage!

Both foes glared at one another, then charged with a roar.

In a blink, moving so fast Pink's eyes could barely follow, both fighters exchanged a blow and kept going, having switched places. For a short, tense moment, they stood in place, two silhouettes under the sunlight.

Then, blood flew from the Black Rabbit's head.

"Food..." the beast said while whimpering. (So this is how I die? Food we all are... and food we shall remain...)

The monster collapsed on his left side, vanquished. Junior let out a victorious roar, as the rabbit regained his original, tiny size. The mimic grabbed the corpse with one hand and immediately swallowed it whole.

Pink couldn't believe it.

They won! Junior won!

The mimic, though, wouldn't leave without exacting a price. 'Sheathing' back its sword on its back, Lord Victor's pet turned to the defeated Red, who had forced himself back on his knees. "Sword." (Give me your sword.)

Red hesitated, for his rapier had been granted to him by Lord Victor for his deeds against the Scorchers. He knew *exactly* what the Mimiczord did to every sword it could get its hands on.

"Sword!" the mimic insisted, its voice turning dangerous.

As a tribute for its service, Red gave Junior his rapier, his eyes turning away. He couldn't bear to look at what he knew would follow.

But Pink, for the sake of true historical accuracy, didn't flinch at the execution. The mimic cruelly broke the rapier in half with its bare hands, threw the remains on the ground, and buried it under the dirt with a gleeful smirk. Junior then left without a sound, satisfied at proving its superiority.

Pink immediately rushed to Red's side, helping him back on his feet and preventing him from collapsing. "It's over," she said, looking at the fence. "It's over."

*Congratulations! For defeating a Black Rabbit, you have taken two levels in [**Bard**]! You earned the [**Extended Song**] Personal Perk.*

+60 HP, +20 SP, +1 AGI, +2 INT, +2 CHA, +1 LCK!

*[**Extended Song**]: Your songs' enhancements last twice as long.*

"Yes..." Red glanced at the rest of his team. Blue had recovered, while Yellow struggled to put back his bones in place. "Are you alright, Rangers?"

"Can't... move..." Black groaned, paralyzed by the lightning. He would need to be patched up by Chocolatine.

"Blue, help him," Red commanded, the kobone rushing to his living brethren's side. "Are the vegetables..."

"Safe and sound," Pink nodded.

"Then... congrats everyone. We have done it. We've won. The Bragging Day Feast is saved." Red chuckled. "Pink, you better write a song about it."

She would. She already had a name for it.

'The Night of the Black Rabbit.'

It would wait until she finished *My Immortal Dragon* though.

Black Rabbit

Type: Beast.

Recommended party level: 5.

Following the golden tradition set by giant rats, bandits, and goblins, Black Rabbits are among the most popular targets of low-level quests. Every adventurer group has a story of hunting one of these pests on behalf of farmers at the start of their career. No matter how many of them are cooked with prunes and mustard, more always come.

Thankfully, they never run fast enough.

Closing Words

Special thanks to my proofreader and first reader, Daniel Zogbi.

Thanks to the amazing patrons who financially supported this book during its publication on Patreon: Filip Passeri, K. William Klaassen, Eldar Kersebaum, Lapha_Denec, antab, Sean Basa, Luminant, Murphy, Aji V, Jeff Gault, James Teeple, BRUNO ASTUR, Dom Ceremonia, Max Collins, Zorathis, ElJako98, Виктор Фон Стыценкофф, Anthony Daniel Martin, RoruRedTailedDolphin, David Hansson, Thaco4, Pablo, Arnon Parenti, Mike Dixon, Mikkel Kolding Christensen, Matthew, Pixie, Sands, K, BlackFire13th, Onigalmasuka, Cade, Kyoma,Jamie McKay, Dillon Rodenbaugh, Bartosz Borkowski, Samuel Lim, Kevin Ramos, Sharrod Brathwaite, Holland Webinger, King Gonflick, Deane L. Uptegrove, Gilium, Jeremy Humphrey, Israel, Letmeinillread, Charles handgis, Rob Riv, Mattijn Jelle Lucas Wagt, Pergamon, Christian Pettersen, Bob Xander, cale lechmere, damien, Elvis Malkic, Nelson Crockett, GenericKane, Jeb, J, Noah Williams, Sikkin, charter, James Short, nicholas Maa, Maxwell Margetts, Colby, Ethan Bell, Vodairo, Arvid Hedebark, Jeb, Filip Passeri, omar crooke, The Golem Crafter, Aubrey Craye, Bob Johnson, Sebin Paul, Tyrell Facey, ParoxysmDK, Zadaine, Johans, Calvin Miner, Sebas Tian, Shirwa, Anthony, Audrick CK, John, Andrew Kahn, DenverDrew, 白酒鬼, Aubrey Craye, SugarRoll, Oskar Nordström, Lucas Oparowski, Owen al-ali Pereira, Trevor Sales, Calvin Miner, Zack, Tycho Green, Augustus, Rory, John Settler, CptJimmy, Sharuy, Christopher Batko, Prateer Panwar, Winston May, Bob Smith, Erik Levin Fisher, DemonKingBaka, Cody Adam Carroll, Ze Feng, Christian Simon, Michael Kilby, PbookR, Guy Smith, Joseph Caywood III, Oskar Paulins, Glader, Filip Passeri, Alawill, Bob Smith, John Carroll, Kenneth C. King, Revive3pls, mohammedd, Bobo Bo, Logan, Nanooki12, Patrick C, Colin Ford, Tab, Alianok, David Madden, Markus Pawlak, Zool, Clarence Odunsi, Gabriel Sontag, Arkeus, Manu, Quentin, John, Tasoula, Andrew Parsadayan, Corgi McStumperson, Daniel Nemtok, Moonspike, Igor Mikulik, C. Wilbs, Hamed Al-Ghamdi, RepossessedSoul, Kevin, Zeuke, Dhalmeida, Parker

Groseclose, Nick, Mackoy, zed, Daniel Mackie, James Walsh, Athra, Chris M, Seadrake, Jim of Trades, Tae, Koen Hertenberg, Enaz the Great, Evan Cloud, Alex Pruitt, Saul Kurzman, Dex, Warwick Robertson, Johnathan, Rhodri Thornber, Marc Claude Louis Durand, Drekin, Bald Guy Dennis, Floodtalon, and Dax.

And thanks to all my wonderful readers on Royal Road.

Vainqueur has been quite the journey. What started as a plot bunny born of my inability to find a LitRPG story with a true dragon main character (instead of a human transformed into a dragon) and loving satire of the fantasy/isekai genre became a full book. I have been amazed by the positive reception it received, which warms my heart always.

I scripted the book so that I could end the story right there on a satisfying note, while keeping the door open for a sequel should I want to explore the world further. As it turned out, I enjoyed writing Vainqueur's adventures so much, that I indeed decided to continue the saga. Too many jokes to tell.

In any case, I hope you enjoyed Vainqueur's tale, and see you soon.